THE PORTUGUESE GAMBIT

P. J. Rands

Cover designed by the author.

This book is a work of fiction. Names, characters, places, and incidents either are products of the author's imagination or are used fictitiously. Any resemblance to actual persons, living or dead, events, or locales is entirely coincidental.

P. J. Rands
Website: www.pjrands.com
Facebook: PJ Rands
Facebook: The Portuguese Gambit

First eBook publication: December 2017. Version 2.0 in January 2018

Frist paperback publication: December 2017. Version 2.0 in January 2018

ISBN: 9781976741067

I dedicate this work to my late friend Conrad Teichert who first encouraged me to write this story, and to my wife and editor Sandi along with our children Spencer, Curt, Drew, and Holly who never stopped encouraging me.

29 And the time drew nigh that Israel must die: and he called his son Joseph, and said unto him, If now I have found grace in thy sight, . . . deal kindly and truly with me; bury me not, I pray thee, in Egypt:

30 But I will lie with my fathers, and thou shalt carry me out of Egypt, and bury me in their buryingplace. And he said, I will do as thou hast said.

GENESIS, CHAPTER 47

CONTENTS

Historical Note

In 1481, King João II ascended the Portuguese throne and reignited the work of his late uncle, Henry the Navigator, to find a sea route to the East Indies by circumnavigating Africa. The mission had become infinitely more urgent and potentially more profitable because the key trading city, Constantinople, had recently fallen to the Ottoman Turks, greatly disrupting traditional trade routes with Asia.

All of Europe believed in the existence of a powerful kingdom ruled by a Christian ruler called Prester John. For centuries, letters and copies of letters purporting to be from Prester John, had circulated among the courts of Christendom. The thinking at that time was that Prester John's realm lie somewhere in Africa. King João, whom modern historians consider the perfect Machiavellian ruler, sought Prester John as an ally against the Turks and in his quest to find the bottom of the Dark Continent.

For a more complete explanation about Prester John and the geopolitical situation at the start of this story, please see the *Expanded Historical Note* at the end of this book.

PART I

West Africa (inland of the Gold Coast)

and

The Sea of Aethiopia off the Ivory Coast

(1483)

CHAPTER 1

Something New

The gasp jolted Mbekah from her stupor. She jerked her head to study the scene at the end of the line of captives. Manu writhed on his back in the gray dirt, clutching an assegai spear buried in his ribs. His eyes bulged; his mouth gaped open. Mbekah sprang to her feet, wincing as the loop of braided hide ripped into her raw ankle. She and the others cowered, drew the connecting cord taut, and dragged the skewered Manu forward a few paces along the trail by his foot which was still in his loop of the cord.

Manu slid along on his back and groaned, then sobbed between gulps of air. One of the three guards yanked the assegai from Manu's side and rammed it into his throat. The assegai's point pinned Manu to the ground and halted the drift of the line of captives. A crimson puddle bloomed in the dirt under Manu's neck.

Mbekah turned away and retched. Others shrieked. The other two guards batted the captives with their assegai shafts until there was only whimpering.

The executioner guard looted for himself the rolled cloth belted around Manu's waist, released his limp leg from the cord, and untied the forked branch bound about Manu's neck that secured him to the captive's neck in front of him in the line.

Mbekah and the other captives watched and wept.

"Go!"

The line of sobbing youths plodded forward.

"Hurry." A guard jabbed the lead captive with the butt of his assegai.

They traveled faster without her limping cousin in the rope. Mbekah shivered at the vision of scavengers brawling for the body. Not a bone to remain. Uncle and aunt never to know their son was dead.

Manu will not be forgotten while I breathe. We hid together when uncle acted the leopard and stalked. We giggled when he found us and tickled.

Tears drenched her cheeks and neck. A moan from behind her. Sighs from ahead and behind. In Mbekah's head she heard the village kinship singer, in the cadence of her gait, chant each family's verse from first parent to dwell in the forest through to the name of a captive in the chain. Manu and his family were linked by blood and memories to her and to each of the remaining captives.

The trail snaked from Mbekah's forested hills into belly-high tan and green grasses and onto a plain where baking brush and sturdy trees seasoned the close-cropped grass. The sky was everywhere—so much grander than in the forest.

Mbekah watched the path, glancing about now and then to spot herds of long-faced wildebeests or striped back-and-whites grazing in the distance. The group startled a thin-necked kor hen from the shadow of a squat bush. The mottled gray fowl sprinted, beat its wings, then locked them for a long glide. It was strange to Mbekah not to stop and search for its eggs.

The guards glanced frequently over their shoulders back along the trail. Ever so quietly, Mbekah sang the death song for her cousin. Others joined her.

"Silence!"

The singing stopped. Her tears did not.

Mbekah thought again about the attack on her village, sudden and brutal in the faint light before goat-milking. Resistance ended after the few men who were not away hunting, were killed. The intruders ransacked huts and shackled her along with other stunned youths, linking them together in single file. In less time than it might have taken to bake a flat millet loaf, the raiders and their enslaved departed. When leaving, Mbekah strained for a last look over her shoulder. Frantic mothers wailed, and bewildered children fussed among the death and debris.

A short time on the trail after the mayhem, most of the raiders disappeared. *To pillage another isolated village?* Three remained to drive them—the captives—*to . . . to where?*

The armed men did not come in daylight with a judgment or revenge to enforce. They did not come boasting and challenging to honorable combat. When victorious, they did not take the heads of the slain. No. These killers are not from our forest. This is something new.

The heat waned. With the sun in their faces, they shuffle-jogged—free right hand on the shoulder of the person in front to reduce the painful impacts of their necks against the forked branches that kept them spaced out in the line. Always in step so the braided leather rope didn't jerk so cruelly at their tender right ankles. Left arms, tied into another rope at the wrists, swung in unison. Mbekah easily kept pace with the others, her legs as long as those of the tallest male in the line.

Mbekah hadn't spoken since the first day on the journey when a guard rewarded her first (and last) words with a stinging blow across her shoulders. *I will live through this. That is what my father would say . . . would have said.*

She kept an eye on where she trod. *I must not go lame.*

The guards too watched the path, slowed them down in rough places, and skirted some spots altogether. She understood the guards' commands, although the accent was foreign, and she determined to obey them, for now. *Did not my father always say to move one's neck according to the music?*

Mbekah shifted the strap of the leather purse slung over her left shoulder and riding on her right hip. She wiped the sweat from her palm on her only clothing—her cloth of many colors which had been rolled and tied like a sash around her slender waist, so her arms and legs moved freely. A gift from her father, it was the cloth the women in the forest made in pale reds and greens, ivory, brown, and orange.

Mbekah lifted her free right hand from the shoulder in front to smooth her dust-caked black hair. Like the other women in the chain, she wore it pulled back revealing most of her ash-brown forehead. They all tied their hair snugly with the ends braided into thin strands that hung from each knot to the nape of the neck. Mother and Foladé, her little sister, were her braiders. She smiled at the thought of the hours they had chatted while the two worked on her hair. *Why did I let myself contend with them the last night we were together? We went to sleep angry. We woke to this!* Foladé was not in the line now. She must have been with the goats and hid when the attack began.

A warm dry breeze pushed the group along, keeping the sweating youths from overheating. A blessing, thought Mbekah, that it was not the season of rain and stifling humidity. She decided the savannah's lavish views did not compensate for its scanty shade. *No shade for the body, no shade for the soul.* She prayed: *There is something in the heaven; let it reach me.*

#

The band stopped. Squatting, Mbekah stole glances at the youngest guard—the one who had stabbed Manu and claimed his cloth. The other two guards called him Yaféu. Lean and muscular, he looked little different from the young men in her village—some of whom were in the rope bonds with her—except that Yaféu's left eye was clouded and did not move with his right eye. Like the young men in fetters with her, Yaféu did not smile.

Is Yaféu also worn out and hungry? Is he tired of this whole affair? Would he rather be hunting or wrestling with friends or teasing one of them about a pretty virgin? Nevertheless, he is here, learning to be what men are in his village. Yaféu's folk will be proud. Bitter, she looked away.

One of the other guards stood and then all were up again and moving. Mbekah concentrated on the path.

Brown bats appeared, swooping and swerving. Long after the sun left the sky the prisoners lay on their bellies in a line and sucked water from a streamlet. Bloated, they trudged on again until the half-moon lit their way from directly overhead.

"Stop," ordered a guard. "We sleep."

Yaféu opened Mbekah's hide purse and gave each captive a piece of raw yam and a few crystals of salt—all looted from their own homes. Another guard gave each a dab of shea butter to rub on their wrists and ankles where the skin had been scuffed away. The anointing stung Mbekah to tears. She knew the ointment was not offered in kindness; like goats, they were valuable property to be cared for.

The mostly-naked captives worked awkwardly to untie their rolled-up cloth belts and spread them on the flattened elephant grass. They lay on their sides, the neck yokes keeping them from sharing body warmth.

Yaféu took a kola nut from a goatskin bag, bit off a chunk, and chewed. The other two guards lay down, leaving Yaféu with the first vigil.

Mbekah closed her eyes and saw the clusters of thatched dwellings in the clearing, her father's hut, and her father sitting with knees out and ankles crossed. He shared a kola nut with his brother. Her mother, aunt, and father's first wife were outside at the mud oven, preparing the afternoon meal. Her sister Foladé watched the baby. In her mind, Mbekah tasted the soft warm flesh of roasted yam. *If only father had been away during the attack!*

Ifé, who was yoked behind Mbekah, sighed in her sleep and rested her wrist on Mbekah's waist, her hand hanging down on Mbekah's stomach.

Out of habit, Mbekah reached for the leopard-spot cowry that had hung from her neck before one of the slavers ripped it away. It was unnatural not to fondle the smooth seashell before sleeping. She would have to live without its protection. *I must rely directly on the Creator.* With that supplication, she dozed off.

Mbekah woke when another guard spoke to Yaféu and replaced him. The new watcher stood, moved around, and chewed kola to stay alert. Mbekah parsed the cacophony of the moonlit savannah. Screeching crickets made it difficult to distinguish the distant howling of the ever-present but rarely seen wild dogs.

She picked an ant from her thigh and flicked it into the night. She thought of her uncle and the other hunters returning to the village and learning of the attack from the mourning women. *Will they think our guards are many or the distance too great to overtake? Can they even follow our tracks? Our rescuers must arrive soon . . . or fail.*

Can we count on rescue? No. Father would tell me not to wait for the sun to wed the moon.

#

A grating across her sore calf wrenched Mbekah from deep slumber. She saw the third-watch guard dragging his spear butt along the legs of the captives in front of her. She sat up. Yaféu, the guard with the dead eye, dropped a strip of dried meat at her feet.

Fingers glided along her ribs and pinched her in the armpit. *Another bulging tick.* Before Ifé, the woman in the line behind Mbekah, could find another parasite to pluck, a guard ordered them to their feet. Mbekah grunted as each stiff muscle came into play in her legs, back, arms and neck. She struggled—left hand in the rope and right hand free—to roll up and secure her cloth about her waist. Yaféu hoisted the hide pack to her shoulder for her.

The lead guard took three paces forward and the captives followed. Mbekah came to tears during her first steps when stiff cord bit into the scab ringing her right ankle. Others shrieked. The line jerked along noisily until the fettered youth synchronized their strides. Mbekah's wrist and ankle sores oozed onto the already sticky hide and another layer of tenacious orange mud formed on her leg loop. The sun peeked above the rim of the savannah over her left shoulder. Mbekah chewed her leathery meal and focused on the trail.

They had traveled for 7 days, seeing no other man or woman. Mbekah had never seen so many browns—orange tinged brown dust swirled here and there; light-brown termite wattles crawled with activity; scruffy, dark-brown wildebeest clipped fields of tan grass; and the occasional gray-brown wood of trees.

Among the browns, gray-green thickets huddled in well-separated low spots while rare groves of small trees commanded the terrain like walled villages. Towering trees, jammed top-down into the earth, beseeched the infinite blue heaven with root-like branches. Mbekah knew the baobab tree because one dominated the clearing in the forest where she had lived her whole life. On the savannah, these giants had the girth of a headman's hut and the height of nine grown men. *Will the song to my village baobab suffice for the spirits of these baobabs on the plain?*

They passed an acacia that had been pushed over, trampled, and stripped of everything but the thorns. A tusked pig and her brood gorged on the fallen seedpods. Black and white birds with orange, horn-like beaks probed for beetles in piles of elephant droppings. The busy birds raised their heads to study the line of humans filing past. As the group moved forward, the burnt-brown piles of dung changed to golden brown, their odor unmistakable. Mbekah observed that no birds attended these fresher leavings. *It will take the rest of the morning for beetles to find the fresh droppings. Then the horn beaks will come for them.*

Ahead, seven elephants, their long nervous noses low and plucking grass, then high and tasting the air. The two with the largest ivory stood ahead of the other five, leaning first on one front leg and then on the other, pivoting to face the other gray giants, then to face forward. The two bulls scrutinized a clan of lions gathered at the carcass of a baby elephant. The largest lion lay, maned head upright and front legs forward, watching the elephants as well as a toothy mob of hyenas that awaited its turn on the carcass. Other lions tore at a gap in the dead elephant's hide to get at the flesh, raising their blood-soaked muzzles from time to time to survey their audience. Vultures circled overhead.

Mbekah reached for the seashell amulet the size of a dove egg and was reminded anew that she would never again enjoy its comfort. Her mother had conferred with the holy man and then walked most of a day to the market village to trade an entire string of tiny, ordinary white cowries for the larger, spotted cowry shell. Father was concerned when mother did not return home that night. The next evening when the holy man blessed the charm for Mbekah, she understood that her mother's two-day walk was as much a part of the gift as the price in white cowries, making the lost amulet all the dearer. *I wish I hadn't been so mean to mother the night before all of this.*

Keeping a watchful eye on the trail, Mbekah lost track of the lions and other scavengers. She prayed with her eyes open and feet moving.

That night, Mbekah woke and tensed at the hallooing of jackals. *I am a goat on a stake. The pacing guard will keep the nasty beasts at a distance.* Fatigued as she was, she forced herself to remain alert long enough to consider her situation. If men from her village were in pursuit, Mbekah had not seen any indication.

On the eighth day, during an afternoon stop, a guard released Bejide from her spot in the rope, gripped her arm, and hauled the limping, crying girl behind a tangle of brush. Yaféu and the other remaining guard tensed, keeping a stricter watch on the squatting captives. Terrified, Mbekah dropped her head into her hands, invoked a blessing for her friend, and listened. She heard nothing from the bushes.

They rested longer than usual before the absent guard returned—alone—and rousted the remaining ten captives to their feet and their journey.

Mbekah wondered if she could have helped her friend somehow before she began to slow the group too much. *My poor Bejide, discarded, most likely her throat slit.*

Bejide was a year younger than Mbekah. The two had often gone with their mothers—both healers—to gather special plants. While their mothers whispered fresh gossip, the girls enjoyed their own secrets. There were lessons in the forest and in the village for the two young apprentices with their mothers and sometimes with the holy man who taught that a healer must treat the soul as well as the body. *Father always said that when you teach a girl, you teach her children and her children's children. Bejide will teach no child. Whom will I teach? I pray thee, Creator, accept Bejide into the village of peace. And let her assure my own father there that I have not quit.*

#

The bare earth yielded to sparse grass, then thick. Trees clustered—not as many as in Mbekah's forest but a pleasing sight nonetheless. The group came to a well-trodden path and followed it to the right. They passed men who carried hunting spears, unlike the short jabbing spears of their guards. They passed women digging roots—mothers and daughters. Two of the women slung babies against their chests. The diggers were not surprised or concerned to see the harrowed captives and their guards. One woman waved and greeted Yaféu by name, calling him nephew.

They stopped near a score of huts while one of their guards went into a hut with two empty purses. Mbekah squatted, facing back along the trail. *The likelihood of our men coming for us is a grain of sand compared to a termite column.* She turned toward the front of the line and studied Kpodo's profile. *Does the oldest male captive have a plan for our escape?*

The guard returned with purses full and they resumed their trek.

On the ninth day, the guards urgently prodded the half-delirious captives along.

Mbekah marveled that any of them could take another step. *The beatings and the fear of execution keep us going.* Mbekah moved her right hand from the shoulder into the armpit of Gyasi, the boy in front of her, to steady him as he struggled to stay upright and moving. She was stronger than some of the boys; along with her mother, sister and half-sisters, she had done much of the family's heavy work.

I carry my captors' stolen purse and drag their wicked ropes. I own nothing but my cloth and my shadow. For family I have but memories. Some memories I am ashamed of. Kpodo, Gyasi, Ifé and the other captives must be my family now.

As the orange sun slid below the horizon, Mbekah picked out faint and then distinct sounds of talking drums. The cadences were ones she'd always known. *The drums announce our arrival.*

As daylight failed, they came to a handful of mud-covered stick houses in a grove of many scores of oil palms on the bank of a river, a river in no hurry. The drumming was more than loud; the percussion throbbed in Mbekah's chest, yet she saw no drums. She saw no women or children.

One of their guards shouted above the repeating rhythms to the headman of a dozen armed men and boys. The headman replied with an accent the same as their guards.

Yaféu smiled for the first time. The guards' spokesman said they were weary and relieved to be home, explaining that the main party would be along in a few days. He believed they had not been followed. The guard muttered something else she did not catch but her skin prickled as the headman approached, ran his fingers over her right shoulder, breast, and thigh. Mbekah set her jaw. The man knelt for a close inspection of her groin.

She closed her eyes and trembled, seeing herself smash a knee into his chin, breaking his kola-stained teeth. *No. Calm. This is not the occasion. Father was right. The rat does not call the cat to account.*

The headman stood, nodded his head and moved down the line of prisoners. The inspection completed, their guards removed the forked braces from their necks and prodded them down the bank and into the river.

"Wash yourselves." Yaféu placed his palm on Kpodo's head and shoved him down into the hip-deep water. Mbekah and the others dunked themselves and remained squatting, their heads above the flow. Guards and captives hunched in the water for a long time listening to the drums, drinking until their bellies stretched tight. Mbekah sniffed the breeze from the far bank. *Many people live in this place.*

Leaving the river, the dripping band moved a hundred paces up a gentle slope, passed between two men with short spears and entered a village through an opening in a thick wall, a wall taller than her by an arm's length. Inside, they came face to face with five drummers, their backs to the side of a dwelling, booming their signal through the gateway out to the countryside. The drumming ceased, and a hush settled on the village interrupted only by the padding feet of the new arrivals on the packed earth.

Ochre dust caked their drying feet. They trudged on along the inside of the wall and its waist-high walkway. *For men to stand on behind the wall and defend the village?* By the light of a fire at the base of the raised walkway, Mbekah observed that the wall and the huts were also ochre. Two women sat by the subdued flames facing the wall, eyes closed. As they passed the meditating pair,

Mbekah spied an indentation in the mud wall that framed the black outline of a turtle-like crocodile. On the shelf formed by the bottom sill sat an assortment of cowries and smooth pebbles. *Offerings. A shrine.* She reached for the spotted cowry that was no longer around her neck and mouthed a curse to ward off the alien spirit.

Villagers greeted their guards as the prisoners trudged in step to an open area—a round meeting place two score paces across. Near the middle of the circle, their ropes were staked at both ends and the traveling guards disappeared. Another line of captives rested in their fetters nearby. One of the boys in that line was from another forest village and kin of Mbekah's father's first wife. Each group studied the other in silence. Four of the girls in the other chain sniffled. Two boys with long sharpened sticks guarded and made it clear that speaking was not permitted.

Gray-white ashes and a few glowing embers remained in the cooking circles at the edge of the open space. Goats on stakes chomped at low stacks of cut grass next to many of the huts. An unseen baby wailed, then stopped. Mbekah imagined her mother giving a breast to her own baby sister. *Mother, please forgive. I love you. Creator, bless my mother!*

A woman at the edge of the clearing studied the newcomers while she lifted and dropped a stout pole into a hollowed-out stump. The woman stopped pounding, ladled oil and pulp from her wooden mortar and disappeared. A tan dog—its skin stretched over its ribs and its nose to the ground—trotted over to sniff at the new arrivals, tickled Mbekah's oozing ankle sores with its wet tongue, lost interest, and moved on.

The woman who had pounded with her pole in the stump came bearing a dried-gourd container. She walked down the line and each one in the chain put in a hand and retrieved a fistful of sticky paste. They ate then licked their palms and fingers. Mbekah observed Kpodo place one hand in front of his mouth while he sucked the food from the fingers of his other hand. She recalled that his prohibition, given to him as a child by their holy man, was to never permit a stranger to see him eat.

Kpodo, the headman's son, was the only married man taken from Mbekah's village. *Will he lead us in an escape? If so, I will follow.*

The food woman left and returned with her gourd. No one refused a second handful. The mashed groundnuts mixed with red palm oil was a feast to Mbekah after so little sustenance for so many days. The captives stretched out on their sides on the packed earth.

"Fssst, Mbekah." Ifé's lips were close to Mbekah's ear.

"Tell," whispered Mbekah, not moving her head.

"You judge we will ever see our families?" This was the first time Ifé had spoken to Mbekah since the start of their woeful journey.

"No, never. We are not the children of debtors like Olubayo and the other two slaves in our village. Nor have we been taken north to the dry lands where the men who praise Allah buy slaves." Mbekah waited a moment. "This is something new."

A boy guard padded down the line past Mbekah and Ifé. Mbekah lay still, eyes shut. She had studied the tethers at each end of the ropes. With a little time, they could work the heavy stakes from the ground. Once loose, they could overwhelm these two boys. *No, it will not succeed. We will not get far with these fetters and we will surely be beaten for the attempt. What is Kpodo planning? He should tell us.*

"I saw your father's body after the attack. He died defending the village. I mourn with you, Mbekah."

"We are linked both in life and in death. Father taught us so when we buried little brother beside the baobab last rainy season." Mbekah lay still and listened. *Where are the guards?*

Ifé went on. "My father and oldest brother were away when the raiders came. Other men were also away. They will gather and come for us. I will be married at the end of next rainy season. Father has the wedding-price cowries for the groom's family."

"Do not think it. This people. There are too many. The watching men and their high wall show they are ready for fighting. Everything has changed for us." Mbekah wanted to sleep.

"Your family proclaimed you ripe for marriage at the last gathering, no?"

It seemed to Mbekah that Ifé would go on all night. "Yes. My first season." Mbekah could picture Ifé wedded and big with child but could not see herself that way, not yet. Though taller than Ifé by a head, Mbekah felt herself even younger than the year that separated them. Her parents had announced their intentions, but Mbekah was certain her small breasts and thin body kept her father from seriously looking for a husband for her this year.

"Olubayo is to be married too," said Ifé.

Ifé must be aware that I know this. Olubayo was in the rope, four people behind, too far away to talk with. Olubayo came to their village as a slave two years before. She was to marry her master. *I cannot stay awake much longer.*

There was a long silence. "Will they force us here?"

"What?" Mbekah regained full consciousness.

"Will they rape us?"

CHAPTER 2

Off the Ivory Coast

Sensing something had changed, Pilot's Mate Lopo Meendez awoke from his nap on the deck of the *Ninho*. He opened his eyes and saw nothing but Rodrigo's scruffy face inches from his own. Smelled nothing but Rodrigo's fish and turnip breath.

"I was about to wake you, Senhor." Gunner's Mate Rodrigo Correia stood and pointed northeast. "Lookout's sighted a sail against the coast."

Lopo raised himself to his knees and twisted around. He popped his chin above the larboard gunwale to scan the tropical ocean northward to the distant shore.

"Onde, where?" Lopo saw the aquamarine sea edged by the low black silhouette of forest against the morning sky but saw no ship. Others on his midnight-to-dawn watch were awakening around him on the deck.

"Mount the guns," roared Pilot Brás Gonçalves from the stern.

Next to the barrel-chested pilot, two helmsmen braced the steering beam to maintain the *Ninho*'s eastward course.

Lopo scurried amidships. He noted Captain Bartolomeu Dias step from his quarterdeck cabin and drop to a knee to peer ahead under the boom of the aft sail. One hand gripped the railing and the other shaded his intense black eyes. Captain Dias squinted at the point indicated by the bow lookout.

Captain Dias bellowed, "One ship, low in the water. Running east southeast. Pilot, hold your course to intercept."

"Steady as she sails," responded Pilot Gonçalves stepping forward from under the quarterdeck overhang to look directly up at the captain who leaned over the railing. "Desgraçoado ship's master will wish he'd never ventured into Portuguese waters."

Avoiding eye contact with Pilot Gonçalves, Lopo clamped his left arm around the mainmast and leaned over the uncovered hatchway.

His two gunnery crews struggled with block and tackle, its taut rope disappearing into the shallow hold.

"Por Deus. You move like besotted cows. Pull together. Heave. Heave. Heave like it's a hogshead of Coimbra wine."

A brass artillery piece, as long as Lopo's leg and twice the girth, inched its way up and out of the darkness. Lopo's men pushed the suspended weapon starboard and lowered it onto a fitted, oak sled to haul forward. They hoisted its twin to the larboard side and brought up two kegs of serpentine powder as well as a score of gray stone balls the size of pomegranates. Their chore in the hold completed, the men scampered up through the hatchway to escape the air below—sour with the odor of bilge and rats. Lopo noted that men on the nearby *São Sebastian*, *Ninho*'s consort caravela, likewise made preparations for battle.

Lopo followed the second cannon as his men muscled it forward. With grunts and heavy breathing, they mounted it, sled included to allow for recoil, atop a thick plank that protruded forward through an opening in the gunwale left of the bow.

A glance over his right shoulder confirmed his dread. With his too-small eyes set too far apart under a thick brow, Pilot Gonçalves bore holes into him. Lopo's eyes met the pilot's and the two glared into each other's core. Pilot Gonçalves widened his pursed lips to a flat smile and nodded slightly. Lopo shuddered and returned to his task.

His two gun crews had time to load before the two caravelas could get within effective range—about the distance of a long crossbow shot. With his sleeve, he dabbed perspiration from his forehead notwithstanding the temperate offshore breeze. He'd never fired the guns at anything but empty hillsides and floating barrels. Indeed, the new pieces had never been fired in anger.

He couldn't flush Gonçalves' vengeful eyes from his mind. *Watching my back whenever the captain's not around is tiresome.*

From his working stance near the bow, Lopo studied the target's square-rigged sails, high sides and towering forecastle. He'd seen many cogs before—the vessels favored in the North Atlantic for their cargo capacity. The pennant was from the Low Countries.

"Mãe de Deus. Sailing back to Europe from anywhere on the Guinea Coast in that barrel bottom of a ship would be hell's own punishment," he said to no one in particular.

No one responded.

He turned his back on his crews to watch an infantry sergeant assist his six men with their matchlock harquebuses. The *São Sebastian* shipped another eight soldiers, all for land duty at the *Mina*. *Our good fortune to have them for today's fight.*

Father Vasco Estevez, a passenger also on his way to a posting at the *Mina*, appeared from his sleeping closet behind the helmsmen. Robed in his sweat-stained, black habit, he stepped into the sun to survey the cause of all the activity.

Amidships, from a leather-bound chest hauled out for the occasion, the cargo master issued a polished cutlass or boarding ax to every sailor not working the cannons.

Lopo returned his attention to his gunnery crews.

"We caught the Castilians here in eighty-one," Rodrigo said from behind the cannon on the other side of the bow. "Their ship was loaded with poached ivory and slaves. Crew fought like devils. We killed two and cut up another ten before they yielded."

"God bless the Pope and King João's diplomacy. We won't see the Castilians again on the Guinea coast. For a few years, anyway." Lopo surveyed the fleeing ship again. "These thieves are Lowlanders."

"Praise the Virgin we have cannon this voyage," said Rodrigo.

The two shallow-drafted caravelas sped at the Dutch cog like matched hounds. Lopo was not surprised to see that the lumbering vessel had no artillery—the weight on its high decks would make it dangerously unstable. The Dutchman's advantage was its tall forecastle, which, he guessed, bristled with crossbowmen.

Lopo had traded peacefully in Rotterdam harbor less than two years before. *We have no quarrel with the Low Countries, but we'll not ignore trespass.*

Lopo turned to see one of his crew, a smooth-faced youth on his first voyage, shiver.

"You all right, Joselinho?"

The boy peered back from his crouching position left of the loaded gun. Wiping a tear with a rub of his shoulder and upper arm, Joselinho croaked, "All right, yes."

"Don't think on it. Just do your duty." Lopo paused for effect, then winked. "And duck behind the gunwale the rest of the time."

Joselinho managed a smile. Lopo forced himself to not tousle the boy's thick hair—light brown like his own and a rare color among a ship full of dark-haired sailors. *Had my nephew survived the pox, he'd be Joselinho's close image.*

Touching crucifix to his lips so Joselinho saw the gesture, Lopo continued. "They won't get near enough to land a single bolt from their bows on our deck."

He'd rehearsed this situation with the captain and pilot. They would use speed and maneuverability as well as the new cannon to harry the lone Dutchman into surrender. Boarding was not a good option. Besides the soldiers, a few workmen, and the priest, the *Ninho* carried a crew of only two dozen.

Lopo looked back over the deck and sixty feet of brilliant sunshine to Captain Dias who had climbed down from the quarterdeck to stand opposite Pilot Gonçalves. Sailors waited to trim sail on command or crouched with the soldiers against the gunwales.

Lopo raised both arms, pointer fingers to the sky, signaling that both cannon were loaded and primed. Captain Dias, jaw set, waved a hand to acknowledge. Lopo turned to concentrate forward, steadying himself with a hand on the gunwale against the action of waves on the speeding hull.

The hunting caravelas drew to a thousand paces on the pirate ship, which made no indication of heaving to. The *São Sebastian* swung south to later curve back, sailing close-hauled to attack the Dutchman's side. Captain Dias gave the order to lower the aft canvas, one of two triangular sails that powered the caravela. The *Ninho* slowed but still advanced on the fleeing ship's stern and starboard quarter.

For a moment, no one spoke. Timbers creaked at every seam and popped at the joints. Rigging shushed in the breeze.

The Portuguese ships closed to two hundred paces on the Dutch cog. The *Ninho* shifted and held a compass point to starboard, aiming the fixed cannon right of the targeted ship.

Lopo turned to watch the stern of his own ship for instructions.

Captain Dias crossed himself and put out his right arm signaling a cannonade wide of the Dutchman. He raised then dropped his left arm. "Fogo".

All eyes on the *Ninho* focused on Lopo. Kneeling beside the left gun, he blew on the smoldering cord, timed the shot with the bow on its way up, leaned away and touched the glowing red spot to the powder hole. The brass piece thundered. It kicked and hurled backward along the plank. Instantly a cloud of burnt sulfur and saltpeter obscured his view. The smoke dissipated in the wind in time for Lopo to see the ball splash menacingly close to the rogue ship. Satisfied, he started his men on the long process of reloading and repositioning the gun. Neither he nor the gunnery crew could hear anything after the blast, so he supplemented every command with an exaggerated gesture.

Captain Dias adjusted the *Ninho*'s course to sight its second cannon on the Dutchman. Lopo's crew wet swabbed the first. He divided his attention between the target, his two gun crews, and the captain. No sign of surrender.

Captain Dias signaled for both caravelas to commence firing. With the resulting smoke, Lopo could observe only the first of his ship's two shots. It and both of *São Sebastian*'s cannon balls crashed into the cog's planking above the waterline.

The *São Sebastian* veered to her right. Soldiers' firearms flashed from her gunwales as she came across the cog's bow. The ragged pops of the eight harquebus shots came to Lopo's ears an instant later. A flight of honed crossbow bolts spewed from the foe's forecastle, falling into the sea or embedding themselves in the *São Sebastian*'s side.

Sailors reefed the mainsail once on the *Ninho*, to keep it from overtaking the foe. Lopo concentrated on his crews' frantic reloading.

Leaping to his feet, Joselinho screamed. "They're striking colors. We've beaten them."

Even his deafened crewmates understood.

"Viva!" cried Rodrigo from behind the other gun.

Men all over the *Ninho* sprang to shout in a riot of sailor's grubby white jerkins and soldiers' green coats. One soldier tapped a flamenco, hands high and clapping. Others whooped and slapped backs. Their sergeant stomped up and down the deck to restore discipline. Estevez the priest stole to the gunwale in front of the quarterdeck ladder and vomited his breakfast to the fish.

Lopo crossed himself, closed his eyes and offered thanks his boast to Joselinho came to pass and that none of the cannon shots fizzled due to bad powder.

Captain Dias cupped his hands around his mouth. "Stand by with the cannon. Sergeant, have the harquebusiers cover the forecastle."

The men on the yielding ship lowered sail and the caravelas came along either side, also dropping their sails. Bronzed, bearded mariners with arms out and hands empty stood on the deck of the cog looking down at the victors.

All afternoon, the Portuguese crews secured the interloping Dutch seamen in chains on the open decks of the two caravelas—chains installed normally to carry slaves to Lisbon. The pilot from the *São Sebastian* and five men from each caravela boarded the cog to sail it on their continued journey eastward. Six of the cog's own crew remained onboard as deckhands.

Lopo oversaw his men as they returned the cannon, powder and shot below the deck and then he reported to Gonçalves. "Ordinance secured, Senhor Piloto."

Gonçalves spat over the starboard gunwale and fixed on Lopo like a bull pawing the earth.

Lopo denied his urge to touch the scab on his own mutilated left ear. *Curse your eyes, Gonçalves. It was you, not I started the fight in São Tiago.* Lopo stood his ground. *You bit away one ear, you'll not get the other.*

"Nice shooting, scholar boy son of a whore. How will you fare when you can't fight with cannon from a hundred paces? When you have naught but a boarding ax and your attacker's foul breath between you?"

Captain Dias leaned over the quarterdeck rail and peered down at his two officers. "Nicely done, Lopo. Gunnery exercises have been worth the pain, no?"

Lopo, looking up, nodded. "They have, yes, o meu Capitão."

Under the captain's scrutiny, the pilot addressed Lopo in a civil tone. "Get some sleep, your watch starts soon."

Sails hoisted, the three vessels picked up the evening's offshore breeze. Captain Dias interviewed the Dutch ship's master but Lopo understood little of their conversation in French. He figured the Dutch master planned to tell his vessel's owners that he surrendered the ship and its cargo of ivory and sea-lion skins after a valiant defense, pleased he had lost none of his men in a hopeless struggle. *If that is his thinking, the master is going to be rudely surprised.*

#

Pilot Brás Gonçalves stood on *Ninho's* deck shaded by the aft sail. His two helmsmen manned the tiller just behind him under the overhang of the quarterdeck. The deck in front of the hatchway was packed with the captured Lowlanders sitting knee to back in irons. Sleeping sailors—the men on Lopo's night watch—cluttered the deck aft of the hatch.

Gonçalves had tired of Pilot's Mate Lopo Meendez. The young officer was naïve about how things were done on the ship. Men on your watch owed you something—part of their pay—for one thing. Lopo didn't collect from his men and that was bad for Gonçalves who did from his. Because he could read, it was Lopo they sent to the navy's new artillery academy for six months. A privileged whelp. *It's clear the little cockroach wants my job. With his throat slit, he'll never get it.*

Gonçalves eyed the bored prisoners then spoke over his shoulder. "Two weeks since I had a woman. One of these Dutch boys will have to do."

"You can't wait a few days?" asked Nunno, the sinuous man at the tiller.

"Me, I can," said Belchior, the stout sailor opposite Nunno on the steering beam. "At the *Mina*, you get a woman when you want. Is it not so, Piloto? And on the return sail we'll have the slave girls." Belchior had been with Gonçalves on his last voyage to the *Mina* and knew the routine.

"It won't be all dice and women at the *Mina*. You'll help with collections—getting true accounts from the pimp takes time and muscle. We may also have to take care of any competition." Gonçalves didn't mention his gold business. It was one thing to keep prostitutes in the village; it was against regulations, but the garrison needed the outlet. Governor d'Azambuja was not going to complain. It was quite another to buy and sell the precious metal from a crown station like the *Mina*; he could hang for that. Besides, he needed no lackeys to deal secretly with the assistant factor at the fort whom he trusted, sort of.

"We can jump Lopo at the *Mina*. In the village," Belchior said.

"Shut your mouth. We'll deal with him when I say." Gonçalves heard the captain's boots on the quarterdeck. Gonçalves stepped back under the overhang. "Shhh."

CHAPTER 3

Palm Wine

Mbekah opened her eyes; someone had tickled her foot. The food woman from the previous night knelt over her. She held a plump bladder and pointed to Mbekah's mouth. Mbekah opened and the woman squirted water, stopping several times for her to swallow.

"It is enough."

The woman touched the cloth under Mbekah. "Pretty."

"From my father."

"Better to hide it."

Mbekah nodded. The woman moved on to Ifé.

Mbekah surveyed the village around them—one edge of the circle of houses in shadow, the other perfectly illuminated. Goats bleated. *If only I could milk our goats for mother again, I would never complain.*

The food woman disappeared with her limp water skin. A new pair of skin-and-ribs boys patrolled the two lines of captives. It would be difficult for Mbekah to talk with the others during daylight.

The food woman brought her gourd. Each captive reached in for a fistful of the oily paste, the same they had eaten before sleeping. The woman returned three times until each captive was fed. She came again with shea for their ankles and wrists.

Mbekah folded her cloth into a small pillow and laid herself down again to hide it with her head. This was the first morning in many they did not have to rise and press on. She yawned and stared at Gyasi's back. The mild taste of groundnut mash lingered. From the sounds, she guessed at what was going on among the mud dwellings: a small girl, most likely, broke sticks for the family oven; another pulverized millet in a scooped-out stone between her legs; a baby fussed (to be held?); dogs worried a he-goat. She closed her eyes and saw her family and the village dogs making those same sounds around her father's three huts.

#

Mbekah jerked awake. *Ifé?* Ifé kneed her in the buttocks again. Mbekah sat up, careful to not move her bound ankle or the wrist rope strung across her belly.

Three men crouched by Olubayo and unfastened her. Two of them hoisted her to her feet and yanked her forward, each gripping one of her arms. The third man followed.

"What? Where?" Olubayo struggled to look back at her friends. "Help. Please."

Mbekah lowered her eyes, relieved it was not her. Ashamed at the thought.

Olubayo faced forward, locked her knees and planted her heels. "No!"

Her escorts wrenched her forward, not missing a step.

Olubayo's legs collapsed. "No. Don't. Please."

They dragged her from the circle and disappeared between two huts.

Mbekah glanced at the whimpering women in the line of captives opposite them. One trembled. Another looked Mbekah in the eye and shook her head.

#

The sun, a yellow snail, slid to mid sky. Their food woman came again with her water skin and gourd. The snail slid onward.

Two men with Olubayo between them emerged from the ring of houses. Blood ran down her inner thighs. With their support, she wobbled to her place in the ropes. She sniffled and stared at her feet.

The men secured her hand and foot, stood, and backed away. They lingered to chat with the two boys guarding them. Mbekah saw them steal glances at her.

She tried for Olubayo's eye but Olubayo covered her face with a forearm and lay back on her cloth. She breathed long and slow and began to whimper.

The shaking-head woman looked at Mbekah and shook her head.

Olubayo? Mbekah had heard of men forcing women, even young girls. Two rainy seasons past, a girl in her village was attacked; so said the whisperers. Her attacker was never found out and the girl went to live in another village.

Yaféu, the slave raider with the bad eye, and another man strode into the cleared area and joined the two men talking with the guards. The group shuffled sideways toward Mbekah, feigning no interest in her or the other captives.

Mbekah closed her eyes and took a deep breath. She clenched her fists and prepared. *Whoever touches me will not soon forget.*

What is happening? She opened her eyes. The men had passed by and on to the head of the line.

Like leopards, two men fell upon Kpodo and one upon Gyasi. The two guard boys threatened Mbekah and Ifé with their sharpened sticks.

"Eee yah." One of Kpodo's assailants jerked back from the struggle, cradling his right hand with his left. "He bites. He bit me." He leaned forward again, knelt on Kpodo's left bicep and walloped Kpodo's cheek with his good hand.

The fourth man removed Kpodo's wife from her spot between Kpodo and Gyasi. He twisted one arm behind her and hustled her away, working to keep her from veering side to side.

Yaféu stood—leaving bitten-hand man alone to hold Kpodo—and faced Mbekah.

"Aawgck."

Yaféu spun back.

Bitten-hand man tore at the rope Kpodo had looped around his neck.

"Yah." Yaféu fell to a knee and ripped Kpodo's death grip from the cord.

Bitten hand rolled away. He held his neck and gasped. He recovered, moved back, and helped Yaféu pummel Kpodo until he lay curled into a bundle—not moving except for the slight rise and fall of his ribs.

The attackers rose to their feet, their chests heaving. Yaféu took two steps toward Mbekah and pounced. Bitten hand slipped her from her ropes and the two men jogged her away.

She had let her vigilance down watching the melee. She hadn't kicked, punched, or bitten anyone. *My only chance since my father's murder.* Elevated slightly and trotted along, she couldn't stiffen her knees to drive her heels into the ochre path.

She silently invoked the Creator, the Great Spirit. *Help me survive. I will survive.*

They retraced their route of the previous night: past the shrine, along the wall, out the gate, and across the river to the guard village. They shoved her into a hut in the palm grove and followed her in.

In the dim light, Yaféu pushed her down.

Her back on the dirt floor, Mbekah kicked at the first face in range. She felt her heel crush bone under flesh. *At last!*

Bitten hands' nose gushed crimson. He bellowed and darted out through the uncovered doorway.

Yaféu and two other men struggled for control over Mbekah. They pinned her arms and spread her legs.

Mbekah bucked her midriff until out of breath.

Outside, men and boys crowded around the opening of the hut to watch.

The headman of the palm-grove guards—the one who had inspected her the afternoon before—entered the room. He stood over her, eyes glazed.

She twisted and bucked again until the big man sat on her thighs. He reeked of wine.

She cried out, "The Great Spirit curse you. And your sons. And your grandsons and—"

Hands clapped over her mouth, immobilizing her head.

She tasted dust and salt. *I step on your face. I piss in your eyes.*

The headman stood and removed his loin cloth then dropped to mount her. He failed. He could not perform. He growled and rose. He turned to the gaping spectators and lunged. The crowd scattered, and he flopped to the ground. He picked himself up, steadied himself, and re-entered the hut, one tentative step after the other.

The hands on her mouth relaxed and pulled away.

The headman stepped to her side. He looked down at himself. Mbekah looked at his limp member.

"Ha!" Immediately she knew it was the wrong thing to say or do.

Hands pressed down on her mouth again.

The headman screamed. He kicked Mbekah's thigh, lifting her middle from the ground for an instant.

Pain blasted her from her leg to her neck. Another blow. This time she felt his toenail pierce skin and muscle. Kick followed bloody kick until two men rushed in and wrestled him from the dwelling.

The mob gathered again at the door, but no one dared enter. No one said a thing.

What now? She lay still but not relaxed. She studied the gawkers at the door. She memorized each face inside the room. *Yaféu, I will dig out your good eye with a stick and then I will kill you. And you, holding man; and you, hands-on-the-mouth man; and your bitten-hand man and your wine-bibbing headman. My people will leave your carcasses for the jackals.* She suppressed a sob but could not squeeze back her tears.

CHAPTER 4

A New Kind of Evil

Mbekah bore a hide purse over her shoulder and balanced a small elephant tusk on her head—sideways so not to poke Ifé in the face or Gyasi in the back. All the captives carried something. They traveled naked because the men of the ochre village had stolen their cloths. She counted this the third day since leaving the village.

The breeze picked up. Mbekah lifted her head and sniffed but could not relate the fresh smell with anything she knew.

Three lines of slaves and their handlers moved along at a comfortable pace. For five days they'd remained in their captors' village, regaining some of their weight. A third line of captives arrived two days after Mbekah's group. As in the village, food was adequate on this portion of their journey. 'Fat goat, enthusiastic buyer' she remembered her father saying more than once.

A clean scent again wafted into her face. It was not the smell of trees or grasses.

Mbekah maintained her pace though every left step was painful because of her leg, cut and bruised from ankle to thigh. She could not put the assault from her mind. Mbekah and the captives had bathed twice during river crossings since departing the village. Even so, she smelled her assailant's foul odor on her own skin.

Why are these men so evil? Is it because they are many and have a high wall? Or was Father right? The heart, not the horns, causes the ram to bully.

Slaves in her forest were treated well enough and eventually became, more or less, part of the owner's family and of the village. She had hoped it would be the same for her group. Like dumping mud on a flame, the men in the ochre village snuffed her hope. Still, she felt fortunate that they only came one time for her and had not been able to force her.

Each day in the village, the food woman lathered a red salve on Mbekah's lacerations and bruised muscles. Mbekah recognized the balm made from the stemless green leaves of the blood plant. Her own mother had taught Mbekah to make it.

On the fourth day, the food woman's face was bruised and her left eye swollen shut. Mbekah touched the woman's battered cheek but the woman avoided her eyes. Men in Mbekah's village hit their wives sometimes but rarely beat them. In the forest, a woman could return to her family and demand the return of her family's wedding cowries if abused.

It is the palm wine. The men there have too much of it.

The last time the food woman came, she whispered that the village council had scolded the minor headman who attempted to rape Mbekah because he had almost crippled her. They said he might have rendered her of little value as a slave. The minor headman was banished to the guard huts on the other side of the river until the slaves were gone. She said Mbekah was spared further sexual assaults, so her leg could heal before the next journey.

Mbekah kept her eye on Kpodo. Despite his calm demeanor, Mbekah knew Kpodo seethed for vengeance. They all did. For the first time in her young life, Mbekah understood the feeling. The men in the ochre village must pay for the murders and the rapes. They must be punished for the theft and the sadness they brought to her village and the misery dumped on her and the other captives. *We must wait for a better moment to exact our revenge. Father would counsel us to be patient. 'Watch the egg to eat the chicken.'*

Mbekah noted that, since the rapes began, the men in the rope avoided looking at the women's faces. Gyasi practically jumped each time she touched him. Kpodo acted as if his wife were no longer present. *Do not fret Kpodo. The calabash still carries water.*

They were not permitted to talk among themselves, but were allowed to sing. Countless times they sang the death song for their slain kinsmen. Mbekah imagined she was home to dance with the village women at her father's burial. She cradled baby sister in her arms and comforted her mother, her sister, and her father's first wife. *Little sister Foladé was not taken in the raid. She must care for mother. How will they know I'm sorry for the wicked things I said the last time I spoke with them? For all the times I was not respectful?*

They came to the top of a grassy sand hill and Mbekah spied the mother of all waters. It was as grand as the sky. Purple and silver light shimmered from the surface near the shore. Billowing white clouds emphasized the deep blue water further out. *What is the song for this water's spirit . . . spirits?*

The company tramped on. At the guards' command they dropped their loads, padded onto the ivory sand, and into water which stung Mbekah's skinless ankles. *What kind of water is this?*

They continued into the gentle surf in step, in a line parallel to the beach. Kpodo, still the first captive in the rope, called cadence. A ridge of water rushed at them, growing all the time. They stopped to watch. Mbekah held her breath. The ridge slowed, reared up, fell toward them and turned to foam. Mbekah's skin tingled when the white, churning water washed through the line. She giggled.

"You bathe. Now," said a guard.

Ifé dunked herself in the waist-deep water and began rubbing her body with her free hand. Others did likewise, careful not to jerk the ropes.

The cool water re-energized Mbekah. She filled her mouth to drink then sprayed the water out. *Salty! What good is such water? And so much of it.*

After the bath, the bound forest youths and their guards moved back to the trail, eyes squinting to see ahead. A cloud floated in front of the low sun, cutting its glare from Mbekah's face. Something glimmered in the distance. Something white and as big as an entire village. A village taller than the baobab tree.

"Step, step, step." They trudged forward in silence except for Kpodo's voice.

Mbekah watched the white village, or whatever it was, grow as they walked, almost forgetting her load.

The pleasant sensations of the ocean fled from her as they approached a grove-sized structure on a low hill. It stood on the opposite edge of a small lake open on one side to the ocean. The walls, if that is what they were, towered as high as three men. *No, four men.* Water surrounded two of the three sides that she could see. One section (a square house?) inside the walls was taller than any part of the walls, taller by the height of two more men. The roof of the tall section was thatched with reddish clay pot sections.

Kpodo ceased calling the steps but the burdened captives continued around the half lake toward the immense white house. Mbekah walked to a beat in her head. Left foot, right foot, left, right in perfect step with the others. Her bound left hand swung forward, back, forward, back.

"This is a new kind of evil." Mbekah spoke quietly. "This village can do what it wants, and others cannot interfere. Yet it draws our guards and their trade like beetles to fresh dung."

Gyasi grunted his agreement.

"What will they do to us in this place?" Ifé paused before

answering her own question. "They will do what they choose. We will never be free again, not in this life."

Mbekah walked for a spell. "I will," she whispered. "I will live free again."

CHAPTER 5

Portugal's Future Among Nations

King João II and two advisors sat astride their chestnut Arabians on the south bank of the Tagus River estuary. Across the broad waterway they could see the docks and the white structures of Lisbon dominated by the tan, reconstructed Moorish castle on the hill above. The king noted the arrival of miniature triangular sails—the first of the city's fishing fleet to return that day from the nearby Atlantic. A multitude of his subjects, ant-sized in the distance, appeared, unloaded, haggled over, and carried off the fresh catch.

King João turned his attention to his companions and the duck hunt in progress before him. However, he had more on his mind than birding.

"Splendid Neblis. From Andalusia, no?" said Bishop Bernaldo de Loronha, Portugal's ambassador to the Holy See.

"Sim," King João agreed. "Falcons as spirited as the Emir of Granada's own. But hold judgment until you see my Northerns fly." *I wonder what useful intelligence the bishop has for us that he could not include it in his written report.*

"No room for doubt." Andrao de Faria, the king's chamberlain, touched the fingertips of his right hand to his high cheekbone for emphasis. "The Icelandics we bought at the

Valkenswaard auction this year are the finest I've ever seen, surpassing even the best Maltese hunting birds. The Dutch know where to get superior falcons."

"Judging from his aviary, the new pope agrees," Bishop de Loronha said.

"Indeed." King João chuckled. "My agents paid dearly a few times to outbid His Holiness in Valkenswaard. Is it a sin to buy from under the Holy Father's powdered nose?"

Ten falconers each steadied a staff, perches for the king's hunting birds. To start the hunt, one of the handlers removed the hood of a white-breasted female Nebli. He released the leg bindings and shoved the staff in the air. King and his guests paused to admire the bird climb high into the morning's aquamarine sky to circle in anticipation of a target.

Near the shore, a score of servants slogged forward in a line, slapping the churned-up water and beating the blue-gray marsh grass with sticks. Dog handlers restrained four hip-high Poodles shaved African lion style.

"We've read your report, Bishop, on the changes in Rome," Chamberlain de Faria said.

King João nudged his horse closer to the other two. "Pope Sixtus' death came not a moment too soon. I fear God's kingdom on earth may not forever survive 'inspired' leaders like Sixtus."

Chamberlain de Faria looked around. "Indeed, Sixtus set a new standard for collecting and spending."

A mallard, flushed from a clump of reeds, lumbered into the air ahead of the noisy waders. The Nebli locked its eyes on the fleeing blur of brown and white and stooped on the waterfowl. One foot crushed the duck's neck and the other foot sank its dagger-sharp talons into the duck's back. Both birds lost altitude before the raptor dropped the duck, back broken, into open water thirty paces from shore. A pale Poodle splashed into the river to retrieve the thrashing bird.

King João followed the action. *What skill the falcon has! What focus! What power! A creature after my own heart.*

Bishop de Loronha broke the silence. "The new pope is boring and harmless, and will do little more than bide his time and die."

"By all the Saints, let it be so," King João said. "Why is the Mother Church's treasury not bulging? Was not Pope Sixtus himself surprised at the cartloads of ducats pouring in to buy his new indulgences for the dead?"

Chamberlain de Faria patted his mount's neck. "Such sums for a parchment from his Holiness! The papacy now has its own money tree. No, its own money orchard!"

"Alas, Pope Sixtus did find a way to spend it. All of it," Bishop de Loronha said.

King João turned his horse to get close to his advisors again. "Wars and politics are not cheap. This I know." *O meu Deus. This I know too well.*

Bishop de Loronha shook his head. "Penniless and finally without a war. Poor fellow. In Rome, they say Sixtus was slain by the peace."

"Such cynicism. But he wins in the end, no? With six of his 'nephews' as cardinals, dead Pope Sixtus will be with us for a long time." *I can learn much from our late pope.*

King João continued. "Let us complain no more about our departed pontiff, may he rest with God. Portugal's trade concessions are secure and the royal coffers full, thanks to Sixtus mediating our peace treaty with the Castilians and for endorsing our exclusive right to the Guinea Coast."

Tall and angular, Bishop de Loronha stood in the stirrups to stretch. "There is another of Pope Sixtus' legacies we cannot ignore—the Holy Inquisition right on our border. The Castilians found ten thousand heretics in Spanish Andalusia last year, mostly 'new' Christians. The conviction rate is remarkable. Eight thousand saying Pater Nosters and paying the fine. Two thousand burned and their property confiscated."

Bishop de Loronha paused. "To be fair, Pope Sixtus attempted to curb the excesses but Castile and Leon stood their ground. It's the Spanish crown that now controls the Inquisition."

"Sim." Chamberlain de Faria nodded. "Plump Jewish converts in the wine press and the inquisitors tramping them for a flow of riches for Fernando and Isabella—silver to finance the reconquest of Granada. Let us pray their Majesties are kept busy with their Jews, new Christians, and belligerent Moors for a long time. We've already had our fill of Castilian aggression."

King João reined in his fidgety mount. "They had better tread the grapes lightly. Who will pay cash money taxes when the Jews, converted or not, are gone?"

King João dismounted. The chamberlain and bishop quickly did the same. The king waived away the squires who stepped forward to hold their horses' reins.

The three led their animals away from the entourage.

Bishop de Loronha said, "With Your Majesty's permission, may I speak of another matter? What of our efforts to find Prester John's kingdom? Of late, my spies in Rome have heard no rumors of your plans."

King João smiled and nodded. "I'm pleased our new projects are still secret. The two Jews we sent overland to India have reported back only once. One is on his way to Jerusalem. The other is traveling to India via Cairo. What do your spies in the papal palace report about others' efforts to contact Prester John?"

"Now and then I learn of missions—all secret, none successful. All agree with our view that the kingdom first to establish an alliance with John's Christian empire will be in the best position to discover and maintain a trade route to the East."

"We will also gain power and influence across Europe if we can secure John as an ally against the Ottoman Empire," Chamberlain de Faria added. "An ally located at the Mohammedans' soft underbelly!"

"It's true," King João said. "Portugal's future among nations depends on our finding Prester John's realm first."

The hunt master brought the limp, green-headed duck for the king to inspect. "We should move further along the shore, Your Majesty. We've hunted out this section."

"Let it be done. We'll follow in a while." King João tugged the reins so his gelding stepped around to shield him and his two ministers from the departing entourage. He looked at Bishop de Loronha and lowered his voice. "We've begun a second effort to find Prester John. Our traveling Jews are too vulnerable for us to rely solely on their eventual success."

"Pray tell," Bishop de Loronha said.

CHAPTER 6

The Village of Two Parts

The procession of guards and captives trudged around the small bay and it appeared to Mbekah that they were going to the village with the massive white walls. However, a river emptied into the bay between them and the walls. Instead of fording the river, the group marched along the bank a hundred paces and veered inland to skirt a lagoon whence the short river flowed.

Mbekah watched a flame flicker to life high in the tower, a signal to all the countryside inland as well as upon the great body of water opposite the land. A faint chorus of frogs greeted them. In the failing light, white birds with stilt legs snaked their necks into the water among the reeds. The frog serenade attained maximum volume.

At the end of the lagoon, the solemn company turned again toward the great water, waded the lagoon's shallow source, and came into a cluster of five score or more huts. The frog song diminished, then ceased to be heard.

The light in the white tower was never far from them during this final stage of the day's march. Mbekah guessed they would arrive at the high walls if they passed through these huts and turned left again. *What terrible men live in the great house with the tower? Why do people in this village live so near it? Foolish rats to dance in the cat's doorway.*

They entered the village in the dark, bearing their loads and dragging their rope along a dividing path. The dwellings on the left had mud walls like those in the ochre village. On the right, they had woven stick walls. Women and girls on both sides of the path turned from their meal preparations to consider the procession.

At every fire Mbekah noted an iron pot. Before the wet season, her father had brought home an identical pot. For it, he traded cowries hoarded over three years selling yams from the family's second field. Mbekah had dug many of the roots herself. Almost everyone coveted her family's pot, one of only two in the village. Her father wondered out loud what distant village made iron pots and how they came to be sold in the forest. Iron weapons and tools, they had obtained for generations from Jenneh in faraway Songhay, but there had been no iron cookware in the forest when he was a boy. The flat-bottomed pot cooked while resting on charcoal separated from the fire or over flames, hung by its sturdy handle. After each use, one of the women of Mbekah's household scoured the pot with sand then rubbed it to a shiny black finish with palm nut oil. *This is a rich village for every fire to have such a pot.*

Men from this village by the lagoon and the great water fell in step with the captives' guards to hear about their journey. They helped herd the bound newcomers into a circular yard fenced by sharpened sticks.

A boy, finger in his mouth, observed from the narrow opening of the corral while two men secured the ropes from each end of the three lines of captives to heavy stakes in the ground.

Mbekah savored the pebble-sized millet cake and flake of baked fish brought to her but her stomach murmured for more.

Sleep did not come quickly. Stretched out in the dung-scented dust of the enclosure, Mbekah listened to their guards chatting with a local who spoke with their same accent. Passing a drinking bladder between them, the men shared tales.

She learned that the village marked the boundary between two nations united under one king. A group from each nation lived there divided by the path the captives had used to enter the village.

The young man told of men with no color in their skin. Since he was a small boy, the strange men had been coming over the ocean in large wooden fish birds with towering white wings. Each time, one fish bird or two at the most came. He said the pale fish-bird men sought gold, ivory, and the hides of certain beasts. They also desired slaves.

The man's words removed one dark riddle from Mbekah's mind, adding another.

Last year the pale men, who call themselves 'Cristowns', arrived in many fish birds—a score less two. They came as an army with splendid weapons, some that thundered. The king of two nations accepted the Cristowns' gifts, and before returning inland to his own village, gave them leave to build a strong house on the finger of land separating the ocean from their lagoon.

In a short time, there was trouble. The Cristowns unloaded building stones from their fish birds. But soon they began to cut blocks from a sacred rock on the peninsula.

"We rushed with spears and knives to the sacrilege. We killed one Cristown and wounded two more before our headman stopped us. More Cristowns joined the stone butchers. We faced each other, weapons in hand, ready at any time to resume the battle."

"What then?" a guard asked.

"Their headman brought more gifts to our village headman. They talked. We returned to our homes."

"And the sacred rock?"

"They chopped it in pieces. The dead stone now forms the front wall of the strong house."

The wine drinkers agreed the Cristowns were wrong to kill the rock.

Mbekah shuddered. *Pale men with no respect for the spirits. Where do they come from? Why do they seek slaves? To feast upon?*

"Now the Cristowns give us cowry shells and purple wine to lie with our women in a long house here in the village. We trade the cowries to other villages for our meat and millet. We drink the wine at night and sleep most of the day."

"A good life," said one guard.

"Our ancient holy man and some of the elders disagree. But our king sent us a young holy man who assures us it's good to trade with the pale men. In the afternoon, I think the old ones are right. After dark, I think the wine is right."

The discussion ended. Or so it seemed to Mbekah.

"Take the bladder. Drink. Eee yow, tomorrow after the trading, I will sell you Cristown wine at a good price. I will teach you Cristown gambling."

CHAPTER 7

Gentle Father

The thirty captives stood in silence a hundred paces from the monstrous fortified dwelling on their right. They had seen the opposite wall the previous afternoon. This morning they waited in three rows facing the path leading to the mysterious stone structure, the ocean at their backs and the lagoon in front. A confusion of seabirds shrilled overhead.

Mbekah's stomach pleaded; they had received neither food nor drink before their guards marched them to their present position between the village and the strong house.

With so many guards on this part of the journey and with their heavy burdens, their captors had not made them wear the neck yokes. For that Mbekah was grateful even though the wrist and ankle ropes were still in place and were checked and rechecked by their guards.

From her spot in the first row, Mbekah turned her head to the right and studied the wall and its iron and wood gate—tall as three men, wide as two with arms spread. *How do they open the heavy door? How do they cross the ditch at the foot of the wall?*

Stacks of elephant tusks, striped black and white hides, and sacks of pepper pods stretched out on the opposite side of the sandy walkway in front of the captives. Between the human and non-human trade goods, the headman from the ochre village balanced on a stool with red markings—surely a symbol of authority like the decorated stools used by leaders in the forest. His counselor and a headman from the Village of Two Parts stood behind. Guards kept vigil at the rear and sides of the formation. The counselor stepped forward, shook out a cloth in the offshore breeze, and squared it on the coarse gray sand before the seated headman.

Mbekah gaped. Her cloth! The cloth of colors she'd received from her father. The cloth she adored. The cloth her sister Foladé, her half-sisters, and other girls in their village had envied.

Why did we quarrel? True, I left them with extra work when I lingered to play the seeds and houses game with father, uncle and cousin Manu. But . . . I loved them <u>all</u>. I <u>love</u> them all.

The sun climbed the cobalt sky forcing Mbekah to shade her eyes with her free right hand whenever she looked at the strong house. Silhouetted heads peered at them from notches at the top of the wall.

Men, women and children from the village gathered and mingled noisily to the left of the captives, leaving a gap of a score of paces.

The crowd fell silent and parted. A man strode through the opening. He seemed to take no notice of the captives. The black contour lines of a full-face tattoo and the long white feather in his left hand gave away his office. This was the village's young holy man. The well-fed man moved behind the seated headman and stood erect.

Following at a distance in the steps of the newly arrived man, a gray-haired man limped through the still-silent villagers. He stooped over a tan gourd supported against his chest with both hands, his face tattoo almost hidden among his wrinkles. Two boys walked behind, each also bearing a gourd. The three left the trail and paused in front of Olubayo—the last captive in the rope with Mbekah, and the one nearest the village.

The three officials turned to watch as did all others present. The old man dipped a small cup into the gourd's opening and handed it to Olubayo. She drank and returned the cup. The old man refilled it and gave it to her again. She emptied it a second time.

The young holy man shouted, "Get him away from the captives," and stepped toward the old man.

The local headman gripped the enraged holy man by the arm to restrain him.

No other person moved to hinder the old man who dragged his bad foot and stopped in front of the next captive.

The young holy man shook his arm loose from the headman's grasp and attempted to bully with his glare.

The old man ignored him. He repeated his kindness with each captive until he stood in front of Mbekah. He peered up into her eyes. "I cannot stop this. What I can do, I am doing. The Great Spirit bless you, sweet daughter!"

"Thank you, gentle father. Thank you. The water is like honey to my parched throat."

The old man and his boys moved on and administered to Gyasi, the boy next to Mbekah, and then to Kpodo's wife and to Kpodo. They disappeared around Kpodo to administer to the captives in the second row.

CHAPTER 8

The Worth of Souls

Mbekah savored the holy man's gift of water. Screeching sounds drew Mbekah's focus back to the wall on the right with its receding shadow. A sliver of sunlight appeared at the top of the gate. The gap grew. The wooden door lowered ponderously, supported by two strange ropes which appeared to be made of interlinked iron loops as big as a child's head. At last, the top edge came to rest on the ground, bridging the ditch.

Ten men with iron-tipped spears marched forth like upright turtles, chests encased and heads covered in shiny metal. A knife as long as an arm hung from each of their waistbands. Another turtle man followed carrying a shaft twice the height of the spears. From a crosswise shaft near the top, fluttered a white cloth dominated by two red bars, one crossing the other and flared at the ends.

A shrine to their guardian spirit? Mbekah uttered an oath to render the demon powerless.

As the turtle men emerged from the shadow of the wall, Mbekah gasped. Their faces were indeed pale—the color of kor hen skin, scalded and plucked. They spread out, forming a line between the slaves and the wall.

Five more Cristowns emerged through the gate, came forward through the line of turtle men, and halted before the cloth spread on the ground. One wore turtle armor and had a red plume in his armored hat.

The second dressed in a heavy black cloth cinched at the waist with a gold rope. A silver amulet—shaped like the red symbol on the white banner—hung from his neck, reaching to his waist. His brown hair formed a ring, leaving the sides and top of his head naked.

The third Cristown, clearly the one in charge, wore no metal shell but slung a short knife and one of the long knives from his belt. A round hat of the brightest red cloth covered his head, flopping down on one side.

The last two in the group of five were also turtle men, but in place of spears they each bore a club fashioned from a hollow iron shaft set in a wooden handle. Near the middle, a smoldering cord dangled. These last two guarded the backs of the first three.

Mbekah glanced again down the line of Cristowns. *With the same long nose and straight hair, how do they know one pale face from another?*

Two dark boys placed a four-legged stool behind the pale headman who seated himself and nodded to the ochre village headman across the cloth. He spoke for all to hear.

Mbekah understood nothing. She heard Ifé's stomach complain and looked in time to see Ifé close her eyes and teeter. Mbekah reached for her in time to keep her upright. Ifé opened her eyes and shook her head violently. The movement drew frowns from the guards facing them.

The black-robed man stepped forward. Using words Mbekah mostly understood, he said, "Headman d'Azambuzha of the Strong House of Sown Zhorzhy da *Mina* authorized us to trade with you this day. He sends his greetings as well as greetings from the second King Zhohwown, good and great Cristown ruler of Portugal, the two Algarvys, and Guinea."

The dark headman said similar polite words to the Cristowns. The man from the Village of Two Parts spoke what must have been the headman's words, but in the speech of the Cristowns. They exchanged bundles, placing them on the cloth between them. The stool boys opened the gifts for all to see. A small knife from the Cristown headman. An ebony amulet from the dark headman.

Mbekah maintained her grip on Ifé's right arm to support her.

The headmen stood. Looking at each other from time to time to point, nod or grunt, they strolled around the stacks of goods. The pale headman hefted a few tusks to look at both sides.

Mbekah wondered when she'd eat again. *The fish-bird men, or the turtle men, or whatever they are. What do they eat when they're not eating people?*

Seated again, the men spoke in lowered tones, waiting after each phrase for their assistants to say the words in the other's tongue.

The Cristown headman raised his voice. He waved his arms, smacked a fist to his other palm, crouched to inspect, touched various tusks, and jumped up. After a pause for the translation, the other man did about the same. So it went.

Mbekah had seen her mother perform the same dance in the market village when she wanted to buy or sell.

After a time, the Cristown man signaled. An aide disappeared into the strong house's opening and returned leading half a dozen dark men carrying trade goods that they arranged around the cloth of colors, her cloth of colors!

The dark headman inspected, counted on his fingers three times and rubbed his cheek. "Not enough. More, by half, of the goat-hair cloth. And where are the mirrors? We must have five mirrors."

A moment elapsed for the translation into the Cristown speech.

The Cristown headman nodded to his aide who again left and returned. He brought the metal mirrors and extra cloth which he placed with the other offered items.

"Enough," said the dark headman.

The two stood and held each other's right hand. They sat.

The dark headman produced a small purse and emptied it onto his palm. Small gold pieces—nose rings, earrings, toe rings, amulets, even lumps—filled his hand.

The three Cristowns straightened with increased interest. Even the two Cristown back-guarders couldn't resist staring.

The gold was returned to the pouch, and given to the head Cristown who bounced his hand a few times to test its heft.

More bargaining, more things offered from inside the walls and another hand-holding.

Mbekah yawned. She struggled to stay alert to keep both herself and Ifé standing.

The two men turned their attention to the captives and bartered anew.

They haggled from their stools. They haggled while dodging through the lines of captives, peering into mouths and squeezing muscles. Two guards from the ochre village stood by to make sure each captive complied with the headmen's requests.

Twice the men stood behind Mbekah to discuss the deal. Both times they handled her sore left calf and thigh, shooting a bolt of pain up her spine.

She wondered why they did not see the evilness of their occupation. Her father's words came to her. *Hyenas cannot smell their own stench.*

The sun reached its highest point when the two headmen smiled and nodded at each other.

The Cristown spoke to his aide who left and fetched six men, each bearing four iron pots by their handles.

Mbekah felt numb. *Iron pots in exchange for people!*

Two of the porters hurried back through the gate and returned, each with three additional pots.

The negotiators stood. Once more, they held right hands and shook them up and down. One score and ten new iron pots sat stacked between them.

One pot for each captive. My father's life and my freedom so a family can be the envy of its village! Mbekah looked to the sky. After a moment of labored meditation, she cried, "Please. Please open the eyes of this people."

All chatter ceased. Those who could see her, stared.

Mbekah beat her chest and wailed.

The ochre village headman screamed at his men. Yaféu, the guard with the bad eye, belted Mbekah with the back of his hand, throwing her to the ground, her left arm supported above her head by the wrist rope.

Stunned, she tasted the blood from her swelling, split lower lip. Her face pulsated with pain. She thought again of the thirty pots. She put her face into the cupped palm of her free right hand and sobbed.

Men and boys from the Village of Two parts rushed forward to lug the ivory and other trade items through the now darkened gateway into the strong house.

Cristown guards lined up with the ochre village guards. One of the latter ordered the captives to precede, one rope line at a time.

Yaféu goaded Mbekah and Ifé helped her stand. Their line shuffled forward.

Mbekah dragged her legs while scanning the lagoon and the grassland beyond through wet eyes. Turning her head to the ocean, she memorized every bleary detail.

Mother must fend for herself without father. I must also fend for myself. She saw they were about to pass through the opening in the Cristowns' wall. *I will not go meekly where the fish-bird men and the hyena men lead.*

At the lip of the wooden door-bridge, she planted her feet in the gravel, stopping the ankle rope's forward movement for those in front of her. *I will not take another step.*

Gyasi, the boy ahead of Mbekah, tripped forward onto Kpodo's wife who tumbled onto Kpodo. "Ouu Yaiy!"

Ifé stumbled into Mbekah's backside. "Wey Ah?"

Mbekah yelped and tottered to her right from a spear-shaft jab to her left side.

Ifé screamed from behind her.

Mbekah half-turned and watched Ifé wrench the spear from the man who had just poked her ribs.

The weaponless guard fell to Mbekah's left and rolled onto his back. He shielded his chest and face with his forearms and hands. Ifé continued to scream and beat him with the butt of his own spear.

Yaféu darted from the head of the line to help the downed guard but Kpodo, recovering from his own fall, seized Yaféu's ankle with his tied left hand.

Yaféu skidded onto his knees, howling in pain, his spear slapping the bridge.

Gyasi bludgeoned Yaféu with his fists.

Other captives grabbed surprised guards, dragging two to the ground and stomping them. A Cristown guard on Mbekah's right swung his spear up to bat Gyasi's back.

"No!" Mbekah flung a fistful of dust and gravel into the guard's face.

The guard clamped his eyes shut and staggered. Kpodo's wife shoved him off the bridge.

Kpodo stood and pivoted to his right away from the hideous entrance. He took a step. His wife pivoted and followed him.

Mbekah pulled Gyasi to his feet so he could also turn and shuffle after them. Mbekah was next in line. Ifé tossed the spear into the ditch and fell in behind Mbekah and so it went to the last captive and all of them were long-stepping away from the walls.

"Step, step, step." Kpodo shouted cadence and the line gained momentum.

The other two lines of captives took advantage of the chaos to turn and race in step ahead of Mbekah's group toward the village.

Mbekah concentrated to keep rhythm. She endured the pain throbbing in her lips, face, neck, ribs, thigh, calf, ankle and wrist.

"Stop them. Don't kill them. Stop them." The headman backed out of the way.

Guards sprinted wide of the three moving masses of captives, attempting to cut them off.

A woman from the village hurried to her two mesmerized children. She arrived first and tackled them out of the path of Mbekah's stampeding group.

Onlookers opened a broad path to allow the captives and their pursuing guards through. More than a few cheered.

Someone in the chain behind Mbekah stumbled, jerking her right ankle in its rope loop. She tumbled into a heap with Ifé on top of her and Gyasi under, enclosed instantly by the larger knot of slippery writhing bodies.

A ring of guards closed in, spears lowered and ready.

The captives untangled themselves and lay on their backs—panting, laughing, crying.

Mbekah's chest bulged and collapsed, bulged and collapsed. *We had to try. We had to try.*

The headman from the ochre village pushed through the crowd to the captives. With flared nostrils and gritted teeth, he flayed Mbekah and her friends with a braid of palm leaf strands.

Mbekah and the others covered their faces. The whip's razor edges sliced their arms and stomachs. Blood splattered them from hair to knees.

Such exquisite pain. Mbekah taunted and the others with her joined in. "Hyena man. Hyena man. Hyena man."

The dark headman swatted. Faster. Harder.

The pale headman leaped into the circle, yelling and shouldering the dark headman aside. The whipping stopped.

The captives chanted. "Hyena man. Hyena man."

Some of the villagers joined in. "Hyena man. Hyena—"

BDOOM.

Silence.

Thunder on a clear day? So close? Stunned, Mbekah stared at one of the pale back-guarders who had followed his headman into the circle. He was pointing his club to the sky. A wisp of black smoke above the iron tube disappeared in the breeze but the smell of burnt egg lingered. *What magic is this?*

The captives released their tensed muscles, lay back, and resumed their heavy breathing.

A crowd of villagers closed in behind the guards.

Mbekah studied the faces peering down at her. Her bloody arms and belly stung. She looked past the faces and searched the bluest of skies. One gray and white bird floated seaward. It whirled once and disappeared over the heads of the silent spectators.

The sky, the people, her sticky hands all faded to nothing.

CHAPTER 9

The White Fortress

"A flicker. I see it. The *Mina*," Gunner's Mate Rodrigo, who acted as bow lookout, shouted.

"Hold northeast toward the light", Lopo told the helmsmen. The *Ninho* fell off a quarter and slowed. Bare feet drummed the deck as men on the night watch scurried to trim the ship's lateen sails. Others, who were trying to sleep on deck, stood to scan the horizon. They felt the breeze across the starboard gunwale with the backs of their necks. Even this close to land, the air from the south carried nothing but the fresh smell of the open ocean. One by one, the off-duty sailors returned to their mats to attempt another half hour of slumber.

Lopo tapped the door of a sleeping cupboard behind the helm. "Senhor Piloto. We see the flame in the tower. Three leagues till São Jorge da *Mina* Castle."

"I know, I know. Such racket! Fetch me when you can see the outline of the tower."

Lopo did not mind the night watch, the coolest time of the day, an important consideration in these tropical waters. Above all, Pilot Gonçalves was not on deck at night sneering over every move or order. Lopo was relieved that the *Mina* would be *Ninho*'s last stop before returning to Lisbon.

After an hour, Lopo ordered the men to start a general cleanup. With buckets of seawater and pumice stones, most hands worked over the deck and gunwales. Others pumped the foul bilge, coiled every rope and stowed unnecessary gear. To finalize, the men tossed buckets of seawater onto each other to wash body and clothes. They doused the captive Lowlanders as well. Captain Dias required that the *Ninho* and crew arrive clean and orderly in all ports.

While they prepared the vessel, Father Estevez set up a confessional in the hold. Two men stood at the hatchway and channeled air into the dark space with a piece of canvas so that priest and sinner would not faint from the stench of urine, mold, and the remaining bilge water laden with dissolved rat feces.

At dawn the two caravelas and the captured Dutch ship approached the fort. Lopo ordered Joselinho, the smallest member of the watch, hoisted up the mainmast in a boson's chair to watch for shoals.

"Fogo", ordered Lopo.

A soldier standing amidships fired his harquebus, discharging a blast of acrid black smoke into the wind. Three pops sounded from the fort in acknowledgement.

Captain Dias and Pilot Gonçalves stood on deck as the *Ninho*, followed by the *São Sebastian*, navigated north into a small bay. Both caravelas dropped mainsails, swung aft sails across their decks to starboard and proceeded west with the flooding tide into the mouth of the Benya River—perhaps the shortest river on the Guinea coast. A cable-length later they entered the Benya Lagoon. The pungency of brackish water and rotting vegetation mingled with the morning's onshore breeze. Brilliant white herons stood knee-deep around the edge of the lagoon, bobbing for their breakfast in the silt and giving little heed to the newcomers.

The captured Dutchman, her keel too deep for the river mouth, anchored in the small bay east of the *Mina* fort. The three newly arrived ships constituted the entire fleet at the fort.

#

"Hoc est enim corpus meum", sang the priest as he raised a wooden platter with four flint-hard biscuits carved clean of their green crusts.

"Amen", chanted the kneeling men on both caravelas, their heads bowed. The two ships were secured together at anchor. At each port on this journey, Captain Dias insisted that a mass of thanksgiving be said before disembarking.

Lopo admired the clean-shaven captain's black cape. His red and blue cap sported a tremendous purple feather with an eye near its rounded tip. The ragged condition of members of the crew at this stage in the voyage contrasted with their captain's shore dress like peahens next to a peacock. Captain Dias was both military commander of the two-ship cargo run and master of the *Ninho*. Lopo focused on the liturgy again.

The cleric continued in Latin. "... Do ye this in memory of Me." He raised a wooden chalice of red wine.

"Amen" chanted the men.

This was Lopo's first voyage with Captain Dias and he was surprised at the show of piety the captain was able to eke from his crew. Shipboard life on Portuguese vessels included daily group prayer and singing the Salve Regina. Outside this routine, Lopo remembered seeing sailors on other ships pray only during perilous times. He wondered if the captain would be so faithful with no priest on board.

After the recitation of the Pater Noster, a crewman acting as altar boy attempted to slice the biscuits but only succeeded in crumbling them into bits. Father Estevez continued the chant—invoking the Lord, Mary, the apostles Peter and Paul, Saint George, Saint Andrew, Saint James, and 'Todos os Santos' in general. He soaked a piece of biscuit in the wine and placed it into his own mouth. In the absence of a choir, Father Estevez himself sang the Agnes Dei.

Lopo had no problem reciting the congregation's part. At last, the crew repeated the Domine three times.

Captain Dias advanced, knelt, and received communion. Every officer, sailor, soldier and other passenger on both vessels also took the wine-dipped crumb on his tongue as the priest said, still in Latin, "May the body of our Lord Jesus Christ preserve your soul unto everlasting life."

Lopo wondered, when Pilot Gonçalves knelt for his sacramental wafer, if the pilot had confessed drinking too much and trying to kill him while in São Tiago. *Did the pilot beg absolution for spreading the lie that I have the evil eye?*

After the mass, Captain Dias, the master from the *São Sebastian*, the pilots from both vessels, and Father Estevez climbed into the two ships' gigs and were rowed to shore.

Lopo and Cargo Master Manoel Vaaz stood at the caravela's gunwale and watched.

"I'm not sad to see our pious passenger leave us. Our loss is the *Mina*'s blessing, I'm sure," Lopo said.

"Capitão Dias has been all too holy himself with the priest on board this trip," said Manoel. "They say the priest has an influential uncle."

"I didn't hear that. Don't want to ever hear such! Capitão Dias is first rate. Knows his duty to God, king, and the ship."

"Sim Senhor." Manoel looked away.

Lopo detected mockery in the man's voice but let it go. He climbed the ladder and leaned on the quarterdeck railing to oversee preparations for offloading the cargo.

With Pilot Gonçalves away, he relaxed. Lopo loved the sea. He loved the sense of urgency and accomplishment among Portuguese mariners. He pictured himself, for the thousandth time, as ship's master.

The first longboats arrived from shore. The crew winched casks of red wine, kegs of gunpowder, sheets of lead, and loaves of precious sugar from Madeira over the side for the garrison. They loaded goods for the fort's trading station called a factory—woolens, cotton goods, iron cooking implements, and polished metal mirrors.

Fifteen replacement soldiers, joking and laughing, left the ships for their new post. Two months of constant exposure to the weather were over for them. A stonemason and two carpenters disembarked with their tools.

The pilot's mate from the *São Sebastian* joined Lopo on the *Ninho*'s quarterdeck. "I was in Governor d'Azambuja's fleet when we arrived here a year and a month ago to build the fort. Capitão Dias commanded a caravela then too."

Lopo saw that the Portuguese stronghold was built at the end of a short, narrow and elevated peninsula that interrupted their view of the Sea of Aethiopia to the south.

"We hurried to build before the people of the village could organize their resistance." The man pointed at the assembly of huts located inland of the fort.

Lopo nodded. He'd heard much of this from his own watch members, but it made sense now that he could see the layout.

"Governador D'Azambuja promised that we would pay a yearly rent to the king of the two nations and give him military support against rivals."

Lopo straightened when Manoel shouted a warning. A keg of powder was about to slip its sling while being lowered over the side. A sailor swung the barrel back over the deck and secured the small barrel. The routine continued.

"This is the best place on the Guinea Coast to trade for gold. Good place for slaves too, though it's dangerous to go inland for them ourselves. Graças a Deus, we can buy them from the coast tribes that come to the fort."

Lopo nodded.

#

"Bom dia, Governador. Dispatches for you from King João carried by his majesty's ship *Ninho* with the *São Sebastian* as escort." Captain Dias bent forward and placed a sealed leather pouch and several letters on the oaken table. "We captured a Dutch ship three days ago just before leaving the Ivory Coast."

"Bemvindo. A pleasure to see you again, Capitão Dias. Sit down, por favor. It's been almost a year, is it not so?"

Captain Dias moved back and sat atop a leopard skin cushion on a low bench. "A year, sim. The letters are from your wife, brother and two sons."

Dias thought the governor looked older than his 42 years. The governor's face and scalp bore the scars of the pox, as he remembered, but his hair, what there was of it, had gone gray since Dias last saw him.

"I saw the captured cog anchored in the bay", said the governor. "What is her cargo?"

"Ivory, sea-lion skins, and a small chest. Gold, most likely. We'll breech the lock when you're available to observe."

"This afternoon. I'll notify the factor to attend."

"I'll hold out eight of the Dutch crew to help my men sail her to Lisbon. It's a clumsy ship for a voyage back to Europe. Those we don't hang will go to Lisbon in chains on the *São Sebastian*."

"You won't have to take the cog back. Tell your men she cannot be sailed back to Europe. We'll burn her for all to see. We want all to think they can't exploit the Guinea Coast without our Portuguese-designed caravelas."

Captain Dias pondered that a moment. "I followed King João's new decree covering pirates on the Guinea Coast. After I had time to learn as much as possible from their captain, I threw him into the sea along with his pilot, pilot's mate, and two men from each watch. I did this in daylight and made sure each member of their crew witnessed the executions."

Governor d'Azambuja leaned his elbow on the right armrest of his throne-like chair. "An awkward business among Christians. But I understand his majesty's position. Let them all go free and they'll be back in a year. Muito bem. Is this a voyage for exploration or just a cargo run?"

"Cargo and replacements. We stopped in Madeira, Arguim and São Tiago in the Cape Verde islands."

Dias remembered this room's newly built bare walls from the year before and noted the added adornment. Behind Governor d'Azambuja's right shoulder hung the escutcheon of the king with its red border and blue cross of the House of Avis. Over his left, hung the escutcheon of the Military Order of Christ with its slotted red cross on a white field. The other three walls bore decorated shields of thick exotic hides along with spears and war clubs received, no doubt, as gifts from local chieftains.

"Still paying your dues carrying freight, Capitão? When is it your turn to lead a discovery expedition?"

"When it pleases his majesty," replied Captain Dias. "Fellow squire Diogo Cão got the last command."

"Ah sim. Months ago, Capitão Cão stopped here for victuals on his way south to new coasts. Two ships—a caravela to get in close and go up the rivers as well as a fat cargo ship to carry supplies for a long voyage."

"The king trusts Cão. These are times for men of experience and perfect loyalty." Captain Dias fingered the peacock feather on the hat in his lap. "It takes courage and leadership to take men thousands of leagues, sailing into the unknown."

Captain Dias continued. "My service and allegiance are impeccable. You will see that it's only a matter of time and I too will . . ."

"Enchanted to see you," Governor d'Azambuja said, cutting short Captain Dias' self-promotion. The governor stood.

"Por favor, you must join us for dinner tomorrow, Tuesday evening. We're all interested in news from Lisbon."

"Obrigado. A kind invitation. Until then, I mean until this afternoon when we breech the chest." Captain Dias, got to his feet then stopped himself. "I almost forgot. You are to open the dispatches immediately. There are urgent instructions. I am to await your orders."

"Very well." Governor d'Azambuja returned to his seat and reached for the sealed pouch. Breaking the embossed wax circle, he removed the top document, unfolded it, and read, mumbling the words to himself.

Captain Dias remained standing. He'd been curious about his unusual orders regarding the official dispatches since the hour he sailed from Lisbon.

"The orders say that the slaves you carry to Lisbon must be treated well while here at the *Mina* and on board your ships." Governor d'Azambuja stopped to study the captain's face. "What do you know of this?"

Captain Dias thought about the question. "Minutes before leaving the dock, the Guinea House steward delivered the dispatches. They're from his majesty's chamberlain. The steward insisted that I witness you opening and reading them upon my arrival. He said you would issue me orders therefrom."

"Indeed. The orders are specific. The slaves are not to be mistreated in any manner. You, I mean we are to assure that our men use the minimum force necessary to maintain order. Furthermore, the slaves are not to be abused or sexually violated in any way under penalty of court martial." Governor d'Azambuja stared again at Captain Dias.

Captain Dias stood a moment. "I've never heard of such a requirement."

"Nor I. But I am required to prepare an affidavit that you have received the order. It states that your pilot, pilot's mate, and possibly others in the crew will be interrogated upon your return to Lisbon to ascertain your and your crew's strict adherence to these orders. The king's factor must send his affidavit that I and my men here have also complied." Governor d'Azambuja stood, a sober expression on his face. "I had better speak with my officers."

"And I, mine." Captain Dias bowed from the waist and left.

CHAPTER 10

The Room of Stone

Three rosy rectangles appeared high on the wall opposite Mbekah's patch of floor. Looking about, she discovered no surprises in the soft light of her second dawning in the Cristowns' strong house. Each woman slept precisely where she had hunched over the day before. And the day before that. Everyone except Kpodo's wife. She trembled in a ball by Mbekah's side; Mbekah thought she had not been there in the cell most of the previous day.

She was a year, perhaps two, older than Mbekah. Everyone knew her father—headman from another village—had three wives, six yam fields, and cowries enough to invest in a good marriage for her. Three moons before the slavers' raid, Kpodo and his parents traveled to her home for the wedding.

Mbekah was digging yams with her sister when Kpodo marched by for the first time with his tender bride a few paces behind. At supper that evening, Mbekah's father told the family, "He who marries a beauty, marries trouble."

Kpodo's bride whimpered and brought Mbekah's thoughts back to the room of stone. The sleeping beauty flinched and squeaked like a swatted puppy, but did not open her eyes. Mbekah stroked the young woman's dust-caked hair.

Up to then, Mbekah had dozed most of the time they'd been in the narrow chamber. It was difficult to do otherwise; the only air and the only daylight came through metal bars and the gate at one end of the long room and through three slots in the wall overhead. She arrived there exhausted from the long days of lugging her load of ivory and ravaged by the whipping at the hands of hyena man. Lines of scabs covered her arms and stomach. Her skin was sticky and stank like she'd gone many days without washing. She reflected upon lessons at her mother's side and decided loss of blood had also increased her need to slumber. *What had caused the nightmares?*

She'd slept enough. She thanked the Creator for that. The only one awake in the crowded enclosure, she strained to understand the sounds from the lagoon.

Not frogs, but the grunts of men. Splashes. Shouts, but not always in the language of my people or of the slave raiders or of the Village of Two Parts. Cristowns and others are at work in the lagoon.

Mbekah was relieved to be awake. Asleep, she had not been in control. She dreamed she and the others fled from the towering walls. They chanted, "Hyena man, hyena man". The turtle men carried iron pots. The hyena man raged and lashed out at her. The scenes went too slow. They went too fast. They were not in the proper order.

I didn't dream the whole time, did I? Everyone sleeps where I remember they slept yesterday. Did I not cup my hands into a wooden pail for food? More than once! Yes, a millet gruel. So sloppy. So delicious. Did not Ifé lift water to my lips with a dipper? Who salved my sores? One of the ancient holy man's assistants. Yes, I remember that too. I was hot and wet. I wanted the dream to stop.

Everyone followed me! We failed but we had to try. The men from our village never came to help us. Yes, we had to try it. I hate that we failed. I love that we tried.

Even so, I will be wiser next time. Father used to say, 'A little subtleness is worth a lot of force.'

Why didn't they kill us when we ran? Because we are valuable. For what? How clever will we be if we're patient and end up roasted and eaten?

Ifé opened her eyes, sat up, and scooted back against the wall where she could lean next to Mbekah. "You're awake."

Mbekah nodded, careful not to pinch her skin on her iron neckband. "I feel better. Sleep has been the healer. I need to bathe."

Ifé studied the room. "I feel worse. At each place we become more the goat and less a child of our mothers."

Olubayo stirred. Her eyes opened and followed Ifé's gestures.

Ifé held up her manacled wrist. "A goat eats and sleeps where its master plants the stake. When the goat is old, the master takes the skin for a purse and the flesh for his belly."

Mbekah contemplated the rectangles of light, now yellow, as they inched down the wall in front of them. Chisel and pock marks in the stones came into focus. More of the women awoke.

Olubayo eased to her feet. "Truly. Each day is worse for us." She shook her head. "What will happen next?" She crouched and looked over Mbekah's lap at Kpodo's wife where she curled on the rough floor like a hut dog. "What did they do with you yesterday? They didn't return you until after I was asleep."

"I don't know. Nothing, I think." Kpodo's wife pushed herself from the floor and wrapped her arms about her knees. "They took me to another room like this one—smaller and with a bed on a wooden platform. There were three of the pale men waiting at the door, laughing and talking. One entered and began to remove his strange clothes. The door flung open and a fat man yelled at the naked man who gathered his clothes and left. The door shut. I lay on the bed all afternoon and evening." Kpodo's wife rocked back and forth on her buttocks, shaking her head.

All the women in the room were now awake and straining to hear.

"I waited. I cried. I slept. A man from the Village of Two Parts woke me and led me back here in the dark."

Olubayo stared at Kpodo's wife. "They didn't rape you?"

Kpodo's wife shook. Muddy tears dripped from her jaw to her breasts to her lap.

Mbekah continued to stroke the young woman's hair.

Ifé said, "They've come for no one since they took you yesterday."

Small groups erupted into conversation.

"The Cristowns are pink like newborn monkeys."

"And hairy like big ones. They stink worse."

No one spoke for a moment.

"They're monsters."

"They're going to cook us."

Mbekah plucked a small pebble from the stone floor. She leaned forward to the extent her chains allowed and ran her fingers over the surface of the paving stones searching for anything solid—bits of twig, a jagged toenail, a seed. She piled them into a tiny heap.

Ifé and Olubayo observed, then examined the floor about them and added to Mbekah's stack. Kpodo's wife lifted her head from her knees to watch.

Mbekah took the largest piece of rock in her collection and etched a line as long as her forearm between her and Ifé.

The women close by fell silent and studied her actions.

She scratched seven shorter lines across the first one.

All the other captives ceased their buzzing. All eyes were on Mbekah.

She distributed four of her piled objects into each of the twelve stalls formed by the lines.

"Houses," exclaimed a captive.

All heads bobbed in agreement.

Mbekah nodded at Ifé. The rectangles of almost-white light were nearing the bottom of the wall opposite from where she crouched waiting for Ifé to play.

Ifé lifted the four markers from one of the six squares on her side of the main line and dropped them, one at a time, into the squares to the right. The last one to receive a marker was the first stall on Mbekah's side.

Mbekah's eyes narrowed. Her chin dipped repeatedly as she swept her gaze to the right along the stalls on her side of the line and back left along the ones on Ifé's side. She took the four markers from the last stall or house on her side—the one on her far right—and placed one each in the first four on Ifé's side.

Ifé moved her hand above her first house which now held five markers.

"Tsuh, tsuh. The third house. Take from the third house." The advice came from a captive from another village.

"The first house is better," Kpodo's wife coached.

Ifé retracted her hand.

Small groups up and down the room debated Ifé's next move. Several more of the women gave suggestions.

Ifé pointed at the houses on the board, one at a time, moving her lips to count and sum up. This done, she scooped up the five objects in her first house, as she'd originally planned, and sowed them one by one in the houses to the right. She completed her turn by removing the two markers in her third house and placing them apart in her 'treasury.' She grinned and looked around the room.

After a short silence the captives huddled again in small groups to argue what Mbekah's response should be.

"Start with the four in your second house."

A tongue clicked twice. "No, no. The third house."

Mbekah's chin bounced at each house while she counted and added in her head. She scanned left and right once more and calculated an alternate move.

Men's voices resonated into the room through the bars. Everyone turned toward the sound. A man from the Village of Two Parts pushed open the screeching gate and leaned against it looking back into the hallway.

CHAPTER 11

Saving Souls

Lopo and Cargo Master Manoel climbed the open stairway inside the fort to a long room used as quarters for visiting officers. Lopo rapped on the oak door, waited a moment, and shoved it open. His nose assured him they'd found their superior officer. He was glad he didn't have to do this alone.

He stepped in from the late morning sunshine and waited for his eyes to grow accustomed. A dozen low wooden frames lined one wall, each topped with a canvas tick stuffed with straw. Compared to officers' accommodations on the caravela, these beds were fit for a duke.

Halfway into the room, Pilot Gonçalves slumped on the floor, his broad back against the white plastered wall, his eyes closed. He inhaled noisily, exhaled quietly.

Lopo approached and noted a torso-sized stain on the sand-colored mattress beside him.

Manoel made a show of pinching his nose. "Por Deus. Even soused, o Senhor Piloto knows enough not to lie in his own vomit."

Lopo extracted Gonçalves' ivory-handled knife from his belt and hid it under a jumbled coat on the floor beside him. "No use getting ourselves sliced up when we wake him."

Manoel found a full bucket and ladle behind the door and dribbled water onto Gonçalves' thinning hair.

Gonçalves shook the water from his head and groaned. Lopo and Manoel hopped clear. Gonçalves wiped away the streamlet flowing down his forehead, adjusted his position against the wall, and snored on.

Manoel ventured his water torture again with the same result.

In the middle of the third ladle, Gonçalves woke and swore. He squinted his undersized eyes at them. "Sons of whores. Get out."

They turned to leave.

"No. Help me up."

The two men hoisted the pilot to his feet and aimed him at the door. They followed his faltering progress out of the room and down the stairs, ready to grab him if he fell. Like a mule returning to the shed, Gonçalves instinctively navigated his way into the next courtyard toward a lone table in a covered walkway against a wall.

A man Lopo judged to be an official of the station lounged in one of two wicker chairs on either side of the table and drank. The seated man watched Gonçalves stagger toward him, saluted with his ceramic flagon, and chuckled. "O Senhor Piloto got enough to drink last night, is it not so?"

Gonçalves wobbled to the table, pivoted, and dropped into the empty chair.

A Guinean orderly, from the Village of Two Parts no doubt, brought another flagon and poured red wine for the disheveled pilot. The orderly backed a few paces away and stood by with clay jar in hand. Two other Guineans cooled the two drinkers with palm fronds woven into spade-shaped fans and fixed to long handles.

No one moved to offer Lopo or Manoel a drink. They stood in the sunny courtyard and waited for instructions. Drops of sweat formed on the back of Lopo's neck and tickled down his backbone under his blouse.

Gonçalves looked up at last and focused on his two subordinates. "Pois?"

Lopo nodded. "The cargo is offloaded, and repairs are going well. We're going to look at the return cargo."

"Check the slaves closely. Looks bad if we lose too many during the voyage." Gonçalves rubbed his face with both hands. He shifted around in his chair and sneered at Lopo. "Por Deus, no sick ones, Senhor Pilot's Mate. Watch the cargo master. He has inspected slaves before."

"O meu amigo. We ship only the fittest negrosinhos from the *Mina*," the other drinker said with mock hurt in his voice. He stood and offered his hand to Lopo and then to Manoel. "I am Baltasar Soares, Assistant Factor. At your service."

"Lopo David Meendez, Pilot's Mate on the *Ninho*. A pleasure to meet you."

"I am Manoel Vaaz. Purser and Cargo Master. At your service."

Gonçalves belched. Wiped his mouth. "If you're quite done, I'd like to finish."

Assistant Factor Soares shrugged and sat again.

"Obrigado," Gonçalves said with exaggerated sincerity. "When you've finished in the cells and at the warehouse, take three days. We officers are quartered on the upper floor . . . but you saw where just now, didn't you?" He raised his drink and paused to stare at it. "You have both earned a flagon and a whore, if there are any of either left when you get around to it. And do join us tonight for azzá if you wish to win some easy money. I know the game to be an honest one."

Lopo said nothing. *One crooked game with you was enough. Would that you'd choked on my ear, pig!*

#

After they inspected the proposed cargo of ivory and malagueta pepper, the fort's clerk sent Lopo and Manoel to the duty officer's room. A sergeant in a washed-out green tunic invited them in where the light was just adequate for Lopo to see a leather satchel and a pair of ivory dice on the table. A burnt cinnamon-skinned boy watched the visitors with interest as he fanned the hefty sergeant seated behind his table.

"Corporal, take our guests to see the slaves." Without getting up, the sergeant handed a diminutive man an iron ring from which dangled half a dozen keys each as long as a man's pointer finger.

Lopo and Manoel strolled behind the chatty corporal who turned now and then to make sure his audience was paying attention. Four blacks trailed close behind them—two warrior types wielded carved ebony clubs as thick and as long as a man's arm, and two smaller fellows who seemed to be errand boys or orderlies. The group entered a short hallway.

Manoel's hand shot up and covered his nose and mouth.

An instant later, Lopo did the same. "Santíssima Mãe de Deus." He stepped out of the procession and braced himself with his free hand on a wall.

"It's the night buckets," the corporal said. "Come boys, get rid of the merda, we're going into the cells."

The corporal unlocked the iron-grate door but most of the inspection group waited outside until the foul-smelling waste was hauled off by the orderlies. The smell of urine and perspiration persisted.

Lopo and Manoel followed the corporal and the two club-wielding men into an elongated room with Negro men crowded against one of the long walls. The two orderlies returned from bucket duty and stepped in behind them.

"Sixteen of Guinea's finest," sang the corporal as if hawking them at auction.

A fly buzzed in Lopo's face while his eyes adjusted. Each captive's neck was looped with an iron band chained to a ring in the wall. The stubby chains allowed for a slave to stand or sit with his back against the wall. Right wrists and left ankles were shackled and secured in like manner.

White eyes stared out from dark faces and followed Lopo as his inspection party walked half-way down the room. The three white men stopped and turned to face the closed-jaw captives.

The corporal jabbered away. Sixteen pairs of unblinking eyes studied Lopo. He looked at the men's feet. He gazed above their heads. Much as he tried he could not keep from peering again into the chained-men's faces.

A few flies hovered but most spent their time creeping under and over the sticky iron bands and open sores about the men's throats, above their hands and at their ankles. Thin lines of scab on some of the men showed they'd been whipped with something light and sharp. *Scourged in the face, not on the back.* Lopo suspected they'd tried to fend off the lashings with their forearms.

Manoel and the corporal carried on their conversation, seeming not to notice the human misery three paces in front of them.

Lopo finished his perusal and looked again into their eyes. He hadn't seen slaves so poorly treated before. Not the ones in Lisbon. Neither had he seen animals abused like this. Maybe they attempted to overwhelm their guards and were punished. They weren't looking at the corporal or Manoel or their countrymen in the inspection group. Lopo was sure each slave in the room studied him. *Why are the slaves staring at me?* His own eyes darted back and forth and verified they had no interest in anyone but him. Lopo backed up until he pressed his back to the wall, scarcely breathing.

"Something wrong, Senhor Meendez?" The corporal moved to Lopo's side and supported his arm.

Manoel grasped Lopo's other arm with both of his hands. "Lopo? You don't look so good."

Lopo turned his head and Manoel's face gradually came into focus. He breathed deeply and stepped away from the wall. "I will be fine," he mumbled. "Go ahead with the inspection."

Manoel checked every slave as the orderlies stretched out legs and arms and forced mouths to open.

The corporal, a head shorter than Manoel, stood a pace behind him and a pace away from the captives. He glanced at Lopo from time to time.

Lopo remained in the center of the room. He spread his feet apart for greater stability and worked to breathe slowly. The shackled men's eyes wondered about him. Implored him. Hated him.

I'm sorry. I didn't know. Just be patient. You will eat well in Lisbon. You'll learn about God. Lopo thought about cheery Sebastian, the Negro slave who worked for the cobbler near his father's vellum shop. Because of Sebastian's sunny disposition, Lopo had always supposed the old fellow had never known trouble in his life. He pictured enthusiastic Negro vendors who thronged Lisbon's plazas. Were they once defeated and morose like these captives? He felt childish to suppose these men had somehow been waiting for a chance to leave their savage ways and join the Christian world. But perhaps their acceptance of God would change them.

Manoel finished and Lopo almost ran from the cell. But he soon found they weren't done. The inspection group moved to another long cell filled with females with the same ash-brown skin as the males just checked.

Chains tinkled, and flies swarmed into the air as the prisoners adjusted positions. The men had been naked and unashamed. The women too were naked but were not so comfortable when the seven men in the group entered. In spite of the chains, some of the women held each other in their arms as best they could. Some turned their backs and stared over their shoulders at Lopo and the other visitors. Others remained in a crouch and covered their private parts with their arms.

Lopo was surprised again. More eyes—curious, cautious, sad. Not one captive showed her teeth. Lopo hung back while Manoel inspected.

Lopo had seen slave women but always wearing clothes. Not the best clothing, but modest. The women in the cell were, well, well-formed. Lopo had young cousins about their age but he'd never seen them naked. God forbid. Not as grownups, anyway. His aunt had tried to make a match for him with women about this old. Portuguese women, of course. But not this shapely. He'd been on a ship away from Lisbon too long. He hadn't expected to be this interested. *Is it right to look at them? They see me staring.* He forced himself to look only at their faces or their feet.

Manoel paused. "This one's nice, eh Lopo?"

Lopo glanced at Manoel and his face flushed. "Por Deus! There's no need to grope them. Just see that they don't have any obvious problems."

"Sim, Senhor." Manoel returned to his task.

Lopo's eyes wandered back to below their necks. He was aroused now. *Mãe de Deus. I shouldn't be looking at them. But I have to. It's my duty.*

One caught Lopo's attention above the rest. At her feet was a grid scratched into the floor and some debris. She was a hand taller than any other woman in the room, yet her breasts were smaller than the others'. She bore the marks of a recent flogging on her arms, abdomen, and thighs. Manacled and naked, she stood straight as a mast and stared back at him.

Studying my very soul. He blinked and looked elsewhere.

#

Lopo finished the baked ackee and returned the olive wood-handled knife to his belt and rubbed his greasy fingers on his trousers. The ackee fruit's yellow flesh tasted like brains, his favorite but he took little pleasure in eating it. The roasted crocodile filet, the first fresh meat he'd eaten since the ship's call at São Tiago, should have been a welcome change. He found the okra slimy. All three were new dishes for him.

He should have savored the fresh food served at an actual table, but he could not. The eyes of the chained men and women intruded into his thoughts. *They will be pleasantly surprised when they arrive in Lisbon. We have so much to offer these savages. Don't we? Maybe not. Have I been naïve? Have I been an idiot?*

After the meal, Lopo wandered around the fort. His recent artillery training had given him a new perspective regarding fortifications. This stronghold, although recently built, had not been constructed with low, slanted walls in the modern style he'd seen in his travels along the coasts of France, England, and the Low Countries. *I see why they built them straight and tall in this place. The crown is not afraid of puny naval artillery or of the primitive weapons of Guineans. The old-fashioned high walls are a statement to the locals that we white men now rule on this coast.*

Lopo came to the *Mina*'s church and stepped through a man-sized hatch cut into one of the tall double wooden doors. He crossed himself and knelt on one knee until he could make out the layout of the chapel in the dim light. It was empty of worshipers and furniture except for a railing a few paces in front of an altar near the opposite end. He stood and advanced. He genuflected before the altar and slid to his right into a kneeling position with his forearms resting on the wooden railing. He closed his eyes and, without beads, struggled through a prayer using his own words.

He wrestled with what he'd always been taught compared to what he'd seen a few hours earlier. He questioned whether Portugal's presence really was the blessing they preached to each other that it was. *Is it thy will, O God, that we convert with sword and school with shackles? I've never doubted the king or the pope. Why start now? On the other hand, why not believe my own eyes? Why not listen to my heart? It is so confusing.*

He lost awareness of the passing of time until his knees began to scream at him in pain. He pushed himself to his feet and paused to admire the altar and the great empty room. The nave was modest by Lisbon standards, but it seemed an archbishop's chapel to Lopo after more than three months away from Portugal's capital city.

Still in contemplation, he returned to the entrance via an outer wall. At one spot, a single candle sent its prayer to *São Jorge*, the dragon slayer saint who was the namesake of the fort. His likeness, mounted on a rearing white stallion with his lance poised to skewer a fire-spewing beast, adorned the wall.

At the back corner, he passed the opening to the small baptistery and headed back to the center of the back wall to the outside doors. He paused to kneel again before leaving and discovered that a priest approached him from the direction of the altar. A tall man, he had a thin face and a short, tapered beard. Lopo frowned. He had hoped he'd been alone during his personal devotions.

"Boas tardes, Pai. I'm Lopo David Meendez, Pilot's Mate on the *Ninho*." Lopo nodded his head and took the priest's sinewy hand, a hand well-suited to wield a sword as his military-religious order might require at times. "At your service."

"Encantado. Chaplain Felipe Alvariz, Order of Christ. I haven't seen you or most of your crew at services these three days. Only Capitão Dias and a young man, José, have attended." Alvariz moved towards the door.

Lopo followed. "I think the men got their fill of masses at sea. It's not often we have a priest with us when we're only running cargo."

They stepped outside into the soft light of late afternoon.

"I haven't seen any of the men myself today." Lopo said.

Chaplain Alvariz fingered the crucifix hanging from his neck. "I trust you'll find them sleeping off last night's pleasures in the barracks hall. The men will be up before the sun sets and they'll head back to the village. Plenty to do over there at night, they say."

"O meu Pai, do you have a moment?" Lopo asked.

They moved to a bench in the long shadow of the church.

Lopo fiddled with the knife in his belt. "I have seen slaves all my life. I speak with them on my street in Lisbon every day. I buy rice pudding and stewed prunes from them in the plazas. I sought the opportunity to sail on the *Ninho*, knowing it would return with slaves. I'm a loyal subject of the king . . ."

"Sim?" Chaplain Alvariz said.

"I saw them today, the slaves in the cells. Is it right? The shackles, the suffering, their families? And what about . . ."

"I see." Alvariz ran his fingers up and down the crucifix's beaded cord. "The answer is not easy, Lopo. Look up, to the horizon, not to your feet in the dirt. If only a few respond to the message of Christ, we succeed. We're not just slaving here. We're saving souls."

Lopo had heard that sermon many times and it had always made sense. The Guineans he'd seen in Portugal went about their business more or less like others. A little less, maybe. Like Jews. No, worse. Like Moors captured at sea or purchased over the border in Castile. But he had seen Guineans—Negroes—at mass in Lisbon. *Is it not a blessing to receive the holy sacraments and be saved in the Kingdom of God?* Negroes in his country had Christian names and spoke Portuguese. A few were free men with families and livelihoods.

Chaplain Alvariz stood, interrupting Lopo's silent deliberations. "Come to the daily mass for Dom Henrique, our departed navigator prince. This evening when the bell tolls. You'll see we have an earnest, if small flock of locals. And we baptize every baby born in the village. We also baptize the slaves when they get to Lisbon. I must go. Will I see you in church tonight?"

"Boas tardes, Pai." Lopo fixed his eyes on Chaplain Alvariz' back as he hurried to his church. *No Father, I've just had my communion with God.*

In the faded black cloth of the retreating priest's cassock, Lopo again saw the defiant eyes of the tall girl in the cell.

CHAPTER 12

A Body and a Bottle

The evening meal finished, servants from the Village of Two Parts cleared the table, replacing silver flagons with carved ebony tumblers. The head servant poured each of the guests two fingers of a burgundy liquid, placed the bottle on the table and retreated.

Captain Dias savored the occasion. Five sat at a table built for a dozen in a room that could have held two such tables side by side under its high, beamed ceiling. Rather than plastered, the walls were lined with oak panels which had not yet begun to darken with age. Candles on the thick table and on the walls bathed the space in warm light. The room was a sovereign's hall compared to his cabin on the *Ninho* and it had been two months since he'd dined with men of his own station. He wiped his knife between his thumb and finger and returned it to its sheath. With his hands still below the table, he pulled a length of blouse from his trousers, rubbed his soiled fingers on the newly exposed cloth, and tucked it back.

Captain Dias knew the governor was well favored by the king. He swirled the liquid in his cup and sniffed it. "Your Excellency, I compliment you on such an exquisite repast all these leagues from civilization."

"We have our luxuries." Governor d'Azambuja raised his

tumbler to salute the king's factor, Rui da Pena, seated at the opposite end of the rectangular table. "O Senhor Factor takes good care of us."

Four of the men at table, including the governor, toasted the fifth, Factor da Pena.

Factor da Pena nodded. "A pleasure to serve, Your Excellency." He turned his high cheek-boned face to Captain Dias. "Por suposto, the wine is always better just after a supply vessel turns up. Your arrival was much anticipated, o meu Capitão."

"What is this we drink? I don't recall anything like it on the *Ninho's* cargo manifest." Captain Dias hadn't felt such fire run down his throat for ages.

Factor da Pena grinned. "It is the same red wine from Coimbra served with dinner, but fortified with alchemists' distilled spirits. You brought us both. We mix it here and spice it with a few herbs. My own recipe. The way we go through the Aqua Ardiente, Guinea House in Lisbon must think we have an unusually active infirmary here."

Captain Dias noted smiles around the table upon disclosure of their little secret.

Governor d'Azambuja leaned forward onto his left forearm, his drink secured in his right fist. "Did you see any Castilian ships on your journey, Capitão?"

"We sighted a sail west of the Canaries but naught else until we captured the Dutchman on the Ivory Coast, just before coming to the Gold Coast."

Chaplain Felipe Alvariz stroked his pointed beard, black like his special occasion tunic. "At last, Their most Catholic majesties Isabela and Fernando respect the Pope's grant of the Guinea Coast to the Portuguese."

Garrison Commandant Gil Pereira slapped his palm on the table. "Pope? Treaty? Bah! The jackals respect our fortifications and armed ships. If we are not vigilant, the Castilians will come again. As will the Genoese and the French. Even our so-called allies, the English. Scavenger dogs. All of them."

Captain Dias raised his tumbler. "Viva King João. May we ever stand with his majesty against Castilla and Aragon."

Factor da Pena seconded.

They lifted their drinks, lowered them, and sipped. The master of the *São Sebastian* and Chaplain Alvariz poured themselves more of the potent mixture.

Governor d'Azambuja looked Captain Dias in the eye. "How is our young king doing with the unruly Duke of Brangança and his brothers?"

The room became silent as all listened for the Captain's response. "It's well known that the House of Brangança believes it is their right to rule the kingdom. Why his majesty puts up with them is a mystery." The Captain continued, "The people side with the king against the excesses and arrogance of the Branganças. He would do well to put them in their place before there's civil war."

Governor d'Azambuja considered this. "Perhaps it is still time for the king to be the owl. His time as falcon will come. He's young but never underestimate him. His decade as co-ruler with his late father has given him a fine perspective of the role he must play."

Chaplain Alvariz coughed into his sleeve. "Has Diogo Cão's expedition returned to Lisbon?"

"Não. Capitão Cão had not arrived by the time I left."

Chaplain Alvariz pressed. "Capitão Cão headed down the coast from here November last. He is either with the fishes or finding things of importance to Portugal to be gone so long."

Captain Dias nodded. "Por certo. Cão will return to Lisbon by heading out to sea and not along the coast so you'll not hear from him as he passes north again. That we are searching for the bottom of Africa and the route to the East is a poorly kept secret, but our mid-ocean path home is still only known to us. Still, we get interlopers trying to take advantage of our discoveries. And it seems others have ideas about how to get to the Orient."

"Pray tell."

Captain Dias sat up straight at this invitation. "There is a mariner named Colom among the Genoese in Lisbon, married into an important family, the Perestrêlos. Colom has sailed most of Guinea, from the bottom of the Sahara to the Gold Coast. He also works as a cartographer with his brother. Colom has assured the king that the best route to Cathay is west from Portugal, across the Ocean Sea."

Governor d'Azambuja cleared his throat. "We know this man. Cristovao Colom was master of a caravela that ran cargo here last fall. He dined at this very table but said nothing of this scheme. What does his majesty say about it?"

"King João is interested but his advisors are certain Colom is wrong about the distance to Cathay. His serene majesty still believes the most promising route is around Africa, if we can find the southernmost tip."

Chaplain Alvariz finished his second drink and wiped his chin and beard. "And what about flanking the Turks and Saracens? Have we found the great Christian empire of Africa yet?"

"Prester John? I don't think so. Não." Captain Dias paused. "Might be a state secret though, if we have found his kingdom."

Factor da Pena spoke. "Moving on to the king's commerce, I have gold, malagueta pepper, ivory, and two score slaves for your return trip, Capitão. I've examined the Negroes myself. Good merchandise—young and healthy."

Three knocks in quick succession reverberated into the dining hall. All eyes shifted to the door. It opened and a young lieutenant from the garrison stepped inside and snapped to attention, his disheveled hair incongruent with his tailored green jacket.

"Begging pardon, o Senhor Commandante. The evening patrol has returned. I wish to pass on their report immediately."

Commandant Pereira remained seated. "Sim. Give the report."

"The patrol recovered the body of a Christian from the lagoon. A boy. Not one of ours, Commandante. The deceased is most certainly one of Capitão Dias' sailors."

"Mãe de Deus. My poor Joselinho. Ayyyyy!"

All eyes returned to the darkened doorway—the direction of the booming lament.

Pilot's Mate Lopo Meendez crossed the threshold into the candle-lit dining hall. He carried, like an offering, a fully-clothed body in his arms.

Captain Dias leapt to his feet, knocking his chair onto its back. He gasped. It was the youngest member of his crew, José Figueroa e Duarte. The boy's head hung back unnaturally, Adams apple to the ceiling and light-brown hair dripping. Arms and legs flopped about each time Lopo moved.

The other four diners were also on their feet. A guard and a handful of black orderlies burst into the room from the serving area.

Lopo raised his face to the rafters and bawled. "Deus. Não. This cannot be true." He shook his head and stared at the boy in his arms.

Chaplain Alvariz rushed to Lopo's side, intoning a blessing in Latin and signing the cross over the limp body.

Captain Dias crossed himself. "Por Deus. What evil is this?"

A soldier pushed his way around Lopo and into the room. His trousers were wet to above his knees and his sleeves a darker green up past his elbows. He stopped dead when he saw that others occupied the room besides the lieutenant and Lopo. He flushed and backed up to leave.

The commandant, in a calm voice, said, "What is it, Corporal?"

The corporal held out an empty wine bottle. "I found this floating in the reeds near the body."

Chapter 13

The Oath

An onshore breeze tousled Lopo's hair. Islands of high clouds drifted shoreward in the clear morning sky. Thirty paces in front of the mourners, curious gulls watched from the edge of the sandy bluff that fell away into the sea. *The same sea and the same birds Joselinho knew back home.*

"In the name of the Father, the Son, and the Holy Spirit. Amen." Father Vasco Estevez crossed himself and nodded to the pallbearers.

Six sailors lowered Joselinho's shrouded body to the bottom of the long, narrow hole, letting the ropes slip smoothly through their hands. They stood, moved to the empty coffin, lifted it to their shoulders, and retreated to behind the two dozen attendees—mostly crew from the *Ninho*.

Three of the soldiers who had recently been passengers on the *Ninho* raised harquebuses and fired once in unison on their sergeant's command.

The blast from the firearms scattered the seagulls and brought a noisy response from the villagers who watched the ceremony from fifty paces back. The wind carried the smell of burnt sulfur and puff of black smoke away toward the lagoon at their backs.

"Retire arms."

The soldiers dropped the butts of their firearms to the ground and maintained them stiffly at their sides.

Lopo stepped forward and dropped a fistful of coarse grey sand into the pit. He crossed himself and closed his eyes. *Go with God, little sailor.*

Captain Dias, Pilot Gonçalves, and Cargo Master Manoel Vaaz took their turns tossing sand while Lopo stood at the foot of the grave.

Lopo continued his vigil as others filed by and scattered their handfuls of grainy earth onto the cream-colored shroud and returned to the fort.

Gunner's Mate Rodrigo Correia filed by last, then joined Lopo. Manoel stood a few paces back.

Lopo, Rodrigo, Manoel and Father Estevez watched in silence while four Guineans with wooden spades closed the grave.

Father Estevez gave each of the laborers five white sea shells. "Obrigado. See you at mass tonight."

The priest turned to the three mariners. "José was at mass in the evening on the day before yesterday, the day he died."

The statement puzzled Lopo. "He didn't have much time after that to get drunk and stumble into the lagoon. They found his body less than an hour after the service."

Even though personally invited to evening mass that day by Chaplain Alvariz, Lopo had found a spot on the parapet of the *Mina*'s wall and had stared out to sea. He continued his attempt at reconciling what he had always believed about bringing the gospel to the innocent savages of the world and what he saw in the cells at the fort that day. He was on the wall when he heard the evening patrol return and saw their soggy burden.

Rodrigo added his opinion. "He's never had more than a cup of wine to drink at a time on this whole voyage—on ship or ashore. Joselinho watched others but never shot the dice himself."

Lopo pondered a moment then said, "Who would want to kill Joselinho?"

#

Pilot Gonçalves and Assistant Factor Soares hunched over a small table in the center of a shack attached to the back of a long hut. A single candle, amid a mound of coins, lit their sorting and counting. A few low stacked columns of the silver and copper money wobbled at Gonçalves' elbow. At both ends of the little room, curtains were pulled aside to reveal a platform topped by a mattress identical to the ones in the guest quarters back at the fort. During the afternoons and evenings, this room was the business end of the only bordello within a thousand leagues. On the bed behind Gonçalves lay half a dozen leather sacks the size of muskmelons: each one tied off at the mouth with a leather thong. No sacks sat on the bed behind Soares because he had handed over the last one to Gonçalves. These were the secret profits since the last time the pilot was at the *Mina*.

Gonçalves looked up when he heard someone out front. He leaned sideways from his chair, parted the entryway curtain, and peered into the dark room, the largest in the Village of Two Parts.

"It's us, Senhor Piloto." Nunno and Belchior threaded their way through the maze of tables and chairs in the deserted hall.

The funeral that morning weighed upon the sailors and few came to join the off-duty soldiers for a night of wine bibbing, women, and dice. Gonçalves insisted that those too drunk to stagger back to the fort be carried by their companions. He had sent the Guinean girls and his Guinean manager home. He wanted no one in the place after closing that night save his inner circle.

The two helmsmen came in through the parted curtains. Soares moved around to the chair at the back of the table, so they could sit in chairs near the doorway.

Nunno removed the floppy beret and black cape from his bony shoulders. "You sent for us?"

Gonçalves studied the pair. "No one saw you that night, right?"

Belchior, cap still in his hand, bobbed his plump head. "Like you told us, we floated him face down in the weeds where the path skirts the lagoon. We emptied the bottle on his head and jerkin and set it next to him. No one was about."

Soares shook his head. "Around here, there's always someone out and about. If not from the fort, then most assuredly from the village. You'll not get away with this, Gonçalves."

"Me? We're in this together."

"It was stupid to kill him. He was lost. He came into the wrong room."

"I . . . we couldn't take that chance. There was gold on the table. The little cockroach always told Lopo everything."

The four sat in silence around the table. Soares glared at him and Gonçalves knew exactly why. Trading for gold could get them both hanged. They had agreed to never mention the gold around his two lackeys, ever. Nunno and Belchior studied their hands or looked at anything but the pilot and the assistant factor.

After all the things he'd gotten away with in his life, Gonçalves wasn't going down over such a trifle. "No one will find out if we keep our mouths shut. Swear to me that you'll not say a word about this. Swear that you'll stop anyone else from witnessing against us."

The three stared at Gonçalves.

He drew his dagger and stabbed it into the table. A few coins tumbled over the edge to the packed-dirt floor. He stood and drew a deep breath into his barrel of a chest. "Swear it now."

CHAPTER 14

Through the Door of No Return

A fresh wind poured through the three slots in the wall above Mbekah's head. A hint of light flickered on the wall in front of the grillwork gate at the end of the room. If others in the room were awake, she could not tell in the dark. She leaned her ear close to Kpodo's wife's ribs to make sure she was breathing. On the other side of Mbekah, Ifé was most assuredly alive. Mbekah brushed her finger over Ifé's nose until Ifé pushed it away, rolled over, and stopped snoring.

Mbekah picked out the sounds that came from outside the room of stone. Men from her forest, caged nearby, moaned from time to time in their troubled sleep. She heard muffled conversations in the hallways, which she did not understand. The night guards, she supposed.

The frogs' serenade in the lagoon was no mystery, but a constant shushing perplexed her. For the past five days, since she had been conscious, Mbekah had studied the sound.

The answer, like dew from heaven, settled on her thoughts. The day before their sale to the Cristowns, she and the other captives bathed in the great salty waters, the same waters that lapped at the walls on two sides of this prison. That day, ridge after ridge of water peaked and tumbled forward into milky foam, which rushed to the shore, shushing all the way.

With the riddle of the sounds solved, she switched to reciting proverbs—the wisdom of her people—she had learned, mostly from her father. One stayed with her. Like the repetitive action of the water ridges, she imagined her father whispering over and over, "*He who will shake the trunk of a tree only shakes himself.*"

#

Mbekah awoke. The sounds of people in motion filled the hallway. Three beams of sunlight illuminated the wall in front of her and the contents of the room were now visible. The other women were already awake but remained still and watchful, like a herd of black and whites at the first sign of a lion somewhere in the tall grass. Their eyes studied the end of the room whence came the noises through the bars of the gate. Mbekah searched Ifé's face for an answer to the new puzzle, but her friend squatted as motionless as a stone and squinted steadfastly toward the end of the room.

Mbekah closed her eyes to concentrate. She spoke for the women closest her to hear. "Iron ropes dragging along the stone floor. A man from the Village of Two Parts calling out, 'Head down. Don't stop.'" She strained to hear more. She again related what she could make out of the commotion. "'Head down. Move on. You! Head down.'" Mbekah opened her eyes and stared at Ifé. "They're moving the men from their room." She shook her head. "Why must they lower their heads?"

The noise ceased. The women waited, silent and alert.

"Where is our food? They have always brought it before now."

Mbekah didn't see who made the question. It was a good one. *Where was the food? And why hadn't the water carriers come?* She settled back against the wall.

Kpodo's wife slid her back down the stone blocks to sit shoulder to shoulder with Mbekah. "They're taking Kpodo. Where? Will they take us too?"

Others spoke in whispers. The whispers became chattering.

One woman spoke stridently for the whole group to hear. "When will they feed us?"

Another added, "This is not good. Why haven't they brought the food?"

Mbekah shut her eyes to see the towering baobab in her village in the forest. She hummed until she found the right pitch and softly sang,

"Stands tall. Waivers not.
Watches over us. Watches our yams in field and barn.
Blesses our millet, blesses our bread.
Blesses our mothers and their milk.
Vigilant, sun time and moon."

Others joined in.

"Stands tall. Waivers not..."

The iron gate swung open and a villager with a club stepped inside to hold it open. A Cristown leaned in and watched while the women intoned their supplication.

Whether they sat, squatted, or stood, the women swayed side to side in perfect rhythm.

Another of the pale men pushed past the first and both leered in at the reverent chorus. Someone shouted in the hallway and the two voyeurs disappeared. The man with the club pulled the heavy gate shut as he left.

The prayer was sung a third time and the women fell silent and somber. Mbekah again heard chains sliding along the stones. She heard the commands to duck heads and keep moving.

#

Governor d'Azambuja leaned forward in his regal chair and dripped sealing wax onto an envelope. He pressed the signet of his ring into the hot drops and held it there for a few seconds. "How are your men taking the ruling of the inquest?"

Captain Dias stood at ease in front of the governor's massive oak table. "No one said anything against it, but I detected incredulity in the eyes and voices of some. I'd say Pilot's Mate Lopo Meendez and most his watch do not believe the boy stumbled into the lagoon and died. I have difficulty accepting it myself. That said, I see that you had no other choice under the circumstances."

Governor d'Azambuja stood and limped around the table, pausing to straighten a zebra hide war shield on the white wall. He half sat on the front edge of the table next to where Captain Dias stood. "The commandante spoke with everyone who was out that night and our sources in the village say no one there admits to seeing or hearing anything. We have other things to worry about, so forget it, Capitão. But don't forget it, if you understand my meaning.

"I will keep my eyes and ears open. Discreetly, of course."

"Good. Would you invite the factor and your purser in, so we can certify the gold and lock the chest?"

Captain Dias came to attention and saluted. He turned to do as bidden.

"One more thing, Capitão. You're returning with only eighteen of the Dutch prisoners?"

Captain Dias paused. "*Ninho*'s deck will be full of slaves. The Dutch sailors will have to work as part of the crew, six of them on my ship. The *São Sebastian* will take twelve, six in irons and six as crew. That's the most we can handle without inviting an uprising."

"I suppose most of the fight went out of them when they saw their officers tossed into the sea. We'll find work here for the remaining Dutchmen while they await other ships. No offense to you, Capitão, but I will not be sad to see you leave. It's been a busy ten days with you here."

"It's true then, o meu Governador, that visits always give pleasure; if not the arriving, so the departing."

"In your case, Capitão, it was a pleasure you arrived, and another that you're taking your troubles and departing. Now let's see the gold?"

#

The sunbeams had reached the bottom of the wall when the iron gate squeaked open again. A pair of water carriers, escorted by two men with clubs, started down the line of women, pausing in front of each.

A group of six followed: two of the pale guards, two more villagers with clubs, and two orderlies from the village bearing iron chains with loops for ankles or wrists. The orderlies unshackled eight women from the wall, the ones who had already been watered, and secured them in the chains. They led them from the room. Mbekah remained with fifteen other very solemn women.

The water givers stopped in front of Kpodo's wife and Mbekah. Each took the dipper from the gourd nearest her and drained it twice as was the routine.

Mbekah whispered, "Where are they taking us?"

The women with the gourds moved on to Ifé and Olubayo. One looked back over her shoulder at the club men. There were no Cristowns in the room at that moment. Though the woman looked at Ifé, whom she watered, she answered Mbekah, barely moving her lips. "You will go through a small door in the wall on the lagoon side. The pale men will put you in their great wooden fish with wings. You will fly over the waters and you will never return."

CHAPTER 15

Except Someone Will Buy It

A Cristown man, two boys, and two club-wielding men came for the last eight women in the stone room. The Cristown did not wear the metal turtle shell and hat Mbekah had noted the first time she'd seen this pale race of men in the bartering field. In his leather belt, he carried two knives in sheaths: a short one with a blade about the length of her hand and a slightly curved one that reached to just below his knee.

The boys placed Kpodo's wife in chains for moving the captives about and did the same in turn with Mbekah, Ifé, Olubayo, and three others. They reached the last slave, a married woman. Mbekah had watched this woman since she first noticed her in another group in the ochre village. Her breasts were swollen, and she seemed in pain at that time. Mbekah heard that the woman had hidden her baby when the raiders attacked her village. The woman cried a lot but had not said much.

They loosed the brooding woman's iron collar and she came to life, screaming and flailing. She slapped the surprised boys several times before they backed out of her reach. With her back to the wall, she tensed and curled her fingers, a panther ready to spring.

Mbekah stiffened and sought how she might help this woman whose situation was more terrible than her own and was about to get worse.

The Cristown gripped the handle of his long knife and nodded slightly at the guards. One inserted himself between the seething woman and the others. He raised his club, ready to punish any who might join in. The other guard crouched low, fixed on the cornered woman's eyes and crept toward her. He feigned lifting his club then dropped it and jabbed her in the belly with its head. The woman collapsed and lay doubled up, speechless, fighting for breath. The boys moved in and put her in the chain.

She finally gulped a breath, then two, then many. She convulsed and sobbed. "You can't take me away. I must go back. My baby. He'll die. My husband will pay you."

The words of Mbekah's father came to her. "*Full-belly child says to hungry child, 'Keep Good Heart.'*" Not that her own situation was so good but Mbekah determined to do what she could in the next few days to comfort the woman without trying to minimize her loss.

The boys pulled the crying woman to her feet and the guards bullied the bunch forward a few steps.

For the second time since her abduction, Mbekah openly defied her captors. She planted her feet and brought the entire party to a halt. She raised both hands in front of her, palms up and arms bent at the elbows. She tilted her head back and spoke in a firm but respectful voice. "Great One. You see us now—weary and hungry and in chains. Where we go, we will help each other, but we ask your watchfulness as well."

Their guards made no move to disturb Mbekah. The mother ceased her crying. Without prodding, the eight women from the forest shuffled lock-step out of the cell to a short hallway. They followed one of the boys into the sunlight and toward a chest-high opening in the wall. Its sturdy door, wide enough for one person at a time, stood open.

"Lower your head," the lead boy shouted.

They slowed. Kpodo's wife bent forward and dropped her head to make it through the hole. Mbekah did the same but needed to steady herself with her hands on the ground. She stepped out onto a ramp and raised herself to her full height. Sun reflecting off the lagoon blinded her for a moment. She scooted forward to make room for the women behind her as they ducked through the doorway one by one. Mbekah squinted to survey the ten paces wide band of shore and the sparkling lagoon. Two magnificent, wooden fish floated atop the calm waters. They were bigger and stranger than she had anticipated but they had nothing that resembled the wings she'd overheard villagers describe. Two smaller boats floated near the shore.

She and the other captives trod down the short ramp to the pebbled shore and into knee-deep water.

"Clean yourselves."

Mbekah sat, immersed herself to her neck in the cool water, and rubbed away the layers of sour sweat. It felt wonderful. She lay back and washed her shoulder-length hair which had long since come unbraided.

The boys helped Mbekah's group of eight into one of the smaller boats where four more villagers held long paddles upright. Mbekah had never seen watercraft any larger than scooped-out logs that carried two or three people. This craft was as wide as five such log boats. When she stood, the sides of the boat came to her thighs.

A pale man in the back of the boat spoke and the dark men, who sat looking at him and the captives instead of where they were going, began to paddle without leaning out over the sides. The pale man guided their boat by moving a stick. They glided toward one of the huge fish with its two upright tree trunks and cords everywhere. She noted, without surprise, an eye the size of a man's chest on the side of the vessel near one end.

"The Cristowns' wooden fish is not for short journeys," Mbekah said to Ifé. "The far shore of the sea waters cannot be seen from here."

Ifé said nothing. She wet her right thumb with her tongue, blew on it, and ran it in a short line from her left shoulder to her bicep where a monkey's tooth in a tiny pouch used to hang from a leather thong. Mbekah knew that Ifé made the gesture out of habit, for the gesture was powerless without the amulet.

Their boat bumped against one of the long, fat fish and men in the boat pushed the chained women up while others pulled them onto its wooden floor. Mbekah saw that this 'fish' was a boat, one that was at least 50 paces long. Their ankle chain scraped along the boards as they moved past a large square hole in the floor and on to the eye end of the huge boat. Cristowns transferred them from their traveling chains to iron loops and chains secured in the open air to the sides of the vessel.

Mbekah sat shoulder to shoulder with Kpodo's wife and Ifé. Two rows of female slaves sat behind, between them and a hip-high wooden wall that probably was there to keep them from falling into the sea. She stared into the faces of three rows of male slaves against the opposite hip-high wall. Above their heads and over the lip of the wooden wall, she saw the upper parts of the strong house that had been her prison for a dozen days and nights.

Mbekah spoke into Ifé's ear. "Much better here in the sun than in that stinking room of stone."

Ifé said nothing.

The Cristown who had come to look at them a few days before, the one with part of an ear missing, was on the boat with them. This one had not leered at her like the other Cristowns and the men in the ochre village. She wondered if others in his land had his green eyes and light brown hair, or his skin—the golden color of a bird lightly roasted on a stick.

Judging from his build, she supposed he was not a warrior, though he was some kind of headman. He labored not himself but told others what to do. He went all over the craft and once she caught him stealing a glance at her. Mbekah feigned not to notice.

The slaves sat or squatted in their irons and observed the activity around them. Mbekah heard a whistle and everyone stopped and stood silently, facing where she had mounted the fish. Another paddle boat approached and came alongside. Three Cristown men climbed up onto the floating marvel. Two of them hefted a small but apparently heavy box with iron reinforcement bands; the other carried a leather purse. The new arrivals waited for a fourth man to climb onto the deck. This man dressed ornately compared to the other Cristowns on the fish. Besides the short and long knives in his belt, he wore a puffy purple loin cloth, as well as dark leggings and a shirt made of a woven fabric. From the side of his cap a purple, strutting-bird feather protruded backward and waved about when he turned his head this way and that.

This man touched a finger to his forehead and his chest, to one shoulder and then the other. Mbekah was surprised that he did not then touch the fetish hanging from his neck. She had noted the same charm on other Cristowns' necks. He surveyed the waiting men about the boat and said something to a gorilla of a man with thinning hair on his head. The gorilla man shouted a command and the pale men returned to their tasks.

The three men with their burdens accompanied strutting-feather headman up a ladder and to the door of a hut which he entered. The three handed their packages in to the headman and descended the ladder to join the others in their work.

In time, strutting-feather man came out of his hut, this time without his long knife or his cap and feather. He climbed down the ladder and strolled to where Mbekah and the other slaves were secured.

The man's outfit seemed impractical. *Is he cold?*

The man with the clipped ear and green eyes came and spoke to him and then left. That confirmed to her that strutting-feather was the top headman. He glanced at her and the other captives before he returned to stand in front of his small room above the far end of the boat. He leaned forward on a railing and observed everyone else at their tasks.

Helpers from the Village of Two Parts returned to shore in the last paddle boat so there were only Cristowns and slaves on the large boat. No, that was not true. An nut-brown man scrambled out through the square hole onto the deck. He joined some of the pale men arranging cords and seemed to be talking and laughing with them in their strange speech. Except that he wore ragged breeches and a jerkin like the pale men, he could have been from any village in the forest or savannah or this shore. Mbekah discovered no indication that he was a slave.

Since she had settled into her spot on the deck, the fish had slowly changed position in the lagoon. At first, she was looking at the Cristowns' stone walls but soon saw the barter field, then the village. At the moment, she was looking inland to the tree dotted landscape beyond the lagoon. She decided that the water in the lagoon had begun to flow into the sea but that something held them from moving further with the current.

The top headman leaned forward over his railing and said something down to gorilla man on deck who shouted to others. Men, including nut-brown man, inserted stout sticks into holes in an upright beam, leaned against their sticks, strained, and turned the beam, walking in a circle. Clipped-ear man shouted and others pulled cords to put up great white cloths on the tree trunks.

The wings!

An almost imperceptible breeze filled the cloths and the fantastic fish boat swam slowly from the lagoon into the short river and into the great waters of the sea. The other great boat followed. Men moved the cloths to the other side and the craft turned. Mbekah could see that they were going away from the prison and the Village of Two Parts.

"Ifé, look at our land—the place of our forest, our village, our families, our ancestors. Will we never see it again?"

Ifé looked a long time but said nothing. She buried her head in her arms and knees and wept.

In her mind, Mbekah sang the farewell song and watched the land slip away until she could no longer tell one tree from another. The last thing she could distinguish was the Cristowns' white structure and its tall house above the walls. They slowly disappeared beneath the blue horizon.

Mbekah tightened her lips and set her jaw. She knew why the raiders came so far to her forest; she knew why they murdered her father and others. *A man does not gather what he does not need except someone will buy it.* Her father had not said that, but it was nevertheless true. The Cristowns were the buyers. She wondered about the thirty iron pots the men of the ochre village received for her and her friends. The price was sufficient to cause men to travel many days to do much evil. *What evil still lies ahead for me and at what price?* Bitter tears evaporated in the wind, but she made no sound.

CHAPTER 16

The Tallest One

Mbekah opened her eyes and stared up into Ifé's face. She couldn't recall ever feeling sick for so long. Weak and hungry, her middle ached from an afternoon and evening of retching. She hadn't been the only one. Most of the captives succumbed to the frightening illness soon after losing sight of the shore.

The pale men drenched the captives with buckets of salt water several times that afternoon to keep their area clean but the stench of vomit lingered. Mbekah still felt a chill from the washings.

With her head in Ifé's lap, she finally dozed after hours of painful stomach spasms. Now she was hungry but wondered if she could keep any food down.

Ifé spoke. "The Cristown man who looks like us spoke to us while you slept. He said the sickness is common with people who go on a big boat for the first time and that you will feel better by the morning when they bring food and water."

Mbekah spoke her father's words as they came to her. "No matter how long the night, the day is sure to come."

Ifé nodded and stroked Mbekah's hair.

A fcw small groups of captives conversed in muted tones. Most slept, a tangle of groaning and mumbling bodies.

Ifé smiled down at Mbekah. "The black Cristown calls himself Paydru. He said it's the same name as one of the first Cristown holy men."

"A strange name. Is he a slave?"

"He is. His master lives in the village where we're going, a village that spreads over the whole side of a mountain next to a river wider than a morning's walk. Paydru works all over the boat and helps the pale men speak to us. He knows their language."

"He is from our forest?"

"He says he is and he speaks like one of us, but I've never heard of any kinfolk he mentioned."

With no moon to diminish the stars, an impossible-to-count number sparkled in the portion of charcoal sky on their side of the great cloth wings. Ifé seemed in good spirits, especially compared to that morning when she cried upon leaving their homeland. Perhaps not getting the boat sickness made the difference. *She takes care of me and forgets her own problems.*

"The men talk about killing the Cristowns if they can get free. They don't say anything about it when Paydru is near. They think he's an informer."

Mbekah hadn't thought about revenge for a day and a night— too many new things had happened to think much about her situation.

Ifé went on. "Why should we kill the Cristowns? They didn't come to our village and murder our fathers and brothers. They haven't raped any of us, so far."

"Do you think the men from the ochre village would have traveled so far to capture us if the Cristowns didn't have a new strong house in their land and iron pots to trade?"

Ifé thought for a moment. "If not to the Cristowns, they could have sold us to the men from the desert."

"Then we would kill the men from the desert. Our men are right. We can't let this happen without a struggle."

"Kpodo makes the most threats. He says it is his right to lead since he is to be headman when his father gets old."

"Boasting is not courage." Mbekah no longer fretted about her sore midriff. "We should have done something to escape on the trail before we came to the ochre village. That's when we needed Kpodo's leadership."

"Quiet. Here comes Paydru and one of the Cristown headmen."

With Ifé's help, Mbekah sat up. Some of the pale men worked quietly about the boat and others curled up in blankets just out of reach of the captives.

Paydru and Clipped-ear man stepped into the narrow pathway between the male and female captives. Both dropped to a crouch and looked into the women's faces. Paydru carried a bucket in each hand and the pale man a sack.

Mbekah studied Paydru. *The teeth smile, but does the heart?*

Paydru said, "This is Lohpu. He is headman of the night workers. You are to be fed in the morning, but we have water and boat bread for those who wish to eat something now."

#

To Lopo, the caravela at night had the appearance of a living thing with dozing bodies everywhere, never completely silent or completely still. Slaves slept in a chain-laced jumble in the front third of the open deck. Off-duty crew napped amidships on the main deck as well as on the quarterdeck beside the captain's cabin above the helm. They huddled in the hold only during a gale because the air down there was rancid and if not exactly lethal, the rats could be.

When Captain Dias walked on his quarterdeck, most of what took place on the *Ninho* was in his full view. Pilot treated pilot's mate accordingly and so forth down the pecking order. For this, Lopo was grateful for he did not wish to deal with Pilot Gonçalves if and when the latter sensed he was free to act without the captain's scrutiny. Even when Captain Dias was in his cabin, Lopo knew he could hear, feel, or smell what was happening on the ship. If the helmsmen held to a new heading, the captain felt it. A stiffer wind, a new swell, dinner served, sails trimmed, slaves exercised, land sighted, the captain knew it. Nature and the crew were all actors perpetually on stage for the captain's pleasure and critique. *Graças a Deus*!

Though this was Lopo's first voyage to the *Mina*, as officer of the night watch, he was given the secret of their return route. Instead of sailing parallel and close to the coast, as they'd done when coming to the *Mina*, Lopo directed his helmsmen to make long tacks southward—away from Lisbon—into the open ocean. After more than a hundred leagues, the *Ninho* and the *São Sebastian* would pick up prevailing winds to push them northwest around the left shoulder of Africa while far out to sea. At that point, they would sail close hauled across the easterlies in a great arc west of Madeira and back east to the Azores on winds out of the west in the northern latitudes. From the Azores they would continue to Portugal on those same winds.

By order of King João, they did not return with the captured Dutch ship in order to perpetuate the myth that only caravelas could sail back to Europe from the Guinea coast. In fact, the trick his countrymen had learned by trial and error in the past fifty years was to venture far from land and use the natural movements of the atmosphere to speed their homeward journey.

If all went well, Lopo would be home in about six weeks. His parents insisted on finding him a bride. He wasn't sure a sailor should have a wife and family to abandon to earn a living and serve the king. Nevertheless, he yearned for the companionship of a virtuous woman—one like his mother—and to have children, especially sons. Other naval officers had families. Why not him? Reluctantly, he'd promised his mother he would be ready to consider a match when he returned from the *Mina*.

He contemplated the naked women who were constantly before him on the open deck—mostly young and about the right age to marry. They weren't another species of human as he'd heard some of his countrymen suggest. When he inspected the slaves for the first time at the fort, he realized that's what he had come to believe subconsciously about the 'savages' brought back as slaves. He looked into their eyes and saw they weren't bestial and crude. They were just black and naked and under duress.

The women are beautiful. Or have I been away from Lisbon too long? What would my mother think if she knew my secret desires for these Guinean women? Surely my father would understand my . . . thoughts. But what about my interest in the one called Bekah? The slave sailor Pedro told me her name. That is different. I feel something more. Her nude body haunts me but there is something other than lust. I want to know about her. She is tall and confident. She is curious. She is angry. I wish I could give her some clothes. No, mother must never know! Back in Lisbon, I will never see Bekah or any of these captives again, except by accident.

Pedro helped Lopo deal with the slaves during his watches and was teaching Lopo a few words in their language. On the king's orders, Pedro also taught the slaves Portuguese words. They will be worth more if they speak some Portuguese when sold. Pedro learned the captives' strange names, strange at least to Lopo.

According to Pedro, he told the slaves about the capital city of Lisbon and about Jesus and Mary and the Saints of God. He explained about the Salve Regina the crew sang each morning when the day watch took over their stations from his men. The slaves wanted to know about the crosses the crew wore about their necks. Pedro told Lopo that most of what he told the captives did not surprise them. He said it hadn't seemed strange to him either when he first learned about Christian amulets and their reverence for God and his spirit helpers.

Lopo was intrigued when he first reported to the *Ninho* to find a slave among the crew. He learned that Pedro's owner received one slave from among the captives on each voyage as payment for supplying a translator and sailor with basic maritime skills. His master had promised Pedro his freedom after the sixth voyage to the Guinea coast. This was his third trip.

Many of the crew talked openly about having their way with the slave women. They grumbled constantly about the orders Captain Dias had Lopo read out loud a few hours after departure from the *Mina*.

"No sexual contact of any kind with this group of slaves," the captain summarized when Lopo had finished reading.

"How could this be," they murmured. A deck full of female captives was an important reason many of them volunteered to run cargo to the *Mina*—that and the prestige that came from sailing the best ships with the most skilled officers and mariners in all Christendom.

Manoel assured Lopo that Captain Dias had never before worried about the crew sharing the women on the homeward voyage and was at a loss to explain the change.

Lopo didn't like talk of taking the slave women. Maybe he thought too much about it. That's what happened on long night watches. He thought too much about too many things.

#

Pilot Gonçalves finished his fourth pewter flagon of red wine, belched, and pushed off the main mast where he'd been leaning and watching the nude girls arrayed in front of him. He steadied himself with his left hand on the starboard gunwale and made his way back to where his two helmsmen manned the steering beam. "I haven't seen Lopo or Rodrigo about. They still asleep?"

"I think so, sim," Nunno whispered. "They must be up on the quarterdeck behind the cabin."

"*O Senhor Capitão* is in his bed. He prays and sleeps this time every afternoon," Belchior added.

"And Pedro?" Gonçalves wasn't sure how their translator would react. "Who's going to keep him silent?"

Belchior looked pleased with himself even if a bit nervous. "Pedro is working for Manoel in the hold. He's got another hour's work down there. Manoel will keep him busy until I signal all clear."

"What about Manoel? He's too friendly with Lopo to trust." Gonçalves hoped Belchior had a good answer because this was risky business; nevertheless, he needed to do it soon.

Belchior smiled thinly. "It will be too late for Manoel to back out by the time he sees what's happening."

The wine sloshing in his belly and spicing his blood made it difficult for Gonçalves to concentrate, so with one arm still braced against the gunwale, he closed his eyes for a long moment to sense as much as he could about the state of the ship and its occupants. "Now is good. Three weeks since the *Mina* and it's time."

"Which one?" Belchior waited.

"The tallest one. She's probably the youngest. From what I've heard, the soldiers at the fort hadn't even had their chance at most of these girls before the king's edict changed the rules for this group."

"I'm beginning to understand, *o meu Piloto*. You think she's a virgin, is it not so?"

"I'll soon find out."

CHAPTER 17

"Sim, Senhor"

Lopo sat with his back against the captain's cabin and gazed at the succession of foaming eddies that stretched back as far as he could see, a hint of the thousand-league furrow the *Ninho* had plowed in the deep-blue ocean since leaving the *Mina*. Even though he was one of few who had a berth, on pleasant days he preferred this spot to that coffin-like sleeping closet on the main deck behind the helm.

He returned his attention to the booklet in his lap. He'd copied the poems by hand, page by page from various books in his math teacher's small library. Lopo no longer needed to open the well-worn little volume to enjoy its contents because he'd memorized each verse. Just the same, he treasured it among the few possessions in his sea kit.

His family had been members of the tannery guild for generations. His uncle and cousins purchased and treated the skins—a smelly business—outside Lisbon. His father sold the tanned hides, parchments, and even vellum in his shop in Lisbon. Purse makers, cobblers, bookbinders, monks, and mapmakers frequented the store. Lopo saved scraps and gave them to Afonso the bookbinder who produced the thin book as a favor.

He caressed its calf-hide binding and turned a page. He read the first line, looked again at the sea, and softly recited the rest of the page's contents. He didn't wish to disturb the other off-duty men who dozed in the warmth of the late afternoon sun.

"Of all that I see,
I desire no other than thee.
And I desire thee such
That for thee I would slay a . . ."

Lopo sensed something was not right—a sound that didn't fit. He cocked his head, straining to hear again and discover what it might be. Muted commotion came from the main deck. A snap followed by silence. He knew instantly that someone had slapped bare flesh with the cat o' nine tails. A woman's scream was muffled almost before it started.

Lopo jumped to his feet. He reached low to chuck Rodrigo on the head as he leaped over him on his way around the cabin toward the front of the quarterdeck. He paused at the railing to survey the situation below.

Three sailors from the day watch paced in the aisle between the male and female slaves and menaced them with clubs. A fourth, Belchior, stood over the first women with his back to Lopo. The stocky helmsman clenched the handle of the multi-thong whip and held it over his right shoulder, ready to lash out. The chained Guineans eyed the whip, or the clubs if they were nearer, in defiant silence.

Lopo didn't like it but he saw no advantage to the slaves or himself to interfere in this touchy situation. Belchior wasn't his man; nevertheless, Lopo cleared his throat to let him know he stood there watching over his shoulder from twenty paces behind and above him.

Belchior turned his body and head enough to make eye contact with Lopo.

Lopo knew Belchior had to do this to make sure it was him, Lopo, and not the captain who now observed the activity on deck.

A few others on watch stepped from their chores to the center of the ship and stared up at Lopo in support of their crew mates standing among the slaves.

Belchior shook his head almost imperceptibly at Lopo.

The message was clear. *Stay out of this.* Lopo felt a slight bump on his back when the ship rocked and knew Rodrigo and others on his watch stood behind him.

Lopo's men who had been sleeping on the main deck rolled out of their blankets, rose, and backed up toward the quarterdeck to face off against the day watch in solidarity with Lopo.

In the silence, sounds that he normally ignored pushed into Lopo's consciousness. Gentle swells splashed against the bow; board creaked against board. Lopo noted the moderate up and down motion of the caravela. Something moved below him, under the quarterdeck and out of his sight. *The pilot is up to no good.*

What was going on here? Was it just Belchior bullying the slaves? A slight movement among the first few women, the ones immediately in front of Belchior, caught Lopo's attention. *Bekah's friend, Ifay. She's trying to tell me something.* Bekah was not next to Ifay. He'd not seen her locked down anyplace except beside Ifay.

Where is Bekah? What does Ifay mean to say? Lopo looked down and saw Manoel almost directly below him, practically hiding. "Where is Pedro?"

"He's working in the hold." Manoel looked away after his reply.

With her chin and eyes Ifay subtly pointed to the spot under him where the pilot most likely was. *Where he is with . . . Bekah!*

Lopo vaulted the railing and dropped to the main deck on all fours like a cat on the hunt. He spun around to peer into the hollow space under the deck he'd just stood on.

Nunno braced himself with feet wide apart behind the binnacle and one arm over the steering beam.

Behind Nunno, Gonçalves struggled to shove Bekah, bound and gagged, feet first into his sleeping cupboard. He held her practically horizontal.

With her legs bent, she pressed her knees against the doorframe.

Nunno sucked in his breath, squeaking in the process.

Gonçalves paused to look over his shoulder and saw Lopo slip his knife from his sash. The pilot released Bekah and whirled to meet the attack.

She fell, bashed her head and back on the deck, and wriggled about to free herself.

Lopo rushed forward but glanced off Nunno's outstretched leg and banged his shoulder against the starboard wall of the half-enclosed area. He recovered in a crouch, ready to spring at Gonçalves who awaited him with his own blade.

"What's going on?" The captain's voice cut through the sea air from above.

Gonçalves straightened and returned his weapon to its sheath before the captain could get down the ladder from the quarterdeck. He grabbed the cord about Bekah's upper arms and chest and dragged her past Lopo to the open deck where the other slaves huddled. "A punishment for stirring up the other slaves after gruel, *o meu Capitão*."

Captain Dias descended to the main deck. He swept the scene with his suspicious gaze and settled on Lopo who remained near Nunno in the covered stern. "No one takes any of the slaves out of chains for punishment unless I am present."

Lopo nodded, barely containing himself. "*Sim*, *Senhor*."

"*Piloto* Gonçalves?" the captain shouted.

The pilot handed Bekah to Belchior and stood tall. "I understand, *sim*."

CHAPTER 18

"Bluhdadih, Bluhdadih, Yihdadoo"

With a chunk of charcoal, Lopo drew a stick man on the polished plank and held it up for the slaves to study.

"This is a man." He placed his finger on his chest. "I am a man. Pedro is a man." He walked across the deck and touched Kpodo's shoulder. "Kpodo is a man."

The same multitude of eyes that had followed Lopo that first day in the *Mina*'s holding cells, followed his every move on the deck of the *Ninho*. Every pair of eyes from that day was here, every pair but one.

Manoel said he didn't know a single instance where only one of the chained Guineans had taken sick and died by this point in the return voyage—they were less than a week from the Azores, their first port stop since the Gold Coast. Usually it was three or four or more. The woman who died had sobbed constantly, wouldn't eat, wouldn't drink. Pedro said she cried because she'd been taken from her baby by the slave raiders.

Lopo displayed and touched the charcoal drawing again. "Man."

Some of the slaves repeated the word but did so in a mumble. It seemed to Lopo that they were testing the word to see how it would come out of their mouths. A few, like Mbekah, repeated every word or sentence during every lesson. That impressed him. *I wonder if someone I know, who could afford it, had a place in their home or shop for such a bright slave girl.*

Under the captain's orders, Pedro worked an hour each morning with the captives to teach them Portuguese. Lopo did the same in the afternoon on his own initiative. He knew his shipmates thought he only bothered to teach the Guineans in order to increase the value of the cargo in Lisbon. Let them think it. He hoped the unwilling passengers' lives would be easier with more knowledge of where they were going to spend the rest of their lives.

Lopo could call each of the slaves by name using the correct pronunciation. He learned to say the "mm" sound in Mbekah, the "mm" he hadn't detected until a few weeks before when he had been calling her Bekah. Pedro helped him with those details for a time every evening when Lopo stood watch with his men. To practice his new language skills, Lopo sat and spoke with small groups of the slaves after their formal lesson. He did this to learn their language, but he spent a large portion of his chatting time with Mbekah and her friends Ifé and Olubayo and the striking beauty they referred to only as Kpodo's wife. That was their way—not to use her name. Besides, they said, she hadn't grown up with them in their village.

Lopo liked that the slaves were no longer naked. In the more northerly waters, each slave had been given a crudely woven garment against the chill. No more than a large sack with openings for head and arms and extended below their knees, it served its purpose.

Lopo placed the wooden slate in his lap and wiped away the stick man's arms. He drew them again, this time holding an open book. Not one of the students spoke a word or shifted to scrape chains against the deck. He held the board up and gave them time to discover the changes he'd made.

"Read. The man reads," Lopo said loud enough for all to hear.

He saw no comprehension in their faces. Lopo said the words again.

Still nothing in the expressions of his class.

He said the words forcefully. "Read. The man reads the book."

Some repeated the words, but no one showed the least sign of understanding.

He left them abruptly and returned with his tan, leather-bound book of poems.

"Book." He held the book for all to see. He looked into Mbekah's eyes.

She shook her head. "What?"

Lopo read out loud from his book. He let a few of them inspect the book. He read out loud again. He mimicked reading to himself and laughed heartily at something in the book.

They watched in silence.

Mbekah said, "Readih. Zih men reads zih book." She shook her head like the Portuguese to mean 'no'. "What means 'readih'?"

All eyes were on Lopo as he performed the whole routine another time. He again saw no indication of understanding.

"Words!" Lopo pointed to the words in the book. He said it loudly to help them understand. They didn't understand.

He passed the book in front of their noses, pointing to the text.

"Words," he yelled. "There are words in the book. Stories in the book."

Nothing but open mouths, teeth, and expectant stares.

Lopo did his act again. "I read the book." He bobbed his head as he shouted each word. "I. READ. THE. BOOK!" Lopo read them a stanza then looked up from the pages to their amused stares.

Mbekah rose and held out her hand. Lopo gave her his book.

She opened it, cleared her throat, and, while looking into its pages said, "Bluhdadih, bluhdahih, yihdadoo." She chuckled, shaking her entire body in accurate imitation of Lopo's own faked laugh.

The Guineans howled with delight and drummed on the deck with their hands.

She handed Lopo the book, her eyes wide open, arms out, head shaking. She said in a loud voice. "What means 'readih'?"

Lopo turned his back to the group in exasperation. He looked into the face of Captain Dias who leaned his back on the mainmast only six paces away. It appeared that every man aboard the caravela crowded behind the captain to watch the show.

Lopo blushed and stammered. "I, uh. I am . . ."

The captain smiled. "Carry on, Senhor Meendez. Carry on."

Ninho's crew members stamped their feet, slapped each other on the back, and laughed and hooted until some cried.

PART II

The Kingdom of Portugal

CHAPTER 19

Many People, Many Houses

The *Ninho* and the *São Sebastian* left the Atlantic and crossed the sandbar at the mouth of the Tagus River as the sun cleared the hills of the Portuguese mainland. Dias and his pilot knew this stretch of the river to Lisbon and did not wait for a river pilot who mainly served the vessels of other kingdoms. It was now the flood tide and home was but two leagues distance.

Lopo had told the slaves that this was not another stop but their destination. This was the land of the Cristowns. Mbekah had learned that these Cristowns were Portuguese and their land was called Portugal. The *Ninho* was going to the main village of the king of the Portuguese, Lisbon. Seated cross legged on the deck, Mbekah stared out over the low gunwales, inspecting everything as it appeared. They were no longer at sea, but the river's banks were so far apart she could see no detail of the shore except for the hills on the north side. There were other boats on the water, none as large as their own. She saw a dark-skinned man, dark like herself, among the men on a smaller boat going to sea. He was not in chains. Men on other small boats fished with nets in the river. None of the boats had the red cross with serifs on their sails like their own.

They sailed on for two hours until the river opened up to become a lake of great size. She could see many houses together on the north shore and flocks of boats bobbing near that shore. Portuguese people moved about and talked to each other. Some paused to watch them cruise past. A few of the people were dark—what Lopo called black. Like the black man on the small boat she had seen earlier, they dressed as the Portuguese and were not chained. No guard watched the black people as they worked or moved about.

"Black people here are free," said Ifé.

"So many people living together cannot be healthy. The odor is like rotting fish mixed with the dry dung of goats," said Mbekah.

Some houses were big like the one next to the village of two nations where the Portuguese men had fetched them. Some houses were tall and had crosses like the amulet Lopo and others wore from their neck. The boat came closer to the shore where there were many houses below a hill on which stood the biggest house. Lopo had called the big house a castle. The castle had high walls and as many towers as the fingers on both hands. The castle surely had room for many warriors and many slaves. The Portuguese men on their boat pulled down the sails and dropped the monstrous iron hook to grab the bottom and hold the boat in one place in the water.

A small craft with long paddles came out to their boat. The peacock feather fellow—Lopo called him <u>capitão</u>—greeted a new man in fine clothes of red and blue when he climbed onto the deck. The two talked for a while with their mouths and their hands. The new man looked at each of the captives and wrote in a book like Lopo's book, only bigger. He looked at each of the Portuguese men and wrote again in his book. Another crew member named Manoel, Lopo's helper on the boat, handed the new man papers which he studied. Mbekah had learned that looking at a book or at papers was reading.

The new man climbed over the side and back into his small boat and was paddled back to shore. The captain gave orders and the Portuguese crew pushed the sticks around and around a rotating post to lift the iron hook. Men on another small craft came from shore and gave the men on their big boat the end of a rope. Men on the shore, many of them black, pulled the other end of the rope and the *Ninho* floated toward the shore until it bumped against a stone-walled river bank. Next to the bank was a large square field covered with smooth stones and surrounded by large structures including one tall house with crosses on twin towers. They had reached Lisbon. The boat's eyes had found the way to the home of the Cristowns.

#

"Your Majesty, caravelas, the *Ninho* and the *São Sebastian* have arrived from *São Jorge da Mina*. Capitão Bartolomeu Dias commanding."

"How long gone?" asked King João.

"Five months and three weeks. The two ships bring more gold than usual and thirty-six slaves. They have prisoners, Lowlanders from a captured Dutch cog. There is other cargo too. At first look, a handsome profit," said Andrao de Faria, the chamberlain.

"Make sure the other ministers and the members of the Cortes hear about the success," said the King.

"In that case, every spy in the capitol will know about it too."

"So be it," said the king. "We need the support of the merchants, clergy, and nobility in the Cortes. This was only a trading voyage, so no deep secrets will be aired."

"And what of our 'project'?" asked the chamberlain.

"Make arrangements to quietly get our dozen slaves, six for palace service and six for the project," said the king. "We don't need any publicity. We'll train the project six with the four that Captain Cao brought back from the Congo River."

"Won't that be a problem? The Congo Guineans are volunteers, children of nobility," said the chamberlain.

"Congo is 500 leagues further south than the *Mina*. I doubt the two groups even speak the same tongue," said the king. "Wait until you're sure that the new Guineans won't bolt or get violent, then put them with the Congolese. It'll be cheaper that way. We're looking for other slaves that have been in Lisbon for a while to join the group later."

"The male Guineans in the project will start their training in the palace. Our tutors will teach them—Portuguese and the Catechism first," said the chamberlain. "The females will live and take their lessons at the Convento *Todos os Santos*. You being Master of the Order of St. James of the Sword made that arrangement rather easy."

The king mused, "So Dona Ana Mendonça will have their charge. Most appropriate."

"In theory, yes, as prioress there," replied the chamberlain. "But Dona Maria Violante da Cunha really runs that place as the mother superior. She's laced up tight in the rules and regulations, the very opposite of Dona Ana."

"Dona Ana can defend herself well enough. I wager she'll get something out of me for this favor," opined the king. "Do the good sisters know what we're up to?"

No one, not even the two donas, at the convent know our purpose so secrecy is not a problem.

#

Captain Dias was the first to leave the ship.

"Senhor Piloto, we meet in three days to settle accounts at the Guinea House. Bring Lopo and Manoel," said the captain.

"At your orders, sir."

"Lopo will tell you which captives are for the king's service. He can also help translate until they are settled in," said the captain.

Captain Dias directed Lopo to speak with him privately on the stone dock beside the ship.

"You did well on this voyage. I am recommending you for further service on the king's ships."

"*Obrigado*, *Capitão*. I desire only to serve the king," said Lopo.

"I myself will need reliable men who know the Guinea coast and its waters. I will have more than a cargo run someday. A voyage of discovery would be long and dangerous, into unknown waters," said Captain Dias.

"Honored to sail with the *capitão*," said Lopo.

"I will advise the *majordomo* that he engage you to spend a few days helping the king's slaves adjust to their new service. Then you will be free to look for another ship. See you at the settling of accounts meeting in three days," said Captain Dias.

"On your orders," said Lopo.

#

Lopo returned to the ship to oversee the slaves. Lopo leaned over to the cargo master. "Manoel, I have heard of the Lisbon slave auction. I'm glad I will not be there when this lot is sold. At least there are no children to be separated from their parents."

"That's why it's no good to know them. To me, they're cargo. More like pigs than ivory though," said the cargo master.

"Handsome pigs to be so lusted after," said Lopo ironically. "I don't even know how I managed to keep the crew away from such pretty sows."

"I'd stay out of dark alleys near the docks, were I you," warned Manoel. "You're not the favorite officer to some of this crew."

Lopo left the cargo master and approached the captives.

"Your ears, please," Lopo shouted to the curious Guineans still chained to the foredeck.

"You will be divided into two bands. Some will come with me." Lopo pointed to the castle on the hills overlooking the city. "You others will be taken to the Guinea House until you are assigned to good families where you will serve in Portugal."

"If you work hard, if you obey your new masters, you will be happy," Lopo said as sincerely as he could to the expectant faces.

No one nodded in agreement or even in understanding. Pedro, the black sailor repeated Lopo's message in the language of the captives. Lopo dropped on one knee to talk to Mbekah, Ifé, and Olubayo.

"You will come to the king's house, the castle, with me. It will be an honor to serve his majesty. The food is good, and the work is not so hard," said Lopo.

"I think so," said Mbekah in her halting Portuguese. "You are not bad like the other men on the boat."

"Obrigado," said Lopo. "I will help you more if I can."

#

Lopo attached himself to the guards that fetched the dozen captives he indicated for the king's service. They walked the sun-warmed paving stones of the Commerce Plaza and up a narrow path between houses to the castle. The shackled Guineans studied each new thing but made certain to keep up to avoid a beating. Portuguese people and even blacks like themselves were hawking food to everyone that came by. Each transaction involved much talking and a flurry of gestures. A black woman carried a large clay pot on her head. She paused to watch the chained group shuffle past. She looked directly into Mbekah's eyes and said something that Mbekah did not understand.

The pot carrier switched to Portuguese. "Don't be sad. You be the king's slaves."

Ifé spoke to Mbekah. "The Portuguese here are so pale. Much lighter than the men on the boat. These people can't be well with such skin."

A man rode by on a large brown beast with four legs. The animal was bigger and much stronger than the man but behaved itself perfectly. They had seen such riders at each place they had stopped while on the boat but not nearly so close up.

"Horse," said Mbekah, remembering her lessons on the boat.

They passed through heavy wooden doors into the palace. The walls were thicker than a man is tall.

"The king is fearful of his own people," said Ifé.

"Where is the grass? Where are the trees?" asked Olubayo, to no one in particular.

A bald man with a beard came and took charge. They followed him into the center of the palace where there was no roof. He looked at each of the captives carefully and finally spoke with Lopo.

Lopo addressed the captives in Portuguese but also with some words the captives had taught him from their language. Mbekah understood Lopo to say, "The king welcomes you to his home. You will sleep without chains tonight. You will be free to go about certain parts of the palace when you have been here longer and have learned your work."

The bald man looked satisfied. The captives whispered among themselves to figure out what Lopo had said.

Lopo led the guards and the line of captives into a large room with sleeping mats. After the door was closed, the guards removed their shackles. It was the first time in almost four moons that they did not have some kind of bonds on two or three places on their bodies. They separated from each other, hesitantly at first and then each made a point of standing apart from the others as far as the size of the room permitted.

Mbekah said to Ifé and Olubayo, "We'll still have to sleep close together for warmth. It's cold in this place and tonight will be colder."

Men and women were each given a loose blouse that came to their knees to replace the rough sack they'd worn on the ship. They ate from shiny brown clay bowls what Lopo told them was couscous seasoned with oil from olives. When the shiny clay spoons failed, they used their tongues to get at the last particles of food. Lopo ate as lustily as did the captives.

Lopo shook the captives' newly freed hands and said, "Until tomorrow."

#

Lopo re-discovered his way home through the maze of streets, plazas, arches, and alleyways. He stopped once to watch a black man wield a twig broom to clean the walkway and street in front of a row of shops. Lopo greeted the sweeper in the language of Mbekah's people.

The man stared at Lopo. "What?" said the man in Portuguese.

Lopo said, "Boas Tardes."

The man nodded.

From a narrow street, Lopo descended stairs in an arched passageway to a parallel street lower on the hill. His father Guaspar's leather shop was still open with candles lit for the last hour of work that day. Guaspar worked in the *Alfama* district for the same well-to-do clientele that Lopo's grandfather had served before him. Pero, Lopo's older brother, would continue the family business in the same rooms when Guaspar was gone.

News had already reached the shop that Lopo's ship arrived that morning. Even so, the moment of the reunion with father, mother, brother, sister-in-law, nephew and nieces was a pleasant surprise. A warm, physical greeting followed. There was animated conversation with nephew and nieces jumping up and down.

"So brown! Is it healthy to be in the sun so much?" asked his mother. "Your ear! Did someone bite out a piece?"

"How long will you be with us this time?" asked his father.

"The voyage was a success?" asked Pero.

"I shall be here two months or more," said Lopo. "There will be time for all your questions."

All but his father and Pero climbed the stairs to the rooms above the shop. The children wanted to hear about monkeys, lions, and the black Guineans. And about his ear.

"Can I see your knife?" asked his nephew.

Lopo rolled on the floor with the children and let them ride him as he crawled about on hands and knees. Their favorite uncle was home.

"You came with slaves this trip," his mother said.

"We brought three dozen. They are to be sold next week after sufficient time to announce the sale," said Lopo.

"We don't have enough slaves in Lisbon already? Moors and Guineans are everywhere," said his mother.

Soberly, Lopo said, "I played God today. I sent two dozen youths to be sold at the auction. It was my choice who went. People that I like will be sold like kegs of olive oil."

"We will go to the church tonight to thank the Virgin for your return," said his mother.

"Yes, dear Mother. To the church later. How are Father's eyes? Why does he work late when the light is poor?" asked Lopo.

"Guaspar's and Pero's workmanship is among the best. Even so, long hours are required to compete with the leather men who have slaves," said his sister-in-law.

"We will invite all the family on Sunday. A feast," said his mother. "I want everyone to see what a fine man you have become. Maybe someone will know the right girl for you."

Lopo blushed and tickled his nephew till giggles turned to screams.

#

That evening, Captain Dias dined with his wife for the first time in almost six months.

"All the city talks of your profitable voyage," said Dona Branca.

"It's no lie, that. To recover Portugal's expenses, to pay for future exploration, we must make many such voyages," said the captain.

"His majesty must be pleased."

"I pray it so. I must be at the palace for a few months at least to hear what is going on and to position myself for a new command," said the captain.

"Capitão Diogo Cao returned from his voyage three score and more days ago. His report to the king and council was in secret but the whispers on the street assure all it was a success," said Dona Branca.

"I will call upon Diogo and pay my respects. A good man to know these days."

A black servant came into the room and poured more red wine into their goblets and disappeared.

"You look as young and ravishing as ever, o meu Coração," said the captain as he toasted his wife.

"I'm relieved to hear. I was wondering after an absence of so many months. We do hear the most lurid stories about sailors and their captives."

"You know by now that your Bartolomeu is as faithful to you as he is to the king and the Holy Father in Rome," said the Captain.

#

Lopo followed his mother and sister-in-law through the massive oak doors of the nearby Cathedral of Santa Maria trailed by nephew and nieces. Guaspar and Pero had remained home after the evening meal to prepare for another day in the leather shop. In his turn, Lopo genuflected then walked the length of the nave to the rail before the altar and knelt alongside his mother who was already mumbling the rosary. Scores of candles flickered but their light barely illuminated the distant walls and did not reach into the copious nooks and niches of the hall. He was awed by the enormity of the enclosed space after months at sea and in far-flung Portuguese trading stations. He half-heartedly said the Pater Noster, an Ave Maria, then thanked the Virgin for his safe return. He promised to make a generous contribution when he received his pay after the settling of accounts.

The children were restless, so his sister-in-law herded them out into the night air. His mother, eyes closed, fingered her beads and prayed on. Lopo pondered the events of his recent voyage. Captain Dias was evidently happy with his service so he, Lopo, would have other opportunities to sail the Guinea coasts. That would mean more money, respect, promotion . . . with a jolt he pictured Mbekah, Ifé, Olubayo, Kpodo, Gyasi and the other captives chained together on the deck of the *Ninho*. Future voyages down the coast of Africa would also mean more captives, more human beings turned into trade goods, then into revenue for the king and into labor for Portuguese farmers, Lisbon merchants, or into servants for the rich. *Can I let myself be mixed up with all that again? Can I ever forget that I have already helped bring almost two score Guineans to involuntary servitude—God's children violently taken from their homes and loved ones? Worse, I have sent some to be sold at auction. I did not choose Kpodo's wife to be in the king's service. She is starting to show the baby she must be carrying. Capitão Dias had made it clear he did not want her sent to the palace in that condition given the special orders about keeping the crew away from this group of captives.*

Anyway, I was supposed to pick captives I thought would be useful and pleasing to the palace. She is beautiful, but she is weepy and didn't show the curiosity and energy I saw in Mbekah and others. I have likely condemned Kpodo to never see his wife again. What will become of the baby? Lopo added one more vow to his prayers. *I will buy Kpodo's wife at the auction and free her. Is that even done? How much will it take? Where will I get the money?*

CHAPTER 20

First Days in Lisbon

Lopo hustled through the *Alfama* district on his way to Guinea House off the main plaza. Mid-morning sunlight reached down into the labyrinth of narrow streets and stair-stepped alleyways revealing, through open doors and un-shuttered windows, artisans at their benches and shopkeepers organizing their wares. Street hawkers were staking out their spots against sections of wall for the day's business. Powerful scents beckoned him as he passed a spice merchant. No doubt the proprietor would be selling product from Lopo's recent voyage within the fortnight. Deep voices raised a psalm as he strode near the cloisters attached to the cathedral; the monks were only midway through Terce. There was still time for Lopo to make the settling-of-accounts meeting if he kept up his pace and stopped not at all. Even in his haste, Lopo rehearsed the events of the day before.

It had fallen upon him again to divide the captives at the castle into two groups—six for some special project and six to begin learning the skills needed for their new vocations. He accompanied the latter six to the Church of the Madalena where they were sprinkled and given Christian names. Then they were off to their places of labor for Lopo to make introductions. Kpodo, christened as Bastiao, ended up in the royal bakery on the plaza adjacent to Guinea House. Along with bread for the palace, the bakery ovens were used to produce ships biscuit. Lopo had eaten more of this twice-baked, stone-hard biscuit than he cared to think about. He mused if they seeded them with weevil eggs before packing them into the barrels. The crown's monopoly on this essential provision for long sea voyages was a solid source of income. Lopo promised to return from time to time to see how it went with Bastiao. It was a worm destroying his peace of mind that he was involved in separating Kpodo, rather Bastiao, from his beautiful, pregnant wife. Gyasi, now called Amrrique, went into service in the castle kitchen. He would be lifting and moving sacks and barrels until they trusted him enough to let him use a knife to cut and chop.

The majordomo, a bald man with a beard, had explained that few Guineans in the city spoke the same tongue as the newly arrived slaves. "They don't know the city or how to get food. If we split them up, escape is not a problem. Few run, none get away."

Lopo pondered what the project for the other six could be. The majordomo told him to pick the brightest, preferably women over men, other things being equal. There was no doubt for Lopo that Mbekah was the shining star of this group: she and also her friends Ifé and Olubayo made the cut. The majordomo assured Lopo that these slaves would be treated well but couldn't guess why or what the project was when Lopo inquired. *Was this why the women captives had been off limits to the crew?*

When Lopo returned to report to the majordomo, he explained to Lopo that a detachment of guards had come and led the six remaining captives away. "Don't ask me, I have no idea where they were taken," said the majordomo.

Lopo looked away. He might never see Mbekah again.

He came to the plaza and quickly wove his way around and through the bustle and goods piled here and there on the cobble stones, past the palace bakery and on to the main entrance of

Guinea House. At the door to the chief factor's office he greeted Manoel and nodded to Pilot Gonçalves. He learned that Captain Dias would be along later. Rather than stand around in awkward silence with the pilot, he requested that someone show him the captives brought there a few days earlier. When he and Manoel approached the cages, all the Guineans' eyes fixed on the two of them. Lopo thought he saw relief and even hope in their faces when they saw him, someone familiar. These unfortunates now wore a rough smock to cover their nakedness. He stepped close to one of the enclosures and Kpodo's wife came to her feet. He could see that her belly bulged slightly. Her eyes were red, and she sniffled quietly.

"Things will get better, I promise you," said Lopo with all the cheeriness he could summon.

A messenger arrived to bid them return to the chief factor's office. "The capitão has arrived", he said.

#

Captain Dias and the chief factor each produced a key with which an assistant unlocked the sturdy chest containing several leather pouches filled with assorted little lumps of gold. The assistant meticulously weighed the precious metal against lead cylinders on the opposite balance-beam tray. He reported to the chief factor who pronounced the total equal to that stated in the sealed documents carried there from the fort at the *Mina*. Lopo sighed in relief. He was sure the others did the same.

Looking down, as if reading, the chief factor said rather slowly, "I'm happy to certify that all cargo has been inventoried and accounted for. A profitable voyage for his majesty and the Order of Christ." Speaking directly to the captain, he continued. "Please tell me, were any of the acquired females assaulted or abused in any way during the time they were in your possession? Consider carefully before giving your answer."

Captain Dias cleared his throat. "By the Virgin and all the saints, I testify they were not."

The chief factor frowned. "How do you explain the girl who is with child?"

Captain Dias looked the chief factor in the eye. "From her condition, it's evident that she was impregnated before my crew took possession. Her group had been at the *Mina* for only a few days before we arrived so I'm confident that she was inseminated previous to her time there."

The chief factor considered this, then studied the other officers in the room. "Do you also swear this to be true."

The three officers each affirmed in their turn.

"Fine. You will sign your names to this effect at the bottom of his majesty's special instructions."

Again, Lopo was relieved and knew he was not the only one.

They discussed the details of their remuneration and received vouchers to collect it. The chief factor made a few comments to the captain, making it clear that he had read the detailed report of the mission that the captain must've made since returning.

Taking this as a cue to speak, the captain volunteered, "Yes, I've spent most of the past two days in interviews with cartographers, shipwrights, navigators, provisioners, the captain general of the army, the admiral of the ocean-sea, linguists, the treasurer, and leaders from both the Order of Christ and the Order of St. James of the Sword. Reporting is tedious and almost as arduous as the voyage. Chamberlain de Faria sat in on all of the interrogations."

The chief factor stood up, indicating that the meeting was over. As he walked his guests to the outer door of the warehouse, Captain Dias wondered out loud why the special instructions about the women.

"I've asked myself the same question," said the chief factor. "I have no answer for you."

Out in daylight again, the four officers stood in a small circle. "Chamberlain de Faria was pleased with my report," confided Captain Dias. "When he receives the chief factor's accounting, I'm certain I will be recommended for future missions. I will look for you three when my next opportunity comes."

All three thanked the captain.

"What of the captives," asked Gonçalves, "the one they call Bekah?

"Mbekah and several others were assigned some kind of special duty," replied Lopo. "I haven't been able to learn what that is or where they are."

Gonçalves thought for a moment. "And the beautiful one that the chief factor asked about, the one with child?"

"She's in Guinea House in the pens. She is to be sold at the auction, whenever that is," said Lopo. He did not like the question. *Does the pilot have plans for Kpodo's wife?*

#

Bong bong bong sounded the bell high in a tower overhead. Mbekah, Ifé, Olubayo, and four other African girls awoke in a dark room to dress for morning prayers: Matins they called it. They filed silently into a large hall and sat on wooden benches. At the front, there was a detailed carving of men and women in distress viewing three men seemingly being punished—they were mounted on crosses and obviously dead or in terrible pain. None of the Portuguese women seemed too upset about this display. The negro girls knelt when the Portuguese women knelt, but could not make out what to say when the Portuguese spoke in unison. The Africans kept an eye open to know when to sit and when to stand. They filed out again for a slice of doughy bread smeared with lard and cold water in a clay cup.

Mbekah knew the routine by now. Prayers in the morning followed by bread and water. Chores around the convent followed by individual prayers. Language lessons followed by group prayers followed by a hot meal. Lessons about the Portuguese god, holy men and women, and about things in the great hall which they called chapel. Chanting to memorize prayers. A ceremony they called mass in the chapel followed by a cold meal. Washing from a bucket and then sleep.

They had been given new names; Christian names they were told. Mbekah became Josefa, Ifé became Inês, Olubayo became Maria. The other girls, who Mbekah learned were from the household of a king in a place called Congo, were newly named Isabell, Catelina, Sancha, and Lionor. They stumbled over the strange sounds of their new names but were required to use them whenever in the presence of others. They were told their new names would be used when they were baptized, whatever that meant.

The three forest-village girls could not understand the Congolese girls when they used their native tongue. They communicated with the Congolese using hand gestures and the few Portuguese words they knew and were learning every day.

This walled-village within the town of Lisbon was called a convent by the Portuguese. In addition to the women dressed head to foot in plain dark clothing, there were some Portuguese girls residing within the convent walls. These girls dressed in white dresses with blue collars just like the African girls and did the same chores. Mbekah—she still did not think of herself as Josefa—learned that these girls wanted to become nuns like the older women in dark dress. There were other girls of all ages—some who lived in a big room and others who came into the convent in the morning and left in the late afternoon. Those girls attended some kind of instruction and did no chores. Their fathers must be rich, thought Mbekah.

When they were together at chores or in their room, Mbekah, Ifé and Olubayo talked among themselves in their own language.

“Do these Portuguese women have men?” asked Ifé/Inês.

“I don’t think so. I think this is their home all the time. No husbands, no children,” concluded Mbekah/Josefa.

“A village of women with no husbands and no children!” exclaimed Olubayo/Maria.

“I want to have children,” said Inês.

Maria shook her head. “Slaves don’t have children.”

Josefa reminded them, “The bald man with the beard said we will go back to the castle after the lessons. Maybe you will have children with a Portuguese man.”

“Yihay,” said Inês, horrified.

They all giggled.

CHAPTER 21

Borrowing Money

Rodrigo set down his empty tumbler, his first Porto wine of the afternoon. "It's nice to be back in Lisbon even if it's a little dull living with my brother and his family. I'm already thinking about finding another ship. Not a long voyage this time around. England or Flanders, maybe."

The *Carapau* Cantina stood near the docks and was cheap, attracting low-level officers and able seamen. The crowded room smelled like a ship with fresh ocean air off the bay mingled with the aromas of spilt wine, fish guts, and simmering seafood. Lopo leaned forward. "A run north to the Portuguese factory in Bruges is not a bad sailing. I've been twice."

"London town is nice," interjected Manoel. After a pause he too leaned in to speak. "There is scandal about the House of Bragança. Plotting with the Castilians against the king. The duke arrested. His lot running for the border. More arrests to come."

Lopo raised his drink. "I toast King João. My father says his majesty is fighting the excesses of the aristocracy and that it's about time." From the fragments of conversations he could hear from nearby tables, the treasonous Braganças were the main topic at other tables too.

A serving girl dropped a slab of bread and set bowls of fish stew in front of the three and hurried off. Rodrigo admired her backside then ripped off a chunk of the bread. "I thought I'd never ask for another fish dish after our last voyage but here we are eating it of our own free will."

There was little discussion while they sipped the hot stew and mopped up the last drops out of their bowls with their bread. The girl returned, poured them more wine, and moved to another table. Lopo looked around to assure no one was paying any attention to them. He lowered his voice. "I need some information. What will it take to buy one of the Guineans at the slave auction next week?" Lopo noted the surprised look on both of his companions' faces. *This is a strange question for me to ask but I have vowed a vow.*

Rodrigo was the first to speak. "My uncle paid 6,500 reais for two males last year. I hear females are not so expensive. Are you thinking about buying Bekah?"

Lopo set down his tumbler. "Mbekah is not for sale. She has gone into his majesty's service. Doing what, I haven't learned. I will buy the one they call the wife of Kpodo—the most beautiful of the ones we brought from the *Mina*."

"The one with child?" Manoel's disbelief was evident.

Lopo nodded. Again, there was silence as Rodrigo and Manoel seemed to ponder Lopo's plan. "I will have to borrow the reais. This, I have never done. How does one go about it?"

"Jews. That's what I've always heard," suggested Rodrigo.

"Not so much these days," said Manoel. "Lombards are the ones who lend money here in the city now. They are all on the same street in the *Alfama*. But this is loco. What will you do with a slave?"

#

Lopo wandered down the street of goldsmiths and pawn shops checking out each one as casually as he could contrive. He had the name of a money lender from Lombardy, one who had been in Lisbon for decades. Manoel seemed to know about these things. A few days after their meal at the *Carapau*, Manoel had come to Lopo's father's shop to find him and tell him the name. Lopo strolled past several houses displaying three golden balls hanging from a curved iron bar. He found the one with Xemenez *Irmãos* painted above the door. He continued on the street for a few minutes then turned around, marched back, and entered. "May I speak with Senhor Xemenez?"

A stout man armed with both a sword and a dagger left the room and returned, followed by a slight, pale man older in appearance than Lopo's father.

"I am Lopo David Meendez, pilot's mate and son of Guaspar Meendez, the leather craftsman and merchant."

The old man nodded slightly.

"You are Senhor Filipe Xemenez? I've come to borrow money."

Xemenez beckoned Lopo to follow him. Xemenez seated himself behind an eggplant-colored oaken table loaded with leather-bound books. Lopo saw no other chair so was forced to stand to make his plea. The banker listened, then asked. "Why do you need so much?"

"It's . . . I'm . . . I can't say. It's important. It's personal." *This is not going well.*

The banker checked his fingernails and combed back his thinning hair with one hand. "An affair of the heart, no doubt. What have you to pledge against this loan?"

Lopo stared at him.

"A pledge to secure the loan. A thing of value. You give us something of value and we lend you the money if Xemenez *Irmãos* thinks your item is worth more than the loan amount. When you pay us back along with the interest, we'll return your pledged item." After a moment of silence, Xemenez continued. "I see, you have nothing of so great a value. Is that it?"

"No. Nothing worth enough to cover the amount I need."

The two regarded each other in silence.

Lopo spoke again. "I see I'm wasting your time." He turned to leave.

The old banker spoke to Lopo's back. "I know of your father and his business. Does he know you are here, asking for such a sum?"

Lopo turned to face Xemenez. "No. It's private, as I said. I earn a good wage and could pay you back over the next three years."

Xemenez considered this. "With your old established family here in the *Alfama*, I believe you won't disappear on me. Still, an unsecured loan is not the business of Xemenez *Irmãos*. If you're really serious, there is a man who deals in loans like this. They're expensive. You don't pay him back, he doesn't take you before a magistrate, if you know what I mean?"

Lopo did not know.

"He will hurt you. He may sell you. You won't want to get on his bad side, believe me."

The banker's words were settling into Lopo's brain. He had not counted the cost before making the promise to the Virgin. *I made an oath. I owe it to Kpodo and his poor wife. And their baby.* Lopo swallowed hard. "When can I meet this man?"

CHAPTER 22

The Sale

The long shadows of the June morning were receding as Lopo wandered into the open plaza. He wasn't sure how the slave auction would work so he had arrived early to observe the preparations in front of Guinea House from the anonymity of the throng of merchants and laborers in the plaza. He saw the assistant factor supervising the placement of his working table to the side of a low platform on which the auctioneer and captive for sale likely would stand. Lopo inched forward to the outer edge of the area where a few buyers had already congregated before the platform. He heard Castilian, Catalan, French, and Flemish along with his native Portuguese. He wondered why the banker Senhor Xemenez was there moving from group to small group. Lopo hadn't told anyone except his two shipmates how he planned to use the three thousand reais he had borrowed from the contact the banker had given him. *My meeting with Galo, the lender, was ominous.* The slim foreigner hadn't strutted around the room as his nickname 'Galo' suggested, but had quietly, confidently studied Lopo. Lopo signed no document but was required to repeat the terms and conditions of the loan and swear by the Virgin and all the saints to secrecy. *What had he done? What else could he have done to keep his vow?* A dark feeling came over him each time he thought about Galo and the implication of harm to his person or worse if he didn't repay the loan.

A grand oaken door swung open spewing forth a troop of armed men followed by two dozen captives in lock step, dragging their ankle chains. The captives lined up, backs to the wall, squinting in the bright sunlight, oiled skin reflecting the same. Buyers came near to study each man and woman to be sold. The assistant factor's man, a black Guinean, darted about to help with the inspections, forcing open a mouth here, lifting a shift there. In a few cases, captives were released from their chains for a moment and made to walk or trot for the buyers to see. There seemed to be much discussion around Kpodo's wife each time her full belly was viewed. Lopo considered. *Is this good . . . or bad?*

The assistant factor announced that all buyers must register before the auction and a crowd formed in front of his table. Lopo saw that Gonçalves was at the table. *Where did he come from? This is not good!*

When the crowd in front of the assistant factor had thinned and Gonçalves had completed his business there and left, Lopo approached to add his name to the list. The assistant factor, who had met Lopo the week before, seemed surprised. He requested to see the reais Lopo carried in a leather purse before he would certify Lopo as a qualified bidder. Lopo carried the borrowed money plus a thousand reais of his own savings. Lopo stepped to the back of the buyers' semicircle and caught the hard stare of Gonçalves. *Are the two of us interested in the same slave?*

At last, the auctioneer mounted the platform and signaled the first captive be brought to his side. "The minimum bid for this well-muscled man is two thousand reais. Who will bid two thousand reais?"

A Frenchman raised his hand and stepped to the front of the buyers.

"The king should get more than two thousand for this fine male," proclaimed the auctioneer. "Who will pay twenty-five hundred?"

A Castilian indicated he would and moved to the front and next to the Frenchman.

The Frenchman did not budge. "Three thousand," he responded.

A new buyer, a churchman by his habit, moved beside the two bidders and barked, "three thousand, one hundred reais."

Lopo tensed. *Did I bring enough reais?*

The three upped the bid by turns—a hundred reais each turn—until the Frenchman, then the churchman dropped back, leaving the Castilian with the winning offer of four thousand reais. Lopo breathed out. *My four thousand reais should be enough for a pregnant woman.*

Kpodo's wife, the tenth captive to be sold, was pushed up onto the platform. She was beautiful even though she bulged in the middle and whimpered. *Does Kpodo know what is going on out here? His wife for sale? He works just a few paces away in the royal bakery.* The thought stiffened Lopo's resolve. He strode to the front of the pack and announced, "Two thousand reais."

A fellow Lisbon citizen moved to Lopo's side and said, "I bid three thousand."

"Thirty-five hundred", said a voice from the crowd.

Lopo turned to see Gonçalves emerge.

The Lisboan slinked back leaving Lopo and Gonçalves at the front of the semicircle of buyers. They stood in a triangle with the platform as the third side. Lopo scrutinized Gonçalves. *How badly do you want this woman?* Lopo saw only evil in the pilot's face. He glanced at Kpodo's wife whose sad eyes fixed on him, pleading it seemed. *She understands what is happening.*

The auctioneer cleared his throat bringing Lopo back to the action at hand.

"Three thousand, six hundred." Lopo wondered whether his bid showed the weakness of his purse or his shrewdness as a buyer.

Immediately, Gonçalves countered, "thirty-seven hundred". He smirked as he studied Lopo's reaction.

"I bid four thousand", said Lopo. There was a unified gasp from the crowd. It was more money paid for any female so far. A drop of perspiration slid down Lopo's forehead.

"Forty-one hundred reais." Again, Gonçalves stared into Lopo's face.

Lopo knew immediately that Gonçalves saw that he was deflated. *I fail. Had I another hundred reais or another thousand, Gonçalves could still outbid me.* He could not look at Kpodo's wife.

Everyone, including the auctioneer eyed Lopo who bowed his head and shuffled back into the onlookers where he bumped into Senhor Xemenez.

"Anyone at four thousand, two hundred?" cried the auctioneer. Silence. "Sold for four thousand, one hundred reais, then."

#

Manoel shuffled through the open door of the *Cais Taberna* sandwiched between Belchior and Nunno. The two maneuvered him to the back corner where Pilot Gonçalves sat alone imbibing fortified Port.

Manoel seated himself at the table. Belchior and Nunno remained standing behind him.

Gonçalves gestured to the black proprietress to bring another tumbler. He poured out for Manoel who looked nervously about the dark room. "I'm charmed to see you, Manoel. How have you been?"

Manoel sipped, choked, and glanced briefly into Gonçalves' eyes before looking away. "Fine."

Gonçalves kept his eyes on Manoel's eyes. "What keeps you busy these days?"

"Not much. Visiting family, friends . . ."

"The boys tell me you've been drinking with Lopo and Rodrigo." The pilot waited out Manoel while he squirmed on his stool.

"I took a meal with them, sim."

"And I hear you've been to see Lopo at his father's leather shop." Gonçalves enjoyed the look of astonishment on Manoel's face. "One wonders what was so important for you to 'drop by' and chat for just a few minutes."

Manoel couldn't seem to find the words to respond so gazed into his reddish-brown drink. After a moment he stole a look at his interrogator.

"Manoel, we've always been able to talk in the past. Why not tell us what you needed to see Lopo about that required a special trip?"

"Just things. You know."

"No, Manoel, I don't know . . . or maybe I do know. Lopo attempted to buy a slave at the auction this morning. What can you tell us about that?"

Manoel looked startled. "Attempted?"

"Just as I suspected. You know all about this. Where did Lopo get the money for this purchase? Does he have that much saved away or did he get it from his family?"

Manoel shrugged.

Belchior grabbed Manoel's right wrist twisting it and his arm behind Manoel's back. Manoel grunted with pain but said nothing.

Gonçalves counted on Belchior's girth to hide the violence imposed upon Manoel from others in the taberna. "Whose money did Lopo have this morning, Manoel?"

Belchior pulled Manoel's arm higher up his back.

Manoel grimaced. "*Basta*. I'll tell you. Please let go of my arm."

Gonçalves nodded. Belchior relaxed his hold.

"He borrowed it from a man they call the Galo. Three thousand *reais*. The rest Lopo had already."

"I've heard of this *tipo*." Gonçalves mused. "Not someone you'd like to marry your sister." He took a long draught of his wine. "Why would Lopo want to go to so much trouble to buy a pregnant slave?"

Manoel started to shake his head causing Belchior to force his arm higher. Manoel gasped. "He feels guilty. He planned to set her free."

Chapter 23

Queen of the Convent

Mbekah washed down the last bite of her morning bread with water dipped from the barrel in the courtyard of the convent. While Ifé and Olubayo chatted, she counted the Sundays since they had arrived at the convent and figured they'd been there for about a moon or what the Portuguese called a month. Sunday, the Lord's Day, was different from the other days of the week. Priests and people from outside the walls came to mass in the large chapel followed by much visiting in the plaza in front of the complex. During this time, she had seen young men flirting with some of the resident girls when the head nun or her helper were not looking. The head nun, Mother Superior they called her, frowned at everything and everyone in the convent though Mbekah had seen her smile a few times when dealing with the priests or outsiders on Sundays. Mother Superior's helper was Sister Maria Giomar—*lots of Marias in this place*—and she frowned a lot too. Mbekah decided that the resident girls, unlike the novices, must be preparing for marriage someday so they talked to boys whenever they could. *Is that not a good thing?*

Mbekah was getting used to hearing Portuguese—understanding more and more words and phrases—and even had begun to think of herself as Josefa. Ifé and Olubayo were becoming

Inês and Maria to her as well. Inês elbowed her, bringing Josefa's wandering mind back to the courtyard and the sight of Sister Giomar striding toward them. They grabbed their clay pitchers and headed out to the well in the plaza; their first chore each day was to refill the drinking barrels in the courtyard, kitchen, and offices. Half dozen trips to the well were needed to accomplish this duty—pitchers balanced on their heads like when they had lived in the forest. *Why don't the Portuguese carry heavy loads on their heads?* They often met other black girls and women at the well but had to speak with them in Portuguese so it was hard to learn much about them. Josefa understood that some of these women were slaves in Portuguese houses and that others were slaves sent out to carry water for whoever would hire them and bring their earnings back to their masters each night. *How strange that the Portuguese cannot fetch their own water. When do the women of the households learn the news of the day? From their slaves?*

The four Congo girls did not do chores and spent this time with the novices and the other girls in the instruction rooms. *Are they learning the church language we hear during singing and prayers? It's not the same as the language that the Portuguese speak. Does their god not speak Portuguese?*

Drinking water replenished, the three now climbed the stairs to the second floor to begin the worst job—retrieving and emptying the piss and excrement jars filled each night by the nuns. These jars they carried out to a cart that awaited them in the plaza at the same time each morning. Samuel, a cheerful black man, stood by the cart, holding the horse still. As usual, the old fellow had the latest gossip. Today the city was animated about the death in Evora of a man of high rank, a duke from the family of Bragança. People were saying that the king was right to have this man killed because he was trying to overthrow the king. People liked the king, it seemed.

When they reentered the convent for another load of night jars, Mbekah saw Sister Giomar arguing with another nun. Sister

Giomar motioned them over. "Josefa, you will go with Sister Consola here. She has work for you. Inês and Maria will finish emptying the jars."

Sister Consola smiled. "A pleasure to meet you, Josefa. Please follow me."

Josefa shadowed the nun across the courtyard and through a door at the far end, a door she had never seen open before. Inside, there were three more doors. Sister Consola used a small metal tool, that Josefa had learned was a key, to allow them to enter the farthest door on the left. She stepped into a room with two chairs and a sofa not like Josefa had ever seen but familiar just the same. These pieces were covered in animal skins from her homeland—zebra, bongo, and imbabala for which she had not yet learned the Portuguese name.

Sister Consola paused when she noticed Josefa's interest. "This is the antechamber. Visitors wait here to see the prioress."

"Prioress?" The word was new to Josefa.

"She is the queen of this convent. The head woman as you say, at least that's what our normal servant woman calls her."

Josefa scrunched her nose. "Is not Sister Violante, the big mother, the head woman?"

Sister Consola giggled. "Mother Superior Sister Maria Violante da Cunha runs the quotidian activities under the authority of the prioress."

"Quotidian?" Josefa was hearing new words by the minute.

"Ordinary. Day to day." I see that you have not met the prioress. Prioress Ana de Mendonça is a grand lady. She's not 'at home' right now. She sometimes overnights at her family's home, a palace really, and she has much to do outside the convent. She visits wealthy people to ask for money to keep the convent open. You will like her. I love her. She rescued me from Sister Violante and her mean little helper Giomar.

"Rescued?" Josefa found that Sister Consola spoke too fast and used many new words. Still she liked being around this cheery woman.

"Rescue means, uh, hmmm, when you save someone like when you choke on your food and someone beats you on the back until the food is cleared away. Do you understand?"

"I think so, yes." Josefa did not understand but she didn't want Sister Consola to think she was slow. "What chore for me?"

Sister Consola looked confused then laughed. "Not here. In the parlor. Follow me."

I won't ask what 'parlor' means. I'll find out later. Josefa moved on Sister Consola's heels as she pushed through a wall of blue and white beaded cords that formed an entryway into another room. "Parlor!?" Josefa blurted out. It was a question. It was an exclamation. *This is indeed a room for a queen.*

It seemed to Josefa that Sister Consola enjoyed watching her gaze about the space. It was as big as the matins chapel but without the high ceiling, but high enough. Light flooded in from the six tall windows on one side. A great fire and its chimney anchored the far end with a massive table pushed against the wall without windows. A smaller piece of furniture, also against the wall, was the base for books. Josefa had never seen more than one book at a time. Here stood seven books of various sizes! From the white walls hung depictions of various scenes—a woman holding a baby, a stern-looking man in a purple robe, a man in one of those metal turtle outfits on a horse and wielding a long, heavy knife. A long carpet hung prominently on the wall in the center. It had a great tree woven into the green and blue background. Words, Josefa thought they were people's names, were written in thick thread on most of the branches. In one corner stood an item covered top to bottom in a light cloth. It was as tall as a man, as long as a man, and as deep as his extended arm. *A piece of furniture? A cabinet?* The dark wooden floors were adorned with more carpets and several animal skins including one from a very large lion.

Josefa tiptoed around the flattened beast. "You have lions near Lisbon?"

Sister Consola smiled. "You are comical. This lion skin came from Guinea, a gift from his majesty the king. And not the only gift. Prioress Ana's son is the most special gift, if you know my meaning."

Josefa did not know her meaning and it apparently showed on her face.

Sister Consola continued. "Sister Ana was not always a nun . . . she is very beautiful. . .uh, hmm . . . she and the king, you know, were very close . . . a few years ago."

Josefa stared at Sister Consola. "The prioress was the king's wife?"

Sister Consola blushed. "No. Her Majesty Queen Leonor was . . .is his wife. I shouldn't be talking about this. But everybody knows. The mother superior would give me lashes for saying such things. More the better to not be under her foot anymore."

"And this child? Does it live here too?

"No. One of the king's aunts cares for the child, I think.

This was better than instruction time for Josefa but she remembered she was here to do some work. "What chore, please?"

Before Sister Consola could answer, a dark, hairy, waist-high creature scampered into the room, made a straight line toward Josefa, and halted at her feet. It sniffed the air, scratched itself, turned its head sideways, screeched, jumped up and down, screeched again, clapped, and held out a hand to Josefa. Josefa could hardly credit what see saw. It was a tailless almost-a-person ground walker that she knew so well from the forests near her village. A young one.

"What . . . where . . .?" Josefa was too surprised and too pleased to utter more.

"Meet *Guincho*, Prioress Ana's monkey. A gift from another admirer. Give her your hand, she'll give you a tour."

Josefa did and they started off toward the fireplace but she froze when she heard a high-pitched, unembodied shrieking. "Geeenshouu". *Guincho* kept Josefa's hand while he noisily hopped in place and yimped for a moment then tugged her toward the large covered item in the corner. "Geenshoouu" came the eerie scream again.

Half way across the parlor, *Guincho* broke loose and loped on all fours toward the veiled cabinet. She yanked the covering which fell to the floor revealing a sumptuous cage made of bamboo. A gray bird with scarlet tail feathers paced the floor of the enclosure. *Guincho* screeched and danced about in front of the cage while the bird that Josefa knew as a king bird whistled and bobbed.

"Now meet *Bate-boQuinha*, Prioress Ana's African talking bird. We call him *Quinha*, the cleverest parrot in Portugal and the Algarve. Yes, from another admirer of the prioress."

#

Guincho and *Quinha* followed Josefa as she moved about the suite making beds, hanging clothes, mopping and so forth. She had trouble exiting the chambers—because her forest friends wanted to tag along—to return dishes to the convent kitchen and fetch fresh water for the red clay jug that the prioress and Sister Consola used for drinking. For the first time since her capture, she sang other than a song to the spirit of some important feature of the landscape. Sister Consola sat at a small table and wrote in a book.

Josefa crept to where Sister Consola worked. "I'm not certain the poop-cart man is still out in the plaza but I will take your jars and see."

"Oh, thank you so much. I was afraid I'd have to do it myself with our regular woman sick today. You can use the back door, so you don't have to go through the convent courtyard."

Josefa collected the two jars and carefully advanced to the door when she heard a key in the lock and stopped short so she wouldn't get knocked over, jars and all, when the door opened. She heard tapping then a voice. "The prioress will enter now." A pause and then the door swung open. A hefty, armed man peered in, stepped in, then turned and waited for a tall, richly dressed woman to enter. Not a nun from her clothes.

Sister Consola scurried to meet the woman. She arrived and bowed her head slightly. "Reverent Mother, I hope your mission was successful and pleasant."

"Yes. Yes. Of course. I see you found someone to straighten up the place. Well done."

"This is Josefa, one of the new Guineans that arrived last month. Sister Giomar lent her to us." Sister Consola spoke now to Josefa. "Josefa, please meet Sister Ana de Mendonça, Prioress of the *Todos os Santos* Convent and Commandress of the Order of St. James."

Josefa curtsied as she'd seen some of the resident girls do when meeting someone new. "Mother."

"One of the new Guineans?" The prioress looked directly into Josefa's eyes. "You must be here on the king's orders, one of the king's special project girls. You should not be cleaning rooms and emptying night jars. You are a guest of the king and supposed to be learning to read and write, the catechism, and how to live in the king's court."

The prioress turned to her assistant. "Sister Consola, please summon Sister Violante. I'll change into my habit and be ready to remind the Mother Superior of the king's orders with regard to our guests from the *Mina*.

CHAPTER 24

A Wife for Lopo

Lopo woke with a purpose. He hadn't slept well worrying about the loan, the interest, the lender, Kpodo's wife . . . But he had received some good tidings. He had heard from Rodrigo that a crew member from the *Ninho* had recently seen Mbekah and others of the captives from the *Mina* at mass in the chapel of the *Todos os Santos* Convent. It was Sunday and he determined he would go and see for himself.

Lopo already sat eating golden slices—yesterday's bread dipped in egg and fried in olive oil then drenched in honey—when his mother called the rest of the family to break the fast. He yawned. "Mãe, I will attend mass with friends today. I must leave shortly."

"Lopinho, home a few weeks and already we don't see you except for a moment now and then. What takes you all over town on a Sunday, anyway? Sunday is for family, no?"

"Don't worry, I will be home for lunch. I would never miss Sunday afternoon with you."

"Good, but you avoid my question. What church will you visit today?"

Lopo did not want to suffer another interrogation about his romantic life, or the lack of one, and so early in the day. He feared his family learning about his loan and the reason for it. He bounded down the stairs calling over his shoulder, "*Todos os Santos.*"

#

From their spot standing with their backs against the wall midway in the long chapel, Lopo and Rodrigo studied each person who entered to stand at the rear of the ever-growing assemblage. They saw unaccompanied girls in their late teens and early twenties who Lopo guessed were students in residence at the convent. He saw young men who he suspected were there to admire the resident student girls and maybe steal a conversation if they could break loose for a moment after the service. He saw families that were most likely here to see their daughters and other families that probably came from the homes near the church. But he did not see Mbekah or any others of the captives they had transported to Lisbon from the slave castle at the *Mina*.

The service commenced. He had seen nuns but no novices. Lopo started to think he would not see Mbekah when a heavenly chorus of young female voices intoned, "Lord, have mercy . . ." Lopo immediately turned his eyes to the choir loft above and behind the congregation. In back of the chorus of novices but not singing stood seven black girls including Mbekah, Ifé, and Olubayo—all dressed like the novices in blue and white.

#

In the plaza after mass, Lopo, followed by Rodrigo, pushed through the chattering groups until he found a small knot of novices, one of whom he singled out. "I beg your pardon, Senhorita. I am looking for the Guinean girls who were with you today in the choir—Mbekah, Ifé, and Olubayo."

The novice shook her head. "No one by those names lives at the Convent."

"Perhaps they now have Christian names. I am sure I saw the three girls I'm speaking of. What do you call the tall one?

A look of recognition came upon the novice's face. "That one is Josefa."

Lopo grew excited. "Where can I find Josefa right now?"

"She would be near the prioress. Josefa is one of her favorites." The novice searched the throng then pointed towards the other side of the square. "Over there is the prioress, the Mother Superior, today's priest, parents of some of the resident students . . . Josefa might be there."

Lopo grabbed Rodrigo by the arm and took a step in the direction pointed out by the novice then stopped and faced her again. "What are the Guinean girls doing at the convent?"

The novice shrugged. "I think they're going to be nuns. They don't seem to be doing the work of slaves."

The two men made their way to the circle of dignitaries as directed by the novice. Lopo saw that Mbekah and her two friends were indeed among them.

Rodrigo stopped Lopo as they drew near. "Careful Lopo. Mbekah may not be allowed to speak with us."

Lopo nodded. "Hmm. You could be right. Let's wait here to see if we can catch her eye."

In an instant, Lopo could tell Mbekah had seen him. He froze. *Will she want to talk to me?* At first, she brightened then he could see she worried. He watched as she elbowed Ifé who followed Mbekah's gaze, and also saw Lopo and Rodrigo. Olubayo picked up on her two friends' actions and noticed whom they were staring at. A big smile appeared on her face until she looked at one of the nuns who sensed something was going on. The nun stepped in front of the three girls and herded them in closer to the fold. Mbekah looked over her shoulder back at Lopo but allowed the nun to force her away from him and Rodrigo.

#

Lopo trudged up the stairs and opened the door into the rooms above the leather shop.

"Speaking of the King of Rome and here he appears." It was his sister-in-law, Pero's wife.

All eyes fixed upon Lopo who blushed. "You've been talking about me?"

"*Todos os Santos* is a good place to look for a wife, Lopo." It was his mother, grinning.

"It was just mass. I was not looking for a wife."

"And why not? You want to be ship's master someday, Lopo. You need a wife. Not just any wife."

"I'm not ready to marry."

His mother was not deterred. "Even when you're not hungry, if you sit down to a fine meal, you soon find your appetite."

"When I'm ready, I'll look for a girl just like you, Mãe." *But not until I do something about Kpodo's wife and pay back the money I borrowed.* "And by the way, who says I'm going to be a ship's master?"

"Other masters have come from families like ours. Mind you though, they had wives with learning and social graces." His mother was not giving up.

Pero's wife jumped into the conversation. "My cousin Margaida is a student at *Todos os Santos*. Her class of 26 girls graduates next spring. All eligible for marriage, and guaranteed to have good manners."

"You have a cousin at the convento?" Lopo wondered if she could help him contact Mbekah.

"Margaida could introduce you to someone, Lopo," said his mother. "Of course, we would want to know something about the girl before that happens."

"Smell the fish before haggling over the price?" asked Lopo. It was his turn to tease.

Lopo's father stepped into the room. "Pay attention to your mother, Lopo. One of the Colom brothers, Cristovao, married a girl who attended *Todos os Santos*. Senhor Colom told me he met her while attending mass there. A good catch. Her late father was the first governor of Porto Santo. The Coloms are from Genoa, but they've been in Lisbon for years. They come to the shop from time to time for vellum for their fine maps, although Cristovao is often at sea."

"You should follow this Cristovao's example," said his mother.

Lopo was used to his mother's mild harassment but his next question would certainly shock the whole room and increase the pressure on him. No matter, he needed information and, since there were no secrets in his family, he might as well go right to the target, audience or no audience. He turned to Pero's wife. "Your cousin, Margaida. Will you introduce me to her?"

CHAPTER 25

Back Alley Visits

Lopo sat alone in the midst of other crowded tables at the *Carapau* Cantina, his knife stuck erect into the wood to signal he waited for others to join him. Two months had passed since Lopo had seen Mbekah at Sunday mass at *Todos os Santos*. As the novice in the plaza had told him that day, Mbekah was called Josefa by the nuns. The cousin of Pero's wife, Margaida, had arranged for him to meet and talk briefly with Josefa which he had now done three times. He was relieved that she was treated well but perplexed about why, as was she. He kept hearing the words "king's project" but neither he nor Josefa could fathom what that meant. Both of them were beginning to think she was to become a nun. *Will she be sent back to the Mina to minister to her countrymen?*

His interest in Josefa still confused him. It mystified his friends; scandalized his family. His mother prayed for him, sure that Josefa had given him the evil eye. *Should my family be worried? . . . Maybe they should be . . . Maybe I should be worried.*

Margaida had grown to like Josefa which helped calm the family but that didn't stop his mother's prayers for him. It pained him that Josefa could become a nun, the wife of Christ! He could bear her taking vows if that's what she wanted. It was certainly better than being a slave. *I don't think Josefa wants to be a nun.*

He had seen immediately that Josefa's involvement with Prioress Ana de Mendonça was a good thing. Josefa's comments indicated that she was happy to spend time with the grand lady.

Josefa was surprisingly philosophical about her situation. "God has put me here and like a thread, I must follow the needle's path."

Manoel told Lopo that the prioress had the ear of the King. *How does Manoel know so much?*

Thwack. Another knife was thrust into the table. Rodrigo laughed at Lopo's surprise, yanked a stool from a nearby table, and plopped down. Before Rodrigo could utter a word, Manoel pulled up another stool and shouted, "Garçonete, vino."

Lopo and Rodrigo laid their knives flat and the serving girl came for their orders.

Lopo watched Manoel scan the room, no doubt for a contact to milk which is likely why he always knew the affairs of so many in the city. But today Manoel seemed overly nervous, agitated. His eyes darted about and he studied each man entering and each man leaving the cantina. He listened to Lopo and Rodrigo but said little himself.

Their bowls of fish stew came, and the conversation abated. Manoel continued to search the room. "Manoel, something is worrying you?"

Manoel took a long look at the patrons at the tables near theirs. He leaned in and spoke so Lopo could hardly make out the words. "I saw Kpodo's wife. Antonia, they call her. Night before last, I caught sight of the devil twins, Nunno and Belchior, escorting a very pregnant dark-skinned woman that could only have been her. Even in the dark and at a distance I knew exactly who they were. I followed them to the back door of the shop of a prosperous butcher, one with a commission from the palace. They were in there half an hour, no more. I watched them do the same at four other places, each for about the same amount of time.

When she hesitated in the way or sobbed they slapped her, hard enough to stagger her, once knocking her to the cobblestones."

Lopo pushed his half full bowl away. He could no longer think about food.

Manoel went on. "I know the proprietor of the last place they stopped at, so I dropped in to chat with him yesterday morning. As I feared, she is now one of Gonçalves' prostitutes."

Even though Lopo could see where this was going, the word "prostitute", said out loud, bashed him like the kick of a mule. He snatched his knife from the table and rose. "Gonçalves will pay for this." He stomped to the door.

A dozen paces out of the cantina Rodrigo and Manoel caught up and tackled Lopo. With his arms and legs thrashing, it was all they could manage to keep him on the ground. When they got his arms and legs pinned, Lopo let out a frustrated roar that could be heard up and down the river front.

On his back, Lopo ground his teeth. "I will kill that bastard pig. They broke the fight up in São Tiago or I would have stuck him then. Stuck him like a pig. This time, no one can stop me."

#

"You didn't let me finish, Lopo." Manoel had let go of Lopo's arm but sat close just in case he tried to bolt. Rodrigo did the same on Lopo's other side. To calm their friend, the two of them had walked Lopo along the river, around the plaza, and up the hill to the castle before settling down on the scruffy grass at the base of its walls.

"I knew you'd be angry—I was angry—so I listened to the man who was Antonia's last "appointment". You can never know too much. The man said he had told the two bawds that he'd had enough of the pregnant woman. The novelty had worn off for him and he wanted someone not full with child for next week. Someone who didn't weep the whole time."

Lopo's breathing quickened, deep and loud.

"Calm down, Lopo. There's more. Lots more. Shall I go on?"

"Go on, sim," Lopo managed to say through his gritted teeth.

"I figured that if this man was tired of Antonia, that others were too and that Gonçalves might consider selling her. You haven't paid the Galo his money back, right?"

Lopo shook his head. "No."

Manoel nodded. "I'd guessed as much. There's no advantage to paying early. All the interest is still due. Those tipos are sharks."

"Go on, por favor." Lopo was regaining his composure.

"I went to the *Cai*, the taberna whence Gonçalves operates. I told him you might still be interested in buying the woman, for the right price. Skipping the details of the negotiation, Gonçalves will take nothing less than forty-five hundred reais."

Lopo hung his head. "With the loan and my own money, I only have four thousand reais. Maybe my brother . . . But then the whole family would know and . . ."

"I have two hundred you can use," offered Rodrigo.

Manoel continued. "I'll lend you three hundred. I can get it to you tonight. Tonight, because that's when you have to bring the money or Gonçalves says no deal. He'll be at the *Cai* until midnight. He says the woman will be there for the exchange. I bet he's going to work her in the back room right up until you show. He's a pig, a true bastard pig."

CHAPTER 26

Full-Course Dinner

Sister Consola let Josefa into the priory via the door from the convent courtyard. *Quinha*, the parrot, perked up. "Djosefa. Djosefa."

Josefa ran to the bird's cage. Sister Consola was right behind her. "Thanks for arriving early, Josefa. We can use an extra pair of hands before our guest gets here."

"Hands?"

Sister Consola giggled. "Don't worry, we are happy you came with your entire body. What I mean is that you can help us get ready for dinner. You and your hands will help us. You see?"

Josefa looked at her hands and nodded. She smiled.

"Djosefa. Djosefa. Djosefa."

Josefa tossed some almonds into the cage.

"Doctor Astruch is punctual. We'll hear his knock in exactly one-half hour. I don't know how he does it. He must get here early and wait around the corner. We need to pull the table away from the wall and put the chairs around it. We should have done this hours ago."

Josefa lent a hand to move the heavy table. "Doctor means healer, no?" Josefa wanted to meet a Portuguese healer.

"No. I mean, yes. We call our healers "doctor" but Iacob Astruch is a doctor of the law. That means he studied many years at university and has been examined by other doctors about his knowledge. A university is a school for men. He studied at the one in Florence. It's unusual for a Jew to study law, mostly the learned Jews are medical doctors—healers—or they are Hebrew teachers. Doctor Astruch is Prioress Ana's Hebrew tutor."

"Jews? Hebrew?"

"Hebrew is another language. It is spoken by the Jews and it's very fashionable these days. So is Greek. Prioress Ana adores Doctor Astruch. He's so interesting. So wise."

Josefa nodded as if she understood but she wasn't sure she did. "Where do these Jews come from?"

"Doctor Astruch is from Andalusia. But his people originally came from the Holy Land, where Jesus Christ lived."

A black slave, the one who normally served the prioress, entered the parlor followed by a Portuguese man Josefa had never before seen who was followed by *Guincho* the monkey. Sister Consola glanced at the man. "That is Josué. The prioress borrowed him from her mother for the evening. He'll be the mordomo tonight to open the door, fetch food from the kitchen, pour wine, and whatever. Her mother's chef is supervising the convent staff in the kitchen. The food will be very elegant."

Guincho hurried to Josefa, looking for attention. Josefa shook the monkey's hand then got back to work. She watched the others set the table and copied them. "The Jews are Christians?"

"Oh dear, no. It's a long history. We'll talk about it some other time. Most Christians don't like Jews. Doctor Astruch escaped from his homeland on threat of death from Christians. But King João seems to get along with them. Doctor Astruch and several other Jews advise the king including another one who 'heals' his majesty, as you say."

Josefa kept up as best she could. She had to keep her eye on *Guincho* so she wouldn't disturb the items on the table.

Sister Consola lowered her voice. "You mustn't talk about our dinner tonight after you leave here. If Mother Superior learns about us entertaining a Jew, she'll get very exercised. Some of the convent's patrons might not approve, either."

Josefa counted the books standing on the side table against the wall. "Nine books! There were only seven before."

Sister Consola looked impressed. "You don't miss much. Some of her books are gifts but she also borrows them from her family's collection."

The prioress danced into the room. She wore a scarlet and gold silk corset dress that left her neck and the tops of her shoulders bare highlighting a brilliant pearl necklace. "Good evening, Josefa. Lovely to see you. Thanks for helping."

Josefa held up her hands. "I brought my hands."

That stopped the prioress for an instant, but she recovered quickly. "Of course you did. And they're nice hands too." She turned to the mordomo. "Josué, please feed *Guincho* and lock her in her room."

Tat, tat, tat. The sound sent Josué to the back door. Prioress Ana clapped her hands. "It's time everyone."

A reception line formed behind Josué who opened the door, bowed, and stepped aside. A rather small man with a white beard passed by and into the room. Josué announced, "Doctor Iacob Astruch."

The prioress, who was a head taller, took the man's right hand with both of hers. "Bem-vindo, Doctor." They touched cheeks and kissed the air. "You know my assistant, Sister Consola. And this is Josefa *da Guiné*. She lives in the convent preparing to be presented at court.

"Ah, such a beauty. I am Iacob Astruch, at your service Senhorita."

Josefa was surprised that this very learned person was so friendly. *Why would anyone not like this man?*

"Djacob. Djacob."

A big smile appeared on Doctor Astruch's face. "And a good evening to you too, *Quinha* parrot."

#

The dinner and dishes cleared away, Josué brought out a large board checkered with ivory and ebony squares. The prioress and the doctor began to place carved figures on the board. The prioress noted Josefa's interest. "Doctor Astruch and I have our fortnightly game of chess tonight but first he will give me another lesson on strategies and tactics. I love the new style everyone is playing these days—the mad queen." She laughed. "It's about time women's role in statecraft was acknowledged."

After the lesson, their game commenced. The player not studying his next move chattered away with the audience of three—Sister Consola, Josefa, and *Quinha*. Doctor Astruch moved one of his white figures diagonally and knocked down a black horse which he removed from the board. "Bishop takes cavalier." He relaxed and turned to the spectators. "I've heard of the young princes and princesses of the Congo King coming to Lisbon to learn Portuguese. But you are not from the Congo, no?

"I came as a slave. My village was attacked, and I and others were brought to the *Mina* castle and then here against our wishes."

"How fortunate that you are now treated so well."

"I miss my family, my village, the forest . . ."

"Your good treatment here cannot make up for the violence you have suffered. But I see you are not moping over water that has gone past the mill."

Josefa paused. "You are telling me to take advantage of the water still to come, no? My father used to say 'Full child tells hungry child not to fret.' But now I remember that you have had your own sad story."

"Yes. My family was scattered, and our possessions were taken from us by the Castilians. But it's not the first time my people have suffered and sadly, it will not be the last."

The prioress moved her black queen and cried, "Check mate! Too bad because you once taught me that focus is the foundation of strategy. Ha!"

"The student reminds the master. I can only be pleased, though." The Doctor turned again to Josefa. We Jews have the same book that Christians use. Prioress Ana will have to read you the story of a young man who was sold by his brothers into slavery. She should be able to translate it for you from the Hebrew or the Latin. I would tell you myself, but I must return to my home in the judiaria before it gets too late."

CHAPTER 27

The Meeting

Lopo hustled toward the *Cai Taberna*. He did not like being out late at night, alone, and carrying over four thousand reais in coin. He had met Manoel earlier to get the three hundred Manoel had promised. A rendezvous with Rodrigo outside the taberna would bring two hundred more. He trusted Rodrigo to guard his back during the exchange and help get Kpodo's wife, Antonia, out of danger.

He left the *Alfama* quarter and made a beeline across the main plaza toward the tabernas and cantinas that lined the riverbank to the west. Leaning forward, he strode purposefully so no one would think him an easy mark. He remained alert to any movement left or right or for sounds from behind. He had his ship's knife tucked into his waistband, as always, but kept his hand off the ivory handle so not to look defensive or worried. He had also secreted a small dagger on his back below the neck and under his cloak. *One never knows what will happen at night near the docks.*

Having crossed the plaza and followed the river bank a few hundred paces, Lopo veered right, heading away from the river and the safety of the night watchmen near the docked ships. *No moon tonight. Graças a Deus that the taberna is not far.*

Two streets in from the river, Lopo suddenly sensed someone behind him but too late for him to turn about. Crack. A club bludgeoned his left shoulder. He reeled forward. Another blow smashed his right arm and ribs knocking his breath out. His knees buckled and down he went, face on the cobbles. He tried to roll over but a kick to his stomach lifted him off the ground and paralyzed him. A hand on the back of his head and another pinning his arm behind his back left him helpless while a second pair of hands patted his clothes.

"Here's his knife. Epa! And a neat little dagger on his back. Ah yes, and here is the purse. It's heavy!"

"Use his own knife, we're done with him . . . forever."

At the rush of footsteps, the two footpads paused, jumped up, and fled into the blackness, taking his knife, his dagger, and his money. All his money.

#

Rodrigo set Lopo down on a pallet in the back room of the *Carapau*. "You nearly met the saints tonight, my friend."

"You saved my life."

"Most likely. But they got your money. I'd wager that Gonçalves is behind this. He knew you were coming with a big purse to buy the woman Antonia. He knew where and when."

"Oh, my ribs. They broke my ribs. Did you get a look at them?"

"Too dark. A tall one and a stout one. Nunno and Belchior, I'd say. But you can count on them having 'witnesses' to say they were elsewhere."

Lopo was silent for a moment. "Even if we could prove it, Gonçalves doubtless owns the magistrate for this district. My main worry is that I cannot help Antonia. Poor Antonia! . . . My vow to the Virgen!"

"Forget what you can't do, Lopo. Start thinking about the three thousand reais and the thug who wants it back, with usury."

CHAPTER 28

Thug to Thug

Senhor Xemenez stood in front of Gonçalves' table at the *Cai.* "Senhor Bras Gonçalves?"

"I am, yes."

"I am the banker, Filipe Xemenez. Your man told me you have a proposition I should hear."

"Sit down, please. Take a glass with me." Gonçalves poured wine into a tumbler for his guest. "I believe you can arrange a deal for me."

"You wish to borrow some money?" Xemenez sipped but kept his eyes fixed on his host.

"I would like to buy a loan from a colleague of yours. He calls himself the Galo."

Xemenez raised his eyebrows. "Go on."

"I know for a fact that a former shipmate of mine, Lopo Meendez, will have trouble paying back the three thousand reais he borrowed to buy a slave woman."

"But he was not successful. I was at the auction. I seem to remember that you outbid him for the woman, pregnant but a beauty. What has Lopo done with the money?"

Gonçalves cleared his throat. "The word on the street is that he was robbed. Lost it all. Careless fellow! I am willing to pay the loan in full, right now, plus half the usury due."

"Why would you do this, Senhor Gonçalves?"

"It's a private matter. But there's more. No one must know I own the loan. Lopo is to believe he still owes the money to the Galo and the Galo will collect the loan when and how I say. I'll even pay him half the usury he gets when he collects. I will meet personally with the Galo to buy the loan and give him instructions."

Xemenez considered the matter for a moment. "I will pass on your offer."

#

"I've found a ship and leave tomorrow for Santa Maria in the Azores then to London. I'll be pilot's mate on the *São Felipe*. It's the caravela they're loading up over there." Lopo knew he had surprised his friend Rodrigo. His mother had been even more surprised. "I have no choice. The Galo has called in his loan. I can't pay so I'm getting out of town for a few months."

Rodrigo's experienced eye studied the *São Felipe* then Lopo's face. "A good enough ship. Capitão Rosas is a steady man. Do I know the piloto?

"Sancho Marques. Another hard case like Gonçalves but I have no choice. I have to earn some money fast." I can only hope that my ribs mend before we hit rough weather.

Rodrigo spat into the river. "Are you not worried that this man, the Galo, will threaten your family?"

"I gave him the two hundred reais you loaned me after the robbery as a down payment on the interest. I promised him more when I return. I don't know what else I can do. I wish Manoel were here. He knows about these things."

"I will tell Manoel to keep his ears open. I will also let Josefa know you have gone."

#

Sancho Marques, the pilot on the São Felipe, set down his mug of beer and belched. "Thanks for dinner, Bras. I have just enough time for a whore before my ship sails. But first, what is it you need from me?"

Gonçalves looked around before speaking. "You know me too well, Sancho. Yes, I have a way for you to return the favor you owe me."

"I'm listening."

"Make sure your new pilot's mate, Lopo Meendez, does not survive this voyage. And make sure his death is an accident."

CHAPTER 29

Surprise Basket

"I promise you will be happy that you put straw in the alley. You will see. The three wise men's horses will not be able to resist the fodder and the distinguished travelers will leave you something nice, just as they did many years ago when they visited the holy family in Bethlehem, so they could worship baby Jesus." Prioress Ana's warm smile convinced Josefa that there was something to this tradition worth waiting for.

Josefa enjoyed relaxing in the priory with her compatriots Inês and Maria. She had grown to love the parrot *Quinha*, the monkey *Guincho*, the warmth of the fire, the books, Sister Consola, the prioress and her kind way of treating them, and the interesting visitors. She was happy that there had been many opportunities to be in the priory in the past three weeks with so many of the convent students away for the Natal holy days. Josefa appreciated that the prioress had liberated them from many of the chores that the Mother Superior had forced on them, especially the daily emptying and cleaning of chamber jars. She felt that she was learning as much in the priory as in the classes over in the convent. Josefa and the others had learned to play chess and had even played a few times with Doctor Astruch. He assured Josefa that it would be good to know the game when she was at court. She was getting the idea that the three of them from her village were not going to be nuns after all but something more like the princesses of the Congo King—future translators—even though she didn't understand why or who she would translate for. Josefa had begun to learn a little of the language of the Congo from her classmates from there.

Prioress Ana summoned Sister Consola and whispered in her ear. Sister Consola left the room on some errand, Josefa supposed.

Josefa selected a book from the small table. This one had been imprinted with the uniform characters using one of the new machines in the German style. The prioress had told them the new printing process reduced the price of books although the price was still rather dear. Alas, this book was in the Hebrew language—perhaps one of the books Doctor Astruch uses to teach the prioress. She picked another, a hand-written volume in Portuguese that contained poems and sonnets and illuminations. She didn't understand a lot of the words but liked the flow. She did want to improve her Portuguese.

The back door to the priory opened suddenly. Sister Consola leaned in from the alley. "Come. Quickly. You will not believe what has been left."

The prioress stood and addressed the young women. "Go see what is out there."

They rushed to the door and out into the alley. Sister Consola knelt over a sizeable basket, one large enough to hold the day's purchases of vegetables for an entire household. She moaned. "This is not what I expected from the magi. Not at all what I expected."

Prioress Ana winked at Sister Consola. "Well, bring it in and let's see what they have left for us."

Sister Consola looked up at the prioress and shook her head. She did not smile. "I'm afraid this wasn't what we planned.

There's a swaddled baby in this basket! A very tiny, negro baby. I'm not sure it's even alive."

#

Inês was holding the baby boy found in the alley when Sister Consola came in with a Portuguese woman who carried a baby girl, except her baby looked huge compared to the foundling baby. "Here is Tomasa. The palace recommended her to be our wet nurse. Is Moisés still breathing? Can we call him Moisés? Found in a basket and all."

The prioress nodded. "I was thinking of Jesus for his name, because of the season. But you were the first to find him and Moisés fits the situation well; although Lazarus might be even more appropriate."

Maria took Tomasa's baby and Inês handed Moisés to Tomasa. "I dipped my little finger in milk and got him to suck so he's ready for you."

Sister Consola floated about. "Graças a Deus, he's alive. I'm going to the chapel to light candles to the Virgin for him."

Prioress Ana called after Sister Consola. "Not a word of this outside the priory or we may have trouble with Mother Superior."

Tomasa stared down into the face of her new charge as he sucked. "So small. I can't tell how many days or weeks old he is because he's malnourished and maybe has not been fed at all recently. He's even too weak to cry."

Prioress Ana paced in front of the fireplace. "There was no message left with him and no one saw who left him. Can you stay here for a few days, Tomasa, until he is stronger? Josefa, please ask the maid to prepare a bed for Tomasa and the two babies. Near the fire would be good."

#

Doctor Astruch stood up from his chess game with Josefa when the prioress entered the room. "I'm happy to see that the new addition to your household is thriving. How long has it been since he joined you?"

"Fifteen days tomorrow. I was planning to send him home with Tomasa but the girls have taken such a liking to him that I've convinced Tomasa to overnight here for a few months. Her husband drops in for dinner most evenings and we're all adjusting. Olubayo has become so attached to the baby that we put her forward as godmother. But first Olubayo herself had to be baptized so all three of the girls converted. I hear it was a surprise to Mother Superior; she still hasn't found out about baby Moisés. Fortunately, her assistant, Sister Giomar, is deathly afraid of *Guincho* which greatly limits her ability to spy on the priory."

Seated again, Doctor Astruch moved a pawn, then looked up at Josefa who was considering her options. She also moved a pawn.

"Josefa, I can tell you're not concentrating. Should we do this another time?

"Later, perhaps, yes. The prioress said you would tell us the story of Moisés. It's part of Jewish history, no?"

Doctor Astruch pushed the chess board to the side. "Wine, please." He thought for a moment, then began. "When Moisés was born, his people were slaves in a land called Egypt. Pharaoh—that's what the Egyptians called their king—worried that the slaves were growing too numerous to be controlled. He ordered that all their male babies be killed. So during the day, the family hid Moisés by floating him in a tar-covered basket in the reeds in the shallows of the Nile River."

The servant woman brought Port and Doctor Astruch sipped a bit. She left the pitcher on the table. Josefa, Inês, and Maria helped each other understand what had been related so far. Josefa spoke for the group. "What is this 'tar'?

"It's black and sticky and does not melt in water. We use it to help our caravelas stay water tight."

The girls spoke among themselves and Josefa nodded. The Doctor continued. "Baby Moisés was discovered by pharaoh's wife, the queen. She wanted the adorable child as her own. She chose Moisés' own mother to be the nursemaid. It's a long and beautiful story but I'll omit some of it to get to the best part. Moisés grew up believing he was Egyptian but eventually learned he was Hebrew and matured into a righteous man. God spoke to him, instructing him to free his people. He did as he was instructed. He said to Pharaoh 'Let my people go' but Pharaoh refused. As the prophet of God, Moisés punished the Egyptians. Moisés called down a plague of locusts that destroyed the crops. He had God turn all the water in the land to blood. He cursed the Egyptians with painful boils. There were nine plagues and each time Moisés' call to 'Let my people go' was refused. Finally, the angel of death came through and all first-born sons of the Egyptians died on the same night. Pharaoh finally understood the message and let Moisés leave Egypt with all of his people."

Josefa sat up. "Where did Moisés take them?"

"Eventually, they go to Palestine. That's where they were when Jesus lived among them."

Josefa contemplated the tale. "Would God speak to me and help me take my people away?"

CHAPTER 30

A French Game

"Rodrigo! What a surprise. How did you know I was home? No doubt you've been talking to Manoel—he who knows all." Lopo stepped into the narrow street to chat with his old friend.

"Yes, Manoel told me he saw the *São Felipe* unloading at the dock yesterday. How did it go for you?"

"Some weather, but that's to be expected this time of year. Oh, and I almost got myself killed. A cut-throat jumped me near the docks in London. I'll put on something warm and stroll awhile with you." Lopo disappeared into his father's shop and returned with a leather jacket.

"Just so you know, I left a message with Margaida at the convent to tell Mbekah, I mean Josefa, you had to go to sea. I didn't speak with her myself. I hope that was acceptable."

Lopo grabbed Rodrigo's arm and steered him towards the docks. "Of course. My wife's cousin is reliable, and she likes Josefa."

"Have you spoken with the Galo since you returned? Is he giving you any trouble about the loan?"

Lopo pursed his lips. "No, but I need to see the Galo. I have some money for him, a payment. What's new in Lisbon? I heard Diogo Cão sailed on another voyage to find the bottom of Africa. I'm surprised you didn't go too?"

Rodrigo sighed. "I'm waiting to go with you when Capitão Dias leads. If that ever happens. Tell me about the attack on you."

#

Sister Consola hurried Josefa from the antechamber, through the parlor, and into a bedroom. Josefa would have liked to stop and play with Moisés and the animals but Sister Consola was insistent. "The courtyard will be used for the game, leaving little space around it for spectators so the prioress is only allowed one guest. You'll have to tell Inês and Maria all about it. She wants you to wear this dress, so people won't think you're going to be a nun."

Sister Consola held up a green silk dress. Josefa sucked in a large breath. "Such a beautiful gown. It is silk, no? Where did you get it?"

"It was Prioress Ana's when she was your age. She wore it to her coming-out party. I'll tell you about it some other time. Right now, I must get you ready. The coach comes in less than an hour."

#

Lopo and Rodrigo walked while Lopo related the assault on him in London. "I was alone, returning to the *São Felipe* after a drink with the piloto. It almost seemed like the blackguard was waiting for me. Makes no sense. Kill a foreign mariner? You know it's an unwritten rule that we don't carry more than drink money in port unless we go someplace in force. Kill me for the fun of it? Makes no sense."

Rodrigo broke his silence. "You will have to take care until you can discover the truth. Here is the *Carapau*. Let's see if Manoel is having a drink."

Manoel got up when he saw his two friends and joined them as they found another table. "I'm afraid I have sad news for you, Lopo. Antonia, the beautiful, pregnant sex slave. She is dead."

Lopo stared at the floor for a long moment. "I didn't keep my vow to free her. I couldn't. I am to blame."

Rodrigo patted Lopo's back. "God knows you tried. You're in debt up to the gunwales for trying. You can't let this weigh on you. This be on the head of Piloto Gonçalves."

Lopo had another thought. "Did she give birth?"

Manoel sighed. "I heard she had a boy but she never really recovered from the labor of childbirth. She died less than a month later. Gonçalves didn't get any help for her, I'm sure. I haven't heard what happened to the baby. Died or taken to a convent, I suppose."

Lopo considered this. "Does Kpodo know?"

"Who would tell him? No, I think not."

#

Lopo made straight for the alley behind *Todos os Santos* convent. He no longer could help Kpodo's wife, but he would make sure her baby got better than she did. But first, he must see Mbekah or Josefa or whoever she was.

Sister Consola answered the door carrying a very small baby, a black baby. "Yes?"

"I am Lopo David Meendez. A friend of Josefa's. You and I have met before. I need to speak with her. Can you help me find her?"

"She is not here. She is at the palace with the prioress. They went to watch the court game of ball so fashionable in France. I'm afraid she'll be gone until late." Sister Consola saw that Lopo was studying the baby. "This is Moisés *dos Santos*. He was left at our door. We are caring for him until we can find a suitable home for him."

#

“I will show you to your chairs. Follow me, please.” The page led them down a narrow, covered passageway between the outer wall and a waist-high wooden screen that separated the spectators from the courtyard. “You will have a clear view of the action. Please don’t interfere with the ball or the contenders. And pay attention; they hit the ball hard enough to bounce off the back wall and it can bruise you if you don’t duck when it comes your way.”

The prioress and Josefa took their seats. “I think you will find the action interesting and fun, even if you don’t bet on the outcome. They strike the ball with their palms.” The Prioress swung her arm to demonstrate. “*Jeu de Paume* they call it in Paris. How they avoid breaking their hands, I don’t know.”

Josefa nodded.

The prioress winked. “I like to watch the young men who play. A bit young for me but not for you. Such fine figures. You’ll see.”

As the page escorted others past them, they stood to let them by and the prioress introduced them one by one to Josefa.

Josefa wondered if she would ever remember all their names, or any of their names, or how they knew the prioress. Then came one she could never forget.

“Good afternoon, *Capitão* Dias, *Senhora* Dias. May I present Josefa *da Guiné*, one of our students at *Todos os Santos*?”

CHAPTER 31

Finishing School

The heat accosted Lopo as he entered the bakery. He wandered about the warehouse-sized room until he saw the man who seemed to be in charge. "Bom dia. I am Lopo David Meendez. I have come to speak with the slave Kpodo or Bastiao as you call him."

"My name is Rui Estevez, baker. What is your business with Bastiao?"

"I was pilot's mate on the ship that brought him from the *Mina*. I speak a little of his language and his majesty the king requested I help with the slaves' adjustment to their new life." Lopo didn't think stretching the truth was a sin, at least not in this case.

"Perhaps you can help, then. I've had Bastiao isolated and in chains for over a week now. On bread and water rations. Of a sudden, he became violent; smashing crates, shoving barrels. He grabbed a piece of firewood and started for one of my white assistants, gnashing his teeth, his eyes wide and wild. Terrifying. I can't find out what made him loco. It doesn't appear to be anything his intended victim did or said."

Lopo hesitated then gave his opinion. "His wife was also among the captives on my ship. Sold at public auction to an uncouth fellow. She died giving birth. Maybe Bastiao discovered this."

The baker went on. "He's been a fast learner and a good worker. I'd hate to lose him but I'm not sure I can risk removing the chains."

"I'll give you my opinion after I speak with him."

#

Lopo squinted for a few moments in the bright sunlight. It was a relief to be away from the sweltering ovens. He had spent at least an hour with Kpodo speaking in what he knew of Kpodo's native language mixing in Portuguese and gestures. Kpodo indeed had heard about his wife's death and that was what touched him off like one of the cannons on the *Ninho*. But Kpodo seemed resigned, calm; no longer wanting to kill his Portuguese masters. Lopo had recommended that the baker release Kpodo back to work. The baker was leery and asked Lopo to return in a few days to speak again with the slave. He said that he, the baker, would make a judgment at that time what to do with Kpodo. Lopo had decided not to speak of the baby Moisés to Kpodo and of his suspicion that the boy was Kpodo's late wife's baby.

Lopo headed for the *Carapau*. He could use a drink and some company. Perhaps Rodrigo would be there or even Manoel. He was deep in thought when he came face to face with Gonçalves. Lopo was shocked back to the reality of the wharves and the foot traffic on the docks. Yet Lopo's shock was nothing compared to the look of surprise on the pilot's face.

"Olá, Senhor Piloto. Surprised to see me?"

"Surprised, yes. A little. I shouldn't be, though. I did hear the *São Felipe* had returned. Will you be in port very long?"

Lopo scratched his newly shaven chin. He could barely hide his disdain for this man. "Don't know. I am looking for another ship that needs a pilot's mate. Another ship sailing north."

#

The Galo dropped a small purse filled with coins on the table. Gonçalves looked up at the money lender. He saw that his two men, Nunno and Belchior, had also observed the Galo's approach in the candle-lit taberna and that they were moving in behind the Galo's back. "What's this?"

"Your half of the interest on the loan to Lopo Meendez. Our agreement: I collect it and keep half." The Galo turned his head and noted the two men standing behind him.

"You find Lopo and tell him at least a quarter of the loan, the principal, is due by the end of the month. And not a word about my part in this. You understand?"

"And if he doesn't pay?"

"We'll talk about that when the time arrives." Gonçalves dumped the coins onto the table and began to count.

The Galo turned, stepped between Nunno and Belchior, and strode from the room.

#

"My wife and I talked with her at a recent court-ball game here in the palace. She was the guest of Dona Ana de Mendonça. Josefa is her Christian name, your excellency." Captain Dias had arranged this private audience with Chamberlain de Faria because he could see that the king had plans for some of the slaves he had transported on his ship from the *Mina*. He could think of no other explanation for the strange orders that his crew not touch the captives. Or why Josefa was being educated at *Todos os Santos* and going to social functions with such an aristocrat as Dona Ana. Dias went on, "I can see that you are preparing Josefa and her companions for some purpose."

The Chamberlain cut him off. "What do you know about these preparations? Are there rumors?"

"No, your Excellency. But I read the orders granting special treatment to her group of captives while on my ship. I saw her at the game of ball, dressed like a courtesan. I know you are grooming the Congolese youth to be ambassadors and translators for the Congo King so I assumed you have similar plans for the Guineans."

"Have you spoken about this with anyone?"

Dias was now worried that he had set a fox in the gaggle. "No, your excellency. I do not discuss possible state secrets. Not even with my wife. I honor my oath to the king."

Chamberlain de Faria considered the responses Dias had given. "Why do you bring this to me?"

"My wife and I can help. Josefa could become a member of our household for a time. My wife would be the perfect model and teacher to finish Josefa's education as a lady. You could place the other girls in similar situations."

CHAPTER 32

Death of a Duke

Lopo and Rodrigo had finished their port duties. With their sea legs adjusted to land, the two strolled out of the gates of the Portuguese factory, a walled compound enclosing a Portuguese city of almost 2,000 souls within the huge city of Bruges. Though they were in the heart of Flanders, they had spoken only Portuguese and eaten the same food served in Lisbon since their arrival three days earlier. Lopo pointed to the impressive tower of the Church of Our Lady in the distance picking up the evening light of the August sun. "I promised my father I would buy woolen cloth for my mother and sister-in-law. The best woven cloth is to be had in the stalls near the church. We'll also find a good place to eat like the locals."

"You still have coin after your last encounter with the Galo?"

"It's my father's money for this purchase. I did pay the usury due to the Galo. He demanded a part of the loan too. I didn't have it. That's why I flew to this ship when I heard it needed a pilot's mate and that you were going to be in the crew."

Rodrigo fingered the ivory handle of his deck knife and scanned the narrow street in front of them as they progressed. "I'm glad I can watch your back this time around." They continued in silence past a few houses. "You got Kpodo out of chains at the bakery. Did you ever tell him about the baby?"

"Didn't think it would help matters. I did speak to Josefa. She agrees that the baby they call Moisés is probably Kpodo's late wife's baby."

Rodrigo frowned. "But is it Kpodo's baby?"

"Maybe. Maybe not. We don't know how she and her group were treated by their Guinean captors before they arrived at the *Mina* Fort."

Rodrigo was in the mood to talk. "You love Josefa, don't you?"

The question surprised Lopo who shook his head. *How does he know what I'm thinking?* "I don't know. I know it's not a good idea to love a Guinean slave. Especially one for whom his majesty has plans."

#

"You will thank me for this someday." Captain Dias had not anticipated his wife's hostility to the arrangement. "Hosting Josefa in our home pleases the chamberlain and can only help my career. Can only help our status."

"How long will we have her? Are we expected to introduce her to our friends and family? And as what? Servant? Ward? Future courtesan?"

Captain Dias didn't know all the answers. *Perhaps I will speak again with the chamberlain.* "Josefa's studies will continue at the convent. She will spend three long days there each week. When she's in our home, it's important that we treat her like an honored guest. You and I will be her role models. The chamberlain was clear on that point."

Captain Dias decided it was time to change the subject. "I have something we must discuss. I learned about it this morning. Diogo, Duke of Viseu has been executed. The wealthiest and most powerful aristocrat in the realm caught in another conspiracy against his majesty the king. It's been no secret that the duke thought his claim to the throne stronger than João's. But King João is no weakling. Last year the King tried and executed Diogo's treasonous brother Fernando, Duke of Bragança. Now this. Diogo, the king's cousin; the queen's own brother! That part is certain. But there are whispers that the king himself was the executioner. Yes, the king stabbed the duke. Invited the duke to the palace for an intimate dinner then dispatched him."

Senhora Dias took all this in. "Can this be true? The king personally killing his brother-in-law? What will become of the youngest Bragança brother, Manuel?"

"The king has publicly ceded Diogo's ducal titles and estates to Manuel. The king is a genius. Young Manuel is now beholden to King João. Manuel would be a complete fool to be disloyal."

The two contemplated the events for a moment then Senhora Dias spoke. "We must be sure we avoid the Braganças until we know who is in good odor and who in bad."

Captain Dias speculated out loud, "Lisbon and the countryside are calm. The cortes must be pleased. I'm sure the common people will be happy to have one less greedy grandee in the kingdom. We likely will avoid another civil war with Castilian troops tearing up the countryside. Viva King João!" Captain Dias took his wife's hand. "We must be seen to be solidly in King João's camp."

The doorman entered the salon. "Senhorita *da Guiné* has arrived with her baggage. Shall I show her to her quarters?"

CHAPTER 33

Sail West to Go to the East?

Josefa arrived early at the convent, entering in the back through the priory. Before classes, Josefa wanted to play with baby Moisés, *Guincho* the monkey, and *Quinha* the parrot. She hoped to chat with Sister Consola and her two girlhood friends from her village. Maybe she would even get a moment with Dona Ana, the prioress. Josefa, Inês, and Maria had agreed that Moisés should learn to speak the language of their village, so they spoke to him in the baby talk they had spoken to their own little brothers and sisters. *Quinha* paid close attention and was squawking like a Guinean toddler even though Moisés had yet to say a word. With so much attention, Moisés was a happy baby—10 months old, they guessed. Tomasa arrived with her own child in hand just before the girls departed the priory for their lessons. Her child ran to *Quinha*'s cage. Moisés fussed until Tomasa put him to her ample breast.

While the baby suckled, Sister Consola walked the girls to the antechamber. "Josefa, Dr. Astruch has arranged for you to meet his majesty the king's physician. Dona Ana will host an evening for him day after tomorrow. Can you stay after classes then, to dine with us?"

#

"I don't know what to think of his ideas. Is he addled or is he a genius?" Their weekly formal dinner was over and Captain Dias sat in the parlor with his wife, Branca, and their house guest, Josefa, telling about the day-long council he had attended in the castle. "I do know Senhor Colom to be a good ship's master and there is no better navigator in the king's service. He was master of one of the caravelas when we brought the landing force and building materials to construct the fort at the *Mina* two years ago. He's from Genoa though some doubt that. Married to the daughter of Governador Perestrelo."

The mention of Governor Perestrelo perked up Branca Dias. "Governador of what?"

"Governador of the island of Porto Santo near the island of Madeira."

Josefa broke in. "The nuns at *Todos os Santos* speak of his wife Filipa who was a student there."

Captain Dias mused. "There's a certain logic to Senhor Colom's belief that to arrive in the East, you must sail west."

Josefa, who had traveled to Lisbon on board a vessel that had sailed many days out of sight of any land, wondered how much further west the ocean sea extended. "How many days to get to the East by sailing west?"

"Ah, that is the point upon which Senhor Colom's idea stands or falls. The king's council of savants is unanimous that Colom has vastly underestimated the distance."

Branca put down her needlework. "What do you believe, Querido?"

"Above all, I believe the next journey of discovery should be led by one of the king's own squires. Me, for example. And the king should continue down the coast of Africa. The bottom of the continent cannot be much further than we've sailed already."

#

The priory was already set up for the evening with Doctor Astruch and the king's physician when Josefa entered through the antechamber. She scurried into Sister Consola's room to change into the green silk gown given her by Dona Ana. While she admired herself in a looking glass, Sister Consola, who remained in her habit, combed Josefa's ebony hair. "Moisés will spend the night with the wet nurse. He's perfectly content with her. But we must think of the next step. Should Moisés be placed with Tomasa or remain in the priory?"

Josefa sighed. "We would rarely see him if he is not here. Can't you leave things as they are?"

"We're a strange family for a growing child. Nuns for aunts. A monkey and a parrot for uncles." Sister Consola laughed at her own joke. "When the mother superior finds out about Moisés, will Dona Ana want to fight that fight?"

Josefa grew serious. "He needs a father. He looks like Kpodo; he's the slave in the royal bakery they call Bastiao. I wonder if we should tell Bastiao about Moisés?"

CHAPTER 34

Two Women in the Same Hut

The weather was clear but cooler than usual. It was nearing the time when the Portuguese celebrate the birth of Jesus and this was the second time Josefa would be in Lisbon for the festival. Mother Superior was speaking to a gathering of the *Todos os Santos* students including the girls from the *Mina* and the Congo King's court. Another lesson on etiquette. The same as last month. Josefa kept her eyes on the speaker but thought about her dinners with Dr. Astruch and his friend Samuel Amatu, the king's physician. At first it was queer to her that men were the healers among this people. The medical doctor's ideas about healing were strange but eventually she began to find similarities in their thinking and methods. Of course, they had different plants available for their cures than the plants she had studied at her mother's side in the forests near her village. She hoped sometime to go into the countryside with the physician's assistant to see what plants he gathered and how they were prepared. She had kept a keen eye for plants in the city whenever she was out of the convent and had seen some her mother had used. The lecture over, the students filed out of the chapel row by row in silence.

Waiting in line for the afternoon meal, Josefa contemplated her living arrangement. She whispered her concerns in her birth language to Inês and Maria. "I worry that Senhora Dias does not like me. She's jealous, I'm certain. If her husband speaks to me or even nods when I speak, Senhora Dias becomes agitated. It makes me nervous just to be with her, alone or in a group."

The girls stood in silence, listening to the muffled voices of the novices and the other students, then Inês offered advice. "You know that two women in the same hut with one man doesn't work. Not in our village, not here. That's why a man in the forest has a house for each of his wives and another for himself."

With their bowls full of wheat and mutton gruel, the three moved into the convent courtyard to find a place to sit. Josefa responded. "I never let Capitão Dias think I want to be one of his wives. How do they call it here? Flirting. I don't flirt with this man. Not when we're alone, not when Senhora Dias is with us. My father said that two rams cannot stay in the same yard. I'm happy to let Senhora Dias be the only ram."

Maria nodded. "Take care, Josefa. Jealousy is blind and there is no medicine that will cure it."

#

"Be in the street tomorrow before eight hours. She always leaves at eight to walk to the *Convento de Todos os Santos*. Tall and wearing the novice's blue habit, you can't mistake her. Follow and take her when she's alone but not too near to this house." Senhora Dias continued. "Here are the thousand reais. I'll pay your agent another thousand in fifteen days when I learn the girl has disappeared with no trace."

The slave merchant nodded his assurance. "She'll be secured in a cart and on the road north an hour after we grab her and not out of her sack until dark. The next day she'll be walking in the line with my other purchases from the auction."

No, no. Keep her covered, gagged, and hidden in the cart. She must not be out of her sack for at least seven days. The chamberlain and the prioress have eyes and ears everywhere, it seems. Burn her clothes and dress her like your other slaves. Give her a new name. Anything but Josefa which is how she is called now. Tell buyers that she is from the Ivory Coast. She's smart so she must believe she has angered his majesty and that is the reason for her treatment. I never want to see her face again.

#

Lopo pulled Margaida out of the room full of family, food, and noise. He wanted news of Mbekah from his brother's wife's cousin. "How is it with Josefa? I haven't seen her in months."

Margaida smiled. "She seems fine. Living now in the home of your Capitão Dias but still taking classes at the convent most days."

"Capitão Dias! Is she happy there? Have you discovered what his majesty's project is for her and her two friends? Should I visit her at the convent or at the home of the capitão?"

"So many questions. Before I answer, tell me what are your intentions regarding Josefa?"

Lopo hesitated. *I must choose the right way to say this.* "I feel responsible for her being here in Lisbon. She's intelligent and should not be a slave or whatever it is she is now. She should be a free woman."

"Sure, sure. You know what? I think you're in love with her." Margaida studied Lopo's face for more clues about his interest in the girl.

Lopo saw that Margaida was disappointed in his answer but that's all he was going to tell his family.

Lopo's mother stepped out onto the stairway. "Lopo, Margaida, come in. Join the celebration. After all, the party is for you, Lopo. Come and talk to Catalina. We invited her to meet you, my handsome ship's piloto back from the sea."

Lopo's face turned pink. "I'm not a piloto yet. Don't hex my chances by calling me that. Catalina seems nice, but . . ."

"But you're not ready to marry. Is that not it? Your father and I have discussed it. You are as ready as you'll ever be. Please, just be nice to her today. Is that too much to ask?"

Lopo sighed, raised an eyebrow to Margaida, and followed his mother back into the Meendez family rooms above his father and brother's leather shop.

CHAPTER 35

Disappeared

"The Senhorita *da Guiné* is not at the house of the Senhores Dias. Senhora Dias said the senhorita left at eight hours as is her custom. I walked there one way and back another. Only half an hour either way. Should I keep looking?"

Dona Ana looked worriedly at the others in the priory then addressed her man servant. "Keep looking, yes. She's been missing now for half a day. Take Sister Consola with you."

Dona Ana turned to her assistant. "Sister Consola, ask the shop keepers on all likely routes if they have seen her today or any other day. When you discover her normal path, concentrate on those shops. I'm sure they would remember a tall Guinean in a blue habit. Especially a beauty like Josefa. Return here quickly if something useful turns up."

Inês and Maria had been quiet while the prioress gave orders. She glanced at the two girls as if it were the first time she had seen them this afternoon. She took both into her arms. "Think where Josefa might have gone. Think of anything she said lately that would give us a clue about where she might be. I have sent word of Josefa's disappearance to Dr. Astruch and to Chamberlain de Faria. Come, let us pray to São Jorge, Santiago, and the Virgin.

#

Captain Dias embraced his wife. "I came as soon as I heard. Tell me again, from the beginning, about what has happened here today."

"Dona de Mendonça's man came about an hour ago. He said Josefa had not come to the convento today for lessons and his mistress wanted to know if Josefa was not feeling well or if something else arose. I told him that Josefa had left here at eight hours—her normal time—to go to the convento. We looked in her room together. Nothing seems to be missing. No clothes gone. He left, and I sent for you. In the meantime, I have discovered that two thousand reais are missing from the ivory box in my armoire. It doesn't make sense. What will Chamberlain de Faria say?"

"This doesn't look good for us. Let us be careful. I will send word to the chamberlain. Meanwhile, we need to do everything we can to find her. I will go and speak with Pilot's Mate Lopo Meendez myself. He knows the Guineans in that shipload better than anyone. The two of us will go to see Dona de Mendonça together.

#

Lopo and Captain Dias were let into the priory through the door in the back alley. Lopo saw the mother superior leave the priory by the door into the convent courtyard. Following the captain's example, Lopo greeted each person in the small crowd assembled there. After speaking briefly with the chamberlain's man, Lopo was cornered by Inês and Maria. They assailed him in their native language. All others in the room turned to watch Lopo and the two girls. Holding his hands up, in his best Guinean he said, "Calm yourselves. I want you to tell me everything, very slowly."

#

The cart had been motionless for at least half an hour after many hours bumping and jolting along. Josefa had listened but heard little other than the tinkling of chains, the whinnying of a horse and occasional muffled conversations in Portuguese. She smelled fire. A male voice gave orders. "Sit there. Drink this. Eat this." A pair of hands hoisted her, sack cover and all, out of the cart and set her on the ground. A brute of a man, a Portuguese, lowered the cover from off her head but re-tied the opening about her neck. In the sack, her arms and feet remained in iron cuffs. She ached all over. She was still damp from when she pissed herself during the long ride and her stomach growled for something to fill it. She managed to pull her knees to her chest and sit up. Surveying the camp in the dark, she noted seven other Guineans sitting silently in a half circle opposite her on the other side of a small fire. In the flickering light, Josefa saw they were in chains, dusty, and obviously exhausted. Some hung their heads between their knees and others studied her with frightened curiosity. Another Portuguese busied himself near the cart. He spoke to the man guarding her. "Give her water."

Her guard, the brute, stared into her face and whispered. "I will remove the cloth from your mouth. If you scream, if you say anything, I will stuff it in your mouth again. Do you understand?"

Josefa looked around again, searching for options. Finding none, she turned to her guard and nodded.

The man removed the cloth that had kept her silent all day while she suffered in the cart in her sack and under a heavy load of something, blankets or hides she supposed. The man observed her for a moment then fetched a ladle with water and held it to her lips. She choked a few times when he poured the liquid into her mouth too quickly. She drained two ladles but turned her head away when the third was brought.

The man who had been by the cart approached her with some dried fish. "So, you have displeased his majesty the king and now you will be sold to some lucky master many leagues from Lisbon. I will call you Belita. Yes, Belita. Let us hope you maintain your beauty until I can sell you." He handed the fish to the brute. "Keep this one healthy, she's money on the hoof".

The brute broke a small piece from the salty, rock-hard fish and fed her, watching her swallow to judge when to give her another morsel.

While chewing, Josefa took a second look at the other captives, lingering on each face while they returned her stare. The third one, a lean muscular male, held her attention much longer than the first two. One eye was clouded and didn't move with the other eye. *I know this face! How can that be?* She moved her eyes to the fourth captive and the fifth. Then it came to her—the identity of the man with the dead eye. She turned her head back and riveted her eyes upon the face of the third captive. *Yaféu! One of the men who raided my village. One of the men who killed my father. One of the three guards escorting me from my village to the ochre village and on to the great Portuguese house by the sea. He held me down so the drunken man in the ochre village could rape me. He . . .* Josefa looked away to calm herself. She didn't want the gag back in her mouth nor the sack pulled back over her head.

The brute who fed her withdrew his hand. *I must calm myself. Breath slowly. Chew more carefully. Swallow.* Another piece of fish was offered, and she bit into it. She turned again toward the captive named Yaféu. *I swore I would kill you someday. And here you are not ten paces from me.*

#

Even though she had not fallen asleep for many hours, at first light, Josefa opened her eyes. She managed to sit up. The brute was up and stoking the fire. She glanced around until, twisting her neck until it hurt, she saw that the other man was feeding the horse. In the daylight she could see he was dressed rather richly. *He is the head man of this pair.*

Josefa watched the sleeping captives. *They had a long walk yesterday. They will have another today, no doubt.* She saw that the sixth captive stirred and sat up. *Something about her is familiar. Reminds me of my younger sister, Foladé.* The sixth captive yawned and looked straight at Josefa. Josefa couldn't look away, their eyes locked on each other. Josefa imagined her sister in her village, watching the baby, braiding hair, tending the goats. Josefa said, mostly to herself, "Foladé." Her voice brought her back from her daydream and she again focused on the sixth captive in chains opposite her.

The sixth captive dropped her jaw for a moment then spoke. "Mbekah?"

Now it was Josefa's turn. "Foladé?"

Foladé stood up, dragging the captives on either side of her in the chains to half up and struggling for balance. She screamed, "Mbekah".

CHAPTER 36

Sisters

On this, the seventh night since Lisbon, when the sack was dropped from off Josefa's head, she was relieved that her sister Foladé was there, smiling back at her from the other side of the camp fire. Five of the original other seven captives were still in chains; Yaféu was there too. Josefa planned to find Foladé in the future, so she needed to know to whom Foladé was sold or at least the day Foladé left the group. The same for Yaféu. Josefa had unfinished business with the murderer from the ochre village. *A Guinean with a bad eye should not be hard to find.*

Josefa sensed that Yaféu had taken an interest in her as well. He smiled whenever she glanced at him. *He does not remember me. Do the captives talk to each other while they walk? Has Foladé told the others who I am? Surely they are curious about me after that first morning when she and I recognized each other.*

On that first morning when Foladé jumped up upon recognizing Josefa, the brute slapped Foladé so hard that she fell back onto the ground and didn't move for some time. He also bound the cloth strip over Josefa's mouth. Later, he took the gag off long enough to feed her bread—fresh bread. Josefa decided that fresh bread meant they were camped that first night near a village where there was an oven.

It had been difficult for Josefa to be near her sister and not speak with her these past six nights and mornings. At first Josefa wondered why the brute struck Foladé but did not hit her. She decided that the two Portuguese men were keeping her fit and untarnished to get a better price for her. The thought sent shivers through her.

#

That night, the seventh night on the road, Josefa lay awake a long time listening to the others sleeping—breathing, snoring, mumbling, and rattling the chains as they moved. *What does the Creator plan for me? How will I get my freedom? How will I free Foladé? How will I kill Yaféu? What will become of my friends in the convent? What about Lopo? What is Lopo to me? Just a friend?*

After some water and stale bread the next morning, the brute removed Josefa from her rough sack and put her in the chain with the other five slaves. Fortunately, Josefa was right behind Foladé. The man behind Josefa separated her from Yaféu. She was glad to be out of the sack and in the fresh air, notwithstanding that the iron cuff quickly rubbed a raw circle around her right ankle. *Will I be able to choke Yaféu to death while he sleeps? Or perhaps bash his head in with something heavy I can reach while still in the chains? It would have to be while the two Portuguese sleep?*

Interrupting Josefa's vengeful thoughts, Foladé began to sing a song to the spirit of the large baobab tree in their village. Josefa and some of the others sang along. In her mind, Josefa was Mbekah once again, helping their mother with the evening meal. The singing stopped, and they trod along in silence for an hour.

Foladé, in a voice barely more than a whisper, interrupted the silence. "Mbekah. In a moment, quietly tell me if you can hear me"

"I hear you, Foladé. I am happy you are here. I am also sad that you are here. What happened? I must know everything."

"If we speak quietly, with great gaps of silence, the two pale men won't realize we are having a long conversation. We have all day and talking makes the day seem shorter."

Mbekah paused, then whispered. "I know father was killed in the attack when I was taken. What became of our mother, you, and baby brother?"

"There were few of us left after the attack. When the men returned to the ruined village from their hunt, they went looking for you but lost the trail. We survivors were too few to be safe so we became a part of Kpodo's wife's village. Four months ago, the slave raiders returned, killing more and taking a dozen of us this time.

"How is it that the man with the dead eye is with you?"

"He was added to our group of captives when we came to a large village with ochre walls and ochre huts. He is called Yaféu. I like talking with him. He's a good man. We have made a promise to each other that we will marry when that's possible."

Chapter 37

Good News

Lopo and Rodrigo's third stop upon returning to Lisbon was the priory at *Todos os Santos*. The first stop had been at the *Carapau* cantina to see if Manoel had learned anything about Josefa's mysterious disappearance. Manoel had not. The second stop was to speak with Captain Dias at his home. The captain knew nothing new and reported that the chamberlain had also not learned anything about the matter. It had been three months since Josefa vanished. For the past two months, Captain Dias had financed their non-stop search in the villages and estates surrounding Lisbon. They had stopped in at every shop, church, and farm. They had questioned anyone on the road, in the fields, at or on the river. They had found no indication that Josefa passed by or through, alone or with others. Their last hope was that the prioress, Dona Ana de Mendonça, had some news.

At their fourth stop, the two men played quietly with Moisés, who was now walking, while they waited for Sister Consola to fetch Inês and Maria from inside the convent. *Guincho* played with a ball of yarn and the bird *Quinha* spoke every word it knew to get the men's attention.

Dona Ana had apparently heard of their arrival and rushed in through the door from the alley. "What news? Please tell me you've discovered something helpful."

Lopo shook his head and watched the prioress slump into a chair. "It's as if she grew wings and soared away. We were hoping that you had gleaned some clue from your contacts. Capitão Dias said he can no longer fund our efforts. So we both must now return to the sea. I will look for a coaster, a ship that will stop in the ports going north. Rodrigo will go south and then east through the straits to do the same."

Inês and Maria came into the room with Sister Consola. They had heard from her that there was no news. Both of the Guineans had tears on their cheeks but remained silent. Moisés scurried to Maria who picked him up.

Lopo guessed they were all thinking the same thing as he, but no one would say it. *Something bad has happened to Josefa.* They had considered the money missing from the Dias home and, knowing Josefa, had dismissed the idea that she had taken the money and run. They knew others were not so understanding and thought Josefa a thief and runaway.

It was time to change the subject. Lopo took a deep breath. "I think it's time I tell Kpodo about Moisés."

#

When meeting with Manoel at the *Carapau* the previous week, Lopo learned that Gonçalves and his two thugs had gone to sea and wouldn't be around for a few months. Captain Dias had assured the two of them that he, the Captain, was in line for command of a future voyage of discovery and wished to have Lopo and Rodrigo in the company. This would have been a great time to remain in Lisbon for a few months but Lopo was down to his last few reais, and those had been borrowed from Manoel. Lopo did learn that the Galo, the money lender, was looking for him and Lopo knew why. He decided to seek the Galo out before he started hanging around near his family's shop. The meeting with the Galo would not be a good one since Lopo didn't even have money to make an interest payment. But first, he must tell Kpodo about Moisés.

The head baker knew Lopo from his previous visits with the slave Kpodo now known as Bastiao. With Lopo's help, Bastiao had settled down to be one of the bakery's best workers. For this reason, the baker wasn't worried when Lopo asked to see Bastiao. Lopo stood outside of the building to avoid the heat of the ovens within. He watched the slave emerge.

Bastiao squinted in the bright daylight until his eyes adjusted then strode over to Lopo and greeted him in his native Guinean tongue.

Lopo returned the greeting, calling him by his Guinean name, Kpodo, as was Lopo's custom when beginning a conversation. They chatted a moment. Then Lopo switched to Portuguese since Kpodo spoke it better now than Lopo spoke the language of the *Mina* captives. "I have some good news for you, Bastiao."

CHAPTER 38

Belita

Rodrigo stood to embrace Lopo when the latter entered the *Carapau* and came to his table. Manoel left another table and joined them.

Rodrigo waived at the serving menina and pointed to the empty places in front of his two companions. Before she could get to their table, Rodrigo said, "I returned to Lisbon three weeks ago. We sailed as far as Valencia. At each port I sought out the slave merchants and spoke with the other sailors. No one remembers a Portuguese-speaking slave matching Josefa's description."

The menina came to hear their orders. Manoel and Lopo asked for red wine. Lopo waited for her to hustle off. "We stopped in every port going north. We rounded the shoulder and reached La Coruhna in Galicia. I too found out nothing about Josefa."

Manoel belched, wiped his mouth, and leaned in toward the others. "Nor have I heard a single word about the woman. It's very strange. Something like this gets talked about sooner or later. But I have seen Gonçalves and the fat one and the skinny one. They returned from the Low Countries less than a week ago. Gonçalves summoned me day before yesterday to their table at the *Cai taberna*. He had heard we are looking for Josefa and demanded to know what we've learned. He asked about you, Lopo. I told him the truth that I hadn't heard from you in almost three months since you hadn't returned to Lisbon yet. Gonçalves knows about your loan from the Galo and seemed to take pleasure in telling me that the money lender is looking for you."

Rodrigo told them he'd been to the priory at *Todos os Santos* since his return and that they, too, had had no news of Josefa. "Bastiao does come there once a week to play with his son and speak to Inês and Maria in their native tongue."

#

"Tie your dress tight around your thighs, Belita; then put your hands on my shoulders so you don't fall over."

Mbekah did what Tareija told her to do just as the first cart driver began dumping clusters of grapes into the shallow stone pool. More loads of grapes followed, and the two women crushed the purple fruit with their slow dance. Pulp and liquid oozed through her toes and the smell of fresh grapes made her hungry. She plucked a small cluster with one hand and savored the sweet fruit, grape by grape. After a time, they were able to stomp and maintain their balance without holding onto each other. Mbekah did, however, stay near the perimeter of the masonry basin so she could grab the edge when she felt she would otherwise tumble into the juicy mess.

Tareija was not a slave but had befriended Mbekah who she knew as Belita soon after she was bought by the Goterrez family. The Goterrez land was near the castle and village of Ourém. The transaction took place on the afternoon of the ninth day after leaving Lisbon. Her sister Foladé and her betrothed man Yaféu were still in the chain when Mbekah was led away.

Tareija's husband André was a day laborer and came to the farm often. Tareija only came on special occasions when the family needed extra help. The grape harvest and crush had begun and required every available worker.

During the previous six months, Belita worked mostly in and around the big house—in the kitchen, in the garden, in the small animal pens, and helping Senhora Goterrez in a dozen other ways. Since Belita spoke and read Portuguese, which was unheard of for a slave, it wasn't long before she was keeping tallies of the stores in the pantry.

Belita accompanied the family into town about once a week when they attended mass. She sat in the rear of the stone church with the other baptized slaves. She made friends with the few Africans that were in the plaza after mass and asked after her sister and the slave with the bad eye, but she had learned nothing. She had not met a single slave in Ourém who spoke the same or similar language of her forest village.

"Have you had any trouble with the men at the farm? My husband André says the other workers talk about you sometimes."

Belita trod silently while this sunk in. "When the senhora is not around, the senhor and the two sons watch me closely. There is a young priest who comes to the house. He also watches me. I don't like it."

"You're young and beautiful, Belita. It's natural for them to look at you. But it's also not such a good thing. Be careful. Never be alone with any of them. Try to never be far from the senhora." Tareija stopped talking while a cart driver dumped his grapes. He returned to the field and she resumed. "There is an old priest, Padre Mateus. Go into the booth when he is hearing confession. Tell him your worries. He might be able to pressure the men to leave you alone."

CHAPTER 39

The Cure

Chamberlain de Faria pushed away from the table and stood. "A delightful evening, Dona Ana. *Todos os Santos* has done a great job educating the young African girls. His majesty will be especially pleased to hear that Inês and Maria have made such impressive progress. Sad and strange about Josefa disappearing and no clues about what happened."

Ana put her arm in the chamberlain's and escorted him to the priory's door to the back alley. "Why all the mystery about the girls from the *Mina*? Can't you tell me more about what King João has in mind for them?"

"They'll be put into service to the crown. Knowing Portuguese will be a big help to us as will having a favorable opinion of our people."

"And when will this service begin, pray tell."

"Soon, Dona Ana. Soon." With that, the chamberlain stepped out the door and into his waiting coach.

#

"Bom Dia, Belita. The senhor still can't get out of bed for anything other than to relieve himself. He screams with each painful step." Senhora Goterrez sniffed the air. "That smells lovely."

Belita finished slicing the shepherds bread that had just come out of the oven back of the kitchen. She turned to face the senhora. "For how long have his feet hurt now?"

Senhora Goterrez crossed herself. "Seven days today."

"And the Jewish physician from Ourém can do nothing for him?"

"He's been here each day but nothing he does relieves the pain."

Belita reached back into her memory of following her mother into the forest to collect and prepare plants for her role as a healer. She thought about the stories her mother exchanged with other healers. "Senhora, I have heard of this sickness in the villages of the forest where I was born. We have a cure. I've seen the plants and herbs that I need in your country. Give me the morning to find the plant and I'll prepare a poultice for your husband."

#

Belita returned to the kitchen after her morning in the fields searching for the right plant. In her basket she carried a bunch of stems with stiff, blue-gray foliage more like thick pine needles than leaves. She ground malagueta pepper then added the fat needles and mashed the concoction for a few minutes.

Senhora Goterrez heard her and came in to observe the process. "Blue stonecrop. That's what we call this plant. And pepper! I pray this works. Come with me to his bed. I'll let you apply the salve."

Belita spooned a fist-sized portion into a clay bowl and followed her mistress into the master's room. The stench of sweat and chamber pot filled the air.

"Belita has prepared a salve for your feet, o meu coração."

Senhor Goterrez sat up in bed but said nothing.

Belita went to work plastering the mash over Senhor Goterrez' toes. Then she wrapped the area on both feet in long strips of wool. "I'll repeat this tonight and in the morning. It will take one to three days for the pain to go away."

CHAPTER 40

The Letter

Dr. Astruch rushed into the room waving a document. "I came as soon as I read this letter. I'm sure it will lead us to Josefa." He sat at the table and unfolded the paper showing a broken red wax seal. "This letter came to my friend, Samuel Amatu, who as you know is his majesty's physician. The sender is a doctor in Ourém. His majesty's physician maintains contact with most of the Jewish doctors in the realm." Dr. Asturch read so all in the priory could hear.

> "Esteemed <u>Mestre</u> Amatu, physician to His Majesty, the King of Portugal, the two Algarves, and Africa, etc. In keeping with my practice of communicating with you the particulars of my profession here in Ourém, I bring to your attention a singular occurrence, the which took place a fortnight past. To wit: The proprietor of a large estate, <u>Senhor</u> Goterrez, fell ill of what appeared to be gout. The man endured so much pain in his feet that he was forced to retire to his bed, notwithstanding his many duties. I attended him daily and assured him the pain would abate shortly. Seeing the seemingly endless torment of her

husband, the proprietor's wife engaged her scullery servant, a slave from the Guinea Coast, to administer to the wretched man. The slave called Belita went into the countryside and fetched a basket full of the leaves and stems of blue stonecrop with which she concocted a poultice that she applied to the proprietor's ankles and feet morning and night. Within two days, the proprietor was pain free and at his duties again. Needless to say, this man and his wife sing the praises of Belita to all who will listen. I believe this clever Guinean knew, as we know, that the frightful symptoms of the gout often go away on their own in about ten days and that Belita is getting credit for nothing more than employing a placebo. I questioned Belita about her cure. I ascertained that she was learning to be a 'healer' from her mother when she was taken as a slave and brought to Lisbon after being held for some time at the *Mina* Fort of *São Jorge*. Although she has only recently arrived in this place, her knowledge of the Portuguese language is good and she has no problem reading and writing it. Belita seemed guarded about herself so I kept my interview brief but thought it wise to pass on this news to you, esteemed Mestre Amatu. As always, your humble servant, Abraam Govon."

#

Senhora Branca Dias paused her needleworking when her husband rushed into the room. "Excellent tidings, minha querida. The chamberlain has confided in me that they have located Josefa."

Senhora Dias sat thcrc, mouth agape, for a long moment.

"I assure you this is good for us. His majesty and other influential people care very much about Josefa. And the chamberlain knows I've spent a great deal of time and money looking for her."

Senhora Dias composed herself. "I'm so happy," she lied.

"I must find Lopo and Rodrigo and tell them the news. This is confidential, by the way. We don't know yet who was responsible for her disappearance. Or why or how it was done."

#

"Lopo, your Capitão Dias is in the shop asking for you. He wants to speak with you privately." Lopo's brother Pero turned and descended the stairs.

"That's something, when a ship's captain comes for you himself, no?" Lopo's mother continued paring rutabagas for the evening meal. "Go, quick. See what he wants."

CHAPTER 41

A New Gown

Josefa frowned. "Why not the green dress? I love wearing it."

Sister Consola smiled. "It's very elegant but being introduced at court, to the king and queen, is special. A once-in-a-lifetime event. Most debutants never get a chance to return to the castle. This is part of your education. Mandated by his majesty, the king himself, and he has provided money for your gowns for this occasion. Tomorrow, the dressmaker and her seamstresses will come to the convent to measure you and the other girls from the *Mina* and the Congo. You will get to choose the cloth and the dressmaker will propose a becoming style. You, Inês, and Maria will have your fitting here in the priory because Dona Ana wishes to be present. She knows about the royal court and the latest fashions."

"Will you attend also?"

"No, no, no. This fête is not for lowly nuns like me."

"Dona Ana? Will she be there?"

Sister Consola noted a look of concern on Josefa's face. "No. Dona Ana usually doesn't go to affairs when she knows the queen will be present. Remember, Dona Ana had a child with the king. Everyone is content to leave those fish heads buried deep and undisturbed. But don't worry, the chamberlain himself will present you to their majesties. I'm sure that Capitão and Senhora Dias will be there too."

This last tidbit was not welcome news for Josefa. She did not feel comfortable around Capitão and Senhora Dias. She was happy she was not sent back to live with them after her return four months ago from the Goterrez farm.

Sister Consola remembered Josefa's concern. "Oh. I almost forgot about you and the Dias family. Dona Ana will figure out something so you have friends at the presentation. Too bad your gallant young pilot's mate is at sea. Lopo would have made a dashing escort."

Josefa blushed, looked away, and was glad to see *Guincho* scrambling toward her for some attention.

CHAPTER 42

A Future Courtesan

It was a Wednesday evening in June, in the year 1486 by the reckoning of the Christians. The deep blue sky over Lisbon was cloudless with enough wind blowing out to sea to clear the air of the accumulated stench from centuries of catches brought daily to the docks. Not that there hadn't been a catch this day. The fleet of day boats had returned with an ample harvest and there had been the usual scene of fishmongers haggling for the fish and a chaos of seagulls diving and brawling for the heads and entrails tossed back into the river-bay.

For Josefa, the perfume of blooming plants and the songs of birds in the city made her think of her village and of her family there. Her mother. She wished her mother could see her tonight when she would wear her gorgeous yellow silk gown tailored especially for the occasion. Josefa had been in Portugal long enough that she thought like a Christian city dweller as much as like a Guinean girl raised in the forest.

She had also been thinking of young men she met and saw in her day to day movements, especially since she had been back in the safety of the convent. When she was a slave on the road and on the Goterrez estate, she had mostly worried about men. Being a powerless slave with uncertain protections was difficult. Being a female slave was even more precarious. She had remained on her guard every minute during her months away from Lisbon. She heard horrible stories from the other slaves she talked to after Sunday mass in the town. She felt she had been rescued by her Lisbon masters none too soon because the Goterrez men were pushing the limits. They didn't treat her the same as they treated Portuguese women. If it had not been for Senhora Goterrez, she would certainly have had serious attempts on her virtue, as the Christians called it. She recalled how shamefully Kpodo's wife had been used by wicked men in Lisbon and that Kpodo's wife died young at their hands leaving Kpodo's son Moisés motherless before he even knew his mother. She worried about her sister Foladé, not knowing what had become of her. And what about Yaféu with the bad eye? How could her sister be so wrong about someone?

She admired Dona Ana and Sister Consola who were somewhat free of the dominance of men. She understood that aspect of the lure of the convent to Christian women. No, Josefa had not changed her mind about being free again or about returning to her homeland. She would achieve those dreams. But might she also choose the convent or something like it for herself?

On the other hand, she had started to think about *some* men differently. Young, handsome men. Yes, she had come to consider even some of the pale-skinned men of Portugal attractive. That surprised her because so many men had treated her wickedly. In addition to her recent experience in the north, she remembered vividly that men had kidnapped her in front of her own home while murdering her father. The same men killed her cousin Manu and her friend Bejide during the forced march to the ochre village. She would avenge their deaths, she promised herself again. Beastly men in the ochre village abused her and the other captives. Portuguese men chained them in pens in the strong house by the sea. The *Mina*, they called that place. Uncouth men of the caravela's crew were barely restrained from raping her during the sea voyage to Lisbon. She had learned in Ourém that most of the other female slaves had all been violated multiple times during their capture and transport to Portugal. Thanks be to the Creator, to Jesus, to the spirits of the trees and rocks, and to the saints of Jesus she had survived and was still a virgin, as the Christians called that condition.

Still, Josefa longed to gain the attention of a few of the men she saw from time to time. Inês and Maria, even more interested than she was, talked about men all the time. They had nicknames for the attractive single men attending Sunday mass in the convent chapel—muscles, mustache, rosy cheeks, blue eyes, tall one, and so on. But those men only had eyes for the Portuguese girl students who flirted back whenever they got the chance. Inês and Maria had asked her about Lopo and Rodrigo and Manoel. Those three had taken an interest in them and came around when they were not at sea. Josefa was surprised how often her thoughts turned to Lopo. She could see he was smart and kind. And rather handsome even though a part of one ear was missing. Green eyes. She especially liked that unusual trait. But it was his character more than his eyes that attracted her to Lopo.

She calculated that she was eighteen years old using Christian counting. Had she remained in her village, she would be ready to marry so maybe it wasn't so strange that she thought about men. About Lopo.

#

In the fading light of the evening, three carriages caravanned from the convent up to the castle overlooking the city and entered through the main gates while pike men came to attention. Josefa, Inês, and Maria along with the four Congo students in their newly minted gowns swished from their coaches onto the courtyard cobblestones. One by one the girls took the arm of a freshly-scrubbed lieutenant who escorted them into a lobby before a massive set of open doors. The seven young couples stood in line on the left and observed a parade of aristocrats and dignitaries pass them by to be announced into a great hall. After the people of status had all entered and were stationed along the sides of the hall, the debutants filed in and were seated in a single row in the center of the room facing a platform at the far end. Their escorts stood behind them. A herald spoke, and all arose to observe the king and queen enter and take their places on adjacent thrones upon the platform. The king nodded and all who had chairs sat down.

The herald spoke again. "This evening, four daughters from the court of the Congo king and three young women from the *Mina* will be introduced to their majesties. They are students at the Convento de *Todos os Santos.* The Congolese are preparing to be ambassadors for their king while the *Mina* girls are preparing for royal service here as translators and advisors. At the conclusion of the introductions, their majesties admonish all of you to mingle and speak with these exemplary young women. They further request that you invite these students to your soirees and other social events, so they can learn firsthand about our culture and customs. And now, Chamberlain de Faria will make the introductions."

The chamberlain stood and nodded to the first Congolese girl. Her escort stepped forward and brought her to stand in front of the platform. "I am pleased to have your majesties meet Isabell, daughter of the second wife of the Congo King."

With one hand in her lieutenant's and the other hand holding her skirt out, Isabell slowly bowed and curtsied deeply, almost sitting on the floor, then stood. "Your Majesty."

The King studied her. "Welcome to our city and our realm. How do they treat you in the Convent?"

"We are comfortable and well fed."

"What do you study at the moment?"

"Portuguese, Latin, the lives of the saints, history, and astrology."

The king smiled and looked at the chamberlain. Isabell returned to her chair and the second Congolese girl was brought forward. The king interrogated her and then the others in their turn in a similar manner to the first, learning something new with each conversation.

Josefa saw from his demeanor that the king was generally pleased with what he observed and heard. After her introduction, the chamberlain commented, "Josefa is the one who was kidnapped from our streets and sold to work on an estate near Ourém."

The king considered her for longer than usual. "We have followed your odyssey with alarm and great interest. We've heard of your initiative and cleverness. We are pleased you were found and returned us. The convent speaks highly of you."

The queen leaned forward. "My, you are especially lovely, and your gown becomes you perfectly. I commend you on your good Portuguese. I have not heard of your trials until just now. I would like you to attend me soon and tell me more about your 'adventures'."

#

"With your permission, Branca, o meu coração, I will leave you to talk with Senhora d'Allmeyda while I go to greet Josefa and congratulate the chamberlain." Captain Dias wandered off.

Senhora d'Allmeyda fanned herself until the captain was out of ear shot. "I'm told that Josefa da Guiné lived in your home for a time. Their majesties are very taken with her, no? To be invited to attend her majesty is a great honor. Strikingly beautiful. I see that young men are also quite interested. She has surely come a long way since your husband brought her here in irons."

Dona Branca held her fan in front of her mouth and moved her head closer to Senhora d'Allmeyda. "Yes, I saw something of her when she was under my roof. Devious. She has used her beauty and charm to great advantage. I'll wager that more than one man of influence has had her in his bed. I keep an eye on my own husband when she is around."

CHAPTER 43

With the Queen

Queen Leonor moved her white pawn two squares forward. "I'm pleased you play the latest form of chess, Josefa. So much more interesting that the queen gets many powerful moves."

Josefa nodded. It was difficult for her to concentrate on the game and chat with her majesty at the same time. "I learned from Dr. Astruch and we play from time to time." *I wonder if the queen realizes that I play chess with Dr. Astruch in Dona Ana's chambers.* Having moved one of her own pawns, Josefa surveyed the cozy room and the three young women who silently embroidered while they listened to the conversation.

"My ladies in waiting have asked me about the men in your life. Do you have someone special?"

This caught Josefa by surprise. She looked again at the other women in the room. They all looked up from their needle work and blushed when they made eye contact. Josefa blushed. Queen Leonor giggled. Then Josefa and the others giggled.

The ladies returned to their sewing. Josefa focused her eyes on the chessboard but couldn't get her mind off the question. At last, she moved another pawn but kept her head down as if contemplating futurc movcs.

"Well, have you a beau?"

Josefa peered into the Queen's eyes. She stammered. "I, uh. No. I have been invited to some, ah, soirees. I go with the other African girls. I talk with men on these occasions, but . . ."

The Queen smiled. "Sounds pretty tame compared to the gossip about you."

Josefa straightened, opened her mouth, but said nothing. The ladies in waiting gaped open their mouths and glanced at one another. One of them dropped a needle and all of them heard it ping onto the stone floor.

"But. Gossip? I'm practically a nun. What could be so interesting about that?"

"Just as I guessed. Some jealous person started a rumor about you and a sordid love life. Pay no heed. I will squash the innuendos as best I can. Let's put away the game and just talk."

That suited Josefa for she could no longer think about chess strategy. "Obrigada."

"I've loved having you come these past two months. Both his majesty and I are grateful for the herbal tea you made for our son Afonso. Overnight, his stomach was calmed. Afonso also thinks you are wonderful. You are such a treasure! Is there anything I can do for you, besides rumor control?"

Another surprise question for Josefa, this time a pleasant one. "My sister . . ."

The Queen cut her off. "That's right! Your sister was in the group of slaves with which you traveled north during your sequestration. Do you know what has become of her?"

"No, Your Majesty. Foladé was still with the group when I was sold to the Goterrez family, so she must be somewhere north of Ourém. I fear for her."

#

Swallowing the last morsel of breakfast, Lopo descended the stairs, responding to a shout from the shop below. Rodrigo and Manoel stood over the workbench of Lopo's brother Pero, chatting with him as he cut a pattern from a tan scrap of leather. Even though the entire building, indeed the neighborhood, smelled of recently tanned hides, the rich scent was almost overwhelming in this room where hundreds of prepared skins were stored and worked.

Lopo embraced each man in turn. "I was going to look for you this afternoon in the *Carapau*. It appears you've already heard that my ship docked yesterday. You must have something urgent for me."

The two visitors looked at each other, then at Pero. Rodrigo spoke. "Lopo, walk with us."

The three stepped into the street and strolled, catching up on each other's comings and goings of the past six months since they'd last been together in Lisbon.

"Have you seen Josefa lately?"

Rodrigo and Manoel became mute. Lopo worried they were deciding if and how they would relay bad news.

They arrived at a spot with no nearby windows or doors and stopped. Rodrigo and Manoel moved to face Lopo.

Manoel broke the silence. "We've not seen her in months but, we hear things. She goes to the palace. She's favored by their majesties. She also goes to parties in the homes of the wealthy."

Lopo sighed with relief.

Manoel continued. "Forgive me for passing this on to you, but the quiet talk on the street is that she is, uh, has become intimate with one or more men who surround the king."

"Well, Josefa already was friends with Dona Ana's friend, Dr. Astruch. It seems natural she would get to know others."

"Intimate, Lopo. As in sleeping with them!" Manoel looked away as Lopo gasped.

Rodrigo spoke. "We weren't sure we should tell you. We agreed you deserve our candor, even though it might be painful."

Lopo recovered his voice and improvised. "I'm happy she has achieved some stature at court. It's not my business how she behaves. Can we go back now?"

Manoel started again. "That's not all, I'm afraid. The Galo is looking for you. He seemed upset. He said you must speak with Senhor Xemenez at the pawn shop to set up a meeting as soon as you returned."

#

"The evening was rather tedious with the same food and wine and people as at every other soiree this summer. Especially with the court spending the month up river. I'll be happy to see this season done and gone. Don't you agree, minho querido?"

With that question, Captain Bartolomeu Dias returned from his inner thoughts and remembered he was in an open carriage, facing his wife. He hadn't been listening so guessed at the answer. "Quite so. Quite so, Querida Branca."

"What was so important that kept you and the other men in the study for so long?"

"We all wanted to hear the particulars of Capitão Diogo Cão's voyage. Up to now, I've only heard scraps."

"State secrets, I suppose. Surely, you can tell me something about it."

Captain Dias mused a moment. "It's no secret that Cão did not find Prester John. Nor did he discover the passage into the Indian Ocean. That's the most important thing to me. To us, that is. I believe I am next in line to lead a voyage to find the bottom of Africa." They rode a moment in silence. "I shall know soon. We have been invited to join the court in Setubal next week for the boar hunt and running of the bulls."

CHAPTER 44

Lancing the Beast

Athin figure stepped out of the shadow of the *Carapau*'s side wall and into the moonlight. Lopo recognized the Galo and joined him as he backed into the shadow again.

The Galo nodded toward the street in front of the cantina. "Who are the two men who came with you? You were supposed to come alone."

"Friends. They know about the loan and about you. I was robbed near here once, so I don't walk alone any more when I have more coin than I need for a drink. I can pay the usury and a bit more tonight."

The Galo set his jaw and squinted. "Did not Senhor Xemenez tell you that another quarter of the principal is now due? You're already behind on our agreement? I think it's time I visit with your father."

"I have enough for another eighth. Talking with my father will complicate things. I'm afraid he'll go to the authorities. Neither of us wants that, right? Senhor Xemenez knows of my family and that I will pay, eventually."

"A sad story, I'm sure. But I have my own sad story. The man I sold thc loan to dcmands his money."

"The man you sold my loan to? That wasn't part of the arrangement! Does he know who I am?

"His name is not important. Passing on the risk of such a loan is customary. What's important is that he requires his money now and you must pay. Our deal was no authorities. You'll regret it if you try to cheat me by bringing in the law."

"Give me a fortnight. I'll contact Xemenez when I have the money."

#

With the cool Autumn breeze at their backs, the hunters rode up the gentle slope through the cork trees toward the brush-covered summit. It was the king's turn to chase so Captain Dias and Chamberlain de Farias rode two-score paces behind their monarch. A half-dozen armed footmen waited to beat the bushes for boar when he got into position and readied his lance. The chamberlain broke the silence. "So, how did you find the bull run yesterday, Capitão Dias?"

"Ferocious bulls. Impressive lance work. And no serious injuries. Surely, they put only the best riders in when his majesty is in attendance. I see why many desire to be at court whenever they can. But for me, I'd rather be at sea, serving the kingdom." Captain Dias hoped the hint wasn't too brash.

The king reached the edge of the cork tree grove and he and horse disappeared into the tall brush.

"Well said, Capitão. In fact, after dinner this evening, in chambers, his majesty will appoint you to the next voyage to find the route to the *Indias*. Capitão Cão has convinced us that the next voyage will be the one to succeed. We have much to discuss. All of this is confidential, as you well know."

"Of course. I am honored to do as his majesty wishes."

Shouts filled the air and the whole hill turned into unseen, raucous commotion. A squeal pierced the air and a voice from the thicket proclaimed, "Huzzah. A fine boar! Well speared, Your Majesty."

Captain Dias and the chamberlain trotted toward the voices to see the beast that the king had slain.

Chapter 45

Staging

"Why do you not lean more heavily on the Lombard to collect the loan from Lopo?"

Gonçalves sipped from his tumbler of wine while he considered Belchior's question. "I enjoy keeping Lopo off balance. Unsettled. The Galo is the best way to do that for now. When the right chance comes, I, myself will deal with Lopo. No more bungled attempts." Gonçalves also enjoyed keeping his two lackeys off guard—one of the botched tries on Lopo's life was theirs, as they all knew. "It's time we had another chat with Lopo's 'friend' Manoel."

Belchior and Nunno stood to leave. Nunno paused. "We always know where to find Manoel. If he's alone, we'll be back with him soon."

"On second thought, first go and check our sources at *Todos os Santos* and at court. See if there's any news about what the king has in mind for Josefa and her two companions. It's curious how they've been lifted from common slaves to court favorites." Gonçalves' eyes glazed over as he stared across the room into the dim, quiet pub. He mused, "I will have another go at Josefa, now that she's the talk of the town."

#

King João and Chamberlain de Faria lounged on a pile of Moorish rugs and pillows aft of the royal barge as it drifted downriver on the sunny autumn day. They had rehearsed the month's activities in Setubal—the hunt, the entertainment, the business of the realm transacted throughout each event and in chambers at night. They had finished lunch but had not yet dozed off into afternoon sesta. Servants served a meal to the rowers and other crew in the bow so king and chamberlain were quite alone.

The chamberlain took this opportunity to confide in the king. "Most everything has been put in motion for our project. Capitão Dias has his mandate and ten months to get his fleet together to venture south again. Our Congolese ambassadors have been educated and prepared to return to their homeland."

"But what, Chamberlain? I sense there is something troubling you. What is not right yet?"

"The girls from the *Mina*. Will they be amenable to do their part? How do we present it to them? They and others are assuming the girl's future will be akin to that of the Congolese girls. Who can blame them? To maintain secrecy, we've used only vague mentions of their role."

The king nodded.

The chamberlain continued. "I fear I've done my job too well. Instead of becoming dispensable servants to Your Majesty, these girls have become the darlings of Lisbon society. Which in turn has increased people's interest in their future."

The king sighed. "I too am worried about how to stage their involvement. Everyone must see them as willing participants. Otherwise, Leonor, Dona Ana, indeed, the whole court will be outraged."

CHAPTER 46

Going Back: The Gambit

Josefa, Inês, and Maria sat quietly in a room in the castle on the hill. They wore the simple uniform of the students at *Todos os Santos* similar with the habit worn by the novitiates. An area rug in cream and hues of blue along with tapestries on three walls were an attempt to soften the stone floor and walls. Several tall slits in the remaining wall allowed the morning sun to illuminate the chamber.

Dona Ana, in the full regalia of a prioress, paced back and forth. "The chamberlain said his majesty wishes to speak with you today about your future service to the kingdom. I suppose I'm here as your guardian and to help convince you that your duties and station in life here will be an acceptable one. Happy about what you hear today, or sad, I want you to not show much emotion. I can advise you later about what is being asked of you. Trust me, even though you are officially slaves, we can improve the offer with some, let us say, 'appropriate negotiation'. João, I mean his majesty can be generous but we dare not push him too far."

The three young women listened in silence. Their four years in Lisbon had all been designed for whatever the king had in mind for them. This was the moment they would learn the fate they had wondered about all that time. They were well-aware that the manner in which they had been treated and the training they had received were not at all typical for captives brought back from the Guinea coast. They had spent many evenings discussing their situation, often in the company of Dona Ana and Sister Consola. They had been perplexed, often surprised, sometimes grateful, and almost constantly fearful at one level or another. They felt guilty when they saw other Guineans in their various forms of involuntary servitude. They had seen how cruel some Christians could be to people of their race. They had seen how kind others were to them. And everything in between.

A door opened and Chamberlain de Faria entered. "His majesty the king will see you now."

They followed him, single file, Josefa first and Dona Ana last, and were seated at one end of an oak table as long as the room they had just left. King João sat at the opposite end, eyes on the ceiling, dictating to a man who wrote furiously and never looked up. The king stopped, looked across the table and discovered that he had four new subjects in the hall in addition to his chamberlain.

The king promptly rose and came around the table, lifted Dona Ana's hand to his lips and blew softly on the back. "Lovely, as ever, my lady. Thank you for meeting with us today." He took each young woman's hand in turn, placing it in his right hand and covering it with his left. He greeted each by her Christian name. He cleared his throat, causing his scribe to look up from his page seeing that the scene had changed. The scribe put his papers aside, placed a new one in front of him, dipped his quill in his ink pot, and held it in readiness. The king returned to his chair.

At the king's nod, de Faria sat down midway between the two parties. "Your Majesty, we have invited Prioress de Mendonça, and her students Josefa, Inês, and Maria here today to learn about the important mission you have for them. The mission for her students, that is."

Josefa sat up straighter at the mention of 'mission', as did the others.

The king took over. "We have chosen you, from the very day you arrived at the *Mina*, to assist us with a quest of supreme importance to Portugal. We have monitored your progress while you have been in our city and are satisfied that you are ready. We will grant you your freedom and return you to Africa on condition that you serve as embaixadoras and translators between your people and my kingdom. Also, you will help us find the Christian Kingdom of Prester John."

#

Lopo arrived before the others at Guinea House, stepped to the chief factor's open door, and rapped on the jam. "Bom dia, Chief Factor. I have come early for our meeting. I will be next door, in the royal bakery. Will you please send a man to fetch me when the others are ready to meet?"

"Of course, sim."

Lopo made his way through the sacks of grain to the ovens where he spied the head baker. "Bom dia, Senhor Estevez. Tudo bem?"

The baker recognized Lopo from his many visits there in the past four years. "Tudo bem, sim. Bastiao is in the back, tallying the barrels of ships biscuit."

Lopo wandered into the back until he saw the slave. Lopo waited to address him until after he finished counting a stack of barrels and paused to mark his tablet. "Ola, Bastiao. Como estás hoje?"

Bastiao embraced Lopo. "Bem. E você?

Lopo preferred his friends speak to him with the familiar 'tu' but he knew life as a slave had conditioned Bastiao to speak to those above him using the formal 'você'. "I dropped by to say Ola and to learn how things are going with your son Moisés."

"Wonderful. Three years old and he speaks more like an adult than an infant—in two languages! That's what happens when you live in a priory with educated ladies, aristocratic visitors, a talking bird, and a monkey. I see Moisés every Sunday. But Lopo, I haven't seen you there in many months."

"Ay, sim. I have been busy. Give my regards to them from me, por favor."

"They, especially Josefa, ask about you. They are surprised you no longer visit."

A loud voice filled the air. "Senhor Meendez, the Chief Factor says the meeting is about to start."

Lopo welcomed the interruption. He did not know what to say when asked why he no longer went to the convent. His sister-in-law's cousin Margaida had pressed him on the point but he could not bring himself to say he didn't go there because of what he had heard from Manoel—that Josefa was bestowing her 'favors' on influential men in the city.

#

Lopo entered the office where the chief factor, Captain Dias, and his friends Rodrigo, and Manoel were already seated.

After adequate time to exchange greetings and pleasantries, the captain changed his voice to a formal tone and spoke. "What I am about to tell you is a state secret. As you know, revealing such confidential information is high treason for which the penalty is death."

At that statement, the atmosphere in the room grew serious.

"His majesty has commissioned me, as his squire and capitão, to lead the next voyage of discovery. We will sail to the *Mina* making the usual stops on the way. We'll sail on to the village of the Congo king, and then south to where Capitão Diogo Cão placed his last stone marker. From there we will continue until we find the passage into the Indian ocean-sea." He paused for effect.

Lopo and his two friends looked at each other with wide eyes but remained mute. Lopo could see that, unlike he and his friends, the chief factor was not at all surprised.

"We will try something new on this voyage. We will sail in two caravelas and one large não in which we will carry stores for our return trip to Portugal. We will anchor the não in a safe harbor on the Atlantic coast so we can retrieve it on our way home." Again, the captain paused to let this sink in. "His majesty has authorized me to advance you, Lopo, to the position of piloto; you, Rodrigo to pilot's mate; and you, Manoel to gunnery mate but you will also remain cargo master. Congratulations to all of you."

Lopo was elated. Pilot! He had made it to the next rung on the ladder. He saw that Rodrigo and Manoel were equally excited about their promotions.

"My brother Pero Dias will command on the não with you, Lopo, as his piloto. Rodrigo will be your pilot's mate. Manoel will be in charge of the cannon as well as the extensive supplies with an assistant for each office, of course. We sail the first of August, in four months. There is much to do. We will go for a drink today at the *Carapau* and announce your good news so you can start tomorrow. The sailing will be announced as a cargo run to our stations along the coast but we will take care to engage crew members we believe can handle the longer voyage. Report here first thing in the morning to sign contracts prepared by the chief factor's office. He will go over details with you including recommendations for our voyage from Capitão Cão."

Captain Dias stood up and the rest did the same. They noisily patted each other on the back and shook each other's hands until all felicitations had been extended and received.

Lopo took advantage of the lull to speak. "One question please, Capitão. Who will be the officers on the two caravelas?"

"I will be in command on the *São Cristóvão* with other officers to be named. Don João Infante will command on the *São*

Pantaleão with Senhor Brás Gonçalves as pilot. You've all sailed with Piloto Gonçalves before, so we should all get along very well."

CHAPTER 47

A Surprise

The afternoon meal in the convent was over. As was their custom, Josefa, Inês, and Maria retired to the priory for a few hours. Today made two days since their audience with the king, when they had learned of his charge that they would return to their homeland as ambassadors to the court of Prester John. They would have to locate his kingdom first though. Josefa was relieved they could talk to Dona Ana about the directive before formally responding. Moisés slept in another room, *Quinha* strutted in its cage, and the monkey *Guincho* played at their feet. Sister Consola and Dona Ana sat across from them.

Josefa asked what she was sure all three of them were thinking. "His majesty gave us eight days to reply to his request. Does this mean that we may refuse?"

Dona Ana considered her answer. "I suppose you may refuse. That is not a good option, though. No, refusing the king is a very bad option for you. It's better to accept with an appeal that certain conditions be met by the crown. You have become rather dear to certain influential people. Her majesty to name one. Dr. Astruch to name another. And his majesty knows I am your greatest champion. I am sure his majesty wants our support in anything he requires of you."

Again, Josefa was the voice for all three. "We have spoken about nothing else these past two days. We wish very much to return to our homes. But we know nothing of this Prester John. We are unsettled about the whole adventure."

"As advisor to the king, Dr. Astruch knows much about Prester John and why it's so important for Portugal to find him and make him our ally. I will invite the good doctor to meet with us as soon as he is available. He likely knows of your mission already, so he can guide us. Bargaining with his majesty is a delicate dance and we must know as much as possible before we take the first steps."

Guincho stood and gamboled to the priory's outside door. Sister Consola chased after. They heard an urgent rapping on wood before they even got there. Sister Consola opened a small window in the door, peered through, and hurriedly unlatched and threw the door open. The queen entered. Astonished, all jumped to their feet and knelt.

Josefa immediately knew that something supremely important was happening or else the queen would never venture into the domain of her husband's former lover, Dona Ana.

The queen acknowledged each of the five women and even shook hands with *Guincho* whom she acted delighted to meet.

Quinha squawked. "Pretty lady. Pretty lady."

Moisés, rubbing sleep from his eyes, wandered in and got a hug from the royal visitor.

The queen surveyed the cage and the room with its artistic and exotic furnishings. "Dona Ana, forgive my unannounced intrusion. I have heard of your interesting apartments, your menagerie, and that you frequently entertain our dear girls from the *Mina*. What I have for them could not wait."

Dona Ana bowed her head to the queen. "You are most welcome, your majesty."

The queen turned to Josefa. "I have brought you a gift. Rather than tell you, I will show you." The queen turned to the footman that had followed her into the room. "Bring them in."

Foladé stepped tentatively through the doorway and looked about. Josefa focused on her and in an instant screamed. "Foladé."

Josefa and her sister rushed into each other's arms, collapsing onto the floor, laughing, crying, kissing.

In a few moments, Josefa looked up at the group that surrounded them. She noted that another guest had joined the celebration. At first, she couldn't believe what she saw, then she blurted out in horror, "Yaféu?"

CHAPTER 48

No Guards Today

Josefa climbed the street to the castle as soon as she had finished breakfast. Prioress Dona Ana had summoned her from the convent to get her out of lessons and from under the noses of the mother superior and her troublesome assistant, Sister Giomar. Dona Ana had sent Josefa on an 'errand' which gave her the day off to be with Foladé. Foladé and her husband Yaféu had started their lives in service to the queen who had told Josefa she could come and spend time with Foladé. Josefa was pleased to hear that Yaféu would be busy learning his new responsibilities in the kitchen, so she and her sister could be alone together.

Josefa was wide awake even though she had not slept the past two nights. She was no longer sure about her vow to kill Yaféu. Inês and Maria had recognized Yaféu as soon as he showed up in the priory the other night. Inês and Maria were speechless the rest of the evening until the queen took the two lovers away, whereupon, they could not stop talking. Yes, Josefa remembered Yaféu. Yes, she remembered that the boy with the bad eye was one of the slavers who killed her father during the raid on their village. Yes, she remembered they killed her cousin Manu and their friend Bejide during their forced journey to the sea. Inês and Maria wanted to know what Josefa would do about it. Josefa had to confess that she did not know.

As she neared the castle walls, Josefa gained a spectacular view of the city and harbor below. Birds sang. Grass and scattered yellow sea daisies grew on the slope below the fortifications. In the bright morning sunlight, it felt incongruous to Josefa to think about murdering someone. At the same time, it felt loco not to exact revenge on this man who had brought so much evil into her life.

Foladé was sitting by the towering wooden doors as Josefa approached. Josefa hadn't thought about it on her previous visits to the castle, but today it reminded her of the time she spent chained to a stone wall in a barred cell in the *Mina* slave fort. The ordeal had been physically difficult and often painful, but the cruelest part had been the uncertainty—not knowing what would come next, not knowing what her fate would be. Foladé must have gone through the same horrendous experience.

Foladé rushed out to greet her. "I'm joyful to see you, Sister. These past two days have passed slowly. Thanks to the spirits, we have the day to talk. Not like when we were on the road in shackles worrying about our guards. Just you and I today. No chains, no guards. Oh, but her majesty wants you, us, to drop in first thing to visit a moment."

"Fine, but I have something to say to you first."

That grabbed Foladé's full attention.

"The night before the slave raiders came and took me away, I said some bad things to you and Mother. It has bothered me these three years we have been apart. I am sorry. Will you forgive me?"

"Yes, I forgive you for whatever you said. But truthfully, I don't remember it. I doubt Mother remembers. From that time, I only remember the horror of Father's death and your capture."

#

Gonçalves slammed his palm on the table. Belchior and Nunno jumped a few inches up from their stools. All conversation in the pub ceased momentarily as heads turned to look in their direction. The Galo, who sat across from Gonçalves, remained unfazed. "That's the last of it. Lopo paid the last half of the loan last night, plus the interest."

Gonçalves growled. "Where did that meddler get the money? He hasn't been to sea in months."

"I believe our business is now concluded. Let me know if you'd like to buy another credit like this one." The Galo stood, showed his backside, and left.

"Demônios! How was this possible?"

Belchior leaned in. "We know that Lopo will be the piloto of the supply ship for Dias' trip down the African coast. Perhaps Lopo got an advance on his wages."

"Sim. Of course. We shall leave Lopo alone for the time being. The voyage will offer many opportunities. Everyone knows seafaring exploration is a dangerous business. Accidents are bound to occur, não é verdade?" Gonçalves lifted his tumbler and savored the thought.

CHAPTER 49

The Amazing Kingdom of Prester John

Sister Consola opened the door and stood aside to let their invited guest enter. "Bemvindo, Dr. Astruch. Thank you for coming here this afternoon. It would have been careless of us to come to you and risk being seen in the judiaria." She followed him into the parlor.

"Knowing the mother superior, is it not also bad for you if I, a Jew, am seen coming to the priory?"

"Dona Ana can defend us if needs be. Just the same, we don't want to flaunt your presence here either, so we don't mention your visits. Speaking of Dona Ana, she regrets she cannot join us. If you don't mind, I would like to sit in on your conversations with the young women today."

In the parlor, pleasantries were exchanged among the group which included three-year old Moisés, the parrot, and the monkey. They all sat and Moisés climbed onto Maria's lap.

"Yes, I have been informed of his majesty's orders for you three. In fact, he has blessed my visit here today that I may tell you about Prester John." Dr. Astruch removed some papers from his leather portfolio. "In Latin, we call him Presbyter Johannes. Reportedly, he is Christian. All Europe has been aware of this saintly king for centuries, now. The few men who travelled there and returned—it's been at least two hundred years—gave such vague accounts that we don't know its location except that it is somewhere south and east of the Sahara."

Josefa spoke up. "In Africa? He would still be alive after all this time?"

"Certainly, for there is a spring there whose waters, when drunk, renews a man to his youthful prime. No doubt it works for women too. It is said that there are beasts there that have never been seen elsewhere—fantastic beasts that are perfectly tame to the people of John's realm. His majesty desires to ally himself with John for various reasons. He has a mighty army which could help us against the Turks and their Arab dominions. His kingdom is wealthy with cities of gold, so he would be an excellent trading partner and provide a stopping place on our way to and from the *Indias*."

Josefa took advantage of the pause in Dr. Astruch's tale. "How do we know so much about Prester John when no one has seen him for so long?"

"He has corresponded with past popes and other rulers and his letters are widely circulated. I, myself, have read one of the letters in the Hebrew language."

"You believe this? That Prester John's kingdom is really about to be found?"

"His majesty, the king believes it and it has been an important motive for his explorations down the coast of Africa. Our adventurers continually ask African peoples for news of Prester John. Some have told us of a great spiritual leader they call Ogané. He is something like a pope to them. He reportedly dwells twenty moons distance from some of the inland tribes. Ogané sends a helmet and scepter to recognize and confirm new kings in Africa. Ogané sits behind a screen; nothing but his feet are seen. But this next voyage will be less about Prester John and more about finding the passage to the *Indias*. Still, your efforts will be important. And, there will be others with you—with your same mission—when you sail in August.

Inês asked, "How will we do this? Look for Prester John?"

"I don't know. Surely someone will instruct you before the time comes."

Josefa sensed that it was time to move the conversation along. "Dr. Astruch, would you tell us again the stories from your holy book of the boy sold by his brothers into slavery? And about the prophet Moisés?

Chapter 50

The Counter Offer

Prioress Dona Ana de Mendonça, Josefa, Inês, and Maria followed Chamberlain de Faria into the room with the long oak table to find the king and his scribe already seated. When the women sat down, the king came around the table to greet each of them and then returned to his large seat. It had been less than two weeks since they were last in this room and heard the king's plans for them.

Dona Ana had told the young women that such cordial treatment from the king was unusual and showed he was very interested in them and their mission. She had tutored them on how to tactfully get some concessions from him while accepting his charge.

De Faria began. "You have had almost two weeks to consider his majesty's request that you return to Africa and be embaixadoras to the court of Prester John on behalf of the Kingdom of Portugal. We hear that you have been instructed by Dr. Astruch regarding Prester John and have counseled with others, even with her majesty. Do you have an answer for us?"

Josefa breathed deeply and exhaled. "I have been chosen to speak for the three of us. Before making our decision, we have a few questions. You will be providing for our expenses, but you have not mentioned our remuneration."

The king let his chamberlain speak to this point. "Your monthly stipend will be the same as all of our neophyte emissaries."

Inês and Maria nodded their approval to Josefa who continued. "We would need gifts for our families to compensate for the years we have not been in our village to help with the work. In addition to the clothing needed for our mission, we think an appropriate recompense would be two iron pots, two axes, and two knives for each of our families. Also, for each of us four goats, two suits of clothing, and one hundred cowry shells."

Josefa paused to gauge the mood in the room. Dona Ana appeared thoughtful and smiled slightly. The chamberlain and the king did not act surprised or bothered by her requests, so she resumed. "Like Moisés in the Bible, I say 'Let my people go!' In order to return with dignity and so that our people will know we are genuinely happy with our Christian friends, we must bring back with us the others from our village who were also stolen away and carried to this place."

Josefa looked around the room. Dona Ana's mouth was open in shock. De Faria glanced worriedly at the king. The king stared wide-eyed at Josefa. He was not pleased. The scribe was shaking his head.

"Each of these others that return with us must also be compensated in the same way I have detailed for the three of us."

The king stood. "Enough. You demand this of me, your sovereign? And how many of your village have been brought here?"

Later, with Dona Ana's help, Josefa would realize the king was not asking her a question but mocking her request although it sounded to her like a question. Which is why she answered. "My sister, her husband, Bastiao in the ships bread bakery, Bastiao's son Moisés, and about a dozen more. You will need to find out where they are now employed and fetch them here."

Later, Dona Ana explained that the king said no more at this point because he was both too amazed and too livid to speak.

Chamberlain de Faria jumped up and huddled with the king and succeeded in calming him. Then the chamberlain turned to the four women. "Please return to the waiting chamber. We will discuss your petition."

PART III

Seeking Prester John

CHAPTER 51

Sailing South

Once again Mbekah feared for her person. She and the other Guineans returning to the *Mina* with her had been put on the caravela *São Pantaleão* with Bras Gonçalves as pilot. This time Lopo Meendez was not the pilot's mate so she knew she had to avoid any occasion when the evil Gonçalves would have the opportunity to assault her. The ship's master, Don João Infante, seemed to be in tune with his majesty on the treatment of her group which was some comfort, but she remembered that Gonçalves was not impressed with such sentiment on her first voyage with him as pilot.

Mbekah had heard Lopo was back in Lisbon long before her departure on this mission and wondered why he had not come to see her. She missed him on this trip and not just because he always had protected her from Gonçalves and his two vile companions, Nunno and Belchior. Lopo was kind, brave, and handsome. She was nineteen years old—four years older than when she was kidnapped from her village in the forest. A lot had happened in those years. She wondered if she could be happy marrying a man from one of the villages in the forest. *Am I too old to find a suitable mate who has never been married? Most likely. Would I allow someone else to choose a man for me in my father's absence? No.*

And that could be a problem. My uncle and my mother would want me to wed a rich old widower or become the second wife to such a man. No, that isn't for me. I will be an oddity in the forest. A rich, single woman. An aunt but never a mother. She admired the prioress Dona Ana, but she wasn't sure she wanted to end up alone like her. Maybe there would be a suitable husband in Prester John's court if they ever found that kingdom. For the time being, when she thought of love and marriage, Lopo was the man who came to mind. She lamented that she would never see him again.

The fleet of two caravelas and one larger ship called a não had been at sea for four weeks and Mbekah understood that they would be stopping in the port of Funchal on the island of Madeira. In fact, the lookouts expected to see the island of Porto Santo any time. From that point, the island of Madeira was only a few hours sailing distance.

Even though Kpodo was the son of the headman in Mbekah's village and thus, expected to be the headman when they returned, Mbekah was the one her group looked to for leadership. Mbekah and her group of liberated slaves had started using their childhood names instead of the Christian names imposed on them in Lisbon and spoke to each other in their native tongue unless speaking with one of the crew. The most important difference on this trip was that they were not in chains. Also, they did not travel naked or nearly naked. They wore sensible clothing supplied by the king. Moreover, chests of formal clothing accompanied the ambassadors for when they arrived back in their homeland. The four Congolese women that had studied with them in the convent were on the caravela *São Cristóvão* with Captain Dias as master. Over the years, Mbekah and her two fellow villagers had become good friends with the Congolese girls in the convent. Mbekah had taken pains to learn some of their language which she thought might be useful someday.

Mbekah and her group slept and kept to themselves under a canvas awning the crew had rigged for them on the deck behind the forward of two masts. Mbekah had met Don João, the ship's master, a few times previously at socials in Lisbon. His surname, Infante, meant prince but he was not a possible successor to the king nor even a member of the royal family. Many of the Portuguese customs were not logical, she thought. After seeing how the Portuguese men looked at her and the other Guinean women, she made sure that Gonçalves and the other crew members saw that she and Don João were on a first-name basis.

Like Mbekah, Ifé and Olubayo spoke Portuguese and had learned to read and write in the *Todos os Santos* convent. However, few of the others in her party spoke Portuguese to any extent. Her sister Foladé and Yaféu had learned only a little in their short time in Portugal but Mbekah was attempting to teach more including reading and writing. All in all, Mbekah felt the weight of responsibility to get her company back to their village without further abuse by these men who were accustomed to taking liberties with Guineans.

Mbekah had struggled with the idea that her sister Foladé was married to Yaféu, the man who had killed their cousin Manu. Yaféu had been among the men who had done so much to destroy the happiness of many lives including Foladé's. Without telling her about Yaféu's atrocities, Mbekah had quizzed her sister back in Lisbon to see if she knew any of this about her new husband. Foladé was not aware of any of this. Mbekah reasoned that if their cousin Manu had been raised in the ochre village, he too would have become a vicious slave raider to satisfy his tribe's desire for Portuguese weapons and other trade goods. Yaféu apparently did not recognize Mbekah or the others in that band of young captives he had roughly guarded to the *Mina* four years ago. Mbekah had not revealed herself to him as his former captive. She had lost much sleep agonizing over what to do about Yaféu. At last, she had accepted the Christian concept of forgiveness as opposed to vengeance and she was relieved to feel a great liberation and peace. Now that he had been a victim of the nasty business himself, Mbekah hoped Yaféu had become in fact, the person Foladé believed him to be.

Mbekah had explained her change of heart to Ifé, Olubayo, Kpodo, and Gyasi and made them promise to not say anything about Yaféu's past. They reluctantly agreed although the two men said they would keep their eye on Yaféu to see if he had indeed changed his ways. After a month together in close quarters on the ship, Mbekah sensed those four had warmed up to Yaféu and that there would likely be no problems.

Moisés wanted to run about so all the adult Guineans had to remain alert to keep him out from underfoot of the crew and from becoming shark bait over the side. Olubayo had taken a keen interest in the child who saw her as his mother. Kpodo had noted this from the time he started visiting Moisés in the priory of the convent. Mbekah could see Kpodo and Olubayo getting together when they were again in their forest. Olubayo had been a slave in their village and again in Lisbon so this would be a happy situation for her. But what of their ambassadorial mission? Were the three of them really going to traipse about looking for this impossibly perfect king and his magical Christian realm? *I will wait and see how things turn out before I decide.*

"Land." One of the Portuguese sailors pointed to a faint shadow almost directly ahead of the ship. Everyone on deck who was not asleep paused to study the horizon in that direction.

#

Pilot Lopo Meendez was the first on the <u>não</u> to see the speck on the horizon that would soon prove to be the island of Porto Santo, the smaller neighbor to the island of Madeira, their destination. He strolled back to confer with his two helmsmen. They were following the two <u>caravelas</u> which made navigation rather simple. The pilots on both of those ships had been instructed to sail slow enough to keep the não in sight at all times. This first leg of their journey to the Gold Coast of Africa, where the *Mina* castle stood, had been routine. And so, Lopo had lots of time to think. He thought about the challenges the long voyage of exploration held for him. One aspect he did not relish was working with Pilot Bras Gonçalves, especially when the não would be anchored, left behind, and he and his crew would be divided and moved onto the two caravelas. He considered ways to diplomatically avoid being placed on the *São Pantaleão* with Gonçalves as pilot.

He pondered his mother's efforts to get him married. Now that Mbekah was lost to him as the courtesan Josefa in Lisbon's aristocratic circles, he had taken more interest in his mother's matchmaking, albeit without much enthusiasm. The timing of this long voyage came at the right time. He hoped he would have plenty of time to get Mbekah out of his head. "Why was she in my head, anyway?" he wondered. He had not courted her. They had never come to any understanding. He had not even expressed his love for her. Yes, he now realized that he loved her. Too late. She had apparently begun to conquer men of a higher social status than him. He knew that marrying a Guinean would have been out of the norm for him, if it was even possible. But to marry one that had become infamous for her flexible morals was not even to be contemplated. Nevertheless, he had contemplated marriage with Mbekah and now struggled to rid his mind of such thoughts.

Happily, they would not be transporting slaves on the return to Lisbon. He was aware that the Congolese princesses, former students in the convent with Mbekah, were on one of the caravelas. On a few occasions he had seen negroes on both caravelas when they were not too distant. He reasoned they must have been brought aboard at the last moment in the darkness just before they sailed from Lisbon. There was more going on than just the Congolese being returned to their country. He would learn more about that when they re-victualed in Funchal on Madeira in a few hours.

CHAPTER 52

A Surprise Meeting

Remembering the unusual robbery attempt in London and the robbery (and almost deadly assault) the night he went to purchase Kpodo's wife's freedom, Lopo never went ashore alone at night during their week in Funchal. During the day, he kept to streets and alleys where shops were open and people were out and about.

On their last evening in port, Lopo and Rodrigo dressed in their finest and hiked up the hill to the governor's mansion. They and the other officers in their fleet were the guests of honor of the governor and the island's high society. Once they were announced, they entered an enclosed courtyard where the men from the other ships mingled with the local ladies and gentlemen sipping wine or fruit juices.

At various intervals, an attendant called out the names of guests who were poised to join the gathering.

Lopo was pleased that some of the leading couples had brought their single daughters to the fête. "Maybe there is life after love lost," he muttered.

Rodrigo stopped and turned to Lopo. "Love lost?"

Lopo regretted his utterance immediately. "Nothing, my friend. Just an expression." It was a feeble response and he knew Rodrigo would grill him later. "Let us drift toward the grey beard and lady conversing with Capitão Dias. The senhorita at their side looks like she could use some younger company."

The attendant spoke above the din. "Isabell do Congo, Embaixadora." The crowd hushed and swiveled to inspect the unusual new arrival, a black senhorita attired in European courtly clothes. "Catelina do Congo, Embaixadora. Sancha do Congo, Embaixadora. Lionor do *Congo*, Embaixadora."

The four young Congolese split the onlookers as they entered. Captain Dias rushed forward to present them to the governor and his wife. Conversation resumed and Lopo turned to continue small talk with the young women and her parents.

"Amrrique da *Guiné*, Embaixador."

Lopo spun to take in with his eyes what his ears could not believe.

"Josefa da *Guiné*, Embaixadora." There stood Mbekah and Gyasi next to the attendant, shadowed by Ifé and Olubayo—all four exquisitely dressed. "Inês da Guiné, Embaixadora. Maria da Guiné, Embaixadora."

#

Shortly after their arrival, the company was called into a great hall to dine at three long tables set in the manner Mbekah had seen in the homes of the aristocracy, high government functionaries, generals, admirals, and rich merchants. Black servants trooped in and out with platters of food and carafes of wine for each of several courses. Those within earshot of Mbekah seemed to study her every move and several commented on her educated Portuguese. She kept explanations regarding her commission vague as she had been sworn to secrecy about their ambassadorial role in returning to Africa.

After the tables were cleared except for the goblets of Port, the governor rose to address his guests. This gave Mbekah an opportunity to survey the room and observe the invitees seated at other tables. She checked out her three colleagues and noted the people they sat near. Out of the corner of her eye she noticed a young man staring at her. She looked away to avoid staring back but his visage reminded her of someone. "Lopo," she said out loud and moved her head to peer across the room into the green eyes of the man she had been thinking about constantly since their departure from Lisbon. *How can this be?*

#

Lopo and Mbekah strolled in the moonlight down the long street to the cove where the ships lay at anchor. Rodrigo followed far enough back to give them some privacy, a luxury for anyone living on a crowded ship for weeks and months at a time.

At the conclusion of the soiree, Lopo had sought out Mbekah. They air kissed in the European style. He requested to see her back to her ship, so she sent the other ambassadors ahead.

"Embaixadora. This explains the treatment and education you've received. You are an envoy to what court, if I may ask?"

"It's all rather vague. I'm returning to my people and then I am to receive orders which are now sealed. And you, a piloto. Felicitations. I'm happy for you."

"I've heard about your success at court and finding your sister. I am happy for you too. But I never expected to find you on this voyage."

"It's still very secret. We came aboard the *São Pantaleão* just before it sailed. I am returning to my village with the others who were brought to Lisbon with me as well as with my sister and her husband. We have Kpodo's boy, Moisés. We bring gifts from his majesty, restitution for the suffering we've been through. I am exceedingly happy with how everything has turned out."

CHAPTER 53

Pilot, He Gets Drunk

Lopo stood in the bow with pilot's mate Rodrigo whose watch it was. Although there remained two hours until dawn, a full moon bathed the sea and the looming island of *São Tiago*.

"It's loco. Why didn't you tell Mbekah you love her?", whispered Rodrigo.

"You've asked me that a thousand times since Madeira, amigo. I wish I had told her. . . . I'm glad I didn't."

"You've had plenty of time to think about it. Make up your mind, Lopo. After this stop, it's only a fortnight to the *Mina* where Mbekah leaves us to return to her village. Are you going to tell her, or not?"

#

Mbekah studied the low buildings of the port of *Ribeira Grande* as the *São Pantaleão* glided in next to the *São Cristóvão* and dropped anchor. The sun peeked out of the sea and cast long shadows of the ships' masts onto the shore two score paces from the caravelas. Lopo's não, with its deeper draft, came to rest seaward of them. Big River, the name of this modest port, seemed an irony to Mbekah. *Where is this big river?*

She had been concerned all night as Pilot Gonçalves and his two henchmen refilled their cups again and again from the cask of wine in front of the sleeping closets behind the tiller. The trio's wine binge had been muted so far, apparently they did not want ship's master Don João, whose cabin was on the quarter deck above, to know of their imbibing. *Are they up to something?* The crew had been leering at her and the women in her company for the past few days, more so than the usual. Gonçalves had stopped trying to hide his hunger for the women. *Frightening!* Ifé had also noticed and shared her fears with Mbekah for their safety. In the early light of dawn, she feigned sleep whenever one of the crew looked her way. Mbekah hoped that Gonçalves would go ashore at this stop and satisfy his lusts in the village.

In the past weeks Mbekah had reviewed in her mind the conversation in Madeira with Lopo. Lopo listened while she spoke as they sauntered back to their ships from the governor's soiree. Lopo was thoughtful. Considerate. Charming but hesitant. She felt like he had something to say but changed his mind as she opened up to him about her joy in returning to her homeland. At the strand, the shore boat came for her. Lopo looked into her eyes, kissed her hand, helped her into the boat, and was gone.

Just as well. I'm going home. Lopo's returning to Portugal. He can't live in the forest. I can't live in Lisbon.

#

Lopo sent Rodrigo and Manoel to shore with ship's master Pero Dias to arrange for the supplies they would load for the final run to the *Mina*. He would go ashore later after Rodrigo returned aboard. He studied the *São Pantaleão* which stood shoreward three score paces of the não to see what Mbekah was doing. He did not see her nor the other Guineans. Perhaps they were sleeping in the cool of the morning, and therefore were hidden behind the caravela's gunwales. Having woken well before the dawn, he was still tired, so he sat in the shade of the quarterdeck to nap.

#

Mbekah watched as Don João and the cargo master disappeared over the side to be rowed ashore. She had been relieved when Gonçalves had climbed into his sleeping cabinet even though Nunno and Belchior remained on deck. Mbekah had learned from past stops that the fleet would be in port for at least a few days while they took on fresh water and supplies for the next leg of the voyage. At some point during the day, there would be a lot of activity aboard as the victualling began. For now, she felt safe enough to doze off for a few hours.

#

Mbekah opened her eyes as a bony hand covered her mouth, and another clamped her wrists together. Nunno's alcoholic grin filled her vision. Belchior seized her ankles and the two men hoisted her and tiptoed back to the cover of the quarterdeck overhang where Gonçalves stood holding open the door to his sleeping closet. She chomped Nunno's hand. He released it from her mouth for an instant and swore. She shrieked before he could mute her again. She retracted her legs pulling Belchior to her and shoved him onto his back. Before he could stagger to his feet, Mbekah placed her own feet on the deck and pushed with all her might headbutting Nunno in the chin. But before she could break completely free, Gonçalves slammed her against the outside wall of the officers' miniature quarters, knocking her breath from her. Gonçalves began stuffing her into his space.

The commotion woke the Guineans. Gyasi and Kpodo immediately saw the situation and sprinted to Mkebah's aid only to be cut off by half a dozen crew members with knives raised.

Ifé ran to the seaward gunwale and screamed. "Lopo! Rodrigo!"

Another crewman wrestled Ifé to the deck and smothered her mouth with his hand.

Yaféu bowled over the man on top of Ifé who jumped up again and along with Olubayo and Foladé frantically waved and shouted in the direction of Lopo's <u>não</u>.

#

Lopo woke as a crewman shook him. "Come see. Something is not right on the *São Pantaleão*. The Guinean women scream and gesture."

Lopo shot to the side of the <u>não</u> facing the two <u>caravelas</u>. He checked that his deck knife was in his waist band and ordered the two men gawking beside him, "<u>Rápido</u>, row me to the *São Pantaleão*".

CHAPTER 54

The Fight

Lopo scrambled out of the dinghy and up the side of the *São Pantaleão.* Landing on the deck, he braced himself for danger. Gonçalves and half a dozen crewmen stood laughing and pointing at the Guineans huddled together under their awning, the women sobbing.

Lopo's two shipmates dropped in behind him.

Gonçalves feigned surprise upon seeing Lopo. Gonçalves chuckled. "A little fun before we go ashore. It was nothing. Nothing. The girls thought we were serious. Look how scared they are."

Gyasi and Kpodo separated, revealing Mbekah lying on her side, leaning up on one elbow, chest heaving. She scowled at her assailants while she caught her breath. "Pigs! Capitão Dias will hear of this."

Lopo glared at Gonçalves, drew his knife, and launched himself at the smirking brute. The surprised men opened a path for Lopo's charge. Gonçalves caught Lopo's knife arm by the wrist but the impact crashed Gonçalves onto his back and the two grappled and rolled about.

"What goes on here?" Bellowed Don João as he raised his head above the portside gunwale.

The struggling pilots froze. Nunno stepped forward. "Piloto Meendez attacked Piloto Gonçalves with a knife."

CHAPTER 55

The Decision

The last witness left the room. Captain Bartolomeu Dias sighed and took a moment to study the expressions on the faces of Pero Dias, his brother, and João Infante. As masters of the two other ships in the mission, they sat in judgment with Captain Dias. The cargo master from the *São Cristóvão*, acting as scribe, continued to write. Captain Dias had not included the chief factor of the *Ribeira Grande* station. Before the inquest even began, Captain Dias could see that the decision would take into consideration the realities of their voyage of discovery which was a closely-held secret. The Captain dismissed the scribe for the time being.

During the proceedings, Captain Dias had already made his decision but wanted the other two first officers on their respective ships to come to the same conclusion. The success of the mission, and therefore of his future, could depend on their verdict this afternoon. If they failed to reach the *Indias*, he didn't want his two colleagues challenging this action when they were back in Lisbon. "Cavalheiros. Your thoughts?"

Don João began, "The important facts are that Lopo Meendez attacked another officer with a deadly weapon based on appearances only. No one, not Lopo nor Josefa, was in danger of bodily injury at the time. All of the witnesses, those friendly to

Bras Gonçalves as well as those friendly to Lopo Meendez agree on these points."

Don Pero took his turn. "Based on testimony of the Guineans as well as your own estimate of what you saw when you arrived on board, Don João, Lopo's assumption was correct. Gonçalves, against orders, had just attempted to violate Embaixadora Josefa da *Guiné*. Furthermore, Gonçalves and other crew members were drunk on their watch. Men on the *São Cristóvão* also observed the Guineans shouting and signaling for help which is why Lopo had hurried to the *São Pantaleão*."

Don João considered. "Gonçalves' story that he was only teasing the woman, is suspect. Even if correct, he should be reprimanded for that alone. Still, we can't have Lopo taking on himself your prerogative for justice, Capitão Dias."

After a moment of contemplation, Don João spoke again. "It's unusual to take the word of negroes against the word of Portuguese Christians. It's a precedent we may not want to establish. How does his majesty view these Guineans?"

Captain Dias cleared his throat. "I assure you, the king holds these women, especially Josefa, in high esteem. Sealed orders, to which I am privy and which you will receive at the *Mina*, require we treat the Guineans with the utmost care and respect. If the king were here, Gonçalves would be in irons. Whatever castigation he got, the king would be sure that Josefa knew of it, so she would not doubt his esteem for her."

Don Pero spoke. "That's it. We will do what the king would do. It's only a question of what penalty is appropriate. Stripes and a demotion?"

"Yet we cannot allow Lopo's unprovoked assault on another officer go unpunished," suggested Don João. "This voyage is not half accomplished. Discipline cannot be lax or we'll never succeed."

"All good points, gentlemen. We cannot manage the rest of this mission without two of our three pilotos. Nor can we trust

Gonçalves with the Guineans." Captain Dias paused. "I will severely reprimand both. Further, I will move Lopo to the São Pantaleão in which the Guineans will continue to travel. Gonçalves will pilot the não. They can each take their mates and other key crew members with them."

CHAPTER 56

Cruising

Lopo came to sit with the Guineans for an hour or more each day before dawn. His ability to speak their language had improved noticeably in the fifteen days he and Rodrigo had been moved to the *São Pantaleão*. Manoel, as cargo master, remained on the não for accountability of the supplies carried in her hull.

The ships convoyed due east from *Ribeira Grande* on *São Tiago* to the African coast. They veered south, taking advantage of the currents and winds, which eventually carried them around the Pepper Coast at Cape Palmas and again east on the underside of the Ivory Coast. The Guineans welcomed the hot, moist air of the last few weeks of the rainy season. It was the weather of their childhood.

Mbekah asked questions that Lopo could not answer. "Who will guarantee our small group's safety as we travel to our village? How will we live without fear of future slave raiders?"

Lopo asked things that Mbekah could not or would not answer. "Is your ambassadorial title honorary or will you have specific duties among your people? With other tribes? How will you communicate with the fort at the *Mina*?"

She finally replied, "They told us that we would be given more instructions when we reach the *Mina*."

Lopo continually questioned his own decision not to tell Mbekah of his love for her. He loved the Guineans as brothers. But he loved Mbekah more, . . . and differently. *Our paths will part soon, and it was best to keep my passion for her to myself. Does she have the same feelings for me? She brightens when I speak to her. But she is so happy to be going home. Is it possible that I'll see her on the return from our explorations?*

#

Manoel had dealt with Gonçalves for many months on his first trip to the *Mina* four years previous and on many occasions in Lisbon. Manoel hated the bully and remained wary. To survive during this leg of the journey, he kept to himself as much as possible which wasn't easy on a ship only 25 paces long with a beam of 7. Unlike the two <u>caravelas</u>, the bigger <u>não</u> had some space for crewmen to sleep out of the elements other than in the hold. Manoel spent as little time as possible in the hold and never at night. Within a week of their departure from Lisbon, the smell of rat urine and damp wood in the tight space above the cargo was insufferable. Now, in the hot muggy climate, Manoel preferred sleeping in the open air on the raised deck of the elevated bow section.

On a few occasions, when he was slow finding a spot to lay out his cape in the bow, Manoel ended up aft on the main deck in front of the raised stern. Instead of a tiller, the não had a proper wheel to control a rudder. Pilot and pilot's mate spent much of their time at or near the wheel located on the stern quarterdeck.

One evening while they cruised east along the Ivory Coast approaching the Gold Coast and the *Mina* fort, Manoel had bedded down under the ladder steps from the main deck to the quarterdeck. Well into the night watch, he awoke to find a new position. He heard Nunno and Belchior, above at the wheel, speaking in low tones. Manoel lay there listening as he tried to go back to sleep. They sailed with a light breeze at their back, so the conversation was not carried off. Manoel could make out every word. He knew their distinct voices.

Nunno said, "You ever wonder about the dead boy we dumped in the marsh weeds at the *Mina* the last time we were here?"

Belchior said, "Not really. We got away with it, didn't we? Forget about it."

CHAPTER 57

Return to the *Mina*

Mbekah awoke to the boom of a cannon. She had fallen asleep earlier in the midday heat. Standing up, she saw a cloud of grey smoke dissipating into the breeze off the landward side of the *São Cristóvão* several hundred paces ahead. Looking to the shore, she saw the *Mina* fort and the nearby village of two nations. She contemplated their arrival at this evil place with mixed emotions.

In a moment, Mbekah heard the first, second, and third cannon shots, signals from the fort. She had prayed many times to *São Jorge* as well as to the spirits of the ocean sea that they would sail safely back to this coast. They still had a long walk to reach her people in the forest but felt grateful this portion of the journey was now over. She sang the song of homecoming which she had not sung for more than four long years. Her companions joined in, swaying to the rhythm. At the conclusion, she thanked the saint and spirits in a reverent voice while the Guineans as well as the Christians onboard listened attentively.

With the breeze blowing onshore, the three vessels, one by one, steered north toward the mouth of the river east of the fort. Lopo supervised the tillermen as they followed the *São Cristóvão* up the shortest river in the world into the calm waters of the lagoon between the peninsula and the mainland. They dropped sails and anchored within a stone toss of each other and in the lee of the fort's high walls. The não, with its deeper draft, set its anchor offshore.

Captain Dias, came to the rail of his ship and hailed Ships Master Infante who now stood on the quarterdeck above and behind Lopo. "Don Infante. Por favor, join me on shore. Your crew and passengers will remain on the *São Pantaleão* until we discuss arrangements with the governador."

#

The crews and passengers spent the night on the ships with the exception of Pilot Gonçalves. Lopo and Mbekah were visiting on the quarterdeck when a ship's boat rowed into the lagoon carrying Captain Pero Dias and the evil pilot. The two men were set ashore and they disappeared into the fort. Lopo and Mbekah moved farther aft and sat late into the night with their backs against the captain's cabin. They were silent much of the time, knowing they would soon separate, possibly to never see each other again.

The incoming tide swiveled the caravelas on their anchor chains, so the pair faced west. The sight of the fires in the two adjacent villages at the end of the lagoon inspired Mbekah to relate her story in more detail than Lopo had heard before. Lopo sickened again to think of his nation's and his own part in the insidious traffic in people. He worried, as he knew Mbekah did, about the liberated slaves' long tramp back to their home. He was well aware of his country's policy to not venture inland due to the dangers of belligerent tribes and tropical diseases. *Can they trust the slave raiders from the ochre village to take them back?* Lopo also feared for the future. *Can these gentle people ever be secure in their freedom from the grim harvest of souls for the ever-growing European appetite for slave labor?*

#

Lopo perceived a thump against the hull and opened his eyes. His head lay on Mbekah's lap. He smiled up at her as she stroked his hair. The caravelas had swung again with the tide and so they faced the early rays of the sun rising above the tree line.

She whispered, "A shore boat has come from the fort."

Lopo was content. *Por Deus, would that I could remain right here the rest of the morning.*

Rodrigo popped his head around the corner of the cabin. "An orderly from the fort is asking for you, Lopo."

CHAPTER 58

Sealed Orders

Mbekah surveyed the congregation. She leaned close to Ifé. "Lopo is not here?"

Ifé searched the dimly-lit space while they followed the priest's lead. They had attended mass hundreds of times, so it did not take much concentration to keep up. She inched close to Mbekah. "No. Lopo is not here."

Crews and passengers had been herded into the *Mina* chapel for a celebration of thanksgiving. Mbekah understood that their belongings were being moved into their quarters in the fort while they worshipped. Over the years in Lisbon, she had become comfortable with Christian doctrine. She had found many similarities with her own beliefs. But today Mbekah was troubled that there were captives in the fort's cells waiting for transport to Lisbon. *Christians are more like the Allah worshippers regarding slavery. Brutal and permanent. Not like the involuntary and usually temporary servitude to meet the demands of forest justice between villages or between creditors and debtors.*

Back in the daylight, a soldier from the garrison directed them to their rooms. Before he shut the door for them he came to attention and cleared his throat. "The four embaixadores are invited to dinner this evening with the governador and other dignitaries."

#

The food was tasty compared to the ship's fare they'd suffered through the past three months—not as refined as in the homes of the rich in Lisbon or what was served by the governor of Madeira, but good just the same.

This evening Mbekah could see Lopo who was seated as far as was possible from her. He made frequent eye contact with her. He appeared agitated. *What, Lopo? Are you trying to tell me something?*

The Congolese ambassadors were also in attendance and had been introduced to the governor along with Mbekah's group. Mbekah's thoughts were elsewhere as high-ranking men made flowery toasts. *How many free African women have dined in this hall? Are the compliments lavished on us tonight sincere? The governador stares too much. Is he lustful? Is he gauging my determination? I was not being too cautious when I told the others to drink only a little wine tonight.*

At last, the evening concluded, and guests rose to leave. Mbekah saw Lopo heading her way. Before he reached them, the governor stepped in their path. "Senhor Amrrique and Senhoras *da Guiné*. Please remain a few minutes."

Captain Dias and Lopo were shown to seats close to them for what was about to take place.

#

"Capitão Dias carried sealed orders regarding his fleet as well as you four embaixadores from this coast." The governor paused to see that he had everyone's ears. "We can share some of them with you. Capitão Dias will command his three ships on a mission further south to the Congo king where the Congolese travelers will be reunited with their families at court. They are subjects of said king and will be in his service."

Mbekah studied Lopo for any indication he knew what was to be done with her and whether it was something good. But Lopo stared at his hands.

"Amrrique, Josefa, Inês, and Maria, all subjects of his Majesty, King João II, all with the title and office of embaixador or embaixadora, will continue south with the fleet. You will receive further instructions at such time as Capitão Dias determines prudent. The other Guineans in your party are free to return to their homes here with the gifts promised to them."

Lopo could not tell that Mbekah was enraged, although he knew she must be. Not so for the other Guineans. They shook their heads and slumped in their chairs.

Mbekah paused for control, then spoke. "Does his majesty renege on our agreement? We have kept our promises. Will he not keep his? We were promised we would return to our village."

The governor was ready for Mbekah's response. "According to a letter to me from Chamberlain de Faria, the king offered to return you to Africa and that is precisely what he has done."

CHAPTER 59

The New Bargain

Another dawn at the *Mina*. Lopo had spent the night on the guards' walkway high up on the fort's wall. Through a crenellation in the battlements, he had stared out to sea. He was ashamed at the too-clever treatment his king had dealt to Mbekah and her three companions. *They had been led to believe they were returning home. I believed it.* <u>*Dona*</u> *Ana and the queen believed it. It was calculated to not legally be a lie. But it is one. Not honorable!*

Nor was the crown going to see that the others got home safely. *'Free to return to their homes'. Washing our hands of them. Ignoring that they will never get home without an escort!*

He had left the audience with the governor too embarrassed to talk with Mbekah. *What would I have said to her?*

I will breakfast then go to the chapel to think about what I will do.

#

Lopo never made it to the chapel. After eating, a summons came to attend the governor in his office. He washed his face, combed his hair, and tried to appear as if he'd not stayed out all night.

He entered the office and saw that everyone from the previous night's meeting was assembled.

Lopo took his seat, Mbekah rose to address the governor. "We are not satisfied that you are keeping your part of our bargain with his majesty. We therefore are no longer bound to keep the commitments we made in good faith. We renounce our titles. We will not serve as legates for your country." She promptly sat down.

Lopo was astonished. He glanced around the room and found that the governor was not indignant. And no one else acted surprised. Mbekah had told him about negotiating with the king and obtaining concessions—the return of the others and reparations extracted for their suffering. *I comprehend now. The governor was warned to expect something like this.*

The governor plowed ahead. "I regret that you see things so. The king requires your services so I have no choice but to send you with Capitão Dias. Perhaps we can come to an understanding so that you go as freemen instead of in chains. Let us hear all of your concerns."

"Maria has become the mother that the child Moisés lost at birth. She is betrothed to the child's father Kpodo whom you call Bastiao. She will return to our village as his wife and represent Portugal's interests in the forest."

The governor showed no emotion. "Go on."

"We must be assured that our companions arrive home safely. Gyasi, also called Amrrique, will accompany them all the way. When he returns with his report of safe passage, we will be satisfied."

"Demônios! That would take a month or more."

Mbekah nodded. "Yes. I suggest you send an armed escort to guarantee their safety and Gyasi's return."

Captain Dias spoke up. "Governador, we'll need almost that much time to refit and recuperate before we proceed. I can accept that timeframe."

Lopo could hardly believe what he was hearing, and that the governor was still listening.

Mbekah continued. "One more thing. To ensure their future freedom, you must demand that the raiders not return to our region to take slaves. Gyasi can witness your representative's communications with the tribes as they travel north. Furthermore, you must give each of them a token with the escutcheon of his majesty, the king with a safe passage warranty engraved on the reverse side."

CHAPTER 60

The Largest River in the World

They navigated southeast across the Gulf of Guinea, past the uninhabited island of *São Tomé*, known to the Portuguese from previous explorations. A day later they sighted the African coast which ran north and south again. The three ships hugged the coast for another week until they reached the Zaire. As far as the Portuguese knew, it was the largest river in the world. Lopo's watch was at the tiller when they encountered the muddy waters issuing from the great Zaire half a dozen leagues out to sea. The clumsy não was left at the mouth while the two caravelas sailed up the deep waterway. Lopo wondered if Gonçalves was happy for the easy duty at anchor or upset to be left out of the festivities that were sure to take place at the court of the Congo king. For three days they sailed against the current between the river's jungle-covered banks. So deep and wide was the flow that they could navigate around either side of substantial islands. They observed people at every bend and were hailed many times by friendly Africans in dugouts. Their predecessor, Captain Diogo Cão had been in contact three times with the Congo king, spending time in his capital on one occasion. They had exchanged subjects to spend time in each other's kingdoms.

After twenty-five leagues on the river they came to a large eddy on the south bank where stood a large village. Lopo followed the lead of the *São Cristóvão* and dropped anchor.

When ship's master Don João Infante returned from conferring with Captain Dias, Lopo learned that the Congolese women returning on the *São Cristóvão* had informed him that this was the gateway to the capital, *Mbanza Congo*, and that they must travel four days through the jungle to arrive there. Captain Dias had been directed by King João to meet the Congo king. However, fearing that tropical diseases could devastate their company and ruin his chances of finding a route to the *Indias*, Captain Dias was considering whether to make the journey. Runners left for *Mbanza Congo* to alert the king of their presence at the village. They would wait for a reply.

#

Mbekah checked that no Portuguese speakers where within earshot. "The others are not willing to take the risk."

Lopo strolled in silence at her side. "Are you certain Isabell can be trusted? Do the other three Congolese women know of your plan?"

"I have only discussed the escape with Isabell. Her cousin is one of the messengers. When he returns, she will ask him to help."

"You haven't heard the details of your mission. Maybe it will be preferable to striking out in a land you know nothing about. You're more likely to return to your home by remaining with us."

Mbekah switched to her native tongue while they sauntered past a trio of Portuguese sailors drinking palm wine on drum-like stools in front of a large, thatched hut. "That the Capitão has not yet shared the king's orders, makes me think we will not be coming back. There are two passengers on the *São Cristóvão* who were captured further south on a previous voyage by Cão. They are being sent back to their people, so they think."

She switched back to Portuguese. "However, there is also a woman passenger on the *São Cristóvão* from the Ivory Coast. She too has been named embaixadora but she was not set ashore when we sailed by her village hundreds of leagues ago. It's clear she's not going home."

Lopo had nothing to say to refute her logic.

Mbekah took his arm and turned him to face her. "I shall take my chances in this jungle as a free woman."

They spotted a commotion over by the river's edge near the ships' mooring.

Isabell rushed by. "The messengers have returned."

CHAPTER 61

The Feast

The manicongo, the title used for the Congo king by his subjects, arrived midday at the village. He came with more than two hundred in his entourage—bodyguards, warriors, wives, princes, princesses, uncles, aunts, cousins, advisors, chefs, litter bearers, hunters, fishermen, musicians, magicians, dancers, holy men, laborers, and others whom Lopo could not classify.

Upon emerging from the jungle, the manicongo was carried to the head of his procession which snaked through the village to the river landing. Captain Dias came ashore where the two leaders made an ostentatious display of greeting for all to witness.

The ceremony was flawless; Lopo realized that both had been prepared for the occasion over the past few days while the Portuguese awaited the king's coming. The manicongo announced a feast for the next evening. The Portuguese would be guests of honor.

An army of laborers erected a temporary village in the existing community's central circle. Warriors set up a defensive perimeter along the river bank and inside the surrounding wall of vegetation. More people came down thc road and dugouts arrived at the landing with trussed critters, wine skins, fish, and exotic produce of all shapes and colors. New fire pits were dug, and iron pots appeared. An evening meal was served to all the newcomers including the crews on the caravelas, a hint of the banquet to come. Captain Dias and Don João, the master of Lopo's caravela, dined privately with the manicongo.

Their African passengers, except the Congolese who were now home, were ordered to sleep onboard that night.

#

Lopo avoided being seen with Mbekah that day. He sat cross-legged on layered palm fronds at the feast in the midst of comely Congo courtesans. If Mbekah was going to disappear, he wished her good fortune, but he didn't want to be implicated in her flight. He was privy to it and therefore could be found guilty of treason. Nevertheless, he searched for Mbekah until he spotted her in the throng, seated with fellow convent students Sancha and Lionor. He knew Mbekah had learned to speak a little Congolese. Perhaps Isabell was also keeping her distance from Mbekah today.

Lopo savored the fresh food served by women wandering among the invitees with platter after platter of jungle delicacies. If he didn't know a plate, he learned its name. If it was flesh, he elicited a pantomime until he thought he could surmise the animal or had to give up. If it was some other body part, he guessed from its texture, color, and smell. He would soon enough be back to a diet of wormy ship's biscuit and scummy water, so he tried at least a morsel of all that was offered. The Congolese beauties watched him for an expression of delight or disgust. They giggled when he smiled and howled when he grimaced. He mostly smiled.

He sipped the wine in his mahogany tumbler to avoid inebriation but noticed many of the sailors were not so cautious.

The food was cleared leaving just the alcohol. Drummers beat a driving rhythm until modestly-dressed men and women danced into the small circle in front of the manicongo and Captain

Dias. The drumming became syncopated to accompany the performers' increasingly energetic gyrations and leaps.

Catelina, another of the Congolese students at the convent with Mbekah, joined him to translate for his attentive group of ladies. Lopo hadn't considered Catelina attractive before but now thought otherwise. *Por Deus! Me thinks I have sipped too much wine.* He remembered Mbekah and scanned the noisy scene for her. *I see Sancha and Lionor. I do not see Mbekah.*

#

Lopo held the lantern high so he could see the faces of the *Mina* Guineans who were getting ready to bed down on their deck mats after a long evening of too much food and wine. "Where is Mbekah?"

They looked blankly at each other. They shook their heads.

Ifé spoke up. "Mbekah and I went to the feast together, but we separated. I did see her sitting with two of the Congolese embaixadoras, Sancha and Lionor. She did not return with me. Nor was she onboard when I got here. Perhaps she is still with those two."

Lopo tapped on the ship's master's cabin on the quarterdeck.

"What?"

Lopo spoke to the door. "Don João, Josefa has not come back to the ship. All of the other Guineans are onboard."

From behind his closed door, Don João replied. "If she's not back by the morning, we'll send crew to find her."

Chapter 62

Betrayal

Lopo slept little and was up before first light. He sat up and leaned against the back of the master's cabin; the humidity and heat kept him out of his compartment. Mbekah's departure weighed heavily on him. She was out of his life but not out of his heart.

From the bank came a low whistle followed by a voice heard barely above the sound of the river. "Boat, please. I wish to come aboard."

That sounds like Mbekah! Too dark to see for sure. Lopo hurried down to the main deck where two men on Rodrigo's watch were readying a boat to fetch the woman on the shore. "I'm going with you."

As they neared the river's edge, Lopo saw Mbekah standing in front of two of the manicongo's guards. She wore a wrap-around cloth that left one shoulder bare. She carried a bundle tied into a roll with leather cord. If he did not know her so well, Lopo would have mistaken her for a Congolese courtesan.

On the return to the ship, Mbekah spoke to Lopo in her native tongue. "I changed clothes and hid. I joined a small group of women that got an early start for *Mbanza Congo*. We were on the road for only a short time. A troop of warriors overtook us. One of them pointed me out and they marched me back to the village to a hut where the manicongo was waiting. Isbell was with him to translate."

Mbekah paused while they climbed up and into the *São Pantaleão.* She and Lopo crept up to the quarterdeck and around to the back of the cabin. "Isabell convinced the king to not report me to Capitão Dias. Just to send me back as if I had spent the night in her company after the evening's entertainment. Besides the manicongo's circle of advisors, only you know that I took flight. And, of course Gyasi and Ifé. But maybe you have reported my attempt?"

"Only that you were not onboard after the banquet. Don João, tired and a little over the barrel, was not concerned. Said we would wait until morning to see where you spent the night. He likely knows you're here now. Walls are thin. Few secrets on a ship. Good that we have not been speaking in Portuguese."

#

That day and the next, the caravelas were restocked with fresh victuals and sweet water from a spring at the edge of the clearing. Two Congolese guards shadowed Mbekah whenever she was on shore. The manicongo did not want to spoil good relations with King João by allowing Portuguese deserters into his jungle realm.

Isabell managed to run into Mbekah. "Come, let's walk." Arm in arm in the rain, the two friends spoke Portuguese. "I did not betray you, Mbekah. Who did? I do not know. The manicongo seems to know everything that goes on in his court. He has his spies."

"I do not blame you. Your solution worked, Isabell. No one suspects I tried to flee. I pray to the saints and the spirits we shall meet again. Perhaps on my way home to the *Mina*."

"As do I, cara amiga." Isabell reached into the folds of her wrap and pulled out an exquisite necklace of tiny pink cowries, with another cowrie shell the size of her big toe for the pendant. "Is it like the one stolen from you when you were captured?"

Mbekah fondled the gift. "It's magnificent."

Isabell seemed delighted. "My parent's holy man blessed it for you. Is that acceptable?"

"Por certo, sim. It's a treasure. I will wear it along with my Christian fetish." Mbekah slipped her new amulet over her head and into place. She closed her eyes and caressed the large cowrie as she had done so many times with the one her mother had given her. "Creator, I wish to be free." *I will be free.*

The two women arrived where the boats were loading for another row out to the ships. They hugged a long time. When they stood back, each saw that the other had tears streaming down her cheeks.

Mbekah was helped into a boat. On board the caravela, she turned and waved to her friend.

#

The rain let up, the afternoon sun revealed steam rising from the grass and the dark green tangle of trees and bushes behind the village. The caravelas weighed anchors and drifted downstream in the still air. Men with sweeps on both sides of the ships managed a little headway so the ships would respond to their tillers. The river was not treacherous, but they made better time if they stayed out of eddies and away from the banks.

CHAPTER 63

Kidnap Cove

With the morning wind at their back, the two caravelas sailed out of the mouth of the Zaire River and dropped anchor near the waiting não. Lopo watched a boat shove off from the não with its master, Pero Dias, aboard. He was rowed to his brother's ship, the *São Cristóvão*. A cannon boomed from the não, a signal for crew ashore to return. This was still the manicongo's realm, so it was safe for the Portuguese to fraternize with the people living where the river meets the sea. A dozen dugouts pushed off from the south shore, laden with tropical fruit and fresh fish. Besides the African paddlers there were a few of the não's crew riding as passengers.

Among the huts on the shore stood a stone pillar capped by a rectangular head with a bronze cross embedded in the top. This padrão, was placed there by Diogo Cão on his first visit to this spot years before. Chiseled coat of arms and words on the padrão let all know that this coast belonged to Portugal. The fleet carried more such stone markers, each taller than a man, to be planted at prominent landmarks on newly discovered coastline.

In an hour, the three ships were sailing out to sea to give them a comfortable margin from the shore before turning south.

#

After five days cruising the coast, with the shore vegetation getting ever thinner, the ships sailed into the northern mouth of a spacious natural harbor. A long spit of land formed the western side of the inlet, protecting it from rough water. Were this spot in Portugal, there would have been many ships moored next to a city with wharves and warehouses at the water's edge. Hundreds of dark figures gathered on the rocky beach to inspect the floating houses with enormous white wings returning to their country.

The ships anchored and the two canons on each were hoisted out of the holds and positioned on either side of the bows. Sweeps were brought out, so the ships could be maneuvered to aim their canon at any threat. Again, the two masters were rowed over to the *São Cristóvão* to confer with Captain Dias.

The Guineans stood at the gunwales and studied the scene. Compared to the lush green shore at the *Mina*, this place was uninviting. With the master gone, Lopo was senior officer on the *São Pantaleão*. He stood on the quarter deck, above the men at the tiller. Rodrigo paced behind the two gun crews.

Ship's Master João Infante returned to the *São Pantaleão*. He climbed the ladder to join Lopo. "This is *Angra do Salto*, the cove where Cão kidnapped two tribesmen. Back in Lisbon, his majesty treated them like royal legates to his court. After two years, they speak Portuguese and bring gifts to their chief."

They watched a boat launched from the *São Cristóvão* row to the beach with the returning Africans sitting in the bow. As they drew near to their fellow villagers the rowers backed oars gently, so the boat remained in place out of range for spears. One of the returning men stood up and waved. He shouted. They were too distant for Lopo to hear the salutation. A man on the shore stepped forward and shouted back. The conversation continued for some minutes. There was a huddle on the beach. At last, a headman called out and all warriors laid their spears in the sand. The boat moved to shallow water and its two dark-skinned passengers jumped out and splashed ashore. There was much hugging and back slapping, an enthusiastic welcome for their lost tribesmen.

Master Infante turned to Lopo. "We will remain on board tonight to give the two ambassadors time to tell their chief all that has happened to them. We do not know if we will be seen as friend or foe so make sure the night watch is vigilant."

#

The sun was still low in the morning sky when a long, slender raft brought one of the two ambassadors from shore to the *São Cristóvão*. Captain Dias, in his own boat, was rowed to land with four armed sailors wearing steel casques and breastplates. As pre-arranged, a boat from each the *São Pantaleão* and the <u>não</u> joined them carrying six armed men as well. All those awake in the fleet watched the friendly encounter with the chief on the strand.

#

They remained eight days while making repairs and transferring stores from the <u>não</u> to the two <u>caravelas</u>. Manoel went back and forth to the village to trade for sheep, cattle, and dried fish. On the second to last day there, Manoel managed to come aboard the *São Pantaleão*. He cornered Lopo and Rodrigo. In hushed tones, he said, "You will be little surprised by what I've learned but enraged nevertheless. Gonçalves or one of his men killed Joselinho when we first were at the *Mina* fort."

Rodrigo placed his hands on Lopo's shoulders. "Calm yourself." He turned to Manoel. "I've always had a flea behind my ear about them and the murder. Now we know. Can you prove this?"

"No. It would be my word against theirs. But there's no room for doubt. I overheard Nunno and Belchior discussing it. We must keep this to ourselves. I am to remain on the <u>não</u> with Gonçalves and his cutthroats while the you continue south. With only a few men, we are to get along with the natives and collect provisions for when you return from your explorations. It's certain that those three will do little to help with the work. They will be dangerous to live with for months on this ship. And they are the least likely to keep the peace with the village. I pray to the Virgin and *São Jorge* that I will be alive when you are next here."

Rodrigo embraced Manoel. "Be careful, amigo. The não has a skiff, does it not? Take some men for a sail. Fish. Find a woman on shore. Keep away from the evil trio, especially if they start drinking."

CHAPTER 64

Left

The *São Cristóvão* and the *São Pantaleão* sailed on into a south wind, tacking to make progress. Each three leagues traversed only gained them one league further down the coast. The landscape reminded Lopo more and more of the Sahara. Ten days from Kidnap Cove, they sighted the rocky headland where Cão had placed his last padrão. From here on, they would be sailing in waters never before seen by Europeans, as far as they knew.

As they approached the shore, they heard a massive barking chorus and discovered most of the 'rocks' on shore were seals and their pups. Boats were sent to harvest a few dozen of the furry beasts for the table and for skins to trade. Lopo went along for the hunt. The boats were beached, and he climbed up the low promontory to inspect the padrão. In addition to the escutcheon of Portugal, the engraved message was thus: "In the year 6685 after the creation of the world and 1485 after the birth of Christ, the brilliant, far-sighted King João II of Portugal ordered Diogo Cão, cavalheiro of his court, to discover this land and to erect this padrão here."

They overnighted off the point and continued. In two days they sheltered in a spacious, deep water harbor protected by an enormously long and wide spit of sand on the west. North of the harbor cream-colored sand mountains rose practically from the sea. In and about the harbor, the ever-present sea gulls shared the water, sky, and strand with great white pelicans and pink flamingos. Lounging seals blanketed the beach. Most notable were the spouting whales and leaping dolphins. Lopo learned later that Captain Dias had named this bay after Our Lady of the Immaculate Conception.

A curious knot of natives watched the intruders from a distance. A boat came for Gyasi and ferried him to the *São Cristóvão*. The following day Gyasi was rowed ashore with gifts which he dragged up the beach and deposited before returning to the boat to spend the night on the *São Cristóvão*.

The next morning the gifts had disappeared. Gyasi was returned to the beach, dressed like a Portuguese cavalheiro. This time, the boat left him. He stood alone for an hour then hiked over a low dune and vanished.

Lopo, Mbekah, and Ifé observed in stunned silence from the deck of the *São Pantaleão*. Lopo offered, "Gyasi must have received his orders."

CHAPTER 65

Fat Sands

The *São Cristóvão* and the *São Pantaleão* worked their way farther down the African Coast against the wind off the larboard bow. To make good time, they remained at sea, passing by several promising inlets. They were often close enough to shore to note particulars of the landscape. Lopo knew that Captain Dias was naming salient features and his scribe recording their descriptions for the king's map makers back in Lisbon.

Lopo was busy during his watch so had little time to visit with Mbekah and Ifé during the long days of late spring in the southern latitudes they traversed. After they witnessed the abandonment of their life-long friend, Gyasi, on a foreign shore near a village of less-than-amicable strangers, the women were unusually somber.

On the third night out from Conception Bay, Lopo huddled before the main mast with the two women against the strengthening wind. "Master Infante has confided instructions given to Gyasi before he was landed. He is to learn the language and customs of the coastal tribes that befriend him and return to the place of going ashore within six months to watch for future Portuguese ships. He is to teach a few promising youths our language and tell them we wish to trade with them in the future.

Above all, Gyasi must inquire about Prester John and should travel to meet him if that is possible. In which case, he is to leave a written message for the local chief to give to a Portuguese ship's master so King João will know to send future ships to look for him."

Mbekah considered Lopo's report. "If we accomplish what is expected, surely his majesty will require us to remain as embaixadoras to our new allies. If we ever see our home again, we will be elderly and stooped. This is not the freedom promised us."

Ifé waited for Mbekah to finish. "What is to keep us from warning the people about the Portuguese? Why shouldn't we tell them about your wicked castle at the *Mina*? That we have been coerced to visit them? And reveal that you seek slaves in addition to their gold?"

Mbekah weighed in. "What makes his majesty think that we will not be taken captive and violated? Who knows what our contacts will think of us until we can learn enough of their language to inform them of our mission, if we're lucky enough to live that long? We have been used deceitfully by your nation. Why will it be different with a nation on this shore? Does his majesty not understand that some headman will make us his concubine, or his slave?

Ifé added, "Or his dinner?"

They considered the situation for a spell. Mbekah broke the silence. "We will come bearing gifts. Some chief will think we are the gift!"

#

On the fourth day out, Lopo remarked to his watch and the women that it would be Christmas in about a week. Instead of cheering up the crew, the news caused them to soberly contemplate their homes and loved ones five months and thousands of leagues distant.

On the fifth day, the fleet passed two substantial islands, one covered with basking seals and the second crowded with penguins. As the wind freshened and dark clouds lowered the mariners received a gift from the baby Jesus—a wonderfully capacious natural harbor in which to shelter from the storm.

They tarried five days during which there was communication with the *São Cristóvão.* Lopo learned that the woman ambassador on that vessel, the one from the Ivory Coast, was ill and near death. He had seen evidence of habitation on the shoreline. *I'm afraid Mbekah or Ifé will be next to be put ashore.*

On Christmas morning, the storm weakened. A few natives appeared on the beach. A boat from the *São Cristóvão* came for Ifé. She and Mbekah clung to each other long minutes before two crewmen pried them apart and manhandled Ifé over the side into her conveyance. Mbekah shed doleful teardrops into the afternoon. The hull of the *São Cristóvão* blocked Lopo and Mbekah's view of the beach so they could only suppose that sometime that afternoon, Ifé was rowed in and stranded the same way Gyasi had been.

#

The Portuguese vessels stole out of the harbor and discovered another, larger inlet immediately west of the one in which they had just been anchored. They navigated west and a little north to clear the peninsula protecting the greater harbor before turning south.

The next day, the Feast of *Santo Estêvão*, the fleet paused to send a party ashore to plant another padrão marker on a granite promontory. Lopo was relieved that Mbekah was not marooned. *Is there a way to save her from the inevitable?*

The going was difficult again along the coast because of constant contrary winds. Vegetation was scarce and river mouths often dry. The crew began referring to this coast as 'Fat Sands'.

Lopo explained to Mbekah that the name was a euphemism for the devil's abode.

On Epiphany, January sixth of the new year, the clouds lifted enough to give them a view of a mountain range ten leagues inland. That night the storm freshened. Lopo had given up his sleeping berth to Mbekah so he slept behind the tiller under the overhang of the quarterdeck. Rodrigo's watch steered west, away from the coast, following the lantern on the stern of the *São Cristóvão*. Master Infante noticed the change of direction and stepped down from his cabin to confer with Lopo and Rodrigo. "In our last conference, Capitão Dias said that if conditions worsen, we will sail out into the ocean sea to see if there is a north wind to send us south. This idea came from his pilot that such a wind would be similar to the south wind in the northern latitudes that we ride back from the *Mina* to Europe via the Azores."

Chapter 66

Lopo is Certain

The ships, under shortened sail, were tossed about by an angry sea and turbulent air. They did find a north wind to carry them south, the same direction as the storm-pushed deep-sea rollers and they surfed into the unknown. It was almost impossible to sleep in such conditions so Lopo's men spent much of the dark hours assisting Rodrigo's watch.

The tempest outside terrified Mbekah, yet it was worse to remain inside the cupboard space Lopo had yielded to her. Since the temperature dropped as they ventured farther and farther south, Mbekah wrapped herself in a large cape and wedged herself against the two gunwales where they peaked together in the bow. As the ship was running with the wind and the seas, she found that spot to be relatively less bone bruising than other places on board.

Mbekah woke one dawn, after almost a fortnight of raging weather, to the comparative calm of a brisk, chilly breeze and moderately choppy seas. She saw they were under full sail again. The biggest surprise was finding Lopo sprawled out at her feet, sleeping the sleep of the dead. She felt under her layers of clothing for the cowry necklace and thanked the spirit of the ocean sea for their deliverance.

A sailor woke Lopo as the crew mustered to sing the Salve Regina, more heartfelt than normal, thought Mbekah. She held the cross at her breast, and kissed it at the conclusion of the hymn. The day watch took their stations.

At midday, after the ship had been put back into order, Lopo joined Mbekah at the bow. "You might want to retire to the cabin to catch up on your sleep."

Mbekah nodded. "I will sleep in there this afternoon, so you can have it for the night. You have not slept much these past days."

"Graças a Deus, we have weathered the storm. We are sailing east now, back to find the African coast."

"How far until we see land?"

Lopo shrugged. "Five, ten days, depending on how far west we were pushed and the shape of the coast."

#

After ten days there was still no land to be seen. Captain Dias signaled for the *São Pantaleão* to come up beside the *São Cristóvão*. The captain put a speaking trumpet to his mouth. "We're turning north to see if the coast is there."

The São Cristóvão put on full canvas again, sped ahead and tacked downwind to larboard.

After Lopo's duty watch, he sought out Mbekah who was seated behind the master's cabin. He spoke in her native language, using Portuguese when a word or phrase failed him. "I have thought of little else these past weeks than about your orders from the crown." Mbekah turned to face Lopo and he saw he had her full attention. "It's not right to set you ashore against your will. If I cannot prevent it, I will join you."

Mbekah's eyes opened wide. "Will they not arrest you?"

"They will, sim. I must be careful. I will consider the various scenarios and plan how to behave in each."

"It will be dangerous on shore. Even if we survive, we will never see the *Mina* or Portugal again. No, you must not throw away your life and your career to do this."

"Mbekah, I shall come with you. I will never be happy if I lose you."

Mbekah cocked her head. "What do you say? I will miss you too. But I will not want to live if you are put into chains or if they kill you."

"I love you, Mbekah. I am sorry I haven't told you until now. I wasn't sure before. I thought so but I wasn't certain until I saw them take Ifé. I'm certain now. I can't watch that happen to you, Mbekah. I love you and will go with you if I can't stop them from this loco scheme."

They embraced. They leaned back and looked each other in the eyes. Mbekah's tears flowed freely. They embraced again until they heard shouting. They jumped up to looked around the cabin to see.

Crew were running to the bow. One already there cried, "Land. Lots of land."

Chapter 67

Cowherds' Bay

As darkness fell, the two caravelas anchored within easy hailing distance of each other in a wide, open-mouth bay east of an elevated headland.

While Lopo snored beside her in the bow, Mbekah studied the wide beach backed by grassy slopes. From a distance at sea, she had seen grazing cattle tended by dark men. From their moorage, she no longer saw them and wondered if the cowherds had fled with their animals or were just obscured by the night. *Will one of us be set ashore here? How will Lopo manage to come with me? Do I love him? When the girls in my village marry, do they love their husbands? I trusted my father would not match me with a man that was distasteful to me. When a girl, I often thought about the kind of man I hoped to be my husband. I don't remember thinking about loving him. Respecting him, yes. Did Mother love Father? We were happy, I think. Does Capitão Dias love his wife? Does King João love his queen? Does Olubayo love Kpodo? She loves his child Moisés. Love is for poems. Is it for real people too? I think about Lopo more and more. He is the best Portuguese man I know. I would be happy to be his wife. My father would be satisfied with Lopo if he got to know him. I believe I do love Lopo. How do we become man and wife?*

#

Mbekah opened her eyes and saw that the sun was fully above the horizon and Lopo was already on duty with his crew. She peeked over the gunwale to study the landscape. The dark men had retreated with their cattle up the hillsides. They squatted here and there about their herd and appeared to study the newcomers floating in the bay. She remembered her own amazement at the first sight of the Christians' colossal sailing ships compared to anything she had known before. She doubted the men on shore had ever come across pale men like the ones she now traveled with.

Lopo approached. "Bom dia, Mbekah. How did you sleep?

"Bem. Obrigada. What is new today?

Lopo knelt beside her. "The embaixadora on the *São Cristóvão* died two days ago. They buried her at sea. You are the only one now."

"I see. I will be the next to be left, is that not it?

Lopo nodded. "This could be the place. We will try to establish contact with the local people today"

#

Before the sun reached its zenith, two boatloads of sailors landed on the beach. Mbekah watched from the *São Pantaleão* as they moved inland two hundred paces onto the edge of a green field. They set out a blanket and loaded it with bracelets, glass beads, an iron pot, a stack of cotton cloth, and a dagger. The delegation stepped back twenty paces and waited. The cowherds, now joined by others, perhaps their headmen, kept their distance. After an hour, the Portuguese returned to their boats and to the caravelas. Throughout the day, Mbekah watched the offerings but no one ventured down to inspect or fetch them.

#

Day two in the bay dawned. Mbekah fixed her eyes on the field where the gifts had been positioned as the beams of sunlight crept down the cove and finally illuminated the spot. The blanket and its treasures were gone. A good sign. If she had to start her mission here, she hoped it would be among friendly people.

Two boats were sent with water barrels to the mouth of a stream emptying into the bay. Men at arms kept watch while the others went about filling the barrels. A score of the natives approached but kept to high ground. Of a sudden, a shower of arrows and stones were unleashed on the watering party. The Portuguese backed out of range to the sides of the rowboats.

A canon boomed on the *São Cristóvão* and a stone ball arced onto the hillside with a thud above the angry herders. They turned to watch it land and consider anew their chances against the strangers from the sea. A guard on the beach shot a bolt from his crossbow into the knot of attackers. The astonished men scattered screaming and hooting leaving one of their fellows writhing on the ground. Mbekah watched in horror. *This is no way to begin my diplomatic quest.*

#

At eventide, Master Infante and Lopo returned from consultations on the *São Cristóvão*. Lopo knocked on the door where Mbekah was resting. She joined him aft of the master's cabin at the stern which now faced away from the land.

Lopo took Mbekah's hands into his own. "Based on today's events, Capitão Dias agrees that this is not a good location to place you, our last embaixadora. Also, we do not know if we have passed the bottom point of Africa or if this is just another section of coast that runs east before turning south again. We will sail farther to ascertain the truth. You will begin your mission at a later date."

CHAPTER 68

The Meeting

Leaving the belligerent tribesmen of Cowherd's Bay, the little fleet sailed into the second week of February. The line of travel was east by northeast, more or less, for they hugged an irregular coastline. Lopo knew Dias mapped as they cruised and watched for features that would aid future mariners on their way to the *Indias.* Wild olive trees and sparse vegetation reminded Lopo of the countryside near Lisbon. Each day, the most important question for Lopo's fellow officers was whether they had already crossed under the bottom of Africa. But for Lopo, it was whether this was the day and place that Mbekah would be abandoned.

Rodrigo cornered Lopo when the latter sat with Mbekah gazing at the starry sky. "The men on my watch are united in insisting we turn back. We have enough proof that we've rounded the great southern cape of Africa. Supplies are low and the way ahead still a mystery. Will you join me in asking Master Infante to request a meeting with Capitão Dias to determine our course of action?"

"I will, sim. Let's speak with the master after morning muster."

Rodrigo went back to his post beside the tillermen. Lopo looked at Mbekah. "The time will soon be here. We need to make preparations for our journey on land. Think about what we have on the ship that we should take with us. Also, we should stop spending time together when Master Infante is on deck. It will be easier for me to join you if he does not suspect me as your accomplice."

#

After some sixty leagues, the two caravelas dropped anchor in the lee of an offshore island—a safe place to debate the future of the voyage. The ship's master, two pilots, two pilot's mates, and two crew members from each caravela along with Captain Dias separated themselves to a secluded spot.

Rodrigo addressed the captain. "We, the crew from both watches on the *São Pantaleão* respectfully assert that it is time to turn back. We are weary. Our good health is no more."

Captain Dias looked to his own pilot who stood. "I am certain now that we are on a northward trajectory to eventually reach the *Indias*. We can return with honor with this good news for the king."

Each attendee commented, generally in favor of returning. Captain Dias stepped forward. "We are on the last leg of our voyage to riches and fame for Portugal and for ourselves. It would be a shame if we quit with so little left to do. The goal is almost in sight. I can feel it." He turned a full circle, looking into the face of each man there. "It is now time to cast your vote. Yea or nay?"

The vote was eight against two for turning back. Captain Dias spoke again. My scribe will prepare a certificate for all to sign, attesting to his majesty that we turned back at your insistence. But let me beg you, give us one last attempt before we affix our signatures to such a document. Let us sail forward for two more days. If nothing appears to change your minds, I will also sign, and we will begin our journey home."

#

The following morning, they moved to a small island closer to shore and placed another stone pillar, the *Padrão of São Gregório* for it was on his feast day they arrived there. They continued east and north. Lopo waited until the ship's master was locked in his cabin for the night. He came to where Mbekah rested. "In two or three days, we begin our trek. Let us think of it as our wedding day and the beginning of our honeymoon."

CHAPTER 69

Rio do Infante

For two days and two nights the coast ran northeast in almost a straight line. Lopo could see Captain Dias almost continuously on deck of the nearby *São Cristóvão*, searching for a sign he could use to convince his crews to continue the voyage forward. Nothing presented itself. On the morning of the third day, the caravelas approached the outlet of a small river intersecting a long peaceful beach. The *São Pantaleão* cleared the sand bar at its mouth and entered a few hundred paces before dropping anchor. Ship's Master Infante signaled back that the depth of the bar was only slightly more than the draft of his caravela and warned the *São Cristóvão* to remain offshore.

Captain Dias, his two officers, two crew member representatives, and scribe were rowed in to the *São Pantaleão* for what was to be the final discussion about going forward or returning. Upon boarding Captain Dias proclaimed, "I name this river the *Rio do Infante*, Don João, in your honor since you are the first Christian to discover it."

The captain had been given his two additional days during which they had seen nothing to disprove that they had entered the ocean sea of the *Indias*. Neither had they discovered any reason to prolong their expedition further from home. The scribe spread out the document of regression and all signed.

Orders were given to fill the water casks and prepare for the return voyage. Captain Dias and a party of armed men accompanied Mbekah to the sandy bank where they were landed before the ship's boat was sent back to the *São Cristóvão*. Lopo watched as Captain Dias and Mbekah stood off from their escort for an hour. They frequently referred to a parchment which the captain handed to Mbekah. Her posture suggested submission but not enthusiasm. *The capitão is giving her instructions, her commission from the king.*

The boat returned from the *São Cristóvão* with the booty Mbekah was supposed to give to her contacts in this wild place. Captain Dias was rowed to his ship. Mbekah and her entourage hefted their load and tramped inland until Lopo could no longer see them from his perch on the quarterdeck.

Lopo descended to the main deck and watched as his cargo master supervised the loading of the water barrels. The river mouth was full of fish which a few crewmen caught in nets for their supper. Other crewmen gathered bird eggs in the rocks above the highwater line. The tide ebbed, and the surf broke over the shallow sand bar. Lopo calculated the timing to cross over the bar in the morning when the water was deep enough to allow their escape to the sea. In his mind he went over the items in the survival bag he had surreptitiously assembled. *Such good fortune to be anchored in the river! My escape will be ever so simple. Will the fleet sail as planned, or will they remain to search for me?*

#

Just after Lopo turned over the watch to Rodrigo and his men, he observed the return of the shore party. Mbekah was no longer in their company. They boarded their boat and were rowed back to the *São Cristóvão*. As they passed by the *São Pantaleão*, Lopo hailed them. "Did you find any natives?"

"No. But we saw signs of people and their cattle. We left Mbekah and her supplies in a grassy meadow a league and a half west of here. We set up her tent. She will be alright."

All evening Lopo secretly studied the bank to see if he could see his fiancée lurking in the bushes.

Rodrigo took a moment to lean on the gunwale near Lopo. "It's a hard thing they've done to Mbekah. Hard for you too, o meu amigo. I won't ask you your plans. I do want you to know that I plan to be a little deaf and blind after sundown."

CHAPTER 70

Turning Back

After muster and the Salve Regina, Lopo climbed the short ladder to the quarterdeck to confer with Don João Infante, ship's master. "We have about three hours for this high tide to turn. We'll take advantage to cross the bar at that time."

The ship's master nodded. "I know it's a difficult thing for you . . . to see the girl Josefa left behind. You've known her a long time. You were close."

"I have known her for years, sim. I was pilot's mate on the *Ninho* when we carried her and other captives back to Lisbon in '83. I taught her Portuguese. She picked it up quickly. A very clever girl."

"So fortunate for Josefa that his majesty included her in his 'school for embaixadores'. And that her majesty took such an interest in Josefa. She was the talk of Lisbon last year. I heard some lurid stories. I only mention it because shortly thereafter the queen killed that gossip and assured all that Josefa was still the virgin who arrived from the *Mina* Coast."

This was a pleasant revelation for Lopo. "How can you be sure which was true? The first rumor or the last one?"

"The stories of Josefa's passion that were passed around were never substantiated. Once the queen had outed the mean rumors, I realized I had not heard of a single cavalheiro, in or out of court, that had bedded the beauty. I'm sure I would have heard if such was happening. No doubt a rumor started by a jealous wife. To think of it! A beautiful negress outshining all of our local senhoras and senhoritas."

#

The tide turned. For half an hour Lopo's full attention was riveted on getting the *São Pantaleão* over the shallow sand at river's mouth and into the sea to join the *São Cristóvão*. That accomplished, he had time to chat with Rodrigo in whispers. "Graças a ti, caro amigo. Your help last night was timely."

"Não foi nada. I was surprised. I was sure you'd join her on land. Glad to have you still with us."

"It will be a challenge. I'm sure I can manage."

#

The current and wind favored them as they ran southwest and then west by southwest down the coast. They stopped often to survey and make detailed notes. To Lopo, it seemed that Captain Dias was being too deliberate to spite the men who made him stop short of his dream of being the first European to reach the *Indias*. After six weeks they passed Cowherds' Bay and sailed on to a shoreline they had missed when they were out at sea.

After another forty leagues, the winds became confused and progress difficult. Just as they rounded a rocky point and headed northwest for the first time, a torrent slammed into them. Visibility was low so they could not see far enough to locate a safe anchorage. They tacked upwind away from the shore and were happy to make even very modest gains in the tempest. Lopo discreetly slept in Rodrigo's berth in foul weather and on deck otherwise.

#

In less than a day the storm abated. The crew started calling the last point the Cabo das Tormentas. They beat north until they made visual contact with land and continued northwest. The coast was scalloped with huge bays. They tarried in two of those. Sailing out of the second, they rounded a mountain that cut like a razor far into the sea. For seven or eight leagues they navigated due north. They passed a flat-top mountain, at the end of which there was another sheltered harbor. As the sun dipped into the sea, the two ships entered and dropped anchor. A small village of low, domed huts could be seen less than half a mile from the beach. Cattle, small and large, grazed nearby. It was the month of May, autumn at those latitudes.

#

Long after dark, Lopo gave Rodrigo a nod. They leaned on a gunwale as far from sleeping sailors as possible. They could see campfires in the village and the silhouettes of people when they stepped in front of the flames.

Lopo put his mouth to his friend's ear. "Still only your two tillermen that have found us out?"

"As far as I know, sim. I'm certain Don João does not know."

"Giving her men's clothing was a good idea but it's still risky. I don't see any other course than to let her out for a spell most nights. She must stretch and get some fresh air."

CHAPTER 71

Ambassador Lopo David Meendez

The sun had been in the sky three hours when ship's master Don João Infante returned to the *São Pantaleão* from meeting with Captain Dias. Lopo and Rodrigo, assuming he had orders for them, met him as he came up the side and over the gunwale. "If we can make peace with the natives, we will remain here three or more weeks. The capitão wishes to do a full survey on land while we beach the ships and scrape their hulls. "Lopo will take six armed men in our boat and join Capitão Dias' boat in an hour to go ashore to establish contact with the village."

Lopo picked his men for the shore party and gave them instructions. He sat by the door of his compartment and rapped softly. "Open the door a crack." Mbekah did so. "Hand me my dress tunic, breastplate, cutlass, and helm. I'm going with the capitão to meet the locals. If we can get along with them, we'll be here long enough to steal you ashore for a few weeks. We have much work to do here on the ships before we head home."

#

The sun was straight up when the two ship's boats glided onto the sand. Two men remained with each boat. The rest moved up off the sand toward the village and set up for a friendly encounter.

The flag was planted, and a chair was placed behind a blanket spread with the usual offerings.

It was obvious to Lopo that the villagers had been watching because they soon came out to meet them. A short bony man, with feathers in his headband, his waistband, and dangling from his spear, led a wedge of physically similar men carrying spears or bearing platters of food.

Captain Dias, in shining helm and chest armor, stood and advanced alone, empty hands held out as if to hug his opposite. They stopped just out of reach of each other. "We come in peace on behalf of His Majesty King João II, Sovereign of Portugal, the two Algarves, and the Guinea Coast. We have gifts for you." He stepped aside and swept an arm to encompass the items on the blanket.

The leading man from the village studied the newcomers and the gifts. He made a speech about the same duration as the captain's. Whereupon he licked the fingers of his right hand and extended it to Captain Dias. The Portuguese had seen a similar gesture before. They knew it demonstrated that there was no poison on the proffered hand. Captain Dias clasped hands with the headman and smiled. The headman also smiled, and the spearmen relaxed. Not a single word pronounced by the other side was understood but all perceived that peace was in the two leaders' hearts. The headman waved for the platters to be brought forward.

The Portuguese brought two chairs out to the village side of the blanket for the captain and village headman. They sampled the food on the trays. In the absence of a mutually intelligible language, they smiled and nodded a lot.

Lopo watched the ceremony and the following pantomime. The natives' language was a blur of the most unusual sounds from deep in the throat to tongue clicks, lots of tongue clicks. He believed the two leaders agreed to trade and to allow the ships to remain for a season. After an hour, Captain Dias waved Lopo forward. "While we are here, you will stay in the village and learn as much of their language as possible."

Shocked, Lopo stepped forward and tentatively bowed to the headman who waved one of his men forward and spoke to him. This man moved over and kneeled to Captain Dias. Two boys came forward, each leading a fat-tailed sheep and handed the cords to the local man who was now by the captain.

The parties separated. Lopo paced beside and slightly behind the headman. As they came in among the dwellings, boys crowded to touch Lopo's armor, his clothing, and his hands. Dogs joined in the throng; their barking adding to the commotion. *Where are the women and girls?* He could see that to the side of the two dozen huts, there were twice that many bowed-stick frames that could be covered with woven mats to quickly triple the size of the village.

In the center of the village, the headman handed his spear to an attendant and sat on a richly decorated stool. He beckoned Lopo to sit on a mat beside him. Some of the assembled also sat on mats while others remained standing. Lopo reached up and removed his steel headgear. The onlookers gasped when his golden hair appeared in the sunlight. He waited for the clamor to subside, pointed to his chest, and said, "Lopo".

#

While strolling with the headman the next morning, Lopo watched Captain Dias, his scribe, and their escort hike to the base of Table Mountain and begin their ascent. The crew unloaded the *São Cristóvão* and set up camp near the beach. Lopo knew they would next haul the ship onto the sand and lay her on a side to clean and repair the hull. *The stars are in our favor once more. I'll have time to get Mbekah ashore before they do the same for the São Pantaleão.*

Lopo spent the day in the company of the headman, whose name he thought was Tkemet, and two of his sons. Lopo asked about everything he saw. He pointed to the ships and the men at work. "Portuguese." He pointed to the village and the people with their herds. "What do you name them?" He had said that phrase so many times, his hosts had fathomed its meaning.

"Khoi. Khoikhoi."

Lopo repeated. "Khoikhoi." He tried a sentence in Khoisan. "You are the Khoikhoi." Tkemet's sons giggled. Tkemet signaled that Lopo's attempt was acceptable, though he too smiled.

The day went quickly for Lopo and he was exhausted from the work of learning. At dark, he had one more thing to say to Tkemet. He attempted it in his newly-learned idiom. "I. My woman. Not wife. On big boat. Must fetch to here." He drew a picture in the dirt of a dugout and pantomimed paddling. He acted out being stealthy. "Not tell Headman Dias." He pointed to the moon and showed where it must be for the trip to the ship. It took several tries until he felt sure Tkemet understood.

Chapter 72

The Ritual

Before the first light of the morning, Lopo and Mbekah stole into the village. Once again, Rodrigo had made it possible for Mbekah to slip out of her sleeping closet and over the side of the caravela undetected and onto a crude raft Lopo put together: the Khoikhoi did not have dugouts or craft of any kind.

Lopo was excited and nervous. He and Mbekah had not yet consummated their union since declaring their love for each other. They had discussed a wedding and agreed such a ritual was impractical if not impossible. In a few minutes they would be together and alone for the first time.

Tkemet was there to meet them. Lopo sensed that Tkemet approved of Mbekah even though she was a head taller than the headman. A petite woman—Lopo decided she was Tkemet's wife—came out of a hut and led Mbekah away. Tkemet saw the surprised look on Lopo's face. "Not wife, yes?"

Crestfallen, Lopo said, "Yes. Not wife."

Tkemet herded Lopo into a hut where three young men were preparing to leave for their morning's activities. Lopo slept the rest of the morning.

#

Mbekah slept several hours alone. She awoke and heard women's voices at the entrance of her hut. When she emerged, she fairly stumbled over three women sitting on a mat, weaving grass baskets. She smiled. They smiled. From a covered basket, the woman who guided Mbekah the night before, offered her dried meat which she devoured. She drank an entire gourd full of fresh water. By that time, a dozen girls had gathered to inspect the tall stranger. Mbekah sat down on a mat and held out her arms in a friendly pose. Timidly, the girls came to her. They rubbed the sleeves of her cotton blouse and canvas trousers. They stroked her long straight hair. Their own hair was short, stiff, and naturally curly. She placed her palm on her breast and said, "Mbekah".

Lopo found her. The girls scattered. The two frustrated lovers embraced. The weavers pretended not to notice.

"You must not let anyone from the ships' crews see you while we're here. Even from a distance, the men will notice how much taller you are compared to the Khoikhoi women and get curious. We're going to have a hard time keeping the men away from these women. The men have not had women since the bordello near the *Mina* castle. I will have to speak with Capitão Dias now that I see how protective the natives are of their women and girls. I've been accepted here, I think, and even I hardly ever see a female."

"Alert me when the Portuguese are coming and I'll disappear. I'm not ready to walk around naked like the women here, with only a skimpy skin cape for cover. I will figure out something. When will we be together?"

"I will try to learn enough words to say we should have the same hut. They speak such a strange language. I may have to draw it in the dirt."

#

Lopo returned to his question and answer routine with Tkemet. In the afternoon, more short people arrived herding the same long-horn cattle, goats, and fat-tail sheep that the villagers husbanded. In no time, they turned about half of the skeletal frames nearby into huts identical to the ones already there. By nightfall, the village had doubled in size. That night Lopo met the headman of the newcomers. The recently arrived men joined Tkemet's men around the fire. From their gestures and the occasional word Lopo could pick out, he knew they spoke at length about the pale strangers from the sea and their gigantic wooden birds.

#

Mbekah took advantage of her escape from almost constant confinement on the ship for the past two months by going with the women whenever they left the village to scour the country side for food and useful materials. She too learned a few words but mostly followed the example set by Tkemet's wife. Women from the new clan joined them on occasion. They made no secret of their curiosity about her and the pale men she came with.

Eight days after Mbekah's advent in the village, a third clan appeared with its animals. They converted the last stick frames into livable domed huts. The village had grown to three times what it was when the Portuguese first sailed into the harbor below the table-top mountain.

To her surprise, the women helped her gather long sticks, weave panels, and fashion a hut. She wasn't sure but she believed the dwelling was for her. *This is very interesting. I must tell Lopo.*

#

Lopo found Captain Dias resting in his tent. "You and all our company are invited to a feast this evening. They have butchered a steer and some sheep."

The captain stood and stretched. "Is this some special occasion?"

"As you've likely observed, there are now three clans camped over there. I think Tkemet wants to give the other two headmen a chance to look us over. The clans' adult males will join us. They will offer you a dried plant to smoke. To not accept would be an insult to your hosts. Like drinking wine, you'll feel a little intoxicated. I advise you inhale deeply only once or twice."

#

There were no women visible when the Portuguese came single file into the village. They mixed with the natives and formed a circle, three deep, seated on mats and skins. Lopo stood between Captain Dias and Tkemet who were each situated on fancy stools as were the other two headmen on the other side of Tkemet. Lopo interpreted, as best he could, the various stages of the evening.

Village men danced a welcome in the center of the ring. Squirming grubs were offered. Most of the Portuguese, used to weevils and worms in their hardtack, managed to swallow at least one of the fleshy morsels. Bladders of sour goat milk made the rounds. They chewed on tough roots and spit the pithy remains into a basket passed for that purpose. Two kinds of raw meat came skewered on sticks. More dancing to the rhythm of clapped hands and hummed tones followed. Finally, a roll of a dried narcotic was lit and passed among the four leaders.

After two full hours, Lopo helped the captain to his feet and watched as his crewmates filed out and off to their camp or ship.

Tkemet motioned for Lopo to sit on the stool that had been the captain's. The headman was a little wobbly from his smoke. He addressed Lopo in Khoisan. "Now you make woman wife."

A line of women danced into the circle, leading Mbekah who wore nothing but a skimpy cape about her shoulders and wild olive leaves in her hair. Lopo blushed. The clapping grew faster and louder. The dancing frantic. Tkemet's wife stood Mbekah in front of Lopo. He stood. He had recovered from his shyness and couldn't keep his eyes off his spectacular, almost nude bride. A strand of fresh cow intestine was draped on each of their shoulders like a garland. Tkemet said a few words. The newlyweds were pushed to the end of a chanting line of men and women. Lopo and Mbekah held hands and followed the line until they came to a recently constructed hut which they entered. The opening was closed off and the company surrounded the hut and continued their racket for, Lopo knew not how long. He had other things on his mind.

CHAPTER 73

Confession

Eleven weeks had passed since the two caravelas departed the harbor by the Khoikhoi village. They had lingered a full month there at the place Captain Dias named *Cabo da Boa Esperança* for he had hope that he would lead a future expedition around this point and on to the *Indias*. With all the significant landforms, currents, and winds recently visited, the captain prepared a map to inform the king and light the way for future voyages. They had careened the ships; they had filled their holds with fresh water and dried meats—cattle, goat, sheep, fish, and seal. And erected another padrão as evidence of their claim on the harbor and its backcountry for Portugal.

The month was a glorious interlude for Lopo and his bride. His ambassadorial duties kept him in the Khoikhoi camp which he used more to get to know Mbekah than to learn more Khoisan. They successfully kept her presence there a secret from the Portuguese who were generally hard at work those weeks. The honeymooners were treated to a ten-day, escorted tour of the area. They climbed the mesa and visited by land the bay they had sailed in just before arriving at their current safe harbor.

Three weeks previous, they had sailed into the bay within a bay to look for signs of Ifé. They had not found her and had sailed on after three days. Only last week they had dropped into the bay with all the whales, birds, and seals to fetch Gyasi if he was about. Again, there was no sign of Mbekah's fellow villager and embaixador.

Long after midnight, Lopo, Mbekah, and Rodrigo sat behind the tillermen and consulted quietly. Rodrigo said, "Every man on the ship knows that Mbekah is on board. If Don João does not know, he is bound to know soon."

Lopo said, "What will he do about it?"

"Don João will have to do something. You must be ready with your explanation. We will reach Kidnap Bay in less than two days. The não should be there, repaired and stocked with provisions, if Gonçalves has done his duty. If we didn't have you and Mbekah's situation to worry about, we would be planning how to deal with the murderer Gonçalves and his two chums."

#

Rodrigo and his men had taken the evening watch, and all had been fed. Lopo led Mbekah up the ladder and knocked on the ship's master's door. "Begging pardon, o Senhor *do Infante*. I have a matter of great importance to bring to your attention." The master looked past Lopo to Mbekah. He acted surprised but not too surprised. *He already knows.*

"Just a moment, while I put on my coat." The master disappeared into his cabin and returned. "Let's retire to behind my cabin. A favorite spot for you, não é?"

"O Senhor, you can see I brought Josefa back on board after she was set ashore by Capitão Dias. And I have hidden her since that night. We have consummated our marriage."

"Marriage?"

"Yes, we were married by Tkemet in the manner of the Khoikhoi. We will marry again when we can celebrate mass in a Christian church."

"Disobeying orders on a mission for the crown? You know that is a capital crime, sim?"

Lopo kept his voice submissive. "I believe when the situation is understood, allowances will be deemed appropriate."

Mbekah stepped forward. "It is my doing. When I saw that Lopo was in love with me, I took advantage of his gallantry. Although I do love him."

Lopo shook his head. "Thanks, coração, but it was my plan and my doing." He turned again to the ship's master. "Josefa knows she was manipulated by those close to his majesty. She understood she was returning to her own homeland and that from there she was to aid us in our search for Prester John. I think Capitão Dias will understand that she was not going to be a friendly embaixadora for Portugal under the altered conditions forced upon her."

"Lopo, you have put me in a difficult situation. I sympathize with you, but I have my sworn duty."

CHAPTER 74

Crossing the Rubicon

The clouds parted, allowing the full moon to shine through as the *São Pantaleão* cruised into Kidnap Bay. Pilot's Mate Rodrigo Correia had the watch that September night. The night before they had lost sight of the *São Cristóvão*, flagship of their little fleet, and had not established contact during the day. It was no great concern because they knew to rendezvous at the store ship.

Don João felt the change when they dropped anchor within hailing distance of the não and came down to the main deck to survey the situation. The *São Cristóvão* had not proceeded them and there was no evidence that a watch had been posted on the não. "We'll wait until morning before raising the crew of the não. Post a watch and the rest of you get some sleep."

Lopo was not sleepy so he relieved Rodrigo's man on watch. Mbekah joined him in the cool breeze. Lopo put his arm around her shoulder and they silently studied the silhouettes of features on the shore.

Mbekah cocked her head. "The skiff comes from the far side of the não. One man, rowing."

In a moment, Lopo recognized their friend, Manoel.

Manoel was careful not to bump the side of the *São Pantaleão*. He climbed up the rope Lopo put down for him. They embraced. "I am the nightguard. I fell asleep and missed your arrival. I have not alerted the others on the não that you are here."

Lopo kept his voice low. "So happy to see you alive. What of the others?"

Manoel whispered. "All dead except Master Dias, Piloto Gonçalves, and Nunno."

"Dead? What are you saying, Manoel?"

Manoel related the tale. "Shortly after you departed, our so-called embaixadores came aboard with their headman and others of their council. To look around and gauge our strength, I suppose. The next day, they arrived in force, thirty armed men in ten dugouts. We saw them coming and were ready, except our two cannons were not loaded. We killed or wounded about twenty and forced them to retreat. Four of our crew died that day and two more were severely wounded. Both eventually succumbed. We've been at a standoff with the tribe since that day. Needless to say, the não is in pitiful condition and there are no provisions gathered for your return. We fish and spear the odd seal from the skiff which I keep in prime condition. I sail it up the coast from time to time to forage on land. We collect rain water to drink. How is it that Mbekah is with you? Where is the *São Cristóvão*?"

Lopo gave an abbreviated account of their voyage.

Manoel immediately grasped the seriousness of Lopo and Mbekah's position. "You must drop me back on the não and escape on the skiff. I keep water, emergency provisions, and supplies in the skiff. I will say I fell asleep and didn't see or hear anything. You should gain at least a two-day head start. More if the caravelas need to take on fresh water. I will tell Rodrigo goodbye for you."

#

Lopo and Mbekah maintained sight of the shore as they sailed north. The sun came up and they saw the tops of the sails of the

São Cristóvão in the distance approaching the tops of the masts of the two ships already moored in the bay.

"We've crossed the Rubicon. Again." Lopo explained the allusion to Mbekah.

"The stomach has no holiday." Mbekah rummaged through the supplies Manoel had placed in the skiff. She baited and trailed a fish line. "'If you find no fish, you have to eat bread.' We used to say that. With the year-old hardtack we have with us, that saying has new meaning to me."

CHAPTER 75

Trapped

Mbekah managed tiller and sail all afternoon while Lopo slept. Lopo knew that the caravelas would travel day and night, once they got started. To keep ahead in the chase, the couple had decided not to put ashore at night so Mbekah got a quick sailing lesson five days earlier. She had been handling the skiff much of the daylight hours during their run up the coast.

Lopo stirred, then opened his eyes. He lay in the bow and watched Mbekah secretly for a few minutes. *I adore this competent, confident woman, my wife. She has adapted so well to every situation—forest, city, court, ship, colony, Khoikhoi village, matrimony, fugitive . . . She has integrity and fealty rarely seen in the people I have met in my lifetime. She would have been an admirable embaixadora for his majesty, had he dealt honorably with her. She will be a valuable asset to her people if they can accept a female leader. It makes me sad that my family will likely never get to know her. They may never even know of this marriage.*

Mbekah realized Lopo was awake and staring at her. "How did you sleep, coração? Are you ready to take over?"

"I dreamed we traveled many moons into the heart of the continent. We met Ogané and he was indeed the great Prester John. He knew of the Christians in Europe. He was aware how corrupt the Christians Church was right up to the Bishop of Rome. He had correct intelligence about how the Christian kingdoms bicker and war against each other. He knew we sought him. He did not want his people to be soiled by contact with such people. He liked you and me but would not allow us to leave and reveal the location of his rich, peaceful capitol. We became his advisors and lived comfortably at his court."

"Did you see any children? Did they look like you or me?"

"I did not. But I would hope they would favor your side of the family."

"I hope so too, if a girl child."

"I agree. We'll have all girls and they'll look like you."

Mbekah perked up. "There's a stream. I'll steer right into it if it's deep enough so we can top off our cask."

"Go ahead. The bottom is only sand so going aground is not dangerous."

#

Mbekah was the first to wake. Long shadows and fading light told her the sun would soon set. They had pulled the skiff well into the mouth of the stream, until it was too shallow to continue, and into the shade of a dense canopy of leaves. They filled their cask with fresh water and foraged for anything edible besides fish. They found a clearing that showed signs of repeated occupation. Perhaps a fishing camp or an overnight spot for the manicongo's patrols—they estimated they were not far south of the Zaire River. They strolled out to a dune behind the beach where the stream cut a channel through the sand. She flirted with Lopo until he gave in to her charms. They shed what little clothing they wore and came together—something that had been impossible on the *São Pantaleão* and tricky in the skiff. Content, they both dozed off.

She dressed and crawled to the top of the low dune. To her dismay, she spied the two pursuing caravelas heading directly toward them. "Lopo. Wake up. We have company."

He pulled his trousers on and joined her. “They’re coming in for fresh water. They’ll see the skiff. We’re trapped.”

CHAPTER 76

The Patrol

"You've only just begun filling the barrels. What is so urgent for you to leave your task?" Captain Dias had been impatient with Gonçalves since rescuing him off the não. The captain was less than pleased to find no provisions waiting for the fleet and that Lopo had taken the não's skiff from under Gonçalves' nose. Even though the sun was setting, Captain Dias had ordered boats ashore for fresh water immediately upon anchoring.

"Desculpe, o Senhor Capitão. We have discovered the não's skiff. Lopo and the woman must be nearby."

"Boa sorte! Get six men and find them. Do not wait for morning. Go now. Also, take Manoel from the *São Pantaleão* with you. I want Lopo and Josefa back alive. Compreende?"

#

Ship's boats were already in the water when Lopo and Mbekah crawled through the dunes back into the trees. They had returned to the skiff and grabbed a few items for their land escape.

Lopo broke the silence. "They will discover the skiff within minutes of coming into the stream. We will hide down the beach where we can watch the ships from the trees.

Mbekah took charge. This was not her forest, but she had a better sense of the land than Lopo. "Careful where you step. Avoid sand or any soft ground. Even one of your sailors can follow footprints. Careful to not step on brittle twigs. Let's not give ourselves away with noise."

They remained in the shadows while they worked their way a few hundred paces south, keeping an eye on the ships. Lopo climbed into the branches of a tree. "One of the boats is returning to the ships too soon. Four oarsmen and one passenger. A big man. Gonçalves! They're not towing any barrels. They must be reporting the discovery of the skiff."

Half an hour later, Lopo observed the boat returning to the beach. "Four rowing and eight others, including Gonçalves. A search party."

#

Mbekah led Lopo inland, following a narrow path through the vegetation—bushes, low trees, tall trees. "*Mbanza Congo*, the manicongo's capitol, is five days march from the sea toward the rising sun. When we get nearer, we should cross a road. The road will lead us to the city."

"They betrayed you before. Why not again?"

"We hide until we see that your people have come and gone before we reveal ourselves." Mbekah stopped dead. She was listening and searching their surroundings. "Too late."

A score of armed warriors emerged from both sides. Spears ready.

Mbekah held arms out, hands open. Lopo copied her. She spoke words Lopo had never heard before.

"You speak Congolese?"

"I learned a little from Isabell while in the convent and later as part of my escape plan when we were here before."

The patrol leader pushed through his men. Mbekah dropped her arms. He spoke to her slowly, gesturing to aid understanding. Mbekah replied.

Lopo relaxed. "What does he say?"

"He remembers us from our visit last year. He asks if we are with the two floating houses that flew into the bay a few hours ago. At least I think that is what he is asking."

CHAPTER 77

Like a Codfish

The Congolese warriors escorted Mbekah and Lopo back toward the beach to the patrol's makeshift camp in the trees, not the camp in the clearing near the stream that they had seen earlier. Four men were left to guard the pair. The others disappeared. Mbekah and Lopo had no choice but to eat a cold meal and stretch out to sleep.

They awoke in the middle of the night to the commotion of the Portuguese search party being ushered into camp and made to sit across the ground from them. The sailors were not bound but they had been disarmed.

Gonçalves glared when he caught site of Mbekah and Lopo. Nunno scooted over next to his boss. Manoel got up slowly and came over to sit with his friends. "We were searching for you when these spearmen jumped us. We had no choice but to come with them. Capitão Dias has no idea we have been captured. Dias wants you two back alive. Gonçalves wants you dead. Do you know what's going on?" We've had no one to translate."

Lopo whispered, "Does the capitão know you helped us at Kidnap Bay?"

"He's not happy I fell asleep on my watch, but he doesn't know I faked sleeping through your arrival and escape. We all agreed later that you must have swum between the two ships to snatch the skiff."

"Have you any idea what will happen to us if we're sent back to the ships? Has Don João told you anything of the capitão's intentions?"

Manoel shook his head.

The Congolese leader spoke to his men at some length.

Mbekah leaned in. "I didn't catch much of that but I believe at the end he told half his men to stand guard and half to get some sleep."

The guards that remained on watch came to each of the Portuguese and tied their hands behind their backs. They hobbled their feet as well. They did not bind Mbekah.

Lopo and Mbekah slept face to face, belly to belly. They whispered a moment and dozed off.

#

After a few hours of rest, the camp was alive with activity. Each of the captives was hand fed a few bites of dried meat of an unknown variety and got water from a bladder squirted into their open mouths.

Mbekah rose slowly and walked deliberately over to where the patrol leader sat. She squatted beside him, speaking in low tones, sometimes drawing in the sandy soil. During the conversation, she pointed to Lopo and to Gonçalves. The patrol leader studied the two Portuguese men as she talked about them. He nodded and called two of his warriors over to give them instructions.

When Mbekah joined Lopo and Manoel, Lopo said, "Did he agree to it?"

Manoel said, "Agree to what? What are you two up to?"

"I told the leader that Gonçalves had insulted me and assaulted me, that my husband Lopo had saved me, and that Lopo had challenged Gonçalves to a duel. Small knives to the death."

Manoel stared at Lopo. "Are you ready for this? Is that your plan?"

"It's the only way we see to not get sent back to the ships with Gonçalves at the lead of the party."

Mbekah continued. "I told him that Portuguese custom demands that the two fight. Lopo's honor and my virtue are at stake. I think the patrol leader would like to see the foreigners go at each other. I assured him he and his men would be amused."

#

The Congolese spearmen formed a circle. One untied Lopo and pulled him to his feet. He returned Lopo's knife to him. Another did the same for Gonçalves who looked confused. Both were pushed into the ring.

Lopo crouched, held his knife in his right hand with point to the sky, and focused on Gonçalves' eyes, hips, and knife hand. "I will gut you like a codfish. I do it for the murder of Joselinho. I do it for Kpodo's wife Antonia whom you debauched and let die. I do it for robbing and attempting to murder me. I do it for assaulting my wife."

Gonçalves got the picture. He readied his blade and lowered his center of gravity. He slid around right when Lopo slid left. "You have seen your last sunrise, woman man. After I slice you open, I will take your woman myself, then give her to every sailor in the fleet."

It was Lopo's agility against Gonçalves' greater bulk. But Lopo knew his opponent had lost his edge by lying around on the não for most of a year.

The spearmen called out to each other. It was clear they were enjoying the unusual combat. Mbekah guessed they were betting on the outcome. The Portuguese captives watched in stunned silence.

Gonçalves lunged, swiping his knife at Lopo's stomach. Lopo jumped out of the way easily and slashed the big man's wrist as his knife hand came across in front of Lopo.

Gonçalves screamed. The fingers of that hand no longer responded. His knife fell to the ground. He clutched the bleeding wrist with his left hand. "Enough. I yield."

"You can yield when you are dead. Pick up the knife."

"You cannot do this to me. You will be hanged for assaulting an officer of his majesty, the king."

"His majesty will thank me when he hears I've rid his kingdom of a murderer and thief. Do you wish to die fighting, or do you wish to die begging?"

Gonçalves attempted to back out of the cordon of spearmen. They body blocked him back into the fight.

"Pick up your knife. You'll get what Joselinho got. No less."

Gonçalves kept his eyes on Lopo as he bent to retrieve his knife with his left hand. Instead of standing tall, he rushed Lopo and jerked his head up to catch Lopo under the chin.

Lopo sidestepped but was caught by Gonçalves' shoulder and went down. Gonçalves' momentum carried him into the band of guards who checked him with their spear shafts and shoved him back. Lopo recovered, spun and caught Gonçalves in the lower back, thrusting his knife into a kidney up to the hilt.

Gonçalves' eyes bulged. He straightened. He flopped onto the turf, face down. He writhed for a moment. Then he lay quietly panting while he bled out and died.

CHAPTER 78

A New Mission

Both caravelas made their way up the Zaire River to the landing where they had been entertained the year before. They had waited five days for Gonçalves and the search party which eventually emerged from the trees with Manoel in the lead. Captain Dias interrogated the men. They told him they had been detained by a band of warriors of the manicongo. Lopo and Josefa were also captives. For some unknown reason, Lopo and Gonçalves were made to fight to the death and Lopo had prevailed. Half the warriors had immediately disappeared, taking Nunno, Lopo, and Josefa with them. Four days later the sailors were brought to the beach by the stream. At that point, their Congolese guards vanished into the forest. In a private audience with Captain Dias, Manoel disclosed how he learned that Gonçalves and his two men were responsible for the death of crew member José Figueroa e Duarte (Joselinho). He included Gonçalves' multiple attempts to violate Josefa. Since Josefa spoke a little Congolese, Manoel suspected she had convinced the band's leader to allow Lopo, as her husband, to avenge her honor.

Two days after the Portuguese ships moored, the manicongo and his entourage reached the village in the clearing.

He promptly came to the river bank and received Captain Dias when he was rowed in.

After formal greetings and exchange of good wishes, Captain Dias spoke. "We have need of fresh provisions for our journey home."

Isabell translated. The manicongo gestured his approval.

The captain said, "We have also come for two of our crew and Josefa, an embaixadora of His Majesty, King João.

Isabell translated.

The manicongo responded.

Isabell listened and gave the translation to Captain Dias. "The manicongo regrets to inform you that one of the crew, whom you call Nunno, was not fit for the long march to *Mbanza Congo*. He died on the trail."

"And what of Piloto Lopo Meendez and Josefa *da Guiné*?"

"When the manicongo found out that the woman had been sent by your king to search for Prester John, he sent both on their way with an armed escort to the city of the great Ogané. Perhaps Ogané is the famous Prester John. He hopes you are pleased with his assistance in this mission that is so important to your king."

Captain Dias contemplated that revelation for a long moment. "Please ask the manicongo when he expects them to return."

After conferring with the manicongo, Isabell said, "Twenty to thirty months."

Captain Dias gritted his teeth and forced a smile. "Please thank the manicongo for his thoughtful aid and say that I will surely relay to his majesty how helpful he has been."

Isabell passed on the captain's courtesy message.

Captain Dias continued. "I am under orders to hasten back to Portugal. As soon as we have been restocked, we will depart. Muitos agradecimentos." He bowed and stepped back into the row boat.

-The End-

Expanded Historical Note

In 1144, an emissary to Pope Eugene II reported the precarious situation of crusader-held Jerusalem and requested more European military aid. He brought news of a potential ally—a Christian empire in the East ruled by a righteous priest named John.

Jerusalem fell in 1187 and the crusaders were eventually expelled from the Holy Land. Christian efforts to reassert sovereignty in the region continued sporadically for centuries. During this time, increasingly embellished letters, allegedly from Prester John (as the priestly king came to be known), were circulated to the courts of European nobles—a ruse by zealots to convince Christendom's rulers that retaking Jerusalem was possible because the elusive Prester John was ready to help.

In Christian minds, Prester John's realm became a land of wealth, fantastic beings, the Holy Grail, and the Fountain of Youth. For wishful European leaders, Prester John appeared to be a formidable power on the flank of the Islamic Middle East and a necessary stopping place on some future route to the spices and silks of the Far East.

In 1420, Prince Henry the Navigator became Grand Master of the Military Order of Christ, successor in Portugal to the persecuted Knights Templar. Henry wished Portugal to replace Constantinople and Venice and become sole middleman to

Europe's trade with the East. The Order of Christ's wealth financed Henry's systematic explorations into the Sea of Aethiopia, as the South Atlantic was called then, down the coast of Africa—pushing the limits of the known world with each voyage while developing the maritime technology needed to sail long distances and, more importantly, to return.

In 1481, King João II ascended the Portuguese throne and renewed the late Navigator's efforts to find a sea route to the East by circumnavigating Africa. Only the mission was now infinitely more urgent and potentially more profitable because the key trading city Constantinople had recently fallen to the Ottoman Turks, greatly disrupting traditional trade routes with the East. King João, whom modern historians consider the perfect Machiavellian ruler, sought Prester John's kingdom in earnest to further his ambitious plans.

Author's Note

This is a work of fiction inspired by historical events. The Portuguese did send female slaves back to Africa on the voyage that first rounded the bottom of Africa in modern times. These women were dropped off in places far from where they were captured. They were expected to make friends with the locals on behalf of the Kingdom of Portugal and seek information about the location of the realm of Prester John.

The reader will recognize King João II, Bartolomeu Dias, Christopher Columbus (Cristovão Colom) and others as historical figures who are characters in this story. I have endeavored to have them act in accordance with historians' representations of their actions at approximately the correct times modified to accommodate the requirements of my plot.

A few of the place names have changed since the Age of Discovery. The Mina fort passed into Dutch and then English hands and is known today as Elmina. It is located in present-day Ghana. The Zaire River is today the Congo River. Cape Town, South Africa thrives in the spot of the Khoikhoi village.

GLOSSARY OF TERMS, PORTUGUESE WORDS, AND PLACE NAMES

Port. = Portuguese Lit. = literally, Id. = idiomatically, i.e. proper translation. Note: '**ç**' is pronounced like '**s**' in 'silly'. 'j' is pronounced like the 's' in 'measure'.

A mina: (Port.) Lit. The Mine, Id. The Gold Coast
Ackee: The fruit of an African tree
Aethiopia, Sea of: The South Atlantic
Aft: Back of a ship
Agnes Dei: (Latin) Lit. God's lamb, Id. Liturgical prayer to Christ as Savior
Alfama: Residential/commercial district in Lisbon
Algarve: Kingdom within Portugal south of Lisbon
Amigo/amiga: (Port.) Friend/female friend
Aqua Ardiente: (Port.) Lit. burning water Id. Hard liquor
Arguim: **Arguin**, An island off the west coast of Sahara Africa
Assegai: a light spear
Ave Maria: (Latin) Lit. Praise Mary, Id. Liturgical prayer to Mary, mother of Jesus
Azores: island group off the west coast of Portugal
Azzá: (Port.) A gambling card game
Baobab: African tree that appears to have its roots at the top and looks to many to be upside down
Basta: (Port.) Lit. Enough, Id. That's enough
Bem: (Port.) Good or well
Bemvindo: (Port.) Welcome, i.e. a greeting
Benya Lagoon: Tidal pond behind the Mina (Elmina) slave fort
Benya River: Very short river that is the outlet from the Benya Lagoon into the ocean
Boa sorte: (Port.) Good luck!
Boas Tardes: (Port.) Good afternoon, i.e. a greeting
Bolt: An arrow used in a crossbow
Bom dia: (Port.) Good day, i.e. a greeting

Bow: Front portion of a ship or boat

Bragança: City on the northeast corner of Portugal

Cabo das Tormentas: Cape of Storms

Cabo de Boa Esperança: Cape of Good Hope

Cais: (Port.) Dock or pier

Cais Taberna: Dock Tavern

Capitão: (Port.) Lit. Captain, Id. Military leader as well as ship's master

Carapau: (Port.) Mackerel

Carapau Cantina: (Port.) Mackerel Bar

Caravela: (Port.) Lit. Caravel, Id. Portuguese developed sailing ship that, when using lateen (triangle) sails, could sail closer to the wind than square-rigged vessels. Caravelas used during the time of this book were 60 to 75 feet long and steered by a long oar on one side. They had no crows nest. Most crew and passengers slept on the open deck.

Caro/cara: (Port.) Dear or expensive

Castile: Forerunner of Spain

Castilian: Person from Castile

Cavalheiro: (Port.) Lit. Knight, Id. Knight or gentleman

Certo: (Port.) Certainly

Christown: This is what Mbekah heard when the Portuguese said the word cristião (Christian)

Cog: Square-rigged sailing ship popular in Baltic and Atlantic Europe, 50 to 75 feet in length.

Commandante: (Port.) Commander

Compreende?: (Port.) Lit. Understand?, Id. Do you understand?

Conception Bay: Now known as Walvis Bay

Convento: (Port.) Convent

Coração: (Port.) Lit. Heart, Id. Term of endearment to a loved one

Cortes (Port.) Lit. Court, Id. Assembly of Portuguese nobility, clergy, and bourgeoisie called and dismissed by the king at will and at a place of his choosing. Can also refer to an assembly of any one of these groups.

Cowherds' Bay: Present day Mossel Bay

Cowry: Shell of certain small to large sea snails often used for money among some cultures

Cristião: (Port.) Christian

Cutlass: Short, broad slashing sword

Da/Do: (Port.) Lit. Of the, Id. Equivalent to German 'von'
Da Guiné: (Port.) Lit. Of/from Guinea, Id. von Guinea
Demônios: (Port.) Demons!
Desculpe: (Port.) Excuse me.
Desgraçoado: (Port.) Lit. Disgraceful, Id. Despicable
Deus: (Port.) God
Dia: (Port.) Day
Domine: (Latin) Lit. Lord, Id. A liturgical prayer
Don: *Should be Dom.* (Port.) Lit. Respected Mr., Id. Manner to address a man of high birth or office or accomplishment.
Dona: (Port.) Lit. Respected Mrs., Id. Manner to address a woman of high birth or office or accomplishment
Ducat: Gold or silver coin
E: (Port.) And
é: (Port.) Is, i.e. third person singular of the verb 'to be'
Embaixador/Embaixadora: (Port.) Ambassador/female ambassador
Encantado: (Port.) Lit. Enchanted, Id. Enchanted/Pleased to meet you.
Epiphany: Three Kings' Day (January 6th)
Escutcheon: Heraldic shield or coat of arms
Evora: Portuguese city about 80 miles east of Lisbon
Fat Sands: Stretch of coast in southwest Namibia
Fogo: (Port.) Lit. Fire, Id. Command to discharge a firearm
Gambit: Ploy, stratagem, scheme, ruse
Garçonete: (Port.) Waitress or barmaid
Governador: (Port.) Governor
Gout: A form of inflammatory arthritis, a painful condition that often affects the joint at the base of the big toe
Graças a Deus: (Port.) Lit. Thanks to God, Id. Thank God
Graças a ti, caro amigo: (Port.) Lit. Thanks to thou, dear friend, Id. Thank you, dear friend
Guiné: (Port.) Guinea, a traditional name for the region of West Africa on the north edge of the Gulf of Guinea including the countries modern-day countries of Ivory Coast, Ghana, Togo, and Benin.
Gunwale: The upper edge of a ship's or boat's side. Also spelled 'gunnel'
Hatchway: Opening in the deck allowing access to the ship's hold
Harquebus: Also called arquebus. 15th century firearm, precursor to the musket and rifle

Hoc est enim corpus meun: (Latin) Lit. This is my body, Id. Priest says this before distributing the bread/wafer and wine during mass

Hold: Interior cargo space in a ship

Houses: Game played by Mbekah and Ifé in their cell at the Mina fort, a version of an ancient game also known as Oware, Awalé, Ayó, and other names

Imbabala: Small antelope

Indias (Port.) Lit. Indies, Id. East Indies or lands and islands of South Asia and Southeast Asia

Indulgences for the dead: A way to reduce the punishment a person must suffer for their sins

Infante: (Port.) Lit. Infant or prince, Id. A prince in the royal line of succession. Can also mean infant or be a surname. Henry the Navigator was known to the Portuguese as 'o Infante Henrique' because his father was king even though Henry was a younger brother of the man who actually became king of Portugal

Irmãos: (Port.) Brothers

Jenneh: Also known as Djenné. City in the Songhay Empire to the north of Mbekah's forest village

Jeu de Paume: (French) Lit. Game of the Palm, Id. Became the modern game of tennis

João: (Port.) Given name John

Judiaria: (Port.) Lit. Jewish quarter, Id. Jewish ghetto

Kidnap Bay: Angra do Salto. Present day Tombua, Angola

Kola: Fruit/nut of the kola tree containing caffeine which is often chewed alone or in a social setting

Kor: Tan, pheasant-like bird

La Coruhna: City in Galicia (northeast Spain)

Lombard: Person from Lombardy, a region in the northwest of what is now Italy

Larboard: Right side of a ship when looking forward. Now called port or port side.

Lohpu: The name Lopo sounded like Lohpu to Mbekah

Lopinho: (Port.) Diminutive of the name Lopo

Madeira: Large Portuguese island off the northwest coast of Africa

Mãe: (Port.) Mother

Mãe de Deus: (Port.) Lit. Mother of God, Id. Mary, mother of Jesus

Majordomo: (Port.) Steward
Malagueta: (Port.) Type of pepper from Africa that is not as desirable as black pepper from the Indies
Manicongo: King in Congolese
Mast: Tall pole that supports a sail or sails
Matchlock: Early mechanism to fire a harquebus, precursor to the modern trigger
Mbanza Congo: Old name for Manicongo's capitol
Menina: (Port.) Lit. Girl, Id. Waitress or serving girl
Merda: (Port.) Lit. Excrement, Id. Often a swear word
Mestre: (Port.) Lit. Master, Id. Professor or teacher
Meu/minha: (Port.) My (masculine)/My (feminine), i.e. first person singular possessive pronoun
Mina: (Port.) Lit. Mine, Id. In this book, can refer to the Gold Coast and/or the Mina slave fort/castle now known as Elmina
Minha: (Port.) My (feminine), i.e. first person singular possessive pronoun
Minha querida: (Port.) My dear one (female)
Mordomo: (Port.) Butler
Mother superior: In charge of day-to-day operations of a convent
Muitos agradecimentos: (Port.) Many thanks.
Não: (Port.) Lit. Negative response, Id. No
Não: (Port.) A vessel larger than a caravela and therefore used as a supply ship
Não é verdade?: (Port.) Is it not true?
Não é?: (Port.) Is it not so?
Não foi nada: (Port.) Lit. No was nothing, Id. It was nothing
Natal: (Port.) Christmas
Nebli: Peregrine falcon from Spanish Andalusia
Negrosinhos: (Port.) Diminutive for negroes
Northerns: Falcons from northern Europe
O meu Coração: (Port.) Lit. The my heart, Id. My dear (male or female)
O meu Deus: (Port.) Lit. The my God, Id. Oh my God
O/os/a/as: (Port.) The (masculine/masculine plural/feminine/feminine plural)
Obrigado/Obrigada: (Port.) Lit. Obligated, Id. Thanks, Thank you
Olá: (Port.) Hello, Hi
Onde: (Port.) Where
Ourém: Portuguese city about 86 miles north of Lisbon

Padrão: (Port.) Stone pillar to mark newly discovered lands in order to claim them for Portugal

Pai: (Port.) Father

Pater Noster: (Latin) Lit. Our Father, Id. Liturgical prayer from New Testament (The Lord's Prayer)

Paydru: Sound Mbekah hears when Portuguese say the name Pedro

Piloto: (Port.) Lit. Pilot, Id. Second officer under ship's master

Pois: (Port.) Lit. Well, Id. A pause word

Por: (Port.) For or by

Por certo: (Port.) Lit. For certain, Id. Certainly

Por Deus: (Port.) Lit. By God, Id. God!

Por favor: (Port.) Lit. By favor, Id. Please

Por suposto: (Port.) Lit. For supposed, Id. Of course

Port: (wine): Fortified (strong) wine from northern Portugal

Prester: (Latin) Priest

Prioress: Head of a convent, often of aristocratic birth and influence

Quarterdeck: Raised deck covering a portion of the rear of a caravel

Querido/querida: (Port.) Lit. Beloved, Id. Dear or Dearest

Rápido: (Port.) Quick or quickly

Reais: (Port.) Lit. Royals, Id. Portuguese monetary unit

Ribeira: (Port.) River or riverside

Ribeira Grande: Sea port now known as Cidade Velha on the Island of São Tiago (Santiago) in the Cape Verde Islands off the coast of West Africa

Rio do Infante: River named by Dias after the ship's master of the São Pantaleão. This is the place where the expedition of discovery of Captain Bartolomeu Dias turned around and headed back to Portugal. Historians are divided whether this is the Great Fish River or the Keiskamma River

Salve Regina: (Latin) Lit. Hail Queen. Id. Hymn to Mary sung, among other times and places, by sailors in the morning on board ship

São Jorge da Mina: (Port.) St. George of the Gold Coast, the official name of the Mina slave fort/castle now known as the infamous Elmina slave castle which is located on the coast of present day Ghana

São Tiago: (Also Santiago) Largest island in the Cape Verde Islands off the west coast of Africa

Santíssima: (Port.) Most holy
São: (Port.) Saint (masculine)
Sea of Aethiopia: South Atlantic
Senhor: (Port.) Mister or Mr.
Senhora: (Port.) Missus or Mrs.
Senhorita: (Port.) Miss
Serpentine powder: Dry-compounded gun powder used in the 15th Century
Sesta: (Port.) Nap or siesta
Setubal: *A typographical error. Should be Santarém*: Santarém is a Portuguese city on the Tagus River about 50 miles northeast of Lisbon
Shea: Tree indigenous to Africa. Shea butter is a natural fat pressed from the fruit of the shea tree
Sim: (Port.) Yes
Songhay: Empire in sub-Saharan West Africa. Important cities were Timbuktu and Jenneh (Djenné)
Sown Zhorzhy: São Jorge (St. George) sounded like this to Mbekah
Starboard: Left side of a ship when looking forward
Stern: Rear part of a ship or boat
Stoop: To fly or dive down swiftly usually to attack prey
Suposto: (Port.) Supposed
Sweep: A long oar
Taberna: (Port.) Tavern
Terce: (Latin) Lit. Third hour, Id. Fixed time of prayer at the third hour of the day after dawn, i.e. 9 a.m.
Tiller: Handle attached to rudder to steer a ship. In the case of a caravel, which was steered by use of an oversized oar attached to the side of the ship, the tiller refers to the handle section of the steering oar
Tipo: (Port.) Lit. Type or kind, Id. Guy or chap or type of person
Todos os Santos: (Port.) Lit. All the Saints, Id. All Saints
Tu: (Port.) Thou, i.e. second person familiar pronoun
Tudo: (Port.) All or every
Tudo bem: (Port.) Lit. All good, Id. Everything is good.
Two Algarves: Kingdom within Portugal located south of Lisbon referred to also a the Algarve
Valkenswaard: Town in southern Netherlands where falcons were sold and traded
Vellum: Parchment (a type of paper) made from calf skin

Verdade: (Port.) Truth
Vino: *Error. Should be Vinho*: (Port.) Wine
Viseu: Portuguese city about 180 miles north of Lisbon
Viva: (Port.) Lit. Live, Id. Hurrah or Long live [the King]
Você: (Port.) You, i.e. second person formal pronoun
Zaire: Old name for the Congo River
Zhohwown: The name João sounded like this to Mbekah

LIST OF CHARACTERS

Note: 'ç' is pronounced like '**s**' in 'silly'. 'j' is pronounced like the 's' in 'measure'.

Amrrique: See Gyasi.

Ana de Mendonça: Prioress of the Todos os Santos Convent in Lisbon. She was João's lover before he became king and the mother to João's bastard son, Jorge who was taken from her and raised by the king's sister. Nevertheless, she remained a popular and influential woman in Portugal. Also known as Sister Ana de Mendonça, Dona Ana, and Dona de Mendonça

Andrao de Faria: King João's Chamberlain.

Antonia: See Kpodo's wife.

Baltasar Soares: Fictional character. Assistant factor at the Mina slave fort.

Bartolomeu Dias: Squire to the king of Portugal and military captain as well as ship's master. Lead the 1487/88 expedition that discovered the bottom of Africa and therefore the sea route to the East Indies.

Bastiao: See Kpodo.

Bate-boquinha: See Quinha.

Bejide: Fictional character. Friend of Mbekah's. She was executed by the slave raiders because she couldn't keep up with the line of captives in route to the ochre village.

Belchior: Fictional character. One of Gonçalves' crew and his henchman.

Belita: See Mbekah.

Bernaldo de Loronha: Bishop and King João's ambassador to the Holy See.

Bishop: See Bernaldo de Loronha.

Branca Dias: Fictional character. Wife of Bartolomeu Dias.

Bras Gonçalves: Fictional character. Pilot on ship sent to the Mina slave fort in 1484. Also a Pilot on a ship in Bartolomeu Dias' expedition to find the bottom of Africa in 1487.

Captain Cão: See Diogo Cão.

Captain Dias: See Bartolomeu Dias.

Catelina: Fictional character. One of four females from the court of the Manicongo who studied at the Todos os Santos Convent to be an ambassador/translator back in the Congo.

Chamberlain: See Andrao de Faria.

Colom: See Cristovao Colom.

Cristovao Colom: Christopher Columbus. Genoese sailor and mapmaker who lived many years in Portugal. He tried several times to interest King João in his theory that one could reach the Orient by sailing west from Portugal.

d'Azambuja: See Governor d'Azambuja.

Dias: See Bartolomeu Dias.

Diogo Cão: Captain of various expeditions down the coast of Africa on behalf of King João. Predecessor to Bartolomeu Dias.

Diogo, Duke of Visue: Brother of Queen Leonor. Personally executed (stabbed) by King João for attempting to usurp the throne. Brother of Manuel who became the Duke of Viseu.

Don/Dom João: See João Infante.

Don/Dom Pero: See Pero Dias.

Dona Ana de Mendonça: See Ana de Mendonça.

Dona Ana: See Ana de Mendonça.

Dr. Astruch: See Iacob Astruch.

Duke of Bragança: See Fernando II, Duke of Bragança.

Duke of Visue: See Diogo, Duke of Viseu and also see Manuel, Duke of Visue.

Father Estevez: Fictional character. Chaplain on the 1484 voyage to the Mina slave fort.

Felipe Alvariz: Fictional character. Chaplain (head cleric) at the Mina slave fort. Member of the Military-Religious Order of Christ.

Fernando II, Duke of Bragança: Queen Leonor's brother-in-law. Fernando plotted against King João and was tried and executed for treason.

Fernando: King of Aragon: Husband of Queen Isabela of Castile.

Filipe Xemenez: Fictional character. Associate of Xemenez Irmãos. Lombard money lender in Lisbon.

Foladé: Fictional character. Mbekah's little sister. Born and raised in a forest village in West Africa and taken by slave raiders to the Portuguese Mina (Elmina) slave fort 1486 and sold to the Portuguese.

Galo: Fictional character. Loan shark in Lisbon.

Gil Pereira: Fictional character. Commandant of Garrison at the Mina slave fort.

Giomar: See Sister Maria Giomar.

Gonçalves: See Bras Gonçalves.

Goterrez: Fictional family. Family with estate near the city of Ourém that bought Belita (Mbekah) after she was kidnapped from Lisbon.

Governor d'Azambuja: Governor of the Portuguese Mina slave fort.

Guaspar Meendez: Fictional character. Lopo's father. Owner of a leather shop in Lisbon.

Guincho: Fictional character. Dona Ana de Mendonça's chimpanzee.

Gyasi: Fictional character. Born and raised in a forest village in West Africa and taken by slave raiders to the Mina (Elmina) slave fort in 1484 and sold to the Portuguese. Renamed Amrrique in Lisbon.

Henry the Navigator: Uncle to King João II. Head of the Portuguese Military-Religious Order of Christ, successor to the Knights of the Temple (Templars) when they were persecuted out of existence. Called Infante Henrique by the Portuguese. Invested heavily in exploration down the coast of Africa and in the nautical technology to complete these explorations.

Her majesty: See Queen Leonor.

His majesty: See King João II.

Iacob Astruch: Fictional character. Jewish refugee from Castile and trusted advisor to King João.

Ifé: Fictional character. Born and raised in a forest village in West Africa and taken by slave raiders to the Mina (Elmina) slave fort in 1484 and sold to the Portuguese. Renamed Inês in Lisbon.

Inês: See Ifé.

Infante Henrique: See Henry the Navigator.

Isabela: Queen of Castile. Wife of King Fernando of Aragon.

Isabell: Fictional character. One of four females from the court of the Manicongo who studied at the Todos os Santos Convent to be an ambassador/translator back in the Congo.

João Infante: One of the ship's master's in Bartolomeu Dias' 1487 expedition to find the bottom of Africa.

Jose Figueroa e Duarte: Fictional character. A member of Lopo's gun crew/watch on the 1484 voyage to the Mina slave fort. Also known as Joselinho.

Josefa: See Mbekah.

Josué: Butler to the de Mendonça family.

King João II: King of Portugal 1481-1495.

King João: See King João II.

King of the Congo: See Manicongo.

Kpodo: Fictional character. Born and raised in a forest village in West Africa. Son of the village headman. Taken, along with his young bride, by slave raiders to the Mina (Elmina) slave fort in 1484 and sold to the Portuguese. Renamed Bastiao in Lisbon.

Kpodo's wife: Fictional character. Born to a wealthy farmer in a forest village in West Africa and married to Kpodo, the son of a headman in a nearby village. Taken, along with her husband, by slave raiders to the Mina (Elmina) slave fort in 1484 and sold to the Portuguese. Renamed Antonia in Lisbon.

Leonor: See Queen Leonor.

Lionor: Fictional character. One of four females from the court of the Manicongo who studied at the Todos os Santos Convent to be an ambassador/translator back in the Congo.

Lopinho: See Lopo David Meendez.

Lopo David Meendez: Fictional character. Pilot's mate on ship sent to the Mina slave fort in 1484. Pilot on a ship in Bartolomeu Dias' expedition to find the bottom of Africa in 1487.

Manicongo: King of the Congo.

Manoel Vaaz: Fictional character. Cargo master on 1484 voyage to the Mina slave fort as well on the 1487 expedition to find the bottom of Africa.

Manoel: See Manoel Vaaz.

Manuel, Duke of Visue: Brother of Queen Leonor. Younger brother of Diogo. King João gave him the title and lands formerly belonging to Diogo, his older brother. Manuel succeeded João as King of Portugal.

Margaida: Fictional character. Lopo's cousin. Student at the Todos os Santos Convent.

Maria Consola: See Sister Maria Consola.

Maria Giomar: See Sister Maria Giomar.

Maria: See Olubayo.

Mbekah: Fictional character. Born and raised in a forest village in West Africa and taken by slave raiders to the Mina (Elmina) slave fort in 1484 and sold to the Portuguese. Renamed Josefa in Lisbon and later named Belita.

Mestre Amatu: See Samuel Amatu.

Moisés: Fictional character. Kpodo's wife's baby. Orphaned. Likely the son of Kpodo.

Mother Superior: See Sister Maria Violante de Cunha.

Nunno: Fictional character. One of Gonçalves' crew and his henchman.

Ogané: Legendary African emperor whom some thought was Prester John.

Olubayo: Fictional character. Born and raised in a forest village in West Africa and taken by slave raiders to the Mina (Elmina) slave fort 1484 and sold to the Portuguese. Renamed Maria in Lisbon.

Padre Mateus: Fictional character. Kind, reliable priest in Ourém.

Paydru: See Pedro.

Pedro: Fictional character. West African slave working as sailor on the 1484 expedition to the Mina slave fort. To Mbekah, his name sounded like Paydru.

Pero Dias: Brother to Bartolomeu Dias and master of one of the ships in the 1487 expedition to find the bottom of Africa.

Pero Meendez: Fictional character. Lopo's brother. Works in his father's leather shop in Lisbon.

Pope Eugene II: Pope in the 12th Century who was first informed of the existence of the Christian emperor Prester John.

Pope Sixtus IV: Pope that died in 1484. Succeeded by Innocent VIII.

Prester John: Legendary Christian emperor sought after by European nations from the 12th to the 16th centuries.

Prioress: See Ana de Mendonça.

Queen Leonor: Queen of Portugal. King João II's wife.

Quinha: Fictional character. Dona Ana de Mendonça's talking bird.

Rodrigo Correa: Fictional character. Member of Lopo's gun crew on the 1484 voyage to the Mina slave fort. Faithful friend to Lopo. Pilot's mate on 1487 expedition to find the bottom of Africa.

Rodrigo: See Rodrigo Correa.

Rui da Pena: Fictional character. Factor at the Mina slave fort.

Samuel Amatu: Fictional character. Jewish physician to King João.

Sancha: Fictional character. One of four females from the court of the Manicongo who studied at the Todos os Santos Convent to be an ambassador/translator back in the Congo.

Senhor Dias: See Bartolomeu Dias.

Senhora Dias: See Branca Dias.

Sister Ana de Mendonça: See Ana de Mendonça.

Sister Maria Consola: Fictional character. Nun and aide to Prioress Ana de Mendonça.

Sister Maria Giomar: Fictional character. Aide to the mother superior in the Todos os Santos Convent.

Sister Maria Violante da Cunha: Fictional character. Mother Superior at Todos os Santos Convent. She was the actual day-to-day manager at the convent.

Tareija: Fictional character. Friend to Belita (Mbekah) when the latter was a slave on the Goterrez estate in Ourém.

Tkemet: Fictional character. Headman of the Khoikhoi village.

Tomasa: Fictional character. Wet nurse to the foundling baby Moisés.

Xemenez: See Filipe Xemenez.

Yaféu: Fictional character. Slave raider from the ochre village in West Africa.

MAPS

A Mina (São Jorge da Mina) Slave Castle/Fort

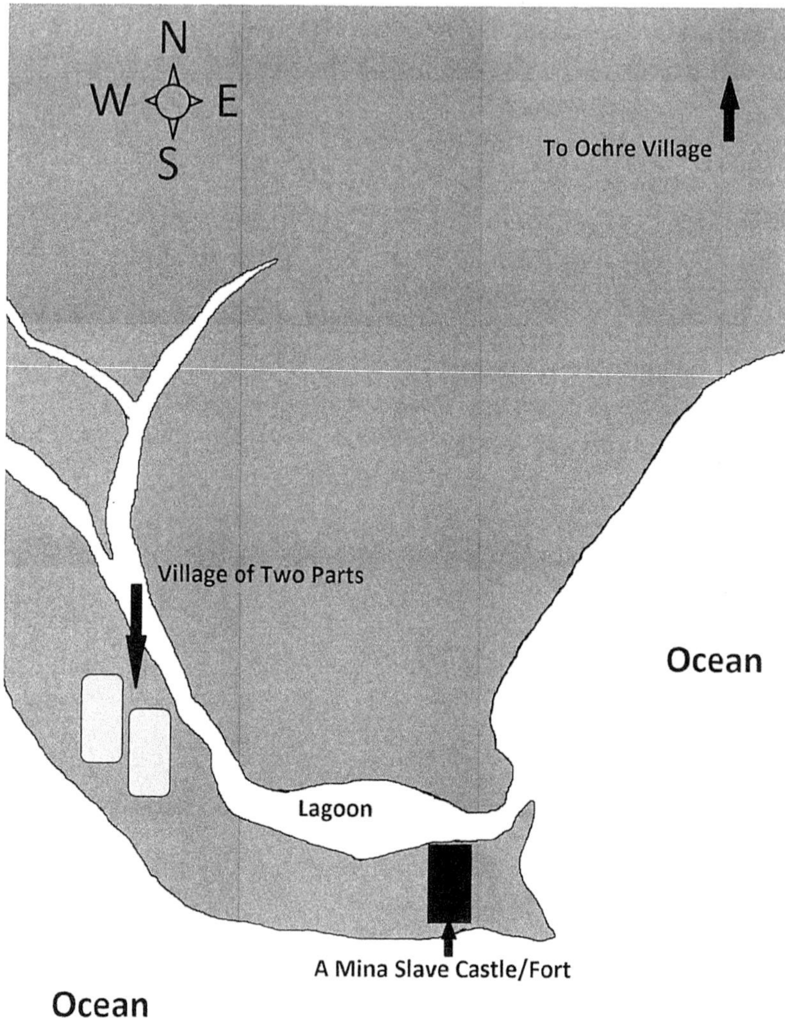

Iberia

La Corunha
France
Navarre
Castile
Aragon
Portugal
Ourém
Santarém
Lisbon
Valencia
Granada
Africa

Africa

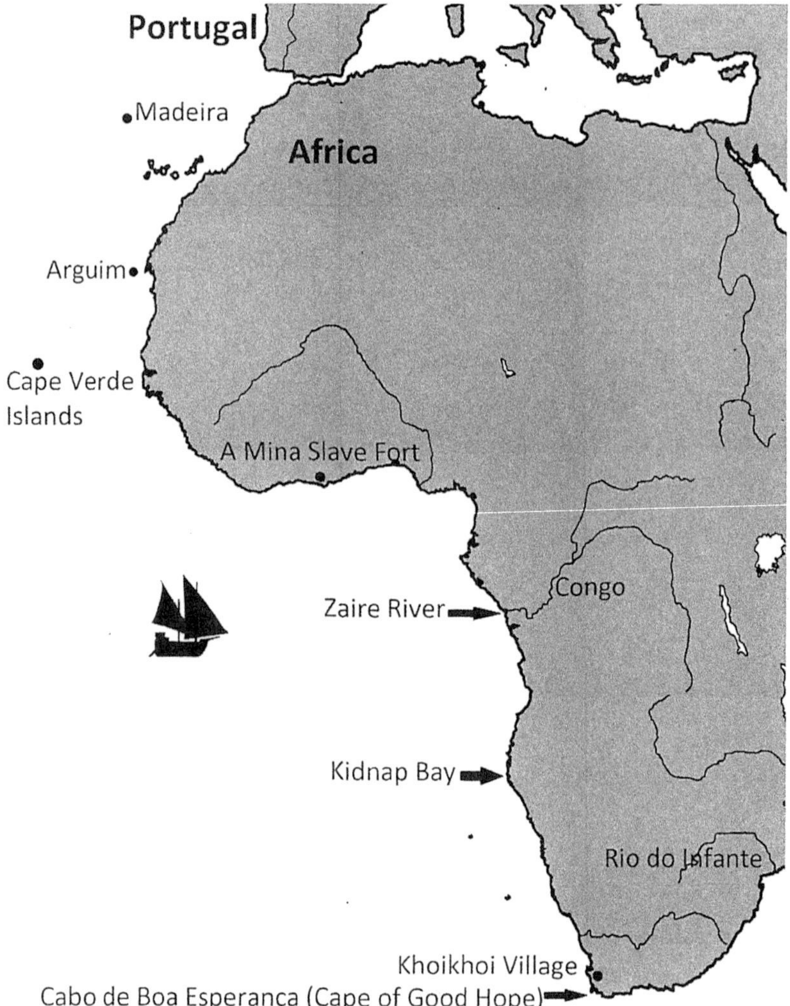
Portugal
Madeira
Africa
Arguim
Cape Verde Islands
A Mina Slave Fort
Congo
Zaire River
Kidnap Bay
Rio do Infante
Khoikhoi Village
Cabo de Boa Esperança (Cape of Good Hope)

Made in the USA
San Bernardino, CA
09 January 2018